Reigning

The Rise Of An English Lawbreaker
Book 3

Malcolm Archibald

For Cathy

Prelude

North Atlantic Ocean, November 1774

"Keep her steady, helmsman!" Captain Bragg had to shout above the scream of the storm that threatened to tear *London's Pride's* masts from her deck.

"I'm trying, Captain!" Isaac Winchester put all his weight behind the wheel, feeling his muscles strain with the effort of holding the ship's head to the wind. For three days, *London's Pride* had battled the gale under topsails only and with her crew praying for deliverance.

Tied to the wheel, Winchester swayed with the violent motion of the ship and peered, narrow-eyed, into the boiling sea ahead. His jaws constantly worked, chewing the remains of a wad of tobacco that had sustained him for hours. "The wind's not easing, Captain!"

"It will," Bragg shouted, more in hope than expectation. "These Atlantic storms always blow themselves out after a couple of days."

David Cupples, the second man on the wheel, said nothing. Laconic by nature, he concentrated solely on keeping the vessel as safe as possible. In common with everybody on board, he knew it was impossible to drive a wooden ship without the danger of her seams opening or something giving aloft. After three days of the wind driving *London's Pride*, Cupples felt she was heavier and slower to answer the wheel.

"We're making water, Captain," Winchester spoke Cupples' thoughts.

"Aye," Captain Bragg agreed. "She's sluggish."

London's Pride responded with less buoyancy at every heavy wave, no longer rising like a cork as she had done even a few hours earlier.

"Bayne!" Bragg's roar battled the scream of the wind. "Check below! She's taking in water!"

Gripping a safety line with his left hand, Joshua Bayne, the first mate, lifted his right in acknowledgement. He did not know whether it was safer above deck or below, but at least beneath decks, he would escape the constant pounding of wind and waves. As Bayne struggled toward the main hatch cover, a rogue wave crashed over *London Pride's* stern and swept forward in a white-foamed rush. Bayne's despairing yell was lost in a hellish cacophony of roaring water and splintering timber.

"That's Bayne gone," Captain Bragg said. A veteran of the Seven Year's War and thirty years at sea, he had experienced too much death to be moved by the loss of a single man.

"Here comes another!" Winchester shook seawater from his head and gripped the wheel with brawny hands.

"Hold hard, boys!" Bragg shouted as another wave crashed over the stern, pressing the helmsmen against the wheel. Bragg knew his ship was low in the water when the sea pooped her, and he had to make an agonising choice. Should he remain in the stern with the helmsmen or check below? He looked forward, where every wave filled *London Pride's* main deck, glanced aloft, and swore. The main upper and fore lower topsails were flapping loose, adding to the ship's distress.

Removing the metal speaking trumpet from its bracket on the mizzen mast, Bragg roared commands.

"All hands," he shouted. "All hands! Make the main upper topsail fast! Clew up the fore lower topsail!"

Swearing, scared, and unwilling, the hands emerged from the stinking dark of the foc'sle. Holding on for their lives, they clambered aloft, some shaking in fear, others pretending nonchalance, and a few, the bravest topmen, throwing themselves up the rigging despite the gale.

A frantic blast of wind blew *London's Pride* onto her beam ends, nearly dipping the larboard lower yard arms into the sea. Cupples swore foully as the gale snapped the ratlines of the mizzen rigging nine feet above the poop. With the sails blown out of their gaskets, *London's Pride* lurched further to larboard, and Cupples heard a rumble below as the cargo shifted.

"Bugger it to damnation and back," Captain Bragg shouted. "Damn these Chesapeake longshoremen; they could no more load a cargo than fly to the moon! Cut away the main lower topsail! We'll work her under bare poles, damn my eyes!"

Leaving the men at the wheel to struggle alone, Bragg dragged himself along the sloping deck, gripping the safety line as mountainous seas burst over the ship. About half the crew obeyed Bragg's orders, working desperately with hatchets and knives, while the remainder fled to the precarious safety of the foc'sle, too scared to return to the deck.

With the last of the sails cut away, the wind exerted less pressure on *London's Pride*, but she refused to right herself. She remained on her beam ends, trapped by the shifted cargo and a tangle of spars and gear. Bragg glowered at the nightmare of white water that roared over his ship's larboard topgallant rail. No seaman, however daring and skilled, could live in that.

"Mr Blackstone!" Bragg came to a hard decision and roared for the second mate. "Jettison the cargo, or we'll be over, damn it! It's shifted to leeward."

Isaac Blackstone was a young man, barely out of his teens, proud of the wedding ring on his finger. He stared at Bragg with his mouth open. "Captain, if we open the hatches, the sea will get in."

"Do your duty, damn you!" Bragg roared.

Huge waves were tumbling over *London Pride's* hull, breaking on the solid English oak. For an instant, master and mate glared at each other as the terrified hands clung onto any handhold and waited for a clear order.

London's Pride made the decision for them. The pressure of the sea carried away a bobstay, and the bowsprit followed, lost to the surging sea. As the waves ripped away the fore topmast, the raffle dragged at the main topgallant mast, and in moments the ship was dismasted and rolling crazily in the mountainous seas. Those hands who had been working aloft vanished with the masts. One moment they were there, and the next, the sea took them, with their cries unheard in the roaring wind.

"Damn my soul!" Winchester said, clinging to the wheel as *London's Pride* gyrated from larboard to starboard and back. "We've got a proper hurrah's nest now."

Cupples nodded, chewing his quid of tobacco, and staring at the maelstrom of raging water surrounding the ship. He glanced at Winchester. "Best make your peace with your maker, Isaac. I reckon we'll be shaking hands with Davy Jones before long."

Winchester staggered as *London's Pride* nearly rolled right over. "Maybe so, Davie, maybe so, but I think the old girl will stay afloat now the masts are gone." He looked up. "Sky's clearing, Davie. The storm's blown itself out."

Cupples spat a mouthful of tobacco juice into the wind. "So it is, Isaac." He forced a grin. "Better late than never. Mebbe we'll see another day, yet."

Before Cupples finished speaking, the storm lashed *London's Pride* with its devil's tail, sending a final wave crashing over the bow to sweep along the deck. When the force of the water smashed a hatch cover and poured into the hold, the ship gave up. She rolled completely over, throwing the men on deck into the sea and trapping those in the fo'c'sle.

Winchester slashed at the rope that tied him to the wheel, hearing a horrific roaring in his ears and feeling seawater rasp and burn in his throat and lungs. When the rope parted, he kicked frantically away from the wreckage to surface thirty yards from the capsized ship.

"Davie!" Winchester shouted, seeing only a chaos of confused water, heaving waves and a mess of cables and spars. Waves rose around him, spindrift-tipped marbled green mountains roaring and hissing. "Davie!"

"Isaac!" Cupples lifted a hand from ten yards away. "Over here!"

Winchester kicked closer, and both men wrapped their arms around a spar, tossing on the already moderating waves.

"She's going!" Cupples said and watched as *London's Pride* sank slowly beneath the surface, taking most of her crew with her. "God in heaven, she's going!"

The storm calmed slowly, leaving a shocked handful of survivors swimming or clinging to pieces of wreckage.

"Where's the captain?" Cupples asked.

"Gone," Blackstone gasped, spitting out seawater.

"We'd best keep together." Winchester was the oldest survivor. "Try to make a raft. "Does anybody know where we are?" He looked hopefully at Blackstone.

"About three hundred miles west southwest of the Scillies," Blackstone said. "Or we were when the storm hit. That storm could have driven us anywhere." He glanced around at the slowly moderating sea. "Gather the spars together, men, and make a sail from some of these scraps of canvas. If we make a raft, the south westerly trades will drive us towards old England."

For the next hour, the survivors collected spars and fragments of wreckage and lashed them together with lengths of cable. One fortunate man found a keg half full of fresh water and another a piece of canvas. Knowing that the alternative was drowning, they worked together, gasping and struggling to keep afloat.

"We're doing well," Winchester encouraged them as the makeshift raft gradually took shape. "Climb on board, lads!"

The survivors dragged themselves onto the collection of

spars and lay there, panting as the waves lifted around them and inquisitive gulls circled.

"A sail," Blackstone croaked. "Fashion a sail and catch the wind."

They raised two spare spars, lodged the ends between the fabric of the raft, and attached the scraps of canvas to create a sail. Within minutes the wind caught the canvas, bellying it out to push the raft in a north-easterly direction.

"We're making progress," Winchester said.

"About half a knot." Blackstone peered ahead. "We'll need better than that, or we'll die of thirst."

The survivors huddled together on the raft, some nursing injuries from the shipwreck, one man praying, and all hiding their fear. Night increased the loneliness as low clouds blanketed every star and the unceasing wind kicked spume from hissing waves.

One man died during the night, rolling into the sea without a sound and vanishing. Nobody noticed his absence until dawn rose red and angry in the east.

"Jacob's gone," Winchester said.

"We'll all be joining him soon," Blackstone said gloomily. He touched his wedding ring, thinking of his wife, Leah, alone in their two-roomed house on the Isle of Dogs.

"Not so!" Cupples said. "Look over there! A sail!" He pointed to the south, where a fine three-master was bearing up on them.

The survivors stood up, raised their hands, and set up a yell, with Cupples and Winchester holding up the sail as a flag.

"She's bearing towards us," Blackstone shouted, his voice hoarse with salt water.

"I know her," Winchester said. "That's *Amelia Jane*!"

"One of Charlie Shapland's ships," Blackstone said. "She's seen us, men!"

Amelia Jane surged toward them, furling her mainsail when close. A group of men stood in the stern with a spyglass fixed on the relieved survivors.

"They're launching a boat," Blackstone said. "We're saved, lads!"

Winchester saw a group of men clustered around the jolly boat, with the ship's mate giving directions, and then a tall man in the stern snapped an order.

"That's Charlie Shapland himself," Winchester said. He saw an officer approach Shapland, and then the group around the jolly boat scattered, and men ran aloft. *Amelia Jane* set her mainsail.

"Wait!" Blackstone shouted, waving frantically. "We're over here!"

Cupples saw Shapland turn his spyglass full onto the survivors on the makeshift raft, and then *Amelia Jane* headed away, with the sea breaking white around her bow.

"Wait!" Blackstone shouted, "Oh, please, God, don't leave us here!" The other survivors yelled and lifted their hands in supplication.

Cupples shook his head. "Shapland saw us," he said as the wind sent a spatter of spray over the raft.

"Why didn't he pick us up?" Blackstone asked, shaking his head. "He's leaving us to die! The rogue's leaving us to drown!"

"Mebbe he was in a hurry," Cupples said. "The reason doesn't matter. All that matters is us trying to reach safety. Put back the sail, and we'll catch this wind." He looked around, where the sea stretched endlessly to a distant horizon and shuddered, knowing the possibility of survival was slim.

Chapter One

J ohn Smith, Lord Fitzwarren, leaned back on his chair, listened to the wind roaring in the flue, dipped his quill in the inkwell, and perused the bill of lading. He smiled, thinking such documents appeared like works of art rather than necessary receipts given by a shipmaster. The bill of lading acknowledged the shipmaster had accepted a quantity of merchandise and promised delivery.

This bill was engraved with a picture of a three-masted ship in both top corners and the name John Smith & Company, Leadenhall Street, London, across the top centre in beautiful copperplate writing. As with all Smith's bills of lading, the first line of printed text ran: "Shipped by the Grace of God in good order and condition" and continued with the ship's name, handwritten, in this instance, "*Martha of Norfolk*, Master William Hood, at anchor in the Chesapeake and bound for London."

"One hundred hogsheads of Virginia leaf tobacco and fifty barrels of tobacco stems for snuff.

And so God send thee, good ship, to thy desired port of safety."

"You're looking very pensive, John." Bess Webb entered the

room. She had been with Smith for over fifteen years and married to him for ten. Dark-haired and of medium height, a white scar disfigured the left side of her face.

"I am," Smith agreed. "I wonder how many more cargoes of tobacco we can ship before this looming war shuts everything down."

"Will it be a war?" Bess sat on her favourite chair beside the fireplace. "I thought it was only some malcontents stirring up trouble."

"I think it'll end up as civil war," Smith said. "My shipmasters inform me the atmosphere in the American colonies is brittle. Unless the authorities there are very careful, the Colonists will be taking to their arms."

Bess screwed up her face. "Whose side are you on, John?"

Smith pushed back his chair and swivelled to face her. "Ours, Bess; yours and mine. Oh, we may appear as part of the British establishment now, with our big houses, this place, and our businesses, but you and I know we'll never be accepted."

Bess touched her scar. "I don't want these people to accept me," she said quietly. "They think their position and money make them superior to ordinary people. No, John, if the Colonists oppose the Crown and the aristocracy, I am wholeheartedly on their side."

Smith grunted. "You're nothing but a Whig, Bess," he grinned. "But nobody wins in a war. Thousands of men are killed, tens of thousands die of disease, trade is disrupted, and ships are captured or sunk. Most of our fortune comes through trade."

"We have the tenants' rents on our lands," Bess reminded.

"We keep the rents low," Smith said. "The only way to win in a war is to make armaments, and I'm not making money that way."

"There is another way," Bess said.

"And what's that, pray?"

"Support the winner," Bess smiled. "As you did in the late war with France."

"I didn't support anybody in the last war," Smith told her.

"You supplied the Royal Navy with grain," Bess said, "and smuggled half the brandy consumed in Kent." The scar on her face writhed as she smiled. "In short, dear John, you played both ends against the middle."

"And that is exactly what I plan to do now, Bess," Smith said.

"I am glad to hear it." Bess shifted on her chair. "I nearly thought you were turning into a Tory."

"Only when it suits me," Smith said. "The impending war will have to wait, Bess. We have other more pressing problems."

"Charlie Shapland and Henry Copinger?" Bess hazarded.

"Shapland and Copinger are two," Smith said, "and another of my ships is overdue." He tapped the bill of lading.

"*London's Pride?*" Bess said.

"I've given up on her," Smith admitted. "Now *Martha of Norfolk* is three weeks overdue with a cargo of tobacco from the Chesapeake. That's the third ship this year."

"Lost with all hands?" Bess asked.

"*London's Profit* and *London's Pride* vanished without a trace," Smith said, "although *Pride* caught the tail end of a hurricane, so that might account for her loss. *Profit* only experienced boisterous weather, which her master should have been able to cope with."

"*Martha of Norfolk* might turn up yet," Bess said. "Her captain, William Hood, is a good man. He's a Down East Yankee, isn't he?"

"From Maine," Smith agreed. "They breed fine seamen in Maine, and he keeps a tight ship. I can't see him losing her without an excellent reason."

"Pirates?" Bess suggested. "Or a mutiny?"

"I haven't heard of a pirate in the North Atlantic," Smith said, "and that intelligence would travel fast. Mutiny is possible, although mutineers have to make landfall somewhere, and I'd hear about it then. No, I think something else. Three ships lost in such a short space of time is too much of a coincidence."

"Mr Abergeldie and the other insurance companies will raise their premiums," Bess pointed out. "And it will be harder for you to recruit crews if you lose too many ships."

Smith nodded. "I know all that," he said. "I want to know why we lost three vessels."

"*Martha* is not lost yet," Bess reminded. "She might still turn up."

"I hope to God she does," Smith said. "I have thirty-two men on her, plus William Hood."

"And a valuable cargo."

"That too," Smith agreed. "We can't afford to lose many more ships and cargoes. The tobacco trade is vastly profitable, but if this liberty business over there blows up, commerce could drop to a trickle, and we'll lose more money." He looked up when somebody tapped at the door. "Come in!"

"Excuse me, Mr Smith." Judd, Smith's secretary, stood inside the door. "A seaman at the front desk wishes to speak to you."

"What sort of seaman?" Bess asked.

"A rather ragged common mariner, Ma'am. He asked particularly to speak to Mr Smith." Judd took a deep breath. "He says he sailed in *London's Pride*, sir."

Smith glanced at Bess with renewed interest. "*London's Pride*? Send him up, please, Mr Judd."

"Yes, sir." Judd withdrew immediately and rapped on the door again three minutes later. "Here is the seaman, sir."

The man was gaunt to emaciation, with ragged clothes hanging from a near-skeletal body and a face burned deep brown by sun and wind.

"Come in, man." Smith extended a welcoming hand. "You look like you've experienced a rough time."

The man nodded and knuckled his forehead. "Rough enough, sir, if you count shipwreck and weeks on an open raft as rough."

"I would, my friend," Smith said. "I've undergone shipwreck

myself." He stepped to the cabinet on the far wall and produced a decanter. "I can offer you Madeira, port, gin or rum."

The man's eyes glistened. "Rum, sir, and you'd be so kind."

Smith poured a generous glass, added two more and handed one to the seaman and another to Bess. "Now, my friend, sit down and tell me who you are."

The man sat delicately on the leather seat of a chair and sipped at his rum. "I am David Cupples, sir, late of *London's Pride* and before that of *Thames Blessing* and the old *Maid of Kent*."

"You've sailed in my ships for some time then, Cupples," Smith said.

"I have, sir, and you've always been a fair employer."

Smith accepted the compliment. "Tell me what happened to *London's Pride*, Cupples, if you will."

Cupples took another draught of rum to strengthen himself for the ordeal of talking to his employer. He related the end of his ship in bold terms as Smith listened and Bess took notes in her firm, neat hand.

"Hurricanes are devilish things," Smith said when Cupples finished his story.

"Yes, Captain." Cupples reverted to a more familiar term of respect as he struggled to convey his point. "But Captain Bragg had its measure. We would have survived the hurricane if the cargo hadn't shifted. That put *London's Pride* on her beam ends, and the sea broke over us."

"That's unlike the dockers at the Chesapeake," Smith said. "In my experience, they are as expert in loading cargo as anywhere in the world." He poured more rum into Cupples' glass and topped up Bess's in response to her hopeful smile.

"Yes, sir," Cupples agreed. "Captain Bragg said something similar."

Smith glanced at Bess, who lifted her eyebrows, dipped her pen in the inkwell and carefully wrote something down. "What do you think happened, Cupples?"

"I can't say for sure, Captain, but some dockers didn't like us."

"Was it this taxation nonsense?" Smith asked.

"I don't rightly know, sir," Cupples said. "I saw other ships loaded in half the time, sir, but they seemed to dislike ours."

"Only *Pride?* Or all my ships?"

Cupples screwed up his face, becoming loquacious as the rum took hold of his ravaged body. "I never heard of any trouble with other ships, sir."

"*London's Profit?*" Smith asked.

"She sailed before us, sir. I didn't see her loaded."

"*Martha of Norfolk?*"

Cupples shook his head. "She was coming into Baltimore as we left, sir."

Smith saw Bess writing assiduously. "Check which dock it was, Bess," he said.

"I will," Bess said.

"And the other disturbing matter," Smith said, pouring more rum into Cupples' glass. "Charles Shapland and *Amelia Jane.*"

"Yes, sir," Cupples said. "*Amelia* had the jolly boat ready to launch, sir. I saw the boys crowding round the boat and the mate, Mr Burgess, giving orders, and then Mr Shapland shouted something, and *Amelia* clapped on sail and bore away."

"Are you sure they saw you, Davie?" Bess asked. "The sea is a big place."

"They saw us, Mrs Smith, sure as I'm sitting here. We was in a raft with a scrap of canvas as a sail, and Mr Burgess was readying the jolly boat, as I told you."

"You saw Mr Shapland countermand the order and sail away." Bess searched for confirmation.

"That's what I think, Mrs Smith."

Bess nodded as Smith put the stopper on his decanter and replaced it in the cabinet.

"How many men were on the raft, Cupples?" Smith asked.

"There were twelve of us, Captain." Cupples' eyes darkened

with memory. "Twelve good men, sir. I knew them all." He mentioned each man as Smith listened, and Bess noted the names.

"Where are they now?" Bess asked.

"They're all dead, Mrs Smith," Cupples said. "They died one by one as we floated across the Atlantic. Isaac Blackstone was last. He died crying for his wife, lying in my arms one day before a French trader picked us up." He looked directly into Smith's face. "Shapland killed them, Mr Smith, as surely as if he thrust a knife into their hearts."

Smith stood up. "I'll deal with Mr Shapland in my own time. The first thing is to get you fed and watered and a new set of clothes."

"And Davie's wages," Bess said.

Smith nodded. "Two month's extra wages for Cupples and the widows of every man in *London Pride's* crew."

As Cupples left the office, Smith walked to the window and looked into the street.

"What do you plan, John?" Bess asked.

"I'm going across to the Chesapeake," Smith said. "But first, I am going to talk to Burgess."

"Not Shapland?" Bess raised her eyebrows.

"No," Smith said. "He can wait."

SMITH FOUND ISRAEL BURGESS SITTING IN THE CORNER OF THE Swan with Two Heads on the Ratcliffe Highway.

"Mr Burgess!" Smith sat opposite. "Is it rum you're drinking?"

"It is." Burgess was a heavy-set man with a florid complexion and a silver ring in his right ear. He watched Smith set two tumblers of rum on the round table and said no more.

"My name is Smith."

"I know who you are," Burgess said. He did not lift the rum.

"You are Israel Burgess." Smith stretched out his legs.

"I am," Burgess said.

"And you are mate of *Amelia Jane*," Smith continued.

"I was," Burgess said again.

"I believe you saw some survivors from one of my ships in mid-Atlantic," Smith said.

"No." Burgess shook his head without meeting Smith's gaze. "I didn't see any survivors."

"One of these men recognised your ship and you," Smith said.

Burgess pushed the rum towards Smith. "Your informant is mistaken, Mr Smith. We didn't see any survivors from any ship. We had a rough voyage and saw few ships. You may ask the captain."

"I will," Smith said quietly. "My survivor mentioned you by name and told me you tried to help."

Burgess looked away. "I'm sorry, Mr Smith. I can't help you."

"My survivor was grateful you tried to help," Smith said.

"I'm glad somebody survived the sinking, Mr Smith," Burgess sounded sincere. "I wish I could help you."

"I wish the same, Mr Burgess." Smith stood. "I don't know the truth yet, but I'll find out." He lowered his voice. "By God, I'll find who was responsible for leaving my men to drown, and when I do, I'll make him pay."

Burgess placed his hands on the table. "Maybe they are already paying, Mr Smith. It's a bad thing to leave men to drown."

"You and I know who is responsible," Smith hissed. "And it was not you."

"Hell mend him, Mr Smith," Burgess said. "Hell bloody mend him."

BESS PASSED OVER TWO MUGS OF COFFEE. "WHAT NOW, JOHN?"

"Now we have questions to answer," Smith said. "Why did

three of my ships sink? Was the cargo on *London's Pride* badly loaded? And if so, why? And why did Burgess lie about trying to help the survivors?"

"How will you get the answers?" Bess asked.

"I'll find out at the source," Smith said. "I'll cross the Atlantic."

Chapter Two

Boston, Massachusetts, British North America, January 1776

"I thought these colonies were English." Captain Fletcher cradled his glass of rum in a huge hand, "but they are anything but. The people are either Scotch or Irish, and they've intermarried with the Dutch, Germans, or even the French, God help us, to create a hybrid race."

Smith listened, saying nothing. He saw Abraham Hargreaves on the nearest table, hiding his smile.

Fletcher continued. "From that bastard breeding has sprung the high-spirited brood that boasts so much of British blood and liberty and who have the damned cheek to talk of chastising Great Britain. There's not an ounce of British blood in them."

"Aren't the Scots as British as the English?" Smith asked.

"No, damn them. They're rebel dogs, gallows bait. Oh, they come crawling to us now, fawning for our acceptance and pleading loyalty to King George. Loyalty!" Fletcher shook his head so hard his wig nearly fell off. "Show a penny to a Scotchman, and he'll plead undying allegiance. Show him two pence, and he'll throw himself into the greatest danger to earn such munificence."

"You think the Crown can buy their loyalty?" Smith sipped at his rum, with his gaze roaming around the public house, examining everybody present.

"Buy a Scotchman's loyalty? Yes, with tokens and smooth promises. But these damned Yankees!" Fletcher shook his head. "They're a troublesome lot with their talk of liberty and their refusal to pay taxes."

Smith shook his head. "Terrible people," he said. "If we all refused to pay taxes, where would we be?"

Fletcher nodded. "I agree, Mr Smith." Lifting his hat, he stood up. "I must leave you now; I have a ship to prepare."

Abraham Hargreaves stepped across to Smith's table. "You keep interesting company, Mr Smith. I wonder what Fletcher would say if he knew you were once the most successful smuggler on the south coast of England."

Smith smiled. "That's only hearsay, Abraham, and it was long ago."

"My father might say otherwise," Abraham replied, smiling. "He has told me many tales of your early days in Kent."

Smith met Abraham's smile. He had spent years working with Abraham's father in the cross-Channel smuggling trade. "I am an eminently respectable merchant now, Abraham, with a fleet of ships and shares in a stagecoach line."

Abraham Hargreaves continued. "My father also told me about the stagecoaches. That's when you were a highwayman, wearing a yellow mask, calling yourself Yellowhammer, roaming the roads and lanes of Kent, holding up coaches and terrorising travellers."

"Your father is repeating hearsay," Smith said carelessly, "if I recall, Lord Fitzwarren was Yellowhammer. Why even his wife proved that in court."

"A woman you subsequently married, my Lord," Abraham Hargreaves said quietly. "That's how you gained the title and lands."

"I never use that title on the western side of the Atlantic," Smith reminded. "And very seldom on the eastern." He looked up as a crowd passed the public house, chanting and shouting loud slogans. "Something's happening out there."

Abraham joined him in looking out of the multi-paned window. The mob was jeering and throwing eggs and dung at a small patrol of red-coated soldiers that limped past under the command of a young sergeant. The soldiers looked angry, but the sergeant kept them under control despite the provocation.

"As you see," Abraham said, "the army is not popular in Boston. Not since the massacre and not before then, either."

"I see," Smith agreed, sipping at his rum. "The lobsters seem to be remarkably self-restrained."

"They're under strict orders not to retaliate," Abraham said.

"I presume the mob knows that?" Smith said dryly. "Or they would not be so bold."

Abraham nodded. "Maybe so. Any repetition of the massacre and there'd be more blood on the street than King George could handle."

"That must be the reason," Smith said. "Show me your city, Abraham."

Abraham tossed back his rum, smacked his lips, and bowed. "This way, my Lord."

"Mr Smith will do nicely," Smith said and grinned. "Blasted Yankee Doodles."

"That's us," Abraham agreed. "Things are different over here, Mr Smith. We're more open to freedom and liberty."

"We?" Smith raised his eyebrows. "You're English-born and bred, Abraham, a man of Kent."

They stepped outside into the cool Boston air, with snow piled in the street and a grey-white blanket of cloud threatening more.

"I know, Mr Smith, but England feels a long way off, and not just in distance." Abraham struggled to find the words. "It's the class system, I think. In England, people are so subservient to the nobility and the king. The elite has all the rights and grabs the land and the power. Ordinary people struggle to survive, while the aristocrats live as they please."

"I've risen from nothing," Smith reminded, playing devil's advocate.

"You have," Abraham agreed. "But only because you side-stepped the system. You didn't obey the restrictive laws or pay the crippling taxes."

Smith grunted, accepting the truth of Abraham's words. "Do you feel more akin to the colonies than to Great Britain now?"

Abraham was silent for a few moments. "No, Mr Smith. I don't feel akin to any colonies. I think we're growing out of any thought of colonialism. I feel like we're a butterfly evolving from a caterpillar. We're ready to take wings and fly, leaving the Old World behind."

Smith nodded. "I like your Boston," he said as Abraham's words planted the seeds of an idea in his mind.

Boston was a settlement of around 17,000 people, beautifully situated on a peninsula between the Charles River and Boston Harbour. Although Smith thought the town was slightly run down, the streets presented a picturesque panorama of undulating roofs, and some public buildings could compare with any provincial centre in England.

"This could be quite a presentable little town," Smith said as Abraham introduced him to the array of wharves on the eastern side. "It undoubtedly has potential."

"Yes, Mr Smith," Abraham agreed.

"Do you think Massachusetts could compete with the world?" Smith threw out a suggestion, wondering how big Abraham dreamed.

"It's not only Massachusetts," Abraham said. "We'd combine all the colonies into one country, bigger than Great Britain or any European country except Russia."

"Ah, I see." Smith eyed Abraham, remembering him as a cheeky young boy who ran riot in Kingsgate and drove his parents to distraction. He had grown into a self-confident young man, eager to test himself against the world.

A platoon of redcoats marched past with muskets on their shoulders and fire in their eyes. When the corporal in charge began to sing, the others joined in, eyeing the passers-by, and clearly hoping for a fight.

"Yankee Doodle went to town,
A-riding on a pony,
Stuck a feather in his cap,
And called it macaroni."

Abraham's face tightened. "Some of the Tommy Lobsters like to rile us," he said. "They laugh at our supposedly rustic manners and ideas."

Smith nodded. He understood that a doodle was a slang term for a buffoon or a country simpleton. The song insinuated that an American colonist believed he could be a macaroni, a man of high fashion, merely by having a feather in his cap. "They're frustrated," he said, "and want to take out their anger on the men who insult and abuse them."

Abraham smiled. "They might get their chance sooner than they realise."

They walked along the Long Wharf that extended into the harbour, and Smith stopped to view the islands offshore.

"Noddles Island, Governor's Island and Bird Island," Abraham named them, pointing to each one.

"I see the harbour is shallow." Smith twirled his cane, pointing to the discoloured water. "How deep are the channels between the islands?"

"Some as deep as five fathoms," Abraham said, "others are three fathoms on the approaches, and only one fathom as we approach Boston Neck and South Boston, skirting the Dorchester Flats."

Smith nodded, digesting the information. "Most are deep

enough for seagoing vessels," he said, "and better than the Thames at low water."

"Are you planning something, Mr Smith?" Abraham asked.

"Only shipping-related," Smith said, tapping his cane on the ground. "Nothing for you to worry about." He shivered. "It's cold here, though."

"This is mild for January," Abraham said. "We get more snow here than London does."

They returned to the town, walked through Boston Common, where groups of men gathered in earnest conversation, and headed to the Bunch of Grapes in King Street, a tavern the British officers had made their own.

"So many redcoats make me uneasy," Smith admitted, remembering the military guard around the scaffold where a pitiless authority had hanged him. He touched the nearly faded scar around his throat where the hempen noose had burned away the skin. "Soldiers and I are not always the best of friends."

"That is in the past, Mr Smith," Abraham reminded. "You are eminently respectable now, one of London's most successful merchants."

Smith shook away the old memories. "Respectability is a mask worn to cover hidden crimes," he said darkly. "While authority hangs little people for minor misdemeanours, it shrugs off the sins of those with money and power." After a glance inside, Smith walked past the Bunch of Grapes and continued his interrogation. "Tell me more about the Americas, Abraham."

"It's an interesting place," Abraham replied immediately. "The scale is immense, everything is painted in bold colours, and the people have strong opinions, whether they are Tories who support the Crown or Whigs who advocate more powers for the colonies." He looked sideways at Smith. "Do you want an example of the Whig point of view?"

Smith twirled his cane, stopped to allow a laden wagon past and nodded. "Undoubtedly, Abraham. This is my first visit to the Colonies, and I mean to experience all I can when I am here."

"I'll take you to church then," Abraham said, smiling.

Smith raised his eyebrows and said nothing as Abraham brought him to the Old South Meeting House. He had expected a quiet place of worship, but a sizeable crowd filled the interior, listening to a tall, handsome man in his mid-thirties.

"That's Joseph Warren," Abraham whispered. "He's a noted firebrand. Listen to what he says, Mr Smith. It will help you understand the feeling here."

"I will," Smith said and settled down in a pew near the back.

"What we want," Warren said, with his strong Massachusetts accent reaching every corner of the room, "is more equality between the American colonies and Great Britain. We are no longer children but fully mature adults, able to stand on our own feet."

The crowd nodded in agreement, some murmuring to themselves and a few raising their hats in the air.

"We will protest to the Crown and the forces of the Crown," Warren continued. "We will write to their representatives in the strongest possible terms, requesting, nay, demanding, our rights as free people. Great Britain boasts of the liberty of the people and a perfect constitution. Let the Crown prove that liberty by extending it to King George's subjects on this side of the Atlantic!"

"He's a good orator," Smith commented as Abraham lifted his voice to cheer.

"He's right," Abraham said. "Every word he says is correct! Massachusetts and the other colonies deserve better. The Crown should not tax us without representation in parliament! That's nothing but tyranny!"

Smith raised his eyebrows without comment as Warren continued.

"If our mild protests, our pacific measures are ineffectual, and it appears the only way to safety is through fields of blood. I know you will not turn your faces from your foes but will undauntedly press forward until tyranny is trodden underfoot."

The audience cheered the words, throwing their hats in the air, with Abraham as enthusiastic as any.

Smith nodded and ran his gaze over the gathering. Most of the men present looked sober and respectable, not the malcontents and wastrels of society he would expect to become involved in such protests.

Warren was speaking again. "We do not want the forces of the Crown in Massachusetts, for standing armies always endanger the liberty of the subject."

Smith watched Abraham's reaction with a mixture of amusement and interest. He could understand why people felt disassociated from central authority when thousands of miles separated the American Colonies from the mother country. Words such as liberty and tyranny seemed to strike a chord.

Smith was thoughtful when the building emptied, with men talking to each other and Warren smiling as he watched them leave.

"Do you think this discontent will lead to violence, Abraham?"

"Undoubtedly," Abraham replied immediately. "Unless the Crown accedes to the Colonists' requests. The people are growing angry at the Crown's tyranny."

"The Colonies have self-government and lower taxes than Great Britain has," Smith probed to see how Abraham would reply.

"And no representation in the British parliament," Abraham said, evidently spoiling for an argument.

Smith nodded. "And no representation in the British parliament," he agreed.

Abraham is my man; enthusiasts are always fertile ground.

Smith stopped at the north-western extremity of the town, from where he could see the slopes of Breeds and more distant Bunker Hill. "You seem quite at home here," he said.

"I am," Abraham agreed, "Since I moved to the Americas, I've opened my eyes to the Crown's tyranny." He stopped outside a shipyard and faced Smith. "You used to fight against such things, Mr Smith. You opposed the Crown's taxes with your smuggling operations and took to the high toby to fight oppressive landowners."

"I haven't forgotten," Smith agreed.

"Are you a Tory now?" Abraham challenged. "Have you joined the ranks of the oppressors since you became a lord, grinding down the ordinary people?"

"What do you think, Abraham?" Smith asked. "Do you think I would do that?"

Abraham considered for a few moments and then shook his head. "No," he said. "You are a man with strong principles."

Smith wondered at Abraham's words. He had long thought himself a man devoid of any principles except what was best for himself. "Thank you, Abraham, and that's what I wish to talk to you about."

Abraham smiled. "I didn't think you had crossed the Atlantic merely to view Boston. What can I do for you?"

"It's what we can do for each other," Smith said. "Do you have somewhere we can talk in private?"

Chapter Three

The woman stood in a doorway in Leadenhall Street, in the City of London. Dressed in shabby-genteel clothes, she looked upwards at the drizzling rain, pulled the three-cornered hat more firmly over her head and waited. Fifty yards from the prestigious offices of the Honourable East India Company, John Smith and Company's headquarters was smaller but equally stylish. Doric pillars supported a pediment above the front door, while an array of tall, multi-paned windows faced the street.

The woman saw candlelight reflected inside the windows and the occasional shape of somebody inside. She watched as a succession of men entered or left the building, all well-dressed, well-fed and seemingly prosperous. She examined each man and discarded them without interest.

At seven in the evening, with the rain persisting and the dark gathering like an ominous cloud, the woman rubbed the stiffness from her legs and crossed the road. She stepped through Smith's front door into a vast, oak-panelled hallway, where models of ships sat within glass cases, and a crystal chandelier hung from an ornately plastered ceiling.

A man in a grey suit and wig approached. "Yes, madam?" His deep voice sounded disapproving.

"I am looking for Mr John Smith," the woman said.

"Mr Smith is abroad at present," the grey man said. "May I enquire about the nature of your business?" His gaze swept over the woman from her head to her booted feet. He analysed her as a respectable matron down on her luck, perhaps a shipmaster's widow seeking money.

"I used to know Mr Smith," the woman said.

"I see." The grey man gave a brief bow. "I am sorry I cannot help you, Mrs..?"

"Rider," the woman said. "My name is Kate Rider. When do you expect John, Mr Smith, to return?"

The grey man shook his head. "Mr Smith has not seen fit to inform me, Mrs Rider. Shall I leave a note telling him you called?"

Kate shook her head. "No, thank you." She dropped in a curtsey. "I'll call back in a few weeks."

"As you wish, Mrs Rider." The grey man opened the door for Kate and watched her walk away.

There's a woman with a story, he thought. *Her past is written in her eyes.*

After a few moments, the grey man closed the door against the evening chill and returned to his station in the inner hall. By the time the long-case clock chimed eight, he had forgotten all about Kate Rider.

SMITH STEPPED ASHORE FROM THE TRIM BOSTON CUTTER AND looked around the wharf. The tobacco town of Baltimore wilted under the lash of a gale, and three lounging men watched him. Only one showed any interest in this middle-aged, granite-eyed man.

"You look lost, stranger." Long-jawed and lean, the watcher pushed himself from a bollard. "What are you looking for?"

"Harry Osborne," Smith said, "and the Eastern Tobacco Wharf."

"You're in luck, stranger." The long-jawed man eyed Smith up and down. "I'm Harry Osborne, and I know the Eastern Tobacco Wharf."

"I am John Smith," Smith introduced himself.

"I thought you might be," Osborne said. "I'll take you to the East Wharf. It's at Fell's Point." Osborne spoke over his shoulder as he led the way. "What's your business in Baltimore, Mr Smith?"

Smith was still unprepared for the directness of colonial speech. "I want to talk to some of the dock workers. Why do you ask?"

"Curious, Mr Smith, curious," Osborne said. "We don't often get important London merchants visiting the dock areas."

"I wish to speak to the foreman or the wharf manager if such a personage exists."

"He's another Londoner." Osborne looked sideways at Smith. "Except you're not from London, are you?"

"Not originally," Smith admitted. "And you're not from Baltimore."

"Not originally," Osborne countered. "How do you know that?"

"I make it my business to know about my employees," Smith said. "And you've been the company agent here for three years."

"I have," Osborne admitted.

"You were born in New York, worked in coastal traders, sailed on a privateer in the last French war, and became a ship's agent five years ago."

Osborne nodded. "That's correct, Mr Smith." He led them along the Baltimore shore with a long, loping stride.

"Tell me why I've lost three vessels." Smith could also be direct.

"You've certainly had some unfortunate luck recently," Osborne said,

"Two of my ships have gone down," Smith reminded. "And a third was missing when I left London."

"Is that why you're here?"

"That's why I'm here," Smith confirmed.

"I knew people on *Martha of Norfolk*," Osborne said. "The master was a hardnosed bastard but a good seaman."

"What happened?" Smith asked, placing a hand on Osborne's shoulder.

Osborne stopped and faced Smith. "I don't rightly know," he said. "Maybe they hit foul weather."

"*London's Pride* did," Smith confirmed, "but she might have survived if the cargo had not shifted."

"Did the cargo shift?" Osborne asked. "We don't rightly know."

"We do rightly know," Smith said. "A survivor told me."

Osborne looked surprised. "I heard *Pride* went down with all hands."

"There was at least one survivor," Smith said. "David Cupples, and he told me what happened."

Osborne bit into a plug of tobacco. "I'm glad somebody survived," he said, "but it's bad news about the cargo shifting."

"It is," Smith agreed. "Who supervises the loading?"

"Joshua Havering." Osborne was not so jaunty now.

"Take me to him."

They stopped at the Eastern Wharf, where men were loading three vessels. *London River* was one of Smith's, while *Amelia Mary* belonged to Charles Shapland and *Hercules* to Henry Copinger, another London merchant.

"Thank you for the guided tour," Smith said. "We'll speak again later." He stepped onto the pier.

The porters and labourers ignored him as they trundled heavy barrows laden with boxes, rolled barrels and kegs or worked pulleys carrying hogsheads onto the ships.

"Joshua Havering!" Smith roared. "I'm looking for Joshua Havering!"

Some of the labourers looked around, and one pointed to *London's River*. "He's in there," he said and continued to work.

Lifting a hand in acknowledgement, Smith strode up the gangplank and onto *London's River*. Three-masted and only two years old, the ship was in good condition, with her masts and spars cared for and the boatswain inspecting the running rigging. The deck was busy with men as a harassed first mate tried to keep control of a dozen problems simultaneously.

"Mr Kane." Smith knew the mate. "How is the loading progressing?"

"Mr Smith!" Jacob Kane started. "I didn't expect to see you in Baltimore. "We're getting there. These Baltimore men know their job."

"Where's Captain Mortimer?"

"He's somewhere ashore, Mr Smith." Kane gave an uneasy smile.

"When do you expect to see him?"

Kane looked even more uneasy. "When he completes his business ashore, Mr Smith."

Smith nodded. "You're in charge of everything, then?"

"At present, Mr Smith."

"When did you last see Captain Mortimer?"

When Kane said nothing, Smith nodded. "Not for a while. Thank you, Jacob. Now, I want to speak to Joshua Havering."

"Havering's in the forward hold, Mr Smith." Kane stopped to roar orders at a group of men. "Sorry, Mr Smith."

"No need to apologise for doing your duty, Jacob," Smith said.

Havering was a broad man of medium height, with a face pitted by smallpox and a long knife at his belt. He looked round when Smith called his name.

"What do you want?" Havering asked.

"I've come to check your work, Havering," Smith told him.

"The devil you have! Who are you?"

"John Smith. I'm the managing owner of *London's River*. Stand aside."

"I'm busy." Havering turned his back. "You could be Jesus Christ Himself, but I'm in charge of the loading."

Reaching forward, Smith grabbed Havering's shoulder and hauled him back. "Stand aside!" he repeated.

Havering staggered and reached for the knife at his belt but contented himself with a glare as Smith pushed past.

The barrels formed a barrier across the larboard side of the hold, stacked to the deck beams above and jammed from side to side. Ordering the labourers to step away, Smith tapped the bottom row, grunted at the sound, and peered through the small gap in between two barrels. He frowned at what he saw and withdrew.

"Havering, come with me." Smith raised his voice. "Mr Kane!" He pointed to a toiling porter. "Fetch me the mate!"

As the porter hurried to the maindeck, Havering stomped across the hold. Kane pushed him unceremoniously aside.

"Yes, Mr Smith?"

"I want this hold emptied and re-stowed, Mr Kane. Employ a different team. Havering and his men are now unemployed."

"You can't do that!" Havering protested, again placing a hand on the hilt of his knife.

"I can, and I have," Smith said. "Carry on, Mr Kane. Stand aside, Havering!"

When Havering objected, Smith grabbed his sleeve and thrust him against the side of the hold. "Stand there, you murdering bastard!"

"What's the matter with the loading?" Kane looked confused.

"The bottom layer is composed of empty and half-rotted casks," Smith said. "And Havering had left a sizeable gap between the casks and the hull. Given any sort of a blow, the ship will heel to larboard; the top layers will shift sideways, put pressure on the bottom layer and break the rotted wood."

Kane stared at Havering in shock. "Why?"

"Let's find out why," Smith said. "Tell us why, Havering. Were you also responsible for loading *London's Pride* and *Martha of Norfolk*?"

"He was," Kane said. "And *London's Profit*. He supervises the loading on this wharf."

"Well, now I'll charge him with murdering the crew of three fine ships and attempting to murder the crew of *London River*."

"I'm damned if you will!" Havering said, drawing his knife. Slashing at Smith, he jinked sideways, dodged around Kane, and ran up the ladder to the deck above. Smith followed, wishing he was in his twenties rather than fast approaching fifty and softened by a near-sedentary lifestyle.

"Stop that man!" Smith roared, watching Havering disappear among the piled boxes and barrels of the quayside. He lengthened his stride, panting as Osborne joined the chase.

"That was Havering, wasn't it?" Osborne asked.

"Yes, and he's responsible for sinking *Martha of Norfolk*," Smith replied.

Osborne stared at Smith for a second and then increased his speed, following Havering through the streets. They ran beyond the dock area and into the town. After a few moments, Smith stopped, gasping for breath.

"I lost him," Osborne said.

"Where does he live?" Smith gripped his cane and felt for the double-barrelled pistol in his inside pocket.

Osborne nodded. "This way." He led them through a succession of streets, with Smith barely glancing around as he ran. "That house there."

Smith checked his pistol. "I'm going inside," he said. "You can accompany me, wait outside, or return to whatever you were doing. The choice is yours."

Without waiting for a reply, Smith strode to Havering's home, a two-storied brick-built terraced house at the end of stylish Ann Street. Five stone steps led to the panelled front door, which he found locked.

"A fine building for a dock foreman," Smith told himself, "unless Baltimore wages are higher than in London." He picked the lock without difficulty, slid inside the house and closed the door behind him. *You should have fitted bolts, Havering.*

"Havering!" Smith roared. "Is anybody at home?"

When nobody replied, Smith searched the house. He did not know what he was looking for but entered rooms and opened drawers and cupboards, uncaring about the mess he made.

After a search that found some fine clothes and various books, a French flintlock pistol and a nautical cutlass, Smith entered a room that looked like an office and saw a battered desk with three drawers.

That looks more interesting, Smith told himself and tried the top drawer. He grunted when he found it locked.

Much more interesting.

It was only a minute's work to force the lock, and Smith smiled when he looked inside.

Where did a dock foreman get so much money?

Smith counted fifty golden guineas lying loose in the top drawer, with a handful of silver. When he opened the next drawer, he found a bundle of letters tied with a linen ribbon and opened them without shame.

Scanning the letters, Smith nodded when two mentioned the "task to our mutual benefit" and mentioned a sum of "£100 Sterling." Both were signed with the name "Mr Jay".

It appears that somebody has bribed Havering.

Folding one of the letters in his inside pocket, Smith heard the front door open.

"Welcome home, Mr Havering," Smith said to himself, closed the drawers and left the office. He waited for Havering at the head of the stairs.

"What are you doing here?" Havering blustered.

"Waiting for you," Smith said. "We can continue our discussion now."

"Get out of my house!" Havering roared. He eyed Smith up and down, evidently calculating his chances in a brawl.

"We'll talk now," Smith told him.

"I'm damned if we will!" Havering was at least ten years younger than Smith and as hard and fast as a physical job could make him. He pulled his long-bladed knife and launched himself up the stairs. Smith waited until he was within three steps, then kicked out, with his iron-studded boot catching Havering square in the face. As Havering grunted and fell back, Smith followed through by stamping on the man's knife hand and twisting his boot sideways. He heard the crack of breaking bones as Havering screamed and released his weapon.

Pushing Havering down the stairs, Smith lifted the knife and followed. Havering crouched at the bottom of the stairs, cradling his injured hand and with blood oozing from a cut Smith's boot had opened in his forehead.

"Now, Havering," Smith said quietly, "you're going to tell me why you've been trying to sink my ships."

Havering climbed to his feet and spat at Smith. "I'll tell you nothing," he said.

Smith fingered the edge of the knife. "I hope you do," he said. "Many good men died when these ships sank, men who were far better than you'll ever be. So tell me why and who paid you, or I'll kill you very slowly."

Havering looked at the knife and the expression on Smith's face. "I'll tell you nothing," he said, with a quaver in his voice. Pushing himself upright, he swung a massive fist. Smith pulled back his head and blocked with his left hand.

Havering is a brawler with strength and power rather than skill.

Smith feinted with the knife, blocked Havering's defence and tripped him up. As Havering sprawled face up on the floor, Smith squatted on his chest, pinning him down.

"Now, Havering, I'm going to prick out one of your eyes and

ask you again." Smith expected Havering's reaction as he cowered away. "Who are you working for, Havering?"

"I don't know," Havering said, watching the blade Smith passed back and forward in front of his face. "I don't know! I never met him!"

"Did you stow the cargo badly on my other ships that sank?" Smith placed the tip of the blade an inch under Havering's left eye and pressed slightly, breaking the skin.

"Only on two of them," Havering said, high-pitched. "Not on *Martha*."

"What did you do to *Martha*?" Smith asked. He drew the point of the blade upward, with blood flowing down Havering's face.

"I was told to bore holes beneath the waterline and stuff them with wax," Havering said. "For God's sake, don't blind me!"

"You sabotaged *Martha*, knowing the sea would wear away the wax and *Martha* would sink at sea." Smith sliced the skin, creeping closer to Havering's eye.

"Yes." Havering began to weep. "Don't blind me. For God's sake, have pity."

"Why? You had none?" Smith asked and changed the question. "Who paid you to murder these men?"

"I don't know his name," Havering spoke in short sentences as the knife blade touched his eyeball. "I told you, Mr Smith! I never met him!"

"Then how did he give you orders?" Smith applied a little pressure.

"By letter!" Havering screamed. "He gave me orders by letter!"

"Did he order you to sink any ships apart from mine?"

"No," Havering said and began to sob as Smith withdrew his knife. "I want all the money you earned," he said. "That's going to the widows and orphans of the men you murdered, and I want every scrap of correspondence relating to your murders."

"Yes, yes," Havering was suddenly eager to please. "Thank you, Mr Smith. I'll give you everything."

When Smith left the house an hour later, he carried a bag heavy with gold coins and a small bundle of papers, including Havering's signed confession. Havering sat in his office, still shaking as tears joined the congealed blood on his cheeks.

Osborne waited in the street outside, ignoring the rain that fell in a steady downpour.

"It was Havering," Smith told Osborne. "He deliberately stowed the cargo badly in two ships and bored holes in *Martha*'s hull."

Osborne took a deep breath. "The murdering bastard!"

"To be sure," Smith said calmly. "Now I have to find out who gave the orders and why."

"What about Havering?" Osborne asked.

"I've finished with him. I'll tell the local authorities what he's done and hand them his confession. I am sure they'll deal with him as he deserves."

Chapter Four

E dward Hind stood at the back of the cart, staring
contemptuously at the crowd that jeered and threw
rotten fruit at him. Dressed in his customary grey
breeches and tan shirt, he rattled the shackles around his wrists
and ankles and felt the slow rain weeping from above. With his
coffin behind him, the executioner in front and a parson at his
side, Hind knew it was his last morning alive. Although he felt
sick, he attempted to appear nonchalant, hiding his fingers that
twisted around each other.

A gaunt-faced sergeant commanded the soldiers who
escorted the cart. Mainly young men or drink-sodden veterans,
they had joined the army to escape poverty or in a moment of
drunken bravado. Now the youngsters wondered what happened
to the glory the recruiting sergeant had promised, while the
veterans only looked for their next drink.

"Seek forgiveness, Hind," the Church of England parson
pleaded. "If you pray for forgiveness now, the Lord will listen,
even to a sinner like you."

Hind jabbed his elbow into the parson's ribs. "Get away from
me. I've had no time for the Church in life, and I don't want it in
death."

The parson ignored Hind's words. "You can still save yourself," he said. "It's not too late to seek mercy from the Lord."

Hind ducked a thrown cabbage that hit the parson on the chest. "There's the Lord's opinion of you, Parson. Now bugger off and leave me alone."

Busy workmen had erected the gallows the previous night, with the gibbet already in place to take Hind's executed body. Most criminals would blanch at the thought of being gibbetted, with their bodies hanging in a metal cage for the birds and insects to devour slowly, but Hind spat his contempt onto the seething crowd.

"I'll be dead," Hind said, with his heart hammering inside his chest. "They can do what they will with my corpse. It's only meat."

"I'm here to save your soul!" the parson persisted.

"I don't believe in your God," Hind said. "But I'll be dancing with the devil when you're preaching sanctimonious lies from your pulpit."

"You blasphemer!" the parson said as the cart rattled the last few yards to the scaffold. The sun struggled through the low cloud, allowing a single shaft of light to emerge behind the gallows, throwing an ominous shadow down the hill and onto the mob below.

A red-haired woman ran from the crowd, whirled a dead cat by its tail and threw it at Hind. "You'll go straight to hell!" the woman shouted as a thin youth held up a miniature gallows noose in mockery.

"Hang him!" the crowd chanted. "Hang him! Let's see him dance!"

"They don't like you much," the executioner, a long-faced, smiling man, said. He glanced over the crowd. "I've been offered bribes to make you suffer."

Hind shrugged and said nothing.

"It's customary for the condemned man to tip the executioner to make his passage easier," the hangman suggested.

"Go to hell," Hind said and spat in his face.

"You first," the hangman said, wiping the spittle from his face. "I'll ensure you suffer at the rope's end, Ned. You'll dangle and dance before the Devil takes you."

Hind looked away. The woman with the dead cat returned, grabbing hold of the edge of the cart, and throwing a rotten egg with great force until the sergeant of the escort dragged her away and planted a solid kick on her backside.

"You dirty lobster bastard!" the woman screamed. "That man murdered three women!"

"Get back, you old bitch!" the sergeant said, realised the woman was not so old and quite handsome beneath the dirt that smeared her face and patted her shoulder. "Step back, Miss, for your own safety."

The driver halted the cart at the foot of the scaffold, where a twelve-rung ladder stretched to the timber-built platform on which the gallows tree stood.

"We don't get many executions in this part of the world," the hangman said. "You're something of a novelty." He grinned, revealing surprisingly white teeth. "The people should thank you for providing free entertainment." Reaching forward, he fingered Hind's coat. "I'll sell this for a pretty penny after you're gone."

Hind said nothing. He knew one of the hangman's perquisites was the condemned man's clothes.

"Up you go!" The hangman unfastened Hind from the cart, with the sergeant of the escort watching and the soldiers pushing back the crowd.

"Come on, son; I'll help you." The driver took pity on the condemned and guided him to the ladder.

"I can manage," Hind snarled.

"Don't be bloody stupid!" the driver said, slipping something into Hind's fist. "Come on!"

The hangman led the way up the steps, with Hind next and the parson taking up the rear, holding his Bible in his hand.

The red-haired woman screamed her hatred from the foot of

the scaffold, reaching out with hands like claws and encouraging the crowd to follow. "Let's see him dance!" she screamed. "Dance on air, you murdering bastard!"

"Get back!" the sergeant ordered wearily and sent two of his dozen privates to push the woman away.

Infected by her example, more of the crowd rushed forward, grabbing the scaffold. "Hang him! Make him dance!" they yelled.

"What the devil are you doing here?" the hangman asked as the driver eased Hind onto the platform.

"This," the driver said, thrust the hangman's head inside his noose and pulled the lever on the trapdoor. The trap opened with a bang, and as the hangman kicked and choked, Hind unfastened his manacles with the key the driver had passed to him.

"What happens now?" Hind asked as he threw the manacles into the screaming crow.

"Now we run!" the parson said. "Get into the cart! Jump, man, while the crowd distracts the guard!"

Hind leapt into the cart as the driver whipped up the horses, and the parson drew a pistol and fired a shot in the air. "That will make them think," he said. "I hope you noticed the horses were all bloodstock."

"I had other things on my mind," Hind said. "Who the devil are you, and what do you want?"

"You can call me Mr Jay," the parson said as the red-haired woman vaulted into the cart, and the soldiers struggled with the crowd. "I own you now."

The woman thrust a pistol into Hind's back. "You do as we say, cully, or you'll wish the hangman had turned you off."

Hind looked into the woman's eyes and recognised a fellow killer. "Just say the word," he said, rubbing the raw marks the manacles had left on his wrists. Sitting down, he leaned his back against the coffin, extracted a pack of cards from his pocket and shuffled them slowly.

SMITH STAYED AT A SMALL INN, A SEAGULL'S CRY FROM Baltimore docks that night, reading the documents he had brought from Havering's house. They did not give him much information.

The writer had given Havering specific instructions in the first letter, ordering him to stow the cargo "to ensure even a squall would sink *London's Profit*" and telling him that "one hundred sovereigns would ease his conscience." He had signed it with "your friend, Mr Jay." The second letter had ordered Havering to ensure *Martha* sunk at sea, and the third was similar to the first but concerned *London's Pride*.

Smith tucked the letters away and counted the money. Havering had spent about thirty sovereigns, leaving two hundred and seventy, which Smith placed into three piles of ninety sovereigns each.

"Ninety golden boys aren't going far when divided between a full crew," Smith said to himself. "Three pounds a man, and that's all a seaman's life is worth." He shook his head. "I'll do better than that."

With the decision made, Smith began to pace the room, wondering who had given the order to sink his ships.

There was a small list of possible rivals, with Charles Shapland at the top and Henry Copinger a close second. Could a business rival be sufficiently ruthless to deliberately sink ships and drown innocent seamen?

Smith recalled Cupples' words about Shapland leaving *London's Pride's* survivors adrift in the open Atlantic. Yes, Shapland headed the list. But with the growing disquiet over the Crown's actions in the Colonies, Smith wondered if any disgruntled Colonial had begun a campaign against British shipping. Havering had expressed ignorance about the man who employed him, and Smith was sure he had told the truth. The name Mr Jay meant nothing.

Smith paced the room, shaking his head and sick at the loss of lives. Shortly after midnight, he heard a commotion in the streets outside and stepped to the window. He saw a crowd of men hurrying past in the night-dark streets, decided it was nothing to do with him and retired to bed. Images of sinking ships and drowning mariners haunted Smith's dreams, so he woke out of temper and with a throbbing headache.

"Did you hear the news, sir?" The hostess was plump, blonde, and pretty, with bright blue eyes and a habit of brushing against Smith every time she passed.

"I did not," Smith admitted.

"You must have heard the disorder last night," the hostess insisted.

"I certainly heard that," Smith agreed.

"It was a murder, sir, a terrible murder."

Even before the woman continued, Smith guessed who the victim was. "That's terrible," he echoed her words. "What happened?"

"It was Mr Havering, sir. You won't know him, with you being a visitor to Baltimore, but he's a foreman down at the docks."

"That's a responsible position," Smith said. He felt nothing for the death of Havering, for anybody who condemned seamen to drown deserved to die.

"A mob raided his house last night," the hostess said. "They hauled the poor man outside, tarred and feathered him and hanged him from a tree."

"Why was that?" Smith asked.

"To be sure, sir, I don't know. I can only think it was a party matter, sir. Mr Havering may have been a Whig, and the mob were Tories, or perhaps the other way round."

Smith nodded and began to eat his mutton and eggs. "I am sure you are correct, Madam," he said.

"Well, sir," the hostess sat opposite Smith, wiping her hands on her apron. "I am not political, not at all, sir, and all I can say is a plague on both their houses."

"With that, I heartily agree, Madam," Smith said. "The best thing to do with politics is to avoid them."

When Smith left the boarding house, he passed under the body of Havering, swinging gently from a branch. The man's face was nearly unrecognisable under its coating of tar, and feathers drifted slowly to the ground.

BEFORE HE LEFT NORTH AMERICA, SMITH INVITED OSBORNE into a coffee house. He ignored the specks of blood on the agent's cuffs and his damaged knuckles.

"Mr Osborne," Smith said. "I am one of the most successful London tobacco merchants, yet the Glasgow syndicates outperform me. Why is that?"

"Partly because ships from the Clyde have less distance to sail to reach the Chesapeake than London ships," Osborne said, "but not only that. John Glassford has fifty ships in his tobacco fleet, while you have eighteen, and you charter some of them."

"Owning all his ships will allow Glassford to plan his schedules better," Smith agreed.

"Yes, Mr Smith," Osborne said. "There are other, more significant reasons, too. Glassford and others, such as William Cunningham and Company and Speirs, Bowman, have established chains of stores throughout Virginia, with Scottish factors, sometimes even family members. They purchase tobacco direct from the planters, so when the Glasgow ships arrive, the cargo is already ready to load."

Smith was taking notes. "That's good business practice," he said. "It will reduce turnaround time and hence wages. I'll look into buying tobacco stores in the Chesapeake."

Osborne nodded. "Shall I keep my eyes open, Mr Smith?"

"Do so. Pay whatever the seller asks without quibbling. We'll recoup the purchase price with excess profits."

"Yes, Mr Smith," Osborne said.

Smith finished his coffee and stood up. "I'll leave things in your hands, Osborne." When he left the coffee shop, Smith looked back over Baltimore. A crowd of men glowered back at him, some carrying long rifles.

This place is simmering with trouble. My discussions with Abraham might be the key to expansion here. I'll keep my feet in both camps.

Chapter Five

"What's happening?" Bess asked when somebody pushed against her.

"The Lord Mayor is passing," Smith explained as a file of scarlet-coated guardsmen pressed back the crowds on either side of the street.

Smith and Bess watched as six matched horses hauled the coach up the Strand, with the liveried driver sitting with an ornate wig and the Lord Mayor glancing at the citizens.

"That's the way to travel," Bess said. "That coach cost over a thousand pounds to build." He repeated the figure. "A thousand pounds! Most people won't earn that in twenty years' work!"

"The Aldermen all subscribed to pay for it," Smith watched the heavily ornamented coach roll past. "And now the Corporation is going to buy it." He grinned. "How would you like to travel in that and reign over London?" Smith asked.

"I doubt I'll get the chance," Bess said. "You once wished to be Lord Mayor," she reminded him. "Have you abandoned your political ambitions?"

"They're dormant at present," Smith told her. "I've been too busy building up the shipping and transport companies."

Bess smiled. "Successfully," she said. "You don't need political power as well. You can reign happily as managing owner."

"Maybe," Smith watched the coach roll past and pictured Bess sitting inside. It would be a fitting climax to a life that started with her following the drum. "Maybe."

MR JAY LEANED AGAINST THE BAR, CONTEMPLATING THE clientele.

"They're quiet enough at present."

"Give them time." Hind stood at his side with a pewter tankard in his hand. "Give them time."

A fire flickered inside a cracked brick fireplace, sending blue smoke up the flue to add to the dense smog that pressed down on the dingy streets of Bermondsey. Men and women crouched close to the fire, some holding tankards, others with small glasses and a few hoping for charity from their companions. Two men arm-wrestled at a circular table, with a stubby candle at each side, so the stronger could press the other's hand onto the flame.

"Interesting clientele," Mr Jay observed.

The serving girls were agile, moving from table to table, avoiding the inevitable groping hand with practised ease and slapping the more persistent customers.

"Let's hasten things a little," Mr Jay said and signalled to the barman. "Give me half a dozen bottles of rum."

The barman frowned. "Let's see your gold, mister."

Mr Jay produced a heavy pocketbook and emptied two sovereigns onto the counter. The barman scooped up the money before Mr Jay changed his mind.

"Here." The barman produced six bottles of rum. "I normally serve from the barrel," he said.

Mr Jay lifted his voice. "Free rum!" he shouted. "Over here!" He raised a bottle and stepped back from the expected rush. Hind watched cynically as most customers hurried to claim their drink, with only the two arm wrestlers remaining where they were.

Mr Jay poured rum into a succession of glasses, with men and women jostling each other in their eagerness to claim a second and third glass. As Mr Jay had anticipated, they began to argue, pushing one another aside.

"What are you trying to do, Mr Jay?" Hind asked. He began to shuffle his cards, watching the mob while standing out of their way.

"Assess potentials," Mr Jay said. He poured rum into proffered glasses, fended off too-willing hands and ignored a be-ribboned prostitute's hopeful request for custom.

"Ah, here we are," Mr Jay said as a verbal dispute escalated into blows. "Stand back, Hind. I want to see what develops."

Still shuffling his cards, Hind moved away. "It's no skin off my nose," he said.

The original altercation expanded, and the two combatants' companions joined in. Mr Jay saw the first punch thrown, and then somebody lifted a stool as a weapon.

"Keep clear of us, damn your hide!" the taller arm wrestler growled as a stray arm knocked over one of the candles.

The man with the stool swung, missed, and staggered onto the back of the smaller arm-wrestler.

"We warned you!" Both wrestlers stood, with the taller lifting the candle and thrusting it into the face of the nearest man.

Mr Jay watched as the two arm wrestlers attacked the mob, felling them with fists and boots, throwing them aside as if they were made of paper. Within minutes, the two men had cleared the pub, leaving a bemused barman, Hind and Mr Jay watching.

"That was well done," Mr Jay said as the two victors surveyed the wreckage, with three men and one woman groaning on the floor.

"Who the devil are you?" the shorter of the two men asked.

"You can call me Mr Jay," Mr Jay said. "I may require men like you."

"HONEST MERCHANTS, SUCH AS US," SMITH SAID, "ARE constantly at war with the criminal element." He glanced at the clock, which read one in the morning. The embers of the fire had long since died, and the servants in their Leicester Square house had retired to bed hours ago. Link boys patrolled the streets outside, hoping for late-night pedestrians to convey through the dangerously dark streets.

"That's the price of honesty," Bess agreed.

"Ship owners with ships berthed in the River Thames are fighting a losing battle against pillagers," Smith said. "We have the noblest port in Britain here, stretching along the river, and one of the busiest in the world, yet it's amazingly inconvenient. The stretch between Limehouse and the Tower is as crowded as any street, so ships are anchored tier beside tier, and hardly even a wherry can pass through."

Bess did not stifle her yawn. "I know all this," she said. "We've lived in London for years."

Smith ignored her lack of interest and continued. "The overcrowding creates problems of access and adds to the difficulty of unloading each vessel, as you can imagine."

"Quite," Bess said and examined her ring. It was a fine pearl set within two Indian rubies in a band of gold. She held it up, so the candlelight reflected from the red stones, sparkling in the room.

"We unload the vessels into lighters and barges," Smith explained, "and that also delays the time they sit uselessly in the river."

"Quite so." Bess stopped examining her ring and turned her attention to the brass candlesticks on the ornate mantelpiece. "I know all this, John."

"And that's when they are most at risk," Smith said and frowned. "I don't believe you are paying heed to my words, Bess."

"I'm not," Bess admitted calmly. "I should be in my bed."

"This is important," Smith allowed a hint of irritation to enter his voice.

"Yes, my love," Bess said, "but I know all this already. In a moment, you'll tell me that the ships are prey for half the thieves and pillagers of the river." She adjusted one of the candlesticks until it stood in line with its companions. "You'll tell me about the crooked lumpers who unload the vessels and the watchmen and Revenue Officers who take bribes to look the other way."

Smith's irritation vanished as he listened, for Bess was correct.

"And when I nod in astonishment at your extensive knowledge." Bess stepped back to check her mantelpiece was as perfect as possible, "you'll tell me about the Night Plunderers, Light Horsemen, Scuffle-Hunters and Mudlarks that haunt the river, robbing poor merchants blind."

"I was coming to them," Smith admitted, smiling.

"Then," Bess continued, facing him, "you will say that sugar, rum, coffee and tobacco are the chief targets of these river pirates."

"Indeed," Smith nodded.

"Why?" Bess said, having effectively halted Smith in mid-tirade. "Why tell me these things that I already know?"

"I was setting the scene," Smith conceded her point. "We both know about these plunderers and pillagers, and our profits suffer because of them. Now I intend to turn a disadvantage into an advantage."

"How?" Bess was suddenly interested. She withdrew to her customary seat and raised her eyebrows. "Tell me more, husband, dear."

"I intend to recruit some of these unfortunates to our cause," Smith told her. "We have a constant rivalry with other companies, so rather than having these thieves rob our vessels, I'll have them pilfering our rivals."

Bess gave her slow smile. "Now that's a good idea," she said.

"Be careful down by the river, John. You're not as young as you once were."

"I've found that out recently," Smith admitted. "Too much port, rum punch, rich food and insufficient exercise."

"That's true for me as well," Bell said ruefully, slapping her stomach. "I'm no longer the trim girl that turned men's heads." She looked in the mirror above the fireplace, touched the white scar that ran down her left cheek to her lip and sighed. "I'll never get my youthful looks back."

Smith stepped across to Bess and kissed her. "You're always beautiful to me."

"Oh?" Bess returned the kiss. "Would you care to prove it, kind sir?" She took his hand. "It looks like I'll have to bribe you to get to bed this morning."

"Oh, Bess," Smith said, snuffing the candle and allowing her to escort him from the room. "All you had to do was ask."

———

SMITH SWUNG HIS CANE AS HE WALKED ALONG THE RIVERBANK. He knew he was in territory as dangerous as any in Western Europe, and with night closing in, the possibility of being attacked, robbed or murdered increased by the minute. After years of building up his companies and travelling between city offices and home, the tingle of danger exhilarated him. Smith felt the weight of the pistol in his pocket and smiled.

Just like old times.

To Smith's right, ships lay in the river, some with watchmen pacing the deck or sitting in the stern, hoping for a quiet night. He saw surreptitious movement in the muddy river and stepped into the shadow of a warehouse to watch. Three slender youths slithered across the mud and swarmed up the hull of a recently arrived brig.

That's the first of them; soon, the Thames will be full of predators, searching for anything they can find.

Smith waited in the shadows, listening to the whisper of the river and the wind singing through the ships' rigging. He saw other figures haunting the riverside, heard somebody crying and then the three youths reappeared, each with a bag tied across their shoulders. The central boy was tallest, with a soldier's scarlet coat over his shoulders and a tarred cord holding up his torn buckskin trousers. A gleam of light reflected from tarnished silver braid on the three-cornered hat on his head. A young girl joined them, padding on bare feet and with her tousled hair descending to her shoulders.

"You lads!" Smith stepped from the shadows and addressed them sharply. "What do you think you're doing?"

The youths stopped, eyeing Smith with truculent suspicion. When they realised he was alone, their confidence increased, and they spread out. "Minding our own business," the tallest said. Smith guessed he was fourteen, a wiry youngster with teeth like tombstones in an abandoned cemetery.

"You're a bunch of thieves," Smith said pleasantly and smiled as the spokesman pushed back his hat and treated him to foul-mouthed abuse.

"Is that any way to address a gentleman?" Smith asked, swinging his cane.

"What do you want?" The youths spread out further, nerving themselves to attack him.

"I want to talk to you," Smith said. The boy on the right crouched while the diminutive girl on the left slipped a knife into her hand. Smith smiled at the spokesman. "What's your name, my young friend?"

"None of your business," the boy in the three-cornered hat spiced his words with obscenity, either in an attempt to shock Smith or because he knew no better.

The girl moved first, dropping her booty, and lunging forward simultaneously. Smith swung his cane hard, catching her across the knuckles and forcing her to drop the knife. As she gasped, Smith jabbed the edge of his cane into her throat, sending her reeling back, choking. The boy on the left was fractionally slower, allowing Smith time to recover, and thrust the point of his cane into his groin. When the boy doubled up, Smith cracked him over the head.

With both attackers disabled, Smith continued his conversation.

"I see you have been busy robbing ships," he said, ignoring the two stricken youths.

The spokesman eyed his companions and scratched his head under the hat. "So?"

"So, how would you like to earn some extra money?"

The girl was retching, trying to catch her breath. Smith put his boot on her knife to restrain any temptation.

"Doing what?" The youth in the hat looked at his comrades and then at Smith, who swung his walking cane, smiling.

"Stealing from ships," Smith told him. The boy on the right was straightening up, still holding himself. Smith swung his cane again, slashing at the boys' legs until he backed off. "I know a man who will give you a fair price from your plunder as long as you steal from certain ships."

Smith knew that London had scores of pawn shops and ship's chandlers who would buy stolen goods but at prices that did not cover the danger of thieving. A pawn who gave decent money was every thief's dream.

The boy in the hat gave a slight nod. "Maybe," he said distrustingly.

"Maybe," Smith repeated and turned away. "Of course, if you're not interested, I can find another thief. London is infested with them." Stooping, he picked up the knife and stepped back towards the shadows.

"I didn't say I wasn't interested," the spokesman said.

"Then let's talk," Smith said, facing him again. "Your companions can remain here. What's your name?"

"Peter Brown," the boy said after a slight hesitation. "What's yours?"

Smith smiled. "That's not your real name, but it will do. Come with me, Peter Brown." Turning quickly, Smith stalked away. He heard Peter's bare feet pad after him and led him to a locked and bolted shop a hundred yards from the Thames.

"Where are you taking me?" Peter asked. "Here, no funny business now!"

Smith nodded. "You are right to be suspicious, Peter." He turned suddenly, checking they were alone. "If you are honest with me, you'll be safe. If you try to deceive me, I'll gut you and leave you as an example. Do you understand?"

Peter looked into Smith's eyes and shuddered. "Yes, mister."

"You call me sir," Smith told him. He unlocked the shop's side door, stepped inside, scratched a spark from his tinder box and lit a candle that sat on a shelf. "Come in."

With fear replacing his truculence, Peter hesitated until Smith dragged him into the shop. "Abraham Reeves runs this establishment," Smith said. "In future, you will bring everything you steal to him, and he'll give you a fair price."

"Yes, sir." Peter looked around as Smith ushered him into the small room behind the front shop.

"Sit," Smith ordered.

The room had a battered round table and two wooden chairs. Peter sat down, looking uneasy and glancing at the exit. Smith kicked the door shut and sat opposite.

"Take your hat off," Smith ordered, and the boy obeyed. His short hair was dark and matted.

"Show me what you stole tonight," Smith said.

Peter produced two lengths of cable and a marline spike.

"Rubbish," Smith said. "No pawn would give more than sixpence for that."

"It's the best I could get," Peter defended himself. "The watchman nearly caught us."

"Rubbish," Smith repeated. "You can do better than that. I want you to target certain ships."

"Why?"

"Because I say so," Smith said. "I want you to rob *Amelia Jane, Amelia Mary, Amelia Margaret* and *Amelia Martha*."

"Don't you like the name Amelia?" Peter asked.

Smith smiled again. "I wonder if you could recognise the name painted on a ship. Can you read?"

"No," Peter shook his head scornfully.

"You won't be able to write, either," Smith said.

"No," Peter confirmed.

"Can you remember the names I gave you?"

"Yes." Peter repeated them without effort.

"Good." Smith knew that illiterate people often had retentive memories. "Try these. *Lady Amelia, Lady Jane, Lady Margaret, Lady Martha*."

Peter repeated the ship's names. "They're all Charlie Shapland's ships."

"That's correct," Smith said. "Mr Reeves will pay double for any item stolen from one of Shapland's vessels."

"Double?"

"Double," Smith confirmed. "Don't try to cheat him. Reeves is a hard man."

"Yes, sir," Peter said.

Smith slid two silver shillings and a sixpence across the table. "That's for the cables."

Peter gaped at the silver coins and pocketed them instantly.

"If you bring anything from the captain's cabin," Smith said, "Reeves will be more than generous."

"What sort of things?" Peter asked quickly.

"Maps, charts, logbooks, letters, documents," Smith said. "Watches, sextants, compasses, binnacles. Tell all your friends the same." He grinned and tapped his nose conspiratorially. "Mr Reeves and I will make you all rich men, driving carriages through the streets of London and hob-nobbing with the dukes and earls."

Peter had no such illusions. "Nah," he said. "But I might rent a room to myself."

Smith nodded. Renting a room rather than sleeping in the streets or a halfpenny a night ken was the height of Peter's ambition. Smith knew Peter's life would be a constant struggle to survive, with no aspirations beyond survival. Children who grew up in London's rookeries learned pragmatism before they learned to walk.

"That's a start," Smith agreed. "Tell me which ships?"

"Charlie Shapland's ships," Peter said, replacing his hat.

"Quite so," Smith said and tossed over another shilling. "Here, treat yourself and tell your friends."

Peter snatched the shilling before Smith changed his mind. Smith grabbed his arm. "I'll be watching you, Peter Brown!"

Chapter Six

Charles Shapland stood at his office window, looking over the crowded shipping in the river. He took a pinch of snuff, sneezed delicately and frowned when somebody tapped at his door.

"Come in," he shouted and turned around, tucking away his ivory snuff box.

"My apologies for disturbing you, sir." A middle-aged clerk stood at the door. "A woman is asking to see you."

"Is she a young woman?" Shapland asked. He knew by his clerk's choice of words and attitude that his visitor was not from the upper echelons of society. If the visitor had been important, the clerk would have called her a lady rather than a woman.

"Not very young, sir." The clerk knew his master's tastes. "Middling young. I'd say around thirty."

Shapland pursed his lips. "Is she presentable?"

"Reasonably presentable, sir, for the sort of woman she is."

Shapland grunted. "Does the woman have a name?"

"She calls herself Kate Rider, sir." The clerk bowed. "Shall I send her away?"

Shapland nodded. "Yes, send her away; I don't know the

name. Get rid of her." He turned away to continue staring out of the window as the clerk closed the door.

"Mr Shapland will see me; damn your pen-pushing eyes!" a female shouted, and a moment later, the office door crashed open, and a woman barged in, followed by the anxious clerk.

"I'm sorry, sir, I couldn't stop her." The clerk flapped his hands despairingly.

Shapland eyed the intruder. She was tall for a woman, with a strong face that could have been beautiful if circumstances had favoured her, but early poverty had carved deep lines on either side of her mouth. The hair beneath her hat was auburn, severely brushed back and gleaming.

Shapland's gaze lingered on the woman's breasts, which she thrust out a little. He realised with a lift of interest that the intruder had a shapely body beneath the strained face. "Let her remain."

"Yes, sir." The clerk hesitated at the door.

"Leave us," Shapland said and exploded, throwing an empty ink bottle at the clerk. "I said, get out, damn you!"

The clerk left hurriedly, closing the door behind him.

"Now, my girl," Shapland said, recovering his equanimity. "Who the devil are you, and what do you want?"

Kate remained where she was, allowing Shapland to ogle her. "I am nobody's girl," she said. "I am Kate Rider, and we have a mutual acquaintance and a shared ambition."

Shapland's expression darkened as he shifted his attention to Kate's face. "I cannot imagine you would know anybody in my circle of acquaintances," he said, "and you could only dream of my ambition."

"Begging your pardon, sir," Kate said politely, dropping into a curtsey, "but that is not quite correct." She glanced at the unoccupied chair against the far, panelled wall of the room. "May I sit down, sir?"

"No, you may not," Shapland replied as his patience thinned.

"Tell me why you're here and be quick about it before I take a whip to you."

"I am here to propose something to our mutual advantage," Kate was unmoved by Shapland's threat, although her fingertips touched the knife hidden in her sleeve. "You have a business rivalry with John Smith."

Shapland nodded. "There is no secret about that."

"You compete in the whaling trade, the tobacco trade and the political sphere," Kate added.

"Don't tell me what I already know." Shapland glanced at the ornate gold watch he carried in his waistcoat pocket. "Make haste."

"I knew John Smith before he became a London merchant," Kate said. "I know his secrets."

Shapland tucked his watch away. "John Smith married into a title, moved to London and transformed his regional trading business into a successful international concern."

"Do you remember a highwayman known as Yellowhammer?" Kate asked.

"Lord Fitzwarren, I believe," Shapland said. "His wife betrayed him, and somebody shot him when he tried to flee a court of law."

"That's the official story," Kate said.

"Is there another version?" Shapland looked for anything that could further his business interests.

"May I sit down, please?" Kate asked. "My story concerns John Smith."

"You may sit down," Shapland allowed, "and tell me your story."

Kate folded her skirt beneath her and sat straight backed on the chair. "The highwayman known as Yellowhammer was not the late Lord Fitzwarren," she said. "John Smith was Yellowhammer."

Shapland frowned. "That's preposterous."

"But true," Kate said. "And John Smith shot my man, Lighting Bowlt."

Shapland said nothing for a moment and then stood and paced the room, chewing on the feathered end of a goose-wing quill. He pointed the feather at Kate. "You may be correct, Kate Rider. We share an acquaintanceship with John Smith. What is your opinion of that gentleman?"

In reply, Kate showed her teeth and hissed. "I detest the man."

Shapland nodded. "What would you do to damage him?"

"Anything and everything," Kate said. "Anything and everything."

Shapland realised he had chewed the feathers from his pen and replaced it on his desk. "Tell me what you know about this Yellowhammer fellow."

"He was a notorious highwayman about ten years ago," Kate said, "and he vanished the same day Lady Fitzwarren killed her husband."

"I remember him well," Shapland said, sitting heavily. "He robbed me while I was gambling with a group of friends."

Kate nodded. "You're fortunate he didn't shoot you."

"Do you have evidence to prove Smith was Yellowhammer?"

"No, Mr Shapland."

"Without evidence, we can't prove anything," Shapland said. "I am not even sure I believe it."

"It's true, Mr Shapland," Kate insisted, "whether you believe it or not."

"Call me Charles." Shapland leaned back in his chair. He ran his gaze from Kate's head to her feet and back. "Yes, call me Charles, Kate. I think we can work together to bring John Smith down."

Kate dropped her eyes in pretended innocence. "Yes, Mr Shapland." She smiled, keeping her eyes downcast, and amended, "Yes, Charles."

"Do you have anything in mind?" Shapland asked.

"I have," Kate said, nodding. "I undoubtedly have. First, we'll destroy his reputation, then his business, and finally, destroy him."

Shapland raised his eyebrows. "That sounds like an amazingly prolonged process."

"I mean to savour it," Kate said. "I want him to suffer as he sees everything he has built up slowly vanish. I want him to crawl through the rookery of St-Giles-in-the- Fields dressed in rags and without a single friend in the world. I want him to live in such dread that the hangman's noose would be a pleasant relief, and then I will step over him and laugh."

Shapland poured them both a glass of gin. "Do you know, Kate, I rather like you."

Kate smiled and accepted the glass. "Thank you, Mr Shapland."

"Charles," Shapland reminded. "My name is Charles. Come closer, my dear, and we can discuss our tactics."

Kate stepped across the room and perched on Shapland's knee. "Is that better, Charles?"

"Much better," Shapland said, squeezing her waist. "Now, what's the first step in your plan?"

"A visit to Bow Street Magistrate's court," Kate said. "We'll get one of the Runners to watch Mr Smith, day and night. If he puts one foot wrong, the Runner will drag him to the magistrate's court, and we can watch his trial."

Shapland nodded. "How can we persuade the Runner to follow him, Katy?"

"With my charm and your money, Charles." Kate put her head on Shapland's shoulder and pressed her breasts against his chest. "With my charm and your money."

"War!" the cry sounded across London, with men gathering in tight groups on street corners and hurrying into coffee shops and public houses to discuss the situation. "We're at war with the rebels in the Colonies."

"War with the Colonials?" Men in wigs and tricorne hats shook their heads in disbelief. "Why? They're our blood and bone?"

A short man waved a fist. "Why? Because they've attacked the army, by God, and insulted the Crown."

An enormously plump merchant bit through the stem of his clay pipe. "But we freed them from the French! They should be grateful to us, the dogs!"

The short man banged his soft fist against a shop door. "The cowards hid behind trees and shot our men in the back!"

"What do you expect from a rag-tag of transported convicts and malcontents?" the plump man asked. "We'll soon show them, the cowardly scoundrels!"

Smith hurried past the wondering crowds, listening to their anger, confusion, and concern. He had read the signs weeks ago and arranged a special meeting of John Smith and Company's shareholders at their Leadenhall Street offices.

Judd stepped aside as Smith mounted the stairs to the Board Room two at a time, holding his cane under his right arm and trailing his left hand along the polished oak panelling. Smith was first to enter the Board Room, as he intended, and ensured the servants lit the candles and fire. The soft glow spread across the room, with its long central table under the gloriously plastered ceiling and the pictures of the company's ships hanging from the panelled walls. When he heard the steady thump of feet on the stairs, Smith moved to the window and watched the spring rain spatter against the glass and the ornate front of the East India Company offices across the street.

"War again, Bancroft." He knew by the tread that the incomer was James Bancroft, his friend of ten years and the most loyal supporter in company matters.

"War again, Mr Smith," Bancroft said. "We're more at war

than at peace, though a civil war this time, against our own blood."

Smith nodded, remembering Abraham Hargreaves' words. "I wonder if the Colonials think of it as a civil war, or do they see themselves as a different country, grown apart by thousands of miles of Atlantic and different experiences fighting along their frontiers."

Before Bancroft could reply, the door opened, and the other partners filed inside the room. Smith greeted them by name, shook their hands and called a servant to bring in brandy and water. He waited until the partners settled around the table, and a servant added coal to the fire. Judd entered last and settled into a small desk at the bottom of the room with his pen poised, ready to take notes.

"Gentlemen," Smith took his place at the head of the table as his position as senior partner and managing owner dictated. "We have a lot to get through today." He placed a list on the table in front of him. "We are at war again, which means we must make certain precautions to ensure the enemy does not capture too many of our ships."

One man stirred restlessly in his chair, and Anthony Jackson, big-bellied and long-legged, smirked.

"They're hardly an enemy," Jackson said. "A bunch of ragged malcontent Colonials. One whiff of powder, and they'll be begging the king for forgiveness."

Jack grunted. "The Colonies contributed greatly to our victories in North America and the Caribbean during the last war," he said. "I would not discount them."

Jackson continued to smirk. He stretched his legs lazily under the table. "You'll see that I'm correct, Mr Smith. We'll give them a few bloody noses, and they'll crawl to us with their hands raised in supplication."

Bancroft shook his head, glanced at Smith and said nothing.

"I have some points to raise." Smith ignored Jackson. "Firstly, I want all our ships to be armed. We'll need a government licence for that. Secondly, I want letters of marque for the fastest and best."

Jackson frowned. "Is that worthwhile, Mr Smith? A letter of marque would turn our ships into *de facto* privateers. I can't see the Colonists having many ships worth capturing, so we'd be spending money for no reward."

"A letter of marque ship is not quite a privateer, Jackson. Any large armed merchant ship can carry a letter of marque. All it does is allow the vessel to capture an enemy ship while on a legitimate trading voyage. We pay the normal wages to the crew, but they take a share of any prizes the ship takes. In contrast, a privateer sails only to capture enemy ships, carries no cargo, and often the crew are only paid if they capture an enemy." He grinned. "No purchase, no pay, as they say."

"A privateering licence will cost us money," Jackson said, "without any guarantee of a return for our investment."

Smith nodded. "You may be right, Mr Jackson. We'll have a vote on that. Do you agree that our ships should be armed?"

Jackson pursed his lips. "I am not sure. I can't see the colonials being any threat at sea. They won't have warships, and the navy will soon mop up their privateers."

"What will cannon cost, Mr Smith?" Bancroft asked, and Smith handed over the lists Bess had prepared, with the cost of each calibre of cannon, plus gunpowder, muskets, blunderbusses, pistols and cutlasses.

"We'll also have to strengthen the decks to carry the extra weight," Smith reminded, "and train some of the crew."

"That will all cost money," Bancroft said.

"It will," Smith agreed. "But the insurance premiums will come down, and our ships will have a better chance of fighting off privateers."

Bancroft nodded. "Do you expect the Colonials to float many privateers, Mr Smith?"

"I do," Smith said. "They're a maritime people with a long

coastline and seafaring heritage. I also expect the French to become involved."

"The French?" Jackson sat straighter. "Why the devil would they join in?"

"They are jealous of our success," Smith said. "They'd do anything to retaliate for our victory in the last war. Remember the Jacobite Rising in Scotland? The French were behind that, creating a diversion to draw British troops away from Europe – and it worked. The French would love to humble Britain's pride."

Jackson mumbled something and began to tap his fingers on the table. "That would put a different perspective on things, Mr Smith." He shook his head. "No, I can't see the French becoming involved. We whipped them last time, and they won't be keen to fight us again. We'll have the Yankee Doodles back in line before Christmas. No, Mr Smith, I disagree with spending money on armaments and definitely not on letters of marque."

Smith nodded. "That's one point of view. Are there any others before we put these matters to a vote?"

Of the eight other people at the table, four remained silent. Jackson repeated his opposition to arming the ships and applying for a privateer's licence because of the cost. Bancroft supported Smith, and two others raised technical questions about strengthening the vessels.

"I have acquired a small shipyard at Wapping," Smith said. "I thought it best to control all the operations ourselves."

When he had answered all the questions, Smith called for a show of hands on arming the company's ships. Bancroft and five others voted in favour, and Jackson and one other against the proposal.

"Carried by a majority," Smith said. "Now, another vote on the letter of marque. All in favour, please raise their hands."

Only Bancroft raised his hand, and Smith nodded his thanks.

"Motion defeated," Smith said. "We won't be venturing along that road today."

Jackson shuffled his feet as Bancroft scribbled a note on a small pad of paper.

"Do you have other points to raise, Mr Smith?" Bancroft asked.

"We'll need Protections for the hands to ensure the press does not grab them," Smith said. "That will also cost, but we'll look after our men."

"Protections for all the hands?" Jackson queried. "I agree we'll need Protections for the masters, mates, and specialists, but common mariners are two a penny. We can pick them up anytime. This little war won't last, so why waste money?"

"The navy will snap up all the seamen they can," Smith said. "If the navy organises a hot press, they'll take everybody, but a Protection might help."

"Some of our hands have sailed with us for years," Bancroft added. "I would not want to lose them."

"Are there any objections other than that of cost?" Smith asked and again requested a show of hands. As only Jackson and one other objected, the partners accepted the proposal to have Protections for the crews.

"This company exists to make money," Jackson said. "So far, all this meeting has done is give it away. We're scared of shadows."

Smith ignored the interruption. "Next," Smith said. "The navy will organise convoys soon, which will be safer but slow and cumbersome. We are fortunate that the company has several new, fast ships which may be better sailing independently." He smiled. "Convoys are also attractive targets for privateers when one or two naval vessels try to shepherd thirty or forty indepen-dent-minded merchant skippers."

The partners agreed that the faster company ships should sail independently.

Having ships sailing without a convoy won't cost the partners anything, Smith realised.

"Next." Smith ticked off the items on his list. "I know what

it's like to be targeted by the Impress Service. I want to introduce some safe houses where our hands can hide without fear of
the press gangs." He saw the partners look uncomfortable. They
were all from a business background, well-heeled, prosperous
men who had been born into money and probably had never
experienced poverty or fear. Even Bancroft shifted unhappily in
his chair while Jackson tutted disapprovingly.

"They're only sailors," Jackson said. "They're used to moving
from ship to ship."

"The country has to man the fleet," a portly partner named
Pemberton said. "We can't deny them the means."

"Is that more money wasted?" Jackson asked.

"If we have decent mariners," Smith sought an economic
argument rather than a humanitarian one. "Our ships will be
more efficient and sail better with less chance of shipwreck.
Keeping a crew safe is an investment and recruiting landsmen or
the like will reduce our efficiency."

"What will that cost?" Jackson pressed his point, looking to
Pemberton for support.

Smith smiled. "It will cost the company nothing," he said.
"I'll pay for the accommodation."

"Out of your own purse?" Jackson insisted.

"Out of my own purse," Smith assured him and felt the
tension in the room ease.

Once the problem of payment was out of the way, the partners unanimously agreed to the idea.

"Is the meeting complete?" Jackson glanced at his watch. "I
have an appointment with a man in New Jonathan's in half an
hour."

New Jonathan's Coffee House in Sweeting's Alley was a
famous address where stocks and shares were bought and sold.

"That's only a five-minute walk," Smith said, wondering if
Jackson was selling shares in any of his ships. "I won't keep you
more than a quarter of an hour."

The partners settled down, although one or two glanced surreptitiously at their watches as Smith continued.

"For my final point of the day, I wish to approach John Company, the East India Company, with a proposal to build a ship to lease to them. As you know, John Company charters ships rather than owns them, and a charter can be lucrative. If they accept one of our vessels, they might take more, and we'll have a foothold in trade to the Indies."

"The East India Company has a monopoly on trade to the Indies," Jackson reminded.

"They have, and I don't expect to break that monopoly," Smith said. "My object is to build quality ships for them to charter. If we do that, we can tap into their profits, yet let them do the hard work."

"That means spending money to build a ship in the vague hope the East India Company will charter her," Jackson said. "That's speculating a great deal of capital on something that might never happen."

The other partners nodded their agreement with Jackson.

"Does anybody have any comments?" Smith passed around a sheet of paper with the estimated figures and proposed profit. Bess and Judd had worked for hours to calculate the costs.

"None of this is certain." Pemberton backed Jackson. "At a time of war, I'd advise we erred on the side of caution rather than throwing money on a venture that might never succeed."

Smith guessed which way the vote would go as he called for a show of hands. Only Bancroft voted with him, and the partners overwhelmingly rejected the idea.

"That concludes today's business," Smith said. "Thank you, gentlemen." He watched them leave. Bancroft lingered.

"I liked your ideas about Protections and safe houses for the seamen," Bancroft said. "These men need all the help they can get."

"They do," Smith said.

"I didn't like the East Indiaman idea," Bancroft said.

"You voted for it," Smith reminded.

"Only because it had no possibility of being passed." Bancroft grinned, adjusted his wig, and placed a broad hat on top. "You looked so lonely up there that I thought somebody had better support you."

Smith smiled. "Thank you, Bancroft." He extended his hand, and Bancroft took it firmly.

"Here's to a short war and a prosperous peace," Smith said.

"Amen to that," Bancroft replied. He gave a half bow and left the Board Room.

Chapter Seven

With the meeting concluded, Smith began buying arms for the ships, obtaining Protections, and tracing the mysterious Mr Jay, who had ordered the sabotage of his vessels in Baltimore. He sat at his desk in Leicester Square with a mug of coffee in front of him and Bess sitting beside a low fire.

"You might have to return to Baltimore to trace this Mr Jay, who gave Havering his orders," Bess said.

"I imagine so," Smith said. "This war will make crossing the Atlantic more difficult. I feel like we've plugged one leak, but the entire sea is waiting to burst through."

"Do you think Mr Jay is a Colonial with a grudge against British merchants?"

Smith shook his head. "I thought about that, Bess, and decided not. A colonial would have targeted other ship owners, not just me. Anyway, we chartered *Martha of Norfolk*. She was a Baltimore vessel, with a Down East master and most of her crew from the Chesapeake."

"Do you think it was a business rival? Shapland or Copinger?"

"I think that's a possibility," Smith said.

"Shapland would be my first choice," Bess said. "Although I'm not sure why. He's grown wealthy on the sugar trade." Her scar writhed as she smiled. "You'll know the saying, as rich as a West Indian? Well, that applies to him."

Smith nodded. "Shapland also has half a dozen ships in the slave trade, and that's where he makes most of his money."

"You're not going into that filthy trade!"

Smith sipped at his coffee. "No, I'm not, Bess. When the magistrate sent me to the navy as a boy, I was like a slave. I'm not putting anybody through that."

"Nor would I," Bess said softly and changed the subject. "How was the meeting?"

Smith explained the results of the company meeting.

"A partial success then," Bess said. "James Bancroft is a loyal man."

"Anthony Jackson is not," Smith said. He finished his coffee. "I'm going to Jonathan's Coffee House tomorrow, Bess, and maybe often in the next few weeks."

"Why?" Bess asked.

"I'll buy any shares in our ships," Smith said. "I've decided I don't like sharing our company with others and having them decide my policies."

"Other people having shares in the ships spreads the cost," Bess reminded, "and reduces the loss if the ship sinks."

"It also stops me doing as I think best."

Bess smiled. "You are a London businessman now, John, not a Kent smuggler or village merchant. You need to adapt to your new position."

Smith nodded, walked to the window, and stared at the bustle of Leicester Square. "I miss the Spike," he said, referring to their home overlooking the Kent coast.

"We can go there soon," Bess told him. "But now we have accounts to balance, Protection lists to make and cannon to find. Back to work, sir, or I'll take you in hand."

Smith smiled. "You're a hard taskmaster, Bess Webb."

"I know," Bess said and tapped her finger on the table.

Smith sighed. "Come on then, Bess. Let's get on with it."

"So you're Peter Brown." Bess stepped from the doorway of the Spotted Dog public house and put a firm hand on Peter's thin shoulder. "I wondered what you were like."

"I'm not Peter Brown," Peter denied, wriggling to escape. "I'm William Knight."

"You're Peter Brown." Bess held on tightly. "Four foot eight inches tall, with a three-cornered hat with silver braid, torn buckskin breeches too large for you and a battered soldier's coat." She shook him gently. "I know all about you, Peter." She smiled. "John Smith sent me for you."

"Who?" A lifetime of hardship had taught Peter to be suspicious of everybody. He tried to escape, but Bess's grip was too firm.

"John Smith," Bess repeated. "The man you're working for. Abraham Reeves' friend." She fished a silver shilling from her pocket and held it up. "Do you want to earn this shilling?"

Peter's eyes narrowed further. "What do I have to do?"

"Come with me, get washed, put on clean clothes and enter a place of your own," Bess said.

"Washed?" Peter looked shocked at the idea. "I can't do that! Water takes all your strength away."

"Let's see who is the stronger," Bess suggested, "me, who washes regularly, or you, who stinks like a cesspit and has probably never washed in his life."

Peter looked at Bess, felt the power of her arm and decided not to put her to the test. "A shilling?" he said.

"A shilling," Bess confirmed. "This way, Peter. I'm going to change your life for the better."

"How?" Peter asked, looking for an avenue of escape.

"In every possible way," Bess told him. Keeping a firm grip on his shoulder, she steered him to a Hackney coach. "In you go, Peter."

Peter stared at the coach. "I've never been in a carriage before."

"It will be a new experience for you." Bess pushed him in and paid the driver the fare.

"Sixpence every half mile," the driver growled. "That's a shilling in advance." He glared at Peter, "and that little rogue had better not make a mess inside my coach."

When they arrived in Leicester Square, Bess hustled Peter through the servants' entrance and stood him in the middle of the stone-flagged kitchen, surrounded by scandalised servants.

"This dirty little boy needs to be scrubbed," Bess announced. "I want him shining bright and free of any lice or other unwanted guests. Fill a bath with warm water."

Peter watched anxiously as two female servants placed a large tub in the centre of the floor and emptied pails of steaming water inside.

"What are you doing?" Peter asked, glancing towards the door for a hasty escape.

"You'll see," the middle-aged housekeeper told him. "Now, off with your clothes. All of them!"

"No!" Peter shouted and lunged for the door. Bess and the housekeeper had anticipated his move and grabbed him.

"No, you don't, young man!"

The servants gathered round, grim-faced and determined. Peter cringed, tried to escape again, and yelled as half a dozen hands gripped him securely.

Bess held Peter as the servants stripped off his clothes. "Into the tub with him!" she ordered. "And bring scrubbing brushes. This dirt is ingrained!"

"No!" Peter yelled again as Bess and the housekeeper lifted him bodily and plunged him into the water. Peter struggled, complaining as Bess held him and the housekeeper, and one of the maids wielded scrubbing brushes and a large bar of soap.

"Wash everywhere," Bess ordered. "And scrub thoroughly!"

"What shall I do with his clothes, ma'am?" a young maid asked, staring at the scene.

"Throw them into the fire," Bess said. "Use tongs. They're crawling!" She examined Peter's hair. "So is his head. Bring me a razor!" She ignored Peter's wail.

"Keep the hat!" Peter shouted. "That's my badge of office!"

Bess nodded. "Keep the hat," she relented when she saw Peter's anguish at losing his prized possession. Wash it and remove any little strangers." She smiled at Peter. "Now, you little rogue, let's see to you!"

PETER LOOKED DOWN AT HIS NEW, CLEAN CLOTHES AND THE unfamiliar boots on his feet. He scratched at his head, with his cropped hair cleansed of lice for the first time in his life. "Wait till the boys see me. They'll think I'm a real toff."

"Real gentlemen can read and scribe," Bess told him, smiling. She was soaking wet from washing him but was satisfied with the result.

"I don't need that," Peter said, as alarmed at the prospect of reading as he had been at the sight of a bath.

"Oh, yes, you do," Bess told him. "Imagine all the wonderful things you could read."

"What wonderful things?" Peter challenged.

"You'll know what's happening in London, read the labels on bottles, see when people are due to be hanged, read the destination on stagecoaches and everything," Bess said. "And if you don't learn, I'll take a rod to you, and you won't be able to sit for a week."

Peter eyed the stick that Bess lifted. After his enforced bathing, he knew Bess was not a woman to take lightly. "All right," he agreed quickly. "I'll learn to read."

"I know you will," Bess said. "Let's get started, then."

Producing a coin from her pocket, she pressed it into Peter's hard hand. "There's the shilling I promised you for getting washed."

Peter looked at the coin and stuffed it deep in his breeches pocket. "What do I get for learning to read?"

Chapter Eight

C harles Shapland sat with his back to the window, silhouetted against the morning sun. He tasted the coffee, screwed up his face and placed the cup on the scarred table. "This is a strange place to meet," he said.

"It's not a place that John Smith would frequent," Mr Jay said.

"For once, I agree with John Smith." Shapland nodded to the coffee house customers. Most were broken-down businessmen hoping fate would favour them, clerks who had embezzled from their masters, or servants without a position. "It's not a place that any respectable businessman would frequent," he said.

"Indeed not," Mr Jay said, tapping the pistol at his belt. "I also made some other precautions." He nodded to the two men he had recently recruited. One watched Shapland while the other inspected the clientele. "These gentlemen were grenadiers before they took up bare-knuckle fighting."

Shapland nodded, avoiding the basilisk stare of the closest ex-soldier. He did not notice the man sitting beside the door, shuffling a pack of cards.

"Why did you want to see me?" Shapland asked. "It had better be worth my while."

"I brought you my notes from John Smith's last company meeting," Mr Jay said.

Shapland took the small bundle of notes, glanced at them and raised his eyebrows. "These could be useful." He smiled. "We'll meet in more salubrious surroundings next time."

Both men looked over as a drunk shouted something and pointed a finger at Shapland. Mr Jay nodded, and the closest ex-soldier rose from his seat, lifted the drunk by the throat and punched him in the groin. The drunk retched, unable to scream, and the ex-soldier carried him to the door and threw him bodily into the street.

"That might be best, Mr Shapland," Mr Jay said. "I'll see what else I can find for you."

"Do you wish payment for this information?" Shapland asked.

"Not a brass farthing," Mr Jay said.

"In that case, I will leave this establishment," Shapland said. Rising, he walked carefully around the ex-soldiers and into the street outside.

Mr Jay waited a moment and nodded to Kate, who joined him at his table.

"Will Shapland use the intelligence?" Mr Jay wondered.

"I'll encourage him to use it," Kate replied. "He'll do anything to forestall Smith, including spending half his fortune."

Mr Jay smiled. "That's what I hoped," he said. "Drain him."

SMITH ADDRESSED THE PARTNERS IN HIS LONDON WHALE Fishing Company at the Howland Great Wet Dock that men were beginning to call the Greenland Dock. Although the windows were firmly closed, the stench of boiling whale blubber penetrated the room, causing some partners to press perfumed handkerchiefs to their noses. While most of the men present only held shares in the whaling company, a handful were also shareholders in John Smith and Company.

"Gentlemen," Smith said, eyeing each man in turn. "Despite the current unrest in the North American colonies, our trade in the Greenland Seas continues to prosper."

The partners nodded in satisfaction, and James Bancroft tapped his hand on the oval table as a sign of appreciation.

"A large whale is valued at around a thousand pounds sterling, while a full ship of three hundred tons will net us, once we pay all expenses, a clear five thousand pounds."

Again the partners nodded. Anthony Jackson shuffled his feet in a prelude to speaking.

"My lord," he said.

"I don't use that title here, Mr Jackson," Smith said. "I am plain John Smith."

"My apologies Mr Smith." Jackson bowed his head. "I believe we pay higher wages to the hands than other companies."

"We do," Smith agreed.

"And we pay a share of oil and bone money to every member of the crew, whatever their rank," Jackson said.

"We pay a sliding scale depending on the quantity of whale oil and whalebone each ship brings home," Smith explained.

"And we pay a bonus to the crews of the boat that first harpoons every whale captured." Jackson looked around the table to garner support. "We would increase our profit if we paid the same as other companies and lessened the bonus."

"I'll ask Captain Beaton to reply," Smith said. "As our senior captain and commodore of our whaling fleet, he is best qualified. Captain Beaton?"

Beaton was a gaunt man in his late forties, with a face leathered by years of exposure to wind and weather. He stood up slowly and cleared his throat before speaking. "A shipmaster earns three guineas per month each voyage, the mate, harpooner and surgeon one guinea, while the common seamen earn five shillings." He had a harsh voice, more used to roaring orders in an Atlantic gale than speaking across a polished table in a well-heated meeting room. "We also pay a bonus of six shillings per man for every ton of oil boiled in Greenland dock, and a bonus we call striking money for the boat's crew that strikes the first harpoon in any whale we capture."

Jackson listened, frowning. "We spoil the hands," he said.

"We can pick and choose prime seamen," Beaton said, "precisely because we pay premium wages. As we have the best men and ships, we continually have the most successful voyages." He held Jackson's gaze. "The government pays a bonus that depends on the tonnage of each vessel, and which depends on certain stipulations, including carrying a ship's surgeon and taking Greenmen, first voyagers, on each ship."

Jackson grunted.

"Thank you, Captain Beaton," Smith said smoothly. "I have one other point. Mr Bancroft has suggested we invest in the Southern Fishery. I'd like your opinions, gentlemen."

Jackson raised his voice first. "Ships in the Southern Fishery carry a smaller crew and are less exposed to extreme weather yet earn a larger government bonus. I fully agree with expansion there."

"Captain Beaton?" Smith asked.

"I have never sailed on the Southern Fishery," Beaton said. "My knowledge is little greater than anybody here." He scratched a spark from his tinder box and lit a long-stemmed pipe, puffing smoke into the room. "I remember that French and Spanish privateers snapped up most of the Southern fleet during the last war."

"That's a chance any merchant seaman takes," Jackson pointed out. "In any case, neither the French nor the Spanish is involved in this war."

"Yet," Beaton said quietly. "They're not involved yet. Once the French realise the bulk of our army and navy is tied up in the Americas, they'll suddenly decide they agree with liberty for the American colonists. Their ships and privateers will swarm out of their harbours and snap up our vessels from Spitsbergen to the Indies."

Smith listened to the opinions of a few others and asked for a vote. When the majority heeded Captain Beaton's advice and decided not to invest in the Southern Fishery, Smith said the motion had not passed.

"I think you are wrong," Jackson shouted. "We are in the shipping business to make money, not to prove our altruism. The Southern Whaling is the best way forward!"

"The vote has gone against us, Jackson," Bancroft said quietly. "Time to move on."

"I have one more proposal," Smith said. "Our whaling ships sail to the Greenland Seas and Davis Strait in spring and return in late summer. After that, they lie dormant in the Greenland Dock. I propose we apply for letters of marque and float them as privateers during the winter months. We'll keep the hands employed and could make some useful money."

"You've proposed buying letters of marque in your other company, Mr Smith, and the partners outvoted you then," Jackson reminded.

Smith grunted. "That is correct," he agreed.

"I'd be surprised if a blubber boat could capture a single Yankee ship," Jackson said. "They are slow and cumbersome."

"My vessels are also sturdy," Beaton said. "I'll vote in favour. If my men are at sea, they'll get paid, and the navy is less likely to press them."

"This war won't last," Jackson said. "It's a waste of money." He glared at Smith. "If you continue to throw away shareholders' investments, Mr Smith, I'll get rid of my shares in your company's ships."

"I'll buy them," Bancroft volunteered, returning Jackson's glower.

"Does anybody else have any points to add before we vote?" Smith asked. When nobody had, he called for a show of hands, and there were three on each side. "I'll use my deciding vote to agree to the motion," Smith said.

Jackson frowned, opened his mouth, closed it again and relapsed into silence.

"Thank you for your time, gentlemen," Smith said. "I will arrange Protections for the whaling ship's hands. The next meeting will be in six weeks, when we'll discuss how much oil and bone we've sold and how much profit we've made."

Bancroft remained behind when the others left. "Anthony Jackson is not pleased that we pay our men handsomely," he said.

"Anthony Jackson doesn't agree with much we do," Smith said.

Bancroft sighed. "We'd be well quit of his complaints," he said. "I've offered to buy his shares if he's serious about selling."

"I'd buy them as well," Smith said. "Thank you for your support in there."

Bancroft smiled and glanced out of the window. "Let's hope for good prices for the whale oil," he said.

"Amen to that," Smith agreed.

SMITH HEARD THE SHARP FOOTSTEPS BEHIND HIM AS HE walked home from the Greenland Dock. He gripped his cane tightly, tapped his jacket to ensure his pistol was safe and wondered at the prevalence of footpads in London. Life here was as precarious as on the frontiers of the American colonies, with highwaymen on the roads and footpads infesting the streets.

"An honest man takes his life in his hands every time he leaves the house," Smith said to himself and smiled. "It's lucky that I'm not an honest man." He stopped suddenly and heard the following footsteps falter and then continue. The hesitation only lasted for an instant but sufficiently long to confirm Smith's instinct. The man was undoubtedly following him.

Let's see how good you are.

Smith thumbed tobacco into the bowl of his pipe, scraped a spark from his tinder box and puffed out rich blue smoke. He dropped the tinder box, swore loudly, and stooped to pick it up, looking over his shoulder.

The man who followed would not stand out in a crowd. He was of average height and build, with a three-cornered hat pulled low over his head and a long cloak that tapped against his ankles. He crossed the road and sauntered on, swinging a thick cane that Smith instinctively knew concealed a swordstick.

You're no footpad, Smith thought. *If you were a footpad, you'd have struck when I was distracted with my pipe.* He puffed more smoke and walked on. *So who are you, and why are you following me?*

Smith increased his pace slightly, forcing his follower to do likewise, and turned into a side street, watching warily for any real footpads. Once around the corner, he increased his speed again. Smith heard his boots clicking against the ground, with the sound echoing from the surrounding buildings.

A dog barked nearby, joined by another, and a man and woman began a furious, foul-mouthed argument that wakened half the street. Smith walked on, lengthening his stride, and swinging his cane. He stopped to peer into a shop window and listened but heard no other footsteps.

Have I lost him? Or is he watching from a distance?

Smith turned round slowly and surveyed the street, seeing nobody. The dog barking reached a crescendo and died away, while the argument ended in a scream and sudden silence. Smith remained still for a long moment, checking each doorway and side entrance.

He's not there.

Rather than return the way he had come, Smith continued onward, stopping every hundred yards to listen. He had to step into an alleyway when a closed carriage careened past, with the cloaked driver whipping his pair of matched horses.

Some cracksman hurrying home after a successful robbery, Smith thought and smiled. He could appreciate a man robbing the rich. *Godspeed, my friend.*

A Charlie, a night watchman who called the hour and was supposed to control night-time crime, hobbled past, bid Smith a good evening and lifted his lantern to provide some feeble light.

"Good evening," Smith replied. "Keep safe."

The Charlie tapped his stick on the road, wrapped his brown cloak closer around his aged body and hobbled on, hoping not to encounter any criminals.

Moving in a wide circle, Smith approached Leicester Square from the west side, walking in the shadows with his cane gripped firmly and the weight of his pistol reassuring against his breast. The square was quiet, with the trees in the centre rustling in a faint breeze. Smith stepped to his front door, checked behind him, slid the key into the lock and entered.

"Lock the door behind you," Bess reminded. She stood at the arched door between the outer and inner hall with a blunderbuss in her hand. "And draw the bolts."

Smith obeyed, knowing that Bess would not give pointless instructions. "What's the to-do, Bess?"

"A man is watching the house." Bess cradled the blunderbuss like an old friend. "Come upstairs. I've closed the shutters on the ground floor windows." She lifted a brass candlestick and trimmed the candle until the flickering light pooled around her.

Smith followed Bess up the carpeted stairs to the front bedroom, whose tall windows overlooked the garden in the middle of the square.

Snuffing the candle, Bess stepped to the side of the window and peered into the street. "Over there."

Smith stood at the opposite side of Bess. The man stood inside the garden, sheltering under the canopy of trees with his three-cornered hat pulled low over his face.

"He's been there for nearly three hours," Bess said. "He disappeared for a while and returned."

Smith nodded. "He followed me from the counting house for a while, but I lost him."

"Why?" Bess asked. "Do you know who he is?"

"Not yet," Smith said. "But I will."

The man stood still, leaning against the bole of a tree with both hands gripping his long cane.

"If he knows where you live," Bess asked, "why is he following you?"

"I'll find that out, too," Smith said.

"How?" Bess asked.

"I'll go and ask him." Smith watched the watcher for a few moments. "Light the candle, Bess, and put it in the centre of the room so it appears that we're inside."

"What are you going to do?" Bess asked.

"Run over and catch him," Smith said. "I want you to hold his attention here."

Bess smiled. "I'm no longer a young woman to attract a man's eyes." She touched the scar on her face. "Even from a distance."

"I don't believe that," Smith said. "Stand near the window and act as if you are talking to me." He left the room and ran downstairs. Drawing back the bolts, Smith unlocked the front door, slowly counted to ten, then yanked the door open and dashed over the road. He was halfway across the street before he saw a sudden movement in the garden as the watcher reacted. "Stop!" Smith shouted as he clambered over the iron railing.

The watcher did not hesitate but ran through the trees.

"Stop, or I'll fire!" Smith shouted and raised his voice. "Stop, thief!"

The watcher doubled back, moving faster than Smith, but stopped abruptly when Bess strode across from the house, holding her blunderbuss.

"Stop," Bess ordered, "or I'll blow your guts across the square!"

The man stopped and spread his arms wide. "You've got me," he drawled.

"Well done, Bess," Smith said. "Bring him into the house."

The man appeared quite composed as Smith shoved him into the outer hall. The noise had awakened the servants, who crowded around, asking a dozen questions.

"Who's that?"

"What's the to-do?"

"Should I light the fires?"

"Everybody get back to bed," Bess ordered. "Go on!" She waited until the servants had withdrawn. "Now, my man, you can tell us who you are and why you're watching our house." She prodded her prisoner with the muzzle of her blunderbuss, propelling him into the front room.

The man smiled. "Gladly. I am Jack Redpath, an officer attached to the Bow Street Magistrates office."

Bess leaned her blunderbuss on the wall beside her as Smith lit three candles. "You're a Bow Street Runner?"

"That's what some people call us," Redpath said blandly. "We don't use the term ourselves. It's a bit insulting, don't you know?"

"Whatever you call yourself," Smith said, taking Redpath's cane, twisting the top to reveal the blade inside and leaning it against the side of the fireplace. "Why did you follow me home from the counting house and watch the house?"

Redpath shrugged. "Orders," he said. "I was ordered to follow you home, and if I lost you, to stand outside the house and be visible."

"You were ordered to be visible?" Bess repeated.

"That's correct," Redpath confirmed. "My orders were to ensure you knew I was here." He grinned. "You have a reputation, Mr Smith."

"What sort of reputation?" Smith asked, lighting his pipe. He did not offer Redpath any tobacco.

"You are known as a Whig scoundrel," Redpath said pleasantly, "and reputed to have dabbled in smuggling, highway robbery and perhaps other illegal activities."

"A Whig scoundrel?" Smith said. "That part is true, and all

the other compliments can be discounted as hearsay." He puffed smoke into the room and poured them each out a glass of brandy. "Have my business rivals garnered any such interesting epithets?"

"Mr Henry Copinger and Charles Shapland?" Redpath tasted the brandy. "We know Copinger as a shrewd Tory rogue and Shapland as a lewd profligate wretch."

Smith sipped at his brandy. "Do the Bow Street officers have names for everybody?"

Redpath smiled without replying.

"Who ordered you to follow me, Mr Redpath?"

"My superior, Mr Smith, Sir John Fielding, the Bow Street magistrate."

"Who told him to order you?"

Redpath smiled again, saying nothing. Smith realised the officer deflected attention with a smile.

"What was the purpose?" Smith asked. "Why were you following me and allowing me to see you?" He answered his own question. "To unsettle me, I presume. You won't find out anything that you don't already know."

Bess topped up Redpath's glass.

"Why, thank you, Mrs Smith," Redpath said. "I obey orders, Mr Smith; I don't question them."

"You're not saying, then," Smith said and expected Redpath's wide smile. "Well, Mr Redpath, if you aren't going to give anything away, I won't keep you from your duty any longer."

"Oh, John," Bess said. "It's beginning to rain outside. We can't send the poor man out in this weather. He can still spy on us and keep dry if he stays indoors."

"That's very civil of you," Redpath said, accepting more of Smith's brandy.

"I have an ulterior motive," Bess said. "I do like to meet a man who can match John word for word." She smiled. "My husband can get a little superior at times."

Redpath laughed. "He won't get the better of me! I work

with the most vicious criminals in London. A Kent merchant is no match for me!" He drank more of the brandy.

"That's what I wanted to hear," Bess said with a sidelong glance at Smith.

Redpath reached out and ran a finger down the scar on Bess's face. "That's like a knife wound."

"It was a sword," Bess told him.

Redpath raised his eyebrows. "Who wielded the sword?" He glanced at Smith.

"It doesn't matter now," Bess told him. "She's dead."

"I'll have to watch you, Mrs Smith," Redpath said and drank deeply, draining the glass.

Smith looked out the window. "The rain's getting heavier."

"I'm happy to stay here." Redpath glanced at his empty glass. "I'm doing my duty in comfort, and that does not happen often."

"Try this." Smith filled a fresh glass with Jamaica rum.

"Rum, by God," Redpath said. "I could drink this all night."

"Then why don't you?" Bess suggested. "Here's to good health and prosperity!" She lifted her glass in salute.

"Good health and prosperity!" Redpath echoed and tossed back his rum. "That's fiery stuff!"

"Best Jamaica," Smith agreed. "We also have Geneva and Hollands."

"By God, you drink well. I'll try them all."

Bess winked at Smith. "That's a good idea, Mr Redpath," she said and poured another bumper glass of rum.

Within half an hour, Redpath was roaring songs and staggering in an attempt to dance. As the long-case clock struck midnight, he slid to the floor and lay still, snoring in a drunken stupor.

"He's asleep." Bess nudged Redpath with her foot. "He'll wake up with the devil of a sore head."

"Go through his pockets," Smith put aside his hardly touched glass.

"Money." Bess pulled a heavy pocketbook from Redpath's inside pocket. "He has at least twenty guineas in there."

"A sweetener to spy on us," Smith said. "Keep searching."

"A couple of letters," Bess said. "One from the Protestant Association, whatever that is, and this one." She produced a folded note from Redpath's hip pocket and unfolded the stiff paper. "Here we are, John."

The note was short, with Smith's name and address and nothing else.

"That doesn't help much," Bess said. "Whoever wrote that didn't wish to incriminate himself. Or maybe Redpath wrote it himself as a reminder."

"Maybe." Smith held up the paper. "But I doubt it. The paper is of superior quality. We'll keep this and compare it with Shapland's writing." He held it up to the candle. "It's got a watermark as well."

"Let's see." Bess examined the note. "You're right. A W within a diamond. Do you know the company?"

"Not yet," Smith said. "But, by God, I mean to find out."

Chapter Nine

"Now, my young friend." Bess sat at the table beside Peter. "Can you remember what we went through last time?"

Peter looked at the open book, the sheets of paper and the pen-and-ink that Bess had placed on the table. "I think so, Mrs Smith."

"Then let's learn some more," Bess said. "Tell me your alphabet."

Peter sighed and recited the alphabet faltering at the letter R.

"S," Bess encouraged, "and then T."

"S, T," Peter repeated and continued. He grinned when he came to Z.

"You've got it!" Bess said and gave him a brief hug. "Well done, Peter!"

"Can I go now, Mrs Smith? Can I read?"

"Not yet." Bess smiled. "You have only started. There is a whole world waiting for you." She pulled over the pen-and-ink and paper. "Now you'll learn to write the letters."

"Haven't I learned enough?" Peter asked, hopefully.

Bess touched the rattan cane on the table. "Not nearly

enough. Now, lift the pen." She guided Peter's fingers around the stem of the quill and altered the angle, so the feathers pointed away from his right eye. "Dip the nib into the ink well, shake off the excess ink, and we'll begin." She watched the beads of sweat appear on Peter's forehead as he concentrated on the unfamiliar task.

"It's all right, Peter," Bess said gently, smiling. "You're getting better every day."

Peter forced a smile. "I don't feel better."

"You are," Bess encouraged. "Now start again. Dip the pen in the inkwell and write me the letter P for Peter."

SMITH STARED OVER THE LONDON SKYLINE, FROM THE DOME of St Paul's to the grim outline of the Tower. Vessels of a dozen descriptions filled the river, some sailing up to unload their cargoes and others pushing downstream, with a pair of Royal Navy tenders moored in mid-channel. Smith grunted; the tenders contained a human cargo of pressed men, wrenched from civilian life, and forced to fight for the king.

"Did you hear what Shapland is doing now?" Smith asked.

"No." Bancroft stood at his side, puffing at a short clay pipe.

"He's purchased letters of marque for half a dozen of his ships." Smith swung his cane in frustration. "That was our idea, by God."

"It was," Bancroft agreed. "Until Anthony Jackson and his cronies scuppered it."

Smith nodded. "And Shapland's given a proposal to John Company to build three new ships for them to charter."

"That was also your idea." Bancroft removed the pipe from his mouth. "That man is stealing your plans, Mr Smith."

"He is," Smith agreed. "He seems to know what I plan to do before I do it." He walked beside the river, with Bancroft easily keeping pace. "I think he has somebody inside our partnership meetings."

"Anybody can purchase shares in one of your company's ships, Mr Smith," Bancroft reminded. "That gives them access to the partnership meetings."

Smith nodded. "I'll have to be more careful with my words." He walked on, with Bancroft silent at his side.

That's the worst of being chairman, senior partner and managing owner of a company. I must pass my ideas to the partners rather than implement them myself.

"I don't think Jackson is an asset to the company," Bancroft said as they stopped to allow a brewer's dray to negotiate a narrow road. "He seems to vote against everything you propose."

Smith grunted. "I'll keep my eye on Mr Jackson," he said.

THE WORSHIPFUL COMPANY OF STATIONERS OCCUPIED Stationers Hall, a splendid building only a short distance from Leicester Square. When Smith strolled through the courtyard and into the impressive entrance, an efficient official listened to his enquiry and examined the notepaper he presented.

"That is a quality piece of notepaper," the official said solemnly.

"I thought so," Smith said. "Do you know the maker?"

"Alexander Wilkinson," the official replied without hesitation. "A fine company, long established. You'll find them at Lawson's Lane in the City."

"Thank you." Smith lifted his hat in acknowledgement.

"Mr Wilkinson runs the company," the official advised as Smith walked away. "He'll see you in person."

Alexander Wilkinson and Company was squeezed into an ancient building in a mediaeval courtyard. The door opened to a small counting house with a battered counter beneath a hanging circle of candles. When Smith walked in, he saw a man sitting on a tall, four-legged stool.

"Mr Wilkinson?" Smith asked politely.

Wilkinson was a small man with an old-fashioned wig that seemed permanently liable to slide from his bald head. He started when Smith asked his name.

"Yes, I am Alexander Wilkinson."

"I believe your firm makes notepaper like this?" Smith produced the note.

Wilkinson took the paper, felt it between his fingers and held it up to the candles to check the watermark. "We make this paper," he confirmed.

"Do you have a list of your customers?" Smith asked.

"I have," Wilkinson said, catching his wig before it descended to the stone-flagged floor.

"May I have a copy?"

Wilkinson looked downwards, avoiding Smith's eye. "Why?"

"I want to know who wrote these words," Smith told him.

"Ah," Wilkinson nodded. "I generally only share such things with customers, Mr ah, Mr?"

"I am Mr Smith. John Smith."

"Mr John Smith," Wilkinson said without looking up. "I don't believe you are one of our customers, Mr Smith."

"Not yet," Smith said. "I manage a small company, and we use quite a quantity of stationary."

"Ah." Wilkinson displayed a little more interest. "I do not know your company, Mr John Smith. In what type of business are you involved?" He looked up.

"Transport," Smith said. "Shipping, stagecoaches and general goods." He saw Wilkinson's eyes narrow.

"Shipping? John Smith and Company? Are you that John Smith? Lord Fitzwarren?"

"That's me," Smith said with a slight smile.

"My Lord." Wilkinson climbed from his stool, stepped back from the counter, and bowed.

Smith acknowledged with a nod. "I prefer plain Mr Smith," he said. "Do you have a list of your customers for me?"

"Of course, My Lord." Wilkinson was suddenly helpful. He bowed as he withdrew from the counter and bowed again when he returned with a handwritten sheet of paper.

"Thank you, Mr Wilkinson." Smith hardly glanced at the list. He did not like to use his title but pulling rank at times like these could be handy.

"Will you be honouring us with your custom, my Lord?" Wilkinson asked with another bow.

"Stand straight, Mr Wilkinson," Smith snapped. "I'm only a man, the same as you. There is no need to bow and scrape to me."

"Yes, My Lord," Wilkinson said and straightened with sudden shock in his eyes.

"I will consult with my people about giving you my custom, Mr Wilkinson," Smith assured him. "My wife and my secretary deal with such matters, and if either of them contacts you, I am sure you will treat her with the same courtesy you have done with me."

"I shall, My Lord," Wilkinson promised.

Smith nodded. "Thank you for your help."

When Smith returned home, he ran straight to his study. Bess joined him and read through the list of customers. "There are a lot of well-known names here," she said. "But only two that matter to us."

"That's what I thought," Smith agreed. "Henry Copinger and Charles Shapland."

"I'd say one of these two sent Redpath to spy on us," Bess said.

Smith nodded. "I'd agree with you."

Bess reread the note she had taken from Redpath's pocket. "John, I've seen this writing before." Standing up, she strode to the bureau beside the long-case clock in the corner of the room and pulled open the drawer.

"What are you looking for?" Smith asked.

"This." Bess hauled out a crumpled sheet of paper. "Remember Joshua Havering in Baltimore?"

"I do," Smith said.

"And the note you found in his house?" Bess continued. "Look!" She laid the two sheets of paper side-by-side. "It's the same writing."

"Dear God," Smith said. "Mister Jay." He thought for a moment. "That suggests that Shapland or Copinger knows every detail of our operations."

"He has a finger in our pies," Bess agreed.

Smith tapped the paper. "We know Shapland was in North America because Cupples saw him returning. I don't know about Copinger."

"If we find a sample of Shapland's writing," Bess said, "we have him."

"These words mean nothing on their own," Smith said. "Our address and a bland instruction." He shook his head. "We'll need more."

"Yes," Bess said. "I would like proof, though."

"We'll get it," Smith said grimly.

When Bess saw the expression in Smith's eyes, she nearly felt sorry for Shapland.

"MR JUDD." SMITH TOOK HIS SECRETARY ASIDE. "I HAVE AN important job for you."

"Yes, sir?" Judd looked nervous. They stood in Smith's office on Leadenhall Street with sunlight easing through the windows and traffic sounds outside.

"Sit down, Mr Judd, and have a drink with me." Smith poured out two glasses of Madeira.

"Thank you, sir." Judd perched on the very edge of the chair, blinking.

"Here's to health and prosperity for us both." Smith lifted his glass.

"Health and prosperity, sir," Judd echoed.

"Now, Mr Judd, I want you to go to Jonathan's Coffee House and buy shares in my ships," Smith said. "I don't care who's selling, just buy any that come up."

"Yes, sir," Judd said. "Mr Smith," he hesitated. "I'll need money."

"You will," Smith said. "I've opened a bank account for you to use. You know how the system operates as well as I do. If anybody asks, say you're working on your own account. Don't say you're working for me."

"No, sir," Judd looked confused.

"Pass the word that you're interested in buying shares in any of my vessels," Smith said and grinned. "Let it be known that you will pay a high price, and if any of Mr Shapland's shares come up, purchase them as well."

"Charles Shapland?"

"That's the fellow." Smith nodded.

"Yes, sir," Judd said.

"As many shares of my vessels as you can, Mr Judd," Smith said. "Remember not to haggle over the price."

Judd nodded again.

"Take ten per cent of the price from every share you purchase," Smith said, "and keep it in a separate account for yourself."

"That's very generous, sir," Judd said.

"It's an incentive," Smith explained. "Good man, Mr Judd. Off you go." He watched Judd leave the office.

That's three men I've sent to three different coffee houses to buy my shares. That should generate interest.

Chapter Ten

"Here," Smith said. "Here's an example of Shapland's writing." He slid the letter across the table to Bess. "Where did you get that?" Bess asked.

"I bought it from one of his clerks," Smith said. "Shapland pays miserly wages, and I thought it a few shillings well spent. Compare it with that note we found on Redpath."

Bess glanced at the letter's contents, grunted, opened a drawer, and produced the note. "No," she said after a few moments. "It's not the same. Shapland has a smooth script, and Redpath's note is spiky."

"Damn," Smith said softly. "We've already checked Redpath's writing, and it's cramped and untidy. Who the devil sent a Runner to spy on us?"

"It must be Copinger," Bess said. "He was the only other person we know who uses Alexander Wilkinson's notepaper."

"It must be Copinger," Smith agreed. "I knew he was a hard man of business, but I never expected him to be underhand that way." He sighed. "We'll have to watch him as well as Shapland now."

"What will you do?" Bess asked.

"I don't know," Smith admitted. "We suspect Shapland has a

spy in our company, so maybe I should plant one in Shapland or Copinger's." He poured them both a glass of Madeira. "I have Judd buying back our ship shares, but so far, he's been unsuccessful in purchasing any of Shapland's."

"Were you going to send Judd into Shapland's shareholder meetings?" Bess asked.

"That was at the back of my mind."

"Is Judd the best man for the job?" Bess asked. "I always considered him a fellow of distressing mediocrity."

Smith sipped his Madeira. "Would you recognise him in a crowd?"

Bess screwed up her face. "I'd have difficulty recognising him if he walked into this room. He's just Judd. A man with no distinctive personality, a perfect clerk."

"A perfect spy," Smith amended. "He's a man who could walk through a room or attend a meeting without being noticed."

Bess nodded. "I understand your reasoning, John." She smiled. "Here's success to your scheme."

"Success," Smith echoed.

"SHE'S A FAST LITTLE CRAFT," CAPTAIN BEATON SAID, "BUT I don't like her light build."

"It's her light build that makes her so fast," Smith said. "I had a Baltimore company build her from light North American pine, so she dances across the sea. The French design the best ships in the world, so I used a French designer. The combination has given us the fastest ship on the seven seas."

Beaton pressed a gnarled hand against the hull. "What do you intend using her for, Mr Smith?"

"Carrying messages," Smith said. "She can outmanoeuvre any warship and outsail any privateer or merchant vessel ever built."

"She won't last." Bearded and with gold rings in both ears, Beaton had endured thirty whaling seasons in the Arctic and judged ships by the standards of a whaling man. "These frail timbers will strain, her hull will open, and she'll leak like a sieve."

"That is very true," Smith agreed. "I give her maybe five years of life."

"What's she called?"

"*Hermes,*" Smith said. "He was the Greek messenger of the gods."

Beaton nodded. "A fair name," he said. "The Greeks understood the sea. Who will be her master?"

"I'm giving the command to Mungo Campbell. He knows the North Atlantic like his own back garden." Smith smiled, "which it is, of course."

Beaton raised his white eyebrows. "Campbell? The Colonial?"

"He's Nova Scotian, born and bred," Smith said. "And one of the finest seamen I have ever met. He'll drive *Hermes* if anybody can."

"Aye, maybe he will, or he might sail her right into the hands of the rebels," Beaton said. "I would not trust any of them."

Smith killed his smile. "Nova Scotia is as loyal as they come. I'd trust Campbell as much as anybody."

Beaton stepped back to inspect *Hermes'* hull. "I'll take your word for it, Mr Smith. She'll be a fine ship as long as she lasts, and that's my final word on the subject."

THIEVERY!" SHAPLAND COMPLAINED, TOOK A PINCH OF SNUFF, and sneezed. "Every day, it gets worse. The little pirates have robbed my ships blind. They've broken into my cabins, stolen charts, ship's papers, watches, and even personal letters!" He glared at Kate as she lounged on a chair in the office.

Kate sat with her legs on a footstool and a glass of gin in her hand. She hitched up her skirt to distract Shapland. "You'll have to employ watchmen," she said. "Shoot the thieving little buggers on sight."

"I do employ watchmen," Shapland said. "The rogues attacked one of my watchmen. They gagged him, tied him to the mainmast and stripped the captain's cabin of everything, even the brass fittings."

"I hope you got rid of him," Kate said.

"I did," Shapland said dryly.

"Somebody doesn't like you." Kate shifted slightly, out of range of Shapland's snuff-induced sneezing.

Shapland swore again. "John Smith," he said.

"Undoubtedly," Kate agreed. "You'll retaliate, of course. He's attacking your ships. What's his weakness?"

"Does he have one?" Shapland asked.

"He does," Kate said. "Why does he always have full crews when others have to scrape for men?"

"He pays them too much and hides them from the Impress Service," Shapland said.

"That's his strength," Kate said. "Now we'll turn it into his weakness."

"How?" Shapland demanded.

"We'll find one of his safe houses and tell the press," Kate said. "He'll lose a full crew in one swoop, and the hands will lose trust in him. A man like Smith lives on his reputation. If we break that, we'll hurt him."

"How will we manage that?" Shapland asked. "If the Impress Service can't find Smith's hiding places, how can we?"

"We use assets the press don't have," Kate said, smiling. "They are ranting, roaring bullies with as much subtlety as a cannonball. Do I have your permission to proceed my way?" Kate knew that Shapland liked to feel he was in command.

"By all means," Shapland said. "I'll leave that to you." He leaned back in his chair, sliding his gaze from her head to her scuffed boots and back. "You're becoming quite an asset, Kate Rider."

Kate shifted slightly, allowing her skirt to ride higher up her leg. She watched Shapland's interest increase. "I have other plans, Charles."

"Tell me later." Shapland rose and locked the door.

JUDD WAITED OUTSIDE THE ROOM UNTIL SMITH GAVE HIM permission to enter.

"I have that information you requested, sir," Judd said, bowing.

"Did you have any difficulty in obtaining it, Mr Judd?" Smith was always punctilious about treating his secretary with respect.

"No, sir," Judd replied. "I met Mr Copinger's clerk in the coffee shop and asked him. He was most helpful when I offered him the three guineas you suggested."

Smith nodded. "Gold has a way of loosening men's tongues. Sit down, Mr Judd."

Judd looked shocked. "It's not fitting, sir."

"As you wish, Mr Judd." Smith poured out two glasses of brandy and offered one to Judd. "At least drink with me."

"Thank you, sir," Judd said reluctantly. "It's very kind of you."

"Nonsense." Smith accepted the thin package of documents that Judd handed to him. "Does Mr Copinger's clerk have a name?"

Judd looked surprised. "His name is Rogers, sir."

Smith glanced at the documents. "You've brought me a list of Mr Copinger's vessels sailing to the Americas, with the master's name and details of the cargoes."

"Yes, sir," Judd agreed. "The second sheet details the vessels' armaments and crew numbers."

Smith nodded. "I see. You have surpassed yourself, Mr Judd. I am very much obliged to you."

"I am only doing my duty, sir," Judd said, finishing his brandy.

"More than that, I think," Smith replied. "I won't forget, Mr Judd. You may return to your office."

"Thank you, sir." Judd stood, bowed, and left the room.

Smith read through the documents, copied a few facts, and lifted another sheet from his desk.

Ships and escorting vessels of the New York, Newfoundland, and Jamaica Convoys for the forthcoming season.

He read through the lists, circled the ships that interested him and cross-referenced them with the documents that Judd had brought.

There you are, Copinger and Shapland. We'll see how clever you are when the Americans get among you.

Rising, Smith reached for his hat and cane.

———

"WELL, MUNGO." SMITH HELD A HEAVY PACKET UNDER HIS arm. "You've given her a trial run to assess her speed. What do you think?"

Campbell ran his eyes over *Hermes*. "I've raked her masts further," he said, "and added more sails aloft, which squeezes an extra few knots in light winds."

"Won't that be a hazard in heavy weather?" Smith asked at once.

"I won't hoist these sails in foul weather," Campbell said. "I won't endanger the ship."

"I have a message for you to deliver," Smith said. "How soon can you cross the Atlantic to New York?"

Campbell pursed his mouth. "Eighteen days, given a favourable wind," he said. Fifteen with luck."

"Are you ready to leave on the next tide?"

"I am," Campbell confirmed.

Smith handed over the packet he carried. The outside was in a waxed waterproof cover with three separate seals, and Smith had weighed it down with a four-pound cannonball. "I want you to deliver this to Abraham Hargreaves at the address on the cover."

"Yes, Mr Smith." Campbell accepted the packet without question.

"Deliver it in person," Smith said. "Give him my compliments and tell him it will be necessary to proceed with the utmost dispatch."

"Yes, Mr Smith," Campbell said again.

"Repeat what I said," Smith ordered.

"I will give Abraham Hargreaves your compliments, hand over this package and inform him it is necessary to proceed with the utmost dispatch," Campbell said.

"You've got it. I've arranged for a cargo of arms and ammunition to be loaded on *Hermes* tonight. That's for the garrison commander in New York, but the letter is more important."

"Yes, Mr Smith," Campbell said.

"If the enemy or the Royal Navy boards you, throw the message overboard. I want nobody to read it except Abraham Hargreaves."

"I understand, Mr Smith." Campbell was a young man, and Smith knew he was better at sea than speaking to a ship owner.

Smith nodded. "Then I'll leave it in your hands, Captain." He walked away, swinging his cane. As he strode towards Leadenhall Street, a yellow phaeton whizzed past, with the driver perched high above the tall rear wheels.

Henry Copinger, Smith said. Copinger pulled up a few yards past Smith.

"On Shanks's pony, I see, Smith!"

Smith raised his cane in acknowledgement.

Copinger, bare-headed and with his dark hair tied in a queue, laughed. "Maybe you're too old to manage a phaeton, Smith." He whipped up the horses and sped along the road with his wheels a yellow blur.

Smith watched him go. *Too old? We'll see about that, Copinger.*

Chapter Eleven

Bess looked around the small room. "You're keeping it quite clean," she approved.

Peter stood in the corner with his hands folded in front of him. "Yes, Mrs Smith," he said. He was nervous as Bess inspected the room she rented for him.

With a small table and chair, a chest, a bed and a selection of crockery, the room was sparsely furnished but far better than anything Peter had previously known. It was dry, sheltered and had a fireplace with a supply of wood and coal to fight the damp chill of winter.

"Yes." Bess nodded. "You've done well."

Peter visibly relaxed. He had learned that Bess was a formidable woman to cross, verbally and physically.

"Now, let's find out how your reading is progressing," Bess said. "Bring over your books."

"Yes, Mrs Smith," Peter said and carried across his reading books. "I've been reading on my own," he said. "When Madge and the boys are not here."

"Well done," Bess said. "When you are a good reader, you can teach them their letters."

"They would not want to learn," Peter told her.

"Neither did you," Bess reminded. "I had to encourage you."

Peter wriggled on the chair at the memory of Bess's encouragement. "You don't have to encourage me now," he said quickly.

"No," Bess agreed. "You've had Madge and the boys in this room, haven't you? I can smell them."

"Yes." Peter looked suddenly guilty. "They come here at night when they've nowhere else to go."

"Quite right, Peter." Bess approved of helping those in need. "Now, let's get started. We're reading chapter five of *Robinson Crusoe*. You start on the third page, and I'll read the fourth."

Peter grinned. He liked it when Bess read to him from a book. He did not care about the words, only the attention she paid him.

SMITH LIFTED THE PILE OF PRINTED DOCUMENTS FROM HIS desk, glanced at the top copy and scanned the words.

"By the Commissioners for Executing the Office of Lord High Admiral of the United Kingdom of Great Britain and Ireland &c, and of all His Majesty's Plantations, &c

Whereas by an Act of Parliament passed in the 15th year of the reign of His late Majesty King George the Second, it is enacted that the person under the age and circumstances therein mentioned shall be freed and exempted from being impressed into His Majesty's service, upon due proof made..."

"That looks like a genuine Protection Certificate." Bess had been reading over Smith's shoulder. She placed a mug of coffee in front of him. "Don't spill that on the Protections," she warned.

"Thank you. The top document is genuine," Smith told her. "The rest are forgeries. I had a screever copy them, and I want them issued to every man we employ, with their name and description added. When I obtain the genuine article, we can discard these forgeries."

"The Press will ignore them," Bess warned.

"Even a false Protection may delay the Press Gang a little," Smith said. "I'll use every trick I can to protect my crews."

"Will the press gang not know these Protections are false?" Bess asked.

"They'll be rushing," Smith said. "The true seamen might know the difference, but often the press recruits pub bullies and the like who would not recognise themselves in a mirror."

"Why are some men protected and others not?" Bess asked.

"In peacetime, the bulk of seamen on British ships are British," Smith explained. "But in times of war, as the Navy expands and grabs every man they can, merchant ship owners and masters like us resort to substitutes, many of whom can be officially protected."

Bess lifted an enquiring eyebrow. "Tell me more."

"Men over fifty-five or under eighteen are protected while foreigners have a lifetime's protection," Smith said. "That means the navy can't officially press them, but often do. They press landsmen, too, although the law says the navy can't take any who have been at sea less than two years. It's the same for apprentices, who have three years' grace."

"Experienced British seamen are getting hard to find now," Bess commented. "I've noticed some ships going to sea manned by old men and boys, with the rest of the crew made up of foreigners."

"That's usually the case in wartime," Smith said. "The navy's the same. They use the press and every other method they can but never get sufficient hands. On paper, the navy looks good with large numbers of ships, but most are undermanned with untrained men. That's fine when the enemy is equally hard pressed, but not in this war."

"Why is that?" Bess asked.

"Our agents in Europe are concerned that France may join in with the Americans." Smith passed over a letter. "I have a man on the inside who tells me the government is gravely concerned."

Bess glanced at the letter. "I don't see why," she said. "We've dealt with the French before, often enough."

Smith folded the letter, placed it in the bottom drawer of his desk and locked it, attaching the key to a small ring attached to his watch chain.

"Normally, when we fight France, we concentrate on building the navy and finance other countries to fight on land. We only have a small army and send a few battalions to Europe. This time, France has no European war to drain her manpower, so she can concentrate on her navy."

"I see," Bess said.

"If France joins the war, she will send thousands of men to the Americas to train the colonials and teach them how to fight. France will supply the specialist engineers and gunners for any siege and, more importantly, match us ship by ship at sea. Sooner or later, Spain will join France, and both will try to regain some of the Caribbean islands we've taken from them. Then the Netherlands will attach herself to our enemies, and we'll be fighting all of Europe in a war we can't win."

"Do you think so?"

"I do. We have one of the smallest armies in Europe, and unless we use conscription, we have a limit to its size. France will support the rebels to tie down and wear down our resources. As soon as they enter the war, we'll have to divert many thousands of men, plus a sizeable chunk of the navy, to defend the West Indian islands."

"Are those small islands important?"

"Yes," Smith said. "Probably more important than the thir-teen rebellious American colonies."

"Why?" Bess asked.

"Colonies exist for several purposes," Smith explained. "Firstly, they can be used as a repository for criminals. We've sent thousands of unwanted people to the Americas, thieves, poachers, the useless, incorrigibles, religious dissidents, rebels, and anybody we didn't want in Britain."

"That's one reason," Bess said.

"They are also a place for raw materials, timber, fruit, fish and so on."

"That's two reasons," Bess said.

"And a market for our goods," Smith said.

"That's three." Bess held up three fingers.

"As security, such as Gibraltar," Smith continued. "They provide bases for the navy and safe anchorages for merchant shipping during foul weather, or when they have to take on water and stores, or refit."

"Four." Bess added another finger.

"Or just to ensure the French don't have these advantages," Smith said.

"Five." Bess lifted her thumb with a small smile. "We don't like the French, do we?"

Smith did not answer the question. "Add another reason," he said. "Nations have colonies to make money. The thirteen rebel colonies have proved expensive. We've had wars against the French and the native tribes, and although the colonists played a major part in the last war, it still cost Great Britain millions." He shrugged. "The West Indian sugar islands make us money, so ultimately they are more important than the rebellious colonies."

"And we're in another war in the colonies," Bess said, "costing more money."

"Is the game worth the candle?" Smith asked. "Is it worth the country spending millions to force the colonists to be loyal to the Crown? Even if we win with our handful of redcoats, will we need to maintain a large, expensive garrison in the colonies for the foreseeable future?"

Bess shook her head. "So what do we do?"

"I doubt many people care if the Americas rule themselves or King George rules them, as long as the French don't control them." Smith shrugged. "Do you think having a colony on the other side of the Atlantic benefits the ordinary people? I don't."

"That's not what I meant," Bess said. "As far as I am

concerned, the colonists can have the Americas, and I'll throw in a pound of cheese if they want it. I mean, what do we do, you and I?"

Smith smiled. "We do what we've always done, Bess. We rise and make money."

Bess nodded. "Who do we support?"

"Ourselves, Bess," Smith said. "What did the Crown and country ever do for us? Or anybody else? Nothing. So we do nothing for them."

"We're in this for ourselves, then."

"Exactly so, Bess," Smith confirmed.

"Thank God for that," Bess said. "I thought you were turning into a flag-waving Tory patriot, singing God Save the King and helping him to reign over the Americas or some such nonsense." She walked to the window and looked outside. Smith watched her for a moment, knowing she was gathering her courage to ask something.

"John," Bess said a few moments later. "What are we going to do about Peter?"

"Do about him? What do you mean?"

"I'm getting quite attached to the boy. We can't just use him and abandon him," Bess said. "He'll revert to what he was, a filthy, unkempt creature with no hope."

"What do you have in mind, Bess?"

Bess looked uncharacteristically apprehensive. "We never had any children, John."

"No, we didn't," Smith agreed.

"Would you not like to have somebody to leave your heritage to?" Bess spoke slowly, not sure how Smith would react.

"I'd have liked a son or daughter," Smith agreed carefully, guessing where Bess was heading.

"Peter is getting to be a decent young man," Bess continued. "He helps his friends, lets them shelter in the room we rent for him, and works hard at his lessons. I don't know about his stealing."

"He's an accomplished little rogue," Smith could not restrain his smile.

"He could be our accomplished little rogue," Bess said. "We could make him our son, John."

Smith felt his heartbeat increase. "That would be interesting, Bess. How about his real parents?"

"He's never known them," Bess said. "I asked. He doesn't know his real name either."

"He could be lying," Smith reminded. "Lying comes easier to him that telling the truth."

Bess lifted her chin. "I know him better than you, John. He knows he'd better tell the truth to me."

"How long have you been planning this?" Smith asked.

"A few months," Bess admitted. "He has a vague memory of some woman leaning over him, slapping his face and shouting, but he doesn't know if she was his mother." She twisted her mouth. "He remembered the smell of gin."

"Gin alley," Smith murmured. "It sounds like Peter's mother was not the soberest person."

"What do you think we should do?" Bess asked hopefully.

"Keep working on his reading and writing," Smith said and touched her arm. "You know more about such matters than I do. If you think it's right to adopt him, we'll do it." He smiled. "John Smith and Son has a good sound."

Bess touched Smith's arm again. "Thank you, John."

Chapter Twelve

"I bought two shares in *London's Tower* yesterday, sir." Judd stood in front of Smith's desk. "Word has spread that I am buying, and the price has risen."

Smith nodded. "You've done well," he said. "I'll have the shares transferred to my name."

"Yes, Mr Smith," Judd bowed as he left.

Two shares here, two shares there; Judd is adding to my holdings day by day. I already own more than two-thirds of the company's shares. Only Jackson and Bancroft possess sizeable holdings now.

SMITH SENT OUT A DOZEN MEN TO SEARCH FOR SAMUEL Burgess, mate of *Amelia Jane,* paying them a shilling a day, with a half crown bonus for the successful man.

"You can help me, Peter," Smith said and gave instructions that Peter related to his circle of fellow thieves and mudlarks. Smith noted with approval that Peter had purchased a set of old clothes from a pawnbroker and used them when he was thieving, wearing his best clothes when he was off duty.

Maybe Bess is right, and we could bring Peter into the household. He's a sharp young lad with a decent streak to him.

After days of searching, one of Peter's minions found Burgess in a dirty public house a stone's throw from the St Giles Rookery.

"Mr Burgess." Smith pushed into the pub, ignoring the predatory glowers from the ragged denizens.

"Who wants to know?" Burgess looked up from under a tangle of unwashed hair. His eyes were bloodshot, and his face was unshaven.

"John Smith." Smith dragged over a three-legged stool and sat opposite him. "I owned *London's Pride*."

Burgess grunted and said nothing. He drained the contents of a pewter pot.

"I'm still enquiring about the survivors of *London's Pride*, Mr Burgess."

Burgess tossed the hair back from his eyes. He looked sixty years old, although Smith knew he was thirty-eight. "I guessed that, Mr Smith."

"You've had time to reconsider, Mr Burgess," Smith encouraged, "and nobody knows you're talking to me."

"We saw something in the water," Burgess admitted at last. "I don't know what it was."

"You saw the survivors of *London's Pride*," Smith said. "Why did you tell me you hadn't seen the survivors?" He ordered two tankards of ale, tasted his, decided it was a mixture of slops and foul water and laid the tankard aside.

"I've got five children, Mr Smith," Burgess said. "If Shapland got rid of me, nobody else would employ me, and my wife and children would starve."

Smith looked around the public house. Cobwebs hung in silvery threads from the ceiling, nobody had swept the floor in weeks, and half the plaster was missing from the walls. A single candle struggled to find sufficient oxygen in the air to give more than a faint yellow glow. "You're not doing them much good in here."

Burgess grunted and swallowed half the contents of his tankard.

"What happened?" Smith asked.

"Shapland kicked me out." Burgess looked up with his eyes red raw and wild. "The bastard got rid of me just like that. I'm bringing home nothing to the wife now." He drained the tankard. "The best I can do is ship as a seaman with the navy, which won't feed the family."

"I'd employ you," Smith said immediately.

Burgess looked up, with suspicion battling the slight hope in his eyes. "Even when I left your men to drown?"

"You were the only man who tried to help," Smith said. "David Cupples mentioned you by name. Get out of this hole and come back with me; I need experienced men in my ships."

———

"Here's to the arm that holds them when gone,
Still to a gallop inclined, sir.
Heads to the front with no bearing reins on,
Tails with no cruppers behind, sir."

SMITH HUMMED THE JAUNTY LITTLE DITTY AS HE CIRCLED THE carriage. He had often watched young noblemen parade in their phaetons, and Copinger's insults helped him decide to try one. He had commissioned Ebenezer Harrison, one of London's best coachbuilders, to create the finest phaeton possible. Now he viewed the product.

"When did you finish her, Mr Harrison?"

"Last night, Mr Smith," Harrison said with pride. "Do you like her?"

"I do," Smith said. "She looks fast. Very fast."

Phaetons were introduced around 1757 and had grown in

popularity among the wealthy. They were amongst the simplest carriages, consisting of a small body perched on high springs above a lightweight undercarriage and the lack of weight added to their speed. By the mid-1760s, most fashionable young men in London drove phaetons, staring from their lofty perches at the people below. Harrison had built a phaeton with a single seat so high above the ground that Smith could step into the carriage straight from a first-floor window.

He smiled. "I'd like a new coat of silver paint on her, with the name, *Quicksilver*, in black."

"Yes, sir," Harrison agreed at once.

"And a motto on a scroll. *Nemo me impune lacessit.*" Smith grinned 'that's Latin for nobody assails me with impunity, but in my case, it will be "nobody passes me on the road."

Harrison gave a professional smile and wrote down the motto, checking the spelling with Smith. He looked up anxiously. "The extra paintwork will incur more cost, sir."

Smith nodded. "I understand that. I haven't paid you a penny yet, have I, Mr Harrison?"

"No, sir," Harrison said hopefully.

"Send me your account," Smith said. "No, I'll give you a down payment now." Dipping in his pocket, he produced a heavy purse and poured a handful of gold sovereigns into Harrison's hand.

"Thank you, sir," Harrison said. He was relieved, for many titled and entitled men failed to pay their accounts until they were well overdue, or neglected to pay at all, driving businessmen into debt or out of business.

"Let me know how much I owe you when I pick the chariot up," Smith said. "When will it be ready?"

"Thursday, sir," Harrison said. "I'll get onto it right away."

"Thank you, Mr Harrison. I'll collect it in person," Smith said, smiling. As he left the coachbuilder's yard, he stopped again to admire the phaeton. Smith knew merchants were usually sober, professionally minded men who spent most of their time poring over accounts or at the Exchange. He had decided not to lose his personality under the weight of responsibility in pursuing profit.

No, damnit, that's not the reason. I want to grind young Copinger's nose in the dust and curb his arrogance.

"You're no longer in your twenties," Bess reminded him when he told her about the phaeton. "These machines can be dangerous."

"That's the fun of the thing," Smith said. "What's life without an element of danger? Driving a phaeton is the most handsome mixture of dignity and danger."

"You're too old to believe such nonsense," Bess said. "You're reacting to a rival's taunts, John. You should know better."

Smith laughed. "I aim to put him in his place."

Bess shook her head. "Be careful, John."

Chapter Thirteen

Kate sat in the corner of the public house, sipping at her gin, and watching the mixed clientele. As well as the regular dock workers, porters and assorted riffraff, there was a floating population of seamen with their distinctive clothes and language. She shuffled her feet, creating a circular pattern on the dirty straw and sawdust on the floor and leaned back in her chair.

"You're a prime-looking woman," a porter said, leering at her over the rim of a pewter tankard.

"Too prime for you," Kate said, adding a short two-word injunction to send him away.

"Well, you look like a bunter," the porter protested, spreading his hands.

"And you look a dim flat," Kate said. "Bugger off."

"I'll not take that from the likes of you!" the porter said and looked down in sudden alarm as Kate pressed a slim-bladed knife against his groin.

"Stay if you want to lose your equipment, my blustering cove." Kate pressed harder. "Not that there's much to lose."

When the porter swore and backed away, Kate tapped the

knife against her thigh. "That's a clever lad. Now turn around and keep moving."

The porter obeyed, leaving the pub at some speed. Kate surveyed the men in the room, separating the seamen from the rest. She concentrated on a quiet group of sailors that gathered around a circular table, slipped up her skirt to reveal her left calf, adjusted her top, so her cleavage was more visible and waited.

When one weather-tanned seaman noticed her sitting alone in the corner and lifted a hand in greeting, Kate smiled back without moving. She saw the sailor's gaze rove over her exposed leg.

Men are so predictable. He'll step beside me in a moment.

The seamen spoke together for a few moments, with an occasional glance at Kate, and then the tanned man stood and walked over to her, with his buckled shoes clicking on the floorboards.

"Excuse me, miss," the tanned sailor spoke with a West Country burr. "We couldn't help noticing you were all alone there."

"I am." Kate smiled into his brown eyes.

"The boys and I don't like to see a woman all alone," the sailor said. "It's not natural, like, especially on the Highway." The Ratcliffe Highway was a street in London favoured by seamen, prostitutes and men seeking adventure in mildly dangerous public houses.

"I'm all right," Kate said. "You boys are seamen, aren't you?"

"We're all from *London's Fancy*," the seaman said as Kate rose to join them at their table. "I'm Jem; this is Davie, Wat and Taffy."

As the men nodded to Kate, Davie dragged her chair to their table.

Kate settled down, smiling at each man in turn. "I'm Kate," she said. "Are you just off your ship? *London's Fancy*, you said. Is she not one of John Smith's ships?"

"That's right," Jem agreed. "We're one day back from the Baltic with timber."

Kate wriggled her hips slightly on the chair. "Are you boys not worried about the press gangs? They've been very active in the Highway since this war started."

The men exchanged glances. "We'll be all right," Jem said cryptically.

"Will you fight them?" Kate asked, rewarding Davy with a smile for the gin he placed in front of her.

Jem pulled a face. "Maybe, if we have to. Better to run and hide."

Kate smiled. "Well, you know best." She edged closer to Jem. "Tell me about the Baltic. It sounds very romantic!"

Davie, Wat, and Taffy smiled, shaking their heads. "It's cold, bleak and miserable," Wat said. "Like the people there."

"You're better in London, then." Kate placed a hand on Jem's thigh. He was young, with hard muscles and a presentable face. He would do. She looked up as a crowd of women entered the pub. Loud-voiced, brash and adorned with ribbons, they were obviously prostitutes. Kate decided she would have to pick a man before the competition flounced her out.

"It's getting busy," Kate said, allowing her hand to drift further up Jem's thigh. He did not object.

Davie watched her through steady, serious eyes while Taffy and Wat turned to watch the explosion of prostitutes.

Jem responded by putting an arm around Kate's waist. She replied with a professional smile, pressing her leg against his.

Davie looked away as two prostitutes peeled away from the main fleet and sailed towards their table. "We've got company, lads," he warned.

"And right welcome they are," Wat said. He laughed. "You've got your woman, Jem; now we want ours!"

"Come on, Jem," Kate said. "You and I have things to do." She patted the inside of his thigh, ran her hand higher up and smiled. "The first time is free."

"Free?"

"For a handsome young lad like you?" Kate said. "The pleasure will be mine." She lowered her voice slightly as the be-feathered prostitutes descended on the table, each choosing her target. "You're quite right to ignore these young flashtails, Jem. They show a lot and know nothing. Believe me, the older the fiddle, the better the tune," Kate told him, "and I know more tricks than any young novice at this game." Sliding her hand into his, Kate stood up and edged away from the table.

"Where are we going?" Jem asked.

"To a quiet place where we can be alone together," Kate told him. "Don't worry; I don't have a bully waiting to crack you on the head with a cudgel. I'm honest Kate Driver."

The Highway was busy with pedestrians as a smattering of gentlemen mingled with the seamen, labourers, prostitutes, and thieves who crowded the street. Kate kept a firm hold of Jem's hand and guided him up a narrow side street to a baker's shop.

"I've got a room up above," she said. "Come on."

Smiling, Jem followed. "I'm glad I found you," he said.

Kate allowed him to cherish the illusion that he was in charge. She opened the door to the single-room house. She had deliberately furnished it to appear like a prostitute's home, with a prominent double bed, a large mirror, two chairs, a table, and a small collection of bottles. A painted sea chest under the window held a selection of clothes while a pot of soup sat beside the unmade fire.

"Sit down, Jem and make yourself at home," Kate said. "Rum, gin or Madeira?"

Jem bounced on the bed. "Rum for me, Kate. You have a palace here!"

Kate smiled at him. "Thank you, Jem." She handed over a tumbler of rum.

"What do you charge?"

"I told you, Jem, the first time is free." Kate sat at his side and toasted him in gin. "Here's to a short war."

"A short war," Jem said, watching as Kate began to remove her clothes.

"Join me, Jem," Kate invited. She knew no better way of relaxing a man than to ask him into her bed and knew she was skilled at the art of seduction. Fortunately, Jem was sex-starved after weeks at sea and responded energetically.

Kate led him on, drained him, and watched as he slumped face down on the bed, panting. "How much am I worth the next time?" she teased as Jem gradually recovered.

Jem rolled onto his back, smiled, reached into his pocket, and produced a handful of coins. "You're good," he said and dropped the money on the rumpled bed. "You'll have to give me a minute."

Kate laughed, took a shilling, and put the rest back into Jem's pocket. "I can help you recover," she said.

"Whenever you like," Jem said.

Dawn had broken when they emerged from Kate's house arm-in-arm, with Jem smiling in the afterglow of sex and Kate hoping her timing was correct. She heard a church clock chime the hours and pulled Jem closer.

"Where shall we go today, Jem?"

"Go?" Jem looked at her. "Are you staying with me?"

"Unless you have somebody else you wish to see," Kate told him, smiling.

"Breakfast, then," Jem said. "The Spread Eagle does mutton chops and peas."

"Take me," Kate said. She heard the commotion before Jem did, mainly because she was expecting it, and distracted him with chatter for a few moments.

"Take the starboard side, Mr Congreve!" a man shouted. "I'll take the port, and don't let any of the scoundrels escape!"

"Can you hear that?" Jem asked. "It's the Press!" Kate heard the panic in his words. "The press gang is coming."

"Jem!" She grabbed his arm. "What will we do?"

"You're safe," Jem told her. "They won't take you!"

"They'll take you though, Jem," Kate said. "I've just found you, and I don't want to lose you so soon!"

"I'll be all right," Jem calmed his initial alarm. "I know a safe place."

"Jem!" Kate clung to his arm in assumed alarm. "Nowhere's safe from the Press!"

"This place is," Jem said. "Come on, I'll show you." He led her along the Highway and up Atlantic Street, where a church sat in solitary splendour, keeping a disapproving eye on the sins and errors of the city. "In here."

"It's not safe so close to the Highway," Kate said. "The Press raids churches as well."

"It's all right, Kate. Come in here." Jem glanced over his shoulder. A stocky midshipman in his thirties led a gang into Atlantic Street, with a pair of petty officers barking orders and a dozen predatory seamen marching purposefully over the dusty ground. The seamen carried cudgels or cutlasses while others pushed a crowd of unhappy captives before them.

"Hurry, Jem!" Kate ran into the church and glanced around at the array of pews with the altar above. "Where can we hide?" She heard the thunder of feet in the street outside.

"This way," Jem shouted, leading her to the altar.

Kate followed as Jem ran up the steps two at a time, glancing over his shoulder as somebody hammered at the church door.

"Hurry, Jem!" Kate pleaded. It was not part of her plan for the Press to catch Jem in the church.

"In here!" Jem opened a small door at the head of the steps and ushered Kate into a dark corridor. "The vicar comes this way when he preaches." The passage led to a relatively large chamber, with a bookcase full of Bibles and prayer books and two doors leading off. Jem hesitated for a second, checked the doors and gave a distinctive knock on the furthest. Three raps, a pause, then four more.

Three raps, a pause and another four. Kate thought. *I'll remember that.*

A bolt scraped back, and the door opened a crack.

"Open up, lads. It's Jem Diamond from *London's Fancy*."

The door opened into a room larger than Kate had expected, with red brick walls under a vaulted ceiling. Five men huddled on a row of benches, one with a hand on the knife at his belt.

"Come in and shut the door," the knifeman said, and Kate followed Jem inside.

"Who's she?" the knifeman asked.

"A friend," Jem said with a sly smile. "She's not one of the Press."

The men nodded and settled down, listening. One scarred man eyed Kate up and down, winked and produced a bottle.

"Gin," he said. "It'll help pass the time."

Kate thanked him with a smile.

The men grinned back, pleased with their cleverness at avoiding the press gang, and a bearded veteran with a huge pigtail began to sing.

"Cheerily, lads, cheerily! There's a ganger hard to windward;
Cheerily, lads, cheerily! There's a ganger hard a-lee!"

Jem moved close to Kate. "A ganger is a craft carrying the press gang," he whispered.

The singer glared at Jem and continued,

"Cheerily, lads, cheerily, else 'tis farewell home and kindred,
And the bosun's mate a-raisin' hell in the King's navee.

Cheerily, lads, cheerily! The warrant's out; the hanger's drawn;

Cheerily, lads, cheerily! We'll leave 'em an R in pawn!"

Jem nudged Kate again. "An R in the muster book means run or deserted," he explained.

"I see," Kate said. "Where do these other doors lead?"

"That one leads to the dockside," Jem explained. "We come inside and bolt the door, so the press can't get us."

Kate laughed. "What a splendid idea." She took a swallow of the gin. "Do all the seamen know of this place?"

"Only John Smith's crews," Jem said.

Kate handed back the gin. "Now, how shall we pass the time?"

Chapter Fourteen

James Bancroft leaned back in his chair, sipped at the Geneva, and smiled at Bess. "By God, Mrs Smith, you know how to feed a man."

"You're always welcome here, James," Bess said.

"I always feel welcome," Bancroft told her. He looked around the room, with the tall windows overlooking Leicester Square, the ornate plasterwork on the ceiling and the long table laden with food and drink. The other guests were busy eating or drinking, with Anthony Jackson smiling drunkenly, Captain Mungo Campbell speaking in his Nova Scotian drawl and Israel Burgess looking ill at ease. Sir Humphrey Waterson sat opposite Bess, listening to everything and speaking quietly to Lord George Gordon.

Smith knew little about Gordon except he was the Whig Member of Parliament for the pocket borough of Ludgershall, supported the Americans in their quest for independence and had tried to improve the conditions of ordinary seamen in the Royal Navy.

"I'm leaving the navy," Gordon said. He was a thin-faced man with connections to the Scottish nobility, and Smith had invited him to create a political link. "I've no future there since I tried to help the seamen."

"A laudable intention, my Lord," Sir Humphrey said, "but hardly conducive to your maritime career."

"What do you intend now, Gordon?" Smith asked.

"Politics, Smith," Gordon told him. "General Fraser bought me a seat in parliament, and I'll fight to end this pointless war, see the Americans get their liberty and oppose any threat to the Protestant religion."

"I agree with you about the Americans," Smith said. "Is there a threat to the Protestant religion?"

"You're damned right there is, Smith," Gordon raised his voice. "The Catholics were violent in their support of the Pretender, Charles Stuart, in the 40s. Now that he is gone, they'll fix their star on the Americans. The longer this foolish civil war continues, the more chance there is of the Catholics rising in Britain and Ireland. The quicker we grant the colonials their liberty, the less chance there is of a Roman Catholic uprising and the civil war spreading here." He swallowed half a glass of Smith's best port. "That damned Lord North might pander to the Papes, but I won't; you can depend on it."

"I see." Smith nodded. He had never heard of a possible Catholic rising but tucked away the information about buying a pocket borough.

"Enough politics, gentlemen." Bess turned the conversation. "We are here to celebrate Mr Bancroft's birthday."

"Not at all." Bancroft waved a deprecating hand.

"Well, James, it is your birthday," Bess insisted.

Smith lifted a decanter. "Shall we try the port? It's freshly imported from Oporto on the last Mediterranean convoy."

"I have a taste for good port," Bancroft said. He waited until Smith filled his glass and lifted it. "I propose a toast," he said. "A toast to the traitor George Washington, a man who broke his oath of allegiance to the king. May his slaves choke him with his ideas of liberty!"

The assembly cheered and tossed back Smith's port.

Bess stood and called for silence. "I have another toast. To Lord North, for his mishandling of the peace and bungling of the war, may his next glass of wine choke the wretch!"

The men laughed and hammered their glasses on the table.

"Another toast!" Smith said, grinning at Bancroft. "To James Bancroft on his thirtieth birthday."

"Thank you, Smith!" Bancroft replied as a busy servant recharged the glasses.

"Thirty?" Jackson repeated. "I thought you were older, Bancroft." He drank his port and waved the glass to attract the attention of a servant.

"Not yet," Bancroft said solemnly. "I will be next year."

"Come on, Bancroft, and I'll show you my new coach," Smith said. "Excuse us, gentlemen. I'll be back in ten minutes." He raised his voice. "I have a race to win!" As Smith left the room, Jackson waited a moment and followed.

THE THREE CARRIAGES STOOD SIDE BY SIDE IN THE PRE-DAWN darkness. Smith's silver *Quicksilver*, Shapland's red-and-gold *Mercury* and Copinger's *Blue Lightning* were all prime examples of the coachbuilder's art. Each had a team of four matching horses who pawed at the ground, impatient to run. Shapland's team was all black, Copinger's grey and Smith had four brown, all named after ships in which he had sailed.

Smith savoured the view of Appleby Common as it spread around the coaches. Twenty miles south of London, it was an area of rough grassland the local villagers used to pasture their livestock, with scattered trees rustling in the chill Kent breeze.

"You do realise you're very stupid, John," Bess said severely.

"I do," Smith agreed, eyeing the opposition. Shapland was murmuring to his horses, feeding them as he patted the lead horses' necks. Henry Copinger was talking to an elderly coach driver, doubtless picking up a few final tips about fast driving.

"Phaetons are notorious for overturning when driven at speed," Bess continued. She nodded to the crowd that gathered around. "Most of these people are gambling on the outcome, and they all hope to see an accident, especially a fatal accident."

Smith smiled. "Let's hope it happens to Shapland and not to me." He lifted an arm to acknowledge James Bancroft, who stood amidst a crowd of younger men. Anthony Jackson stood a few yards further back in deep conversation with a tall, red-haired woman.

"Let's hope so, John," Bess said. "You are racing twice around the Common; for how much?"

"We're each putting in a purse of a thousand guineas," Smith told her. "The winner scoops the lot, but it's not the money that counts. It's the glory. Shapland has boasted of his coach for months, and now I have the chance to put him in his place."

"Henry Copinger is also racing," Bess reminded. "He's a stalwart thirty-year-old and much more experienced in driving a phaeton."

"Copinger has a fine chariot," Smith acknowledged, "and he is a bold, thrusting man, yet I sense a weakness within him." He grinned. "He won't be a threat."

Bess looked away. "I wish you were more cautious," she said.

"Are you ready, gentlemen?" Shapland strode forward. Three inches taller than Smith and ten years younger, he thrust his brown wig firmly on his head, jammed a broad-brimmed hat on top and smiled. "Conferring with your woman, I see, Smith."

"That's right," Smith agreed. "You have a fine chariot, Shapland."

"As have you, Smith," Shapland countered. "Let's see if you can handle it." He slapped Copinger on the shoulder. "I forgot you would be coming, Copinger."

Copinger was a serious-faced man with startlingly blue eyes. He looked at Shapland without comment and turned away.

"Are you ready, Smith? Are you prepared, Copinger?" Shapland strode across the springy grass, tall, handsome, and confident in his position.

"I'm ready," Smith said as Bess treated Shapland with a smile.

"Good morning to you, Mrs Smith." Shapland gave a slight bow. "I hope you have your purse with you today?"

Bess smiled. "I'll need it to carry home our winnings," she said. "A thousand guineas from you and a thousand from Mr Copinger. I'll be able to buy myself a handsome new wardrobe."

Shapland smiled. "We'll see, Mrs Smith. We'll see." He hoisted himself onto his carriage and sat on the single seat.

Everybody watched as the Appleby Express coach stopped at the edge of the Common to disgorge its quota of spectators. Lucy Beeching had run the company for years, ever since Lightning Bowlt, the highwayman, had murdered her intended, Mr Foreman. Now she waved to Smith and wished him luck.

"We're due to start, John," Bess warned.

"I'm ready," Smith said.

Sir Humphrey Waterson was the referee, a man known to all three participants and who had promised not to gamble on any of the coaches.

"Places, gentlemen, please," Sir Humphrey said.

"Good luck, John." Bess touched his arm and stepped away.

Smith smiled and took his seat, holding the reins and talking quietly to the horses. He saw Copinger leap into his place with his face expressionless.

"Move back, gentlemen and ladies," Sir Humphrey ordered. "Give the competitors space, if you please!" He began to push back the most forward of the spectators, ensuring the immediate area was cleared, with quite a sizeable crowd gathered despite the early hour.

"Good luck, Mr Smith!" Bancroft shouted. "I've got a hundred sovs on you to win!"

"I'll do my best for you," Smith replied with a wave of his hand.

The sun tipped over the horizon, spreading welcome light over the grey morning. Smith saw the trees of the Common in silhouette, branches stark against the paling sky, with the pale rays catching the glossy paintwork of the phaetons.

"Ready, gentlemen?" Sir Humphrey tipped back his hat and lifted a white silk handkerchief. "When I drop this handkerchief, you are free to start. The rules are simple, two circuits of the Common, and the first man to arrive back here is the winner. Nobody else is allowed to interfere in any way. Is that clear, gentlemen?"

"Clear," Smith replied at once.

"That's clear," Copinger said.

"We all know the rules, Sir Humphrey," Shapland said. "Get on with it, man!"

Smith glanced at the route. The beginning was level, with a hundred yards between two copses of trees. After that came a slight incline over rough grass and a gentle left turn around a solitary oak.

Smith nodded. He would remain in the rear, watching how the others drove. He expected Shapland to race into an early lead and stay there with Copinger on his shoulder.

Beyond the oak, the course stretched for half a mile of undulating ground, with some scattered boulders and a few sheep as additional hazards.

I'll pass the oak tree, push the horses past Shapland, and stay in front.

After the undulating straight came a sharp left-hand turn, a dangerously narrow passage between a pile of rocks and a steep downward slope.

That will be the trickiest section of the course to drive but the hardest in which to overtake. If I'm in front at that stage, the others can only watch my back.

With the steep slope negotiated, there remained a broader, but still downward, run to the finishing line.

That will be another stretch where carriages can overtake. I'll ensure

I am well in front by then, for Shapland will press hard to retake the lead.

Once the phaetons passed the finishing line, they would do the whole course again.

Sir Humphrey's lifted his hand high, shouted, "Ready!" and dropped his handkerchief in a flutter of white silk. All three carriages moved forward. Twelve horses pulled, three racing men yelled, reins cracked on rumps and haunches, and the crowd roared in excitement.

"Go on, Smith!" Bancroft shouted, waving his hat in the air. "Go on and win!"

Smith had a momentary image of Judd talking to Jackson and then switched all his attention to the race. Everything else could wait until he had won.

Shapland took the lead, roaring triumphantly as he cracked the reins over his lead horses' rumps and pushed his carriage in front. Copinger tried to overtake, nearly running wheel to wheel until Shapland lashed backwards with his whip, catching the leading grey horse across the muzzle. The horse flinched, pulling away, and Copinger struggled to control his team.

Smith grunted, watching the contest in front. He had planned to hold back and watch, but with Copinger already in difficulties, Shapland pulled a full length ahead, steering his red-and-gold *Mercury* with great skill. Smith guided *Quicksilver* around Copinger's *Blue Lightning* and pushed on, already ten yards behind Shapland.

"Come on, boys!" Smith encouraged his team. He was only dimly aware of the cheering crowd, with some men running alongside the carriages for a short spell and Bancroft waving his hat like a man demented.

The incline was steeper than it had looked from a distance, with the ground rougher, pitted with rabbit holes and molehills. Smith swore as his left rear wheel thumped into a hole, and *Quicksilver* lurched to the side. He regained control with difficulty and saw Copinger creeping up behind him as Shapland eased further ahead.

This race is not going to plan.

Some members of the crowd pressed closer as Shapland rounded the solitary oak and pushed onto the straight. One man waved a brown bottle and shouted obscenities above the grind of wheels and hammer of hooves.

"Get out of the way!" Copinger yelled. "I'm the faster driver!"

Smith cracked his whip without replying, encouraging the horses to greater speed. *Quicksilver* was newer, lighter, and better constructed than Copinger's older *Blue Lightning*, and he inched ahead but was still far behind Shapland's *Mercury*. Shapland swore, flailed his whip and swerved to avoid a sheep, losing ground that Smith gained as both carriages swayed over the bumpy, rising ground.

Despite his words, Copinger had fallen behind, leaving Smith a clear run at Shapland's carriage. Smith managed his horses, steered around a half-hidden lichen-furred rock and eased closer. From his height, he looked down on a small flock of running sheep and drew level with Shapland.

"You'll not get past me!" Shapland roared, whipping furiously.

Without replying, Smith encouraged his team, inching closer to *Mercury*, so his rival had to alter course or risk a collision. Smith's carriage crashed over a hidden stone and edged in front, wheel by wheel.

"You bastard, Smith!" Shapland shouted as Smith pulled into the lead twenty yards before they reached the tight corner.

Smith reduced speed a fraction to negotiate the turn. He steered for the gap between the rocks on his left and the precipitous slope on his right. A group of spectators had gathered there, shouting, and waving their arms as they encouraged their favourites. One man had a dog, which barked furiously and ran alongside the carriages, perilously close to *Quicksilver*'s wheels. Ignoring everything else, Smith concentrated on the passage, had a frightening look at the steep slope and tore through the gap to the long run to the finishing line.

He was in front now, but Shapland was not giving up, whipping his horses in a furious endeavour to regain the lead. Smith maintained his position as they sped down the slope and saw Bess standing beside the finishing line; she shouted something as he swept past and onto the second circuit. Now he knew the course, he increased his speed, standing in the seat and roaring at the horses as he handled the ribbons like a professional.

"Keep going, Smith!" Bancroft encouraged.

Three men sat on the lower branches of the solitary oak as Smith raced past. The Common was a blur as Smith steered around the grazing sheep as if he had driven a carriage all his life and sped up the undulating grassland. A glance behind him confirmed Shapland was twenty yards in the rear, with Copinger a hundred yards further behind and no threat at all.

Smith allowed himself a smile as he pulled around the turn, heard the spectators cheering and drove into the space between the piled-up rocks and the precipice. Once through the gap, it was a straight run home and collect two thousand guineas.

Got you, Shapland!

Smith lifted his head triumphantly just as he heard a loud snap from beneath the carriage.

"What the deuce?" Smith struggled with the steering, swearing as the carriage failed to respond to his demands.

Quicksilver slewed to the side, with the horses screaming in panic as the machine overturned. Smith felt himself flying, let go of the reins and had a nightmare vision of *Quicksilver* and its team of horses on its side as he fell over the precipice. Somebody yelled, and then he landed on his right shoulder and rolled over and over into blackness.

Chapter Fifteen

K ate waited in the shadowed door of a warehouse, watching the docks. It was her fourth night at the same location, with the previous three bereft of any incident. She listened to the drunken bawling of a group of seamen further along the street, saw a brown-coated Charlie deliberately alter his route to avoid the noise and smiled.

During the day, the affluent rule London. At night, they hide behind barred windows and bolted doors, and the drunks, thieves and footpads take over. We live in a city with a dual personality.

Kate stiffened as she saw four youths emerge from one of Shapland's ships. Three boys and a girl slid over the taffrail and down a rope as handily as any foretopman. The tallest waited on the quay until his companions were beside him before loping away, with all four carrying bundles of stolen goods. As they passed the lighted window of a house, Kate noticed that the tall boy held a silver snuff box.

You took the bait, my little fellows. I've been watching you four ignore every ship except Charlie Shapland's.

Kate followed them through a succession of dark streets until they arrived at Abraham Reeves pawnshop, where dim candlelight proved Reeves was still open for business.

Kate found a convenient doorway on the opposite side of the road, slipped into the shadows, and waited. She saw a second candle glow beside the first, and fifteen minutes later, Reeves' door opened, and the four youths emerged, empty-handed and smiling. The girl said something, and the boys laughed.

"Got you, my boys," Kate said, waited until they were twenty yards ahead and then followed.

"I'D LIKE TO SPEAK TO JACK REDPATH, PLEASE," KATE SAID when she entered the Bow Street Magistrate's office.

Fielding, blind but as sharp as any man with perfect sight, nodded. "He's on patrol at present. That's Kate Rider, isn't it?"

"It is." Kate was always impressed with Fielding's ability to recognise people by the sound of their voices.

"Why do you want him, Miss Rider?"

"I have some information that might help him," Kate said.

"And I suppose you want to be rewarded for your information." Fielding gave a slight smile.

"No, sir," Kate replied at once. "Mr Redpath is a friend of mine."

"I see." Fielding's smile broadened. "You may tell me what you have to say, and I will pass the message on to Redpath."

"Certainly, sir," Kate replied. "Abraham Reeves, the pawnbroker, is a fence, sir. He has been accepting goods stolen from Charles Shapland's vessels."

Fielding adjusted the bandage he wore across his eyes. "Can you prove your accusation, Miss Rider?"

"I can, sir if Mr Redpath acts quickly. Among the items he acquired is a silver snuff box that belongs to Charles Shapland."

"Oh?" Fielding's head rose slightly. "I have only your word for that, Miss Rider."

"Not at all, sir," Kate said. "Mr Shapland's name is inscribed on the inside, under the lid."

"Tell me, Miss Rider, how you come by that piece of intelligence," Fielding asked.

"I gave Charles, Mr Shapland, the snuff box," Kate said. "It was a present on his thirty-fifth birthday."

Fielding nodded. "I will pass your information on to Jack Redpath," he said.

"Thank you, Mr Fielding." Kate curtseyed politely as she left the magistrate's office and headed for Bermondsey.

That's taken care of the fence. Now for the thieves.

"CARRY HIM GENTLY!" THAT WAS BESS'S VOICE, DRIFTING from a grey fog. Smith opened his eyes and saw half a dozen faces staring at him. He heard voices, tried to move, and fainted. The darkness was a blessing, relieving him from pain.

What happened? Where am I?

He remembered the crack beneath the carriage and losing control of *Quicksilver.* Then there was the fall, with the splintering of wood and screaming of stricken horses.

"Bess?"

"Lie still," Bess said quietly. She looked down at him with concern in her eyes. "You've taken a bit of a tumble."

"What?" Smith tried to move and groaned as something sharp probed into his side.

"Lie still!" Bess ordered again, but Smith had already drifted into unconsciousness.

When he woke again, Smith was unsure where he was. The ceiling was unfamiliar, and he could not move. He was aware of people nearby but could not see who they were. He lifted a hand and returned to the darkness. Darkness was familiar; he was safe there. There was no pain within the blanket of darkness and no confusion.

But the darkness altered when he returned. He was no longer oblivious, and there was more than darkness. He was back on the scaffold with the rough hempen noose around his neck, trying not to cry as the hangman patted his shoulder.

"It will all be over soon," the hangman said, roughly sympathetic.

"Be brave, son." His father was standing beside him, with an identical rope around his neck. The moisture in his eyes was sorrow for his son, not for himself.

"Father," Smith said, and the hangman pulled a lever. The rope tightened, choking him, and Smith gagged as the rope burned into his neck. Then he was in churning salt water with wreckage around him as his ship sank. Men shouted to an unresponsive God or cursed away their last moments alive as the masts slipped beneath the sea.

The water burned in Smith's throat and chest and roared in his ears as he drowned only a quarter of a mile from shore. Smith knew he had to swim, but the sea was cold and full of flotsam. When a length of cable wrapped around his legs, hampering him, he kicked it away, losing his trousers in the process and struck out for land, except he could not move his right arm.

The water closed over his head, taking him back to blackness. It was easier to succumb than to fight, easier to allow oblivion than to struggle anymore. Death was peaceful, a slow sinking into oblivion to join so many of his shipmates. Death smiled at him, inviting him home. The door was open, with a plethora of friendly faces beckoning him to enter. Death was easy, an escape from this life of turmoil and strain. Death spoke to him with sugared words.

Come, my friend. You've seen me a hundred times; you've shaken my hand within the hempen noose, tasted my sweetness at the muzzle of cannon and forced the door under my sea. Come now, come home.

"John!" That was Bess's voice. "Come back to me, John!"

An image eased into Smith's mind, Shapland's sneering face, laughing with triumph as he pocketed a thousand guineas and walked off, victorious.

"John!" Bess's words were struggling with the peace of death.

He saw the light emanating from her merging with the darkness, creating a fringe of grey, shot through with flecks of pure gold.

I'm waiting. Come home to me.

"No!" Smith shouted and forced open his eyes.

Bess sat at his side, her round face familiar, the old white scar puckering her left cheek and splitting her lip, yet without spoiling her beauty. Concern filled her eyes.

"Are you back with us, John?"

"Bess?" Smith tried to sit up. "What happened?" He looked around in confusion.

"You crashed the carriage," Bess reminded him, "and rolled arse over elbow down the slope."

Smith nodded as the memories returned. "I lost us a thousand guineas," he said.

"You did," Bess agreed, shaking her head. She looked tired and wearied, with her hair hanging loose, unwashed, and her clothes crumpled. "You're a stupid man, John!"

"How long have I been here?"

"Three weeks," Bess told him. "You've wasted three weeks lying in bed, and Shapland's made the most of it."

Smith frowned. "What's the matter with me? I can't move."

"You've smashed two ribs, broken an arm and got a fine collection of cuts and bruises," Bess told him. "The doctor thought you might die."

"I nearly did." Smith remembered the blackness that seemed so welcoming. "Help me up."

"The doctor said you've got to lie in bed for another fortnight at least."

"The doctor can get to hades," Smith said. "Help me up, Bess, damn it!"

"You're a stubborn man!" Bess scolded, putting an arm around his back.

Smith grunted as he moved. "And get some light in this damned room," he said. "I can hardly see."

"The doctor said a darkened room was best."

"The doctor doesn't know a damned thing," Smith said. "I want to see the sun and feel the wind."

Bess nodded and pulled open the shutters, allowing grey light to enter. With a glance at Smith, she threw open the window so cold air poured into the stuffy room.

"That's better," Smith struggled up, accepting the pain. "Light some candles, too." He grinned at her. "You look terrible."

"Thank you. So do you," Bess told him. She rasped a hand across his jaw. "I've been trying to shave you."

"I'm lucky you didn't cut my throat." Smith grasped her arm. "Have you been there all the time?"

"Where the devil else would I be? Somebody has to look after you, fooling around as if you were still twenty years old!"

"Help me get dressed," Smith said. "We have a business to run."

Bess wrinkled her nose. "You're not getting dressed until you've washed," she said. "You're stinking."

"I'll need help," Smith told her.

Bess sighed. "Just like a baby. I'll ring for a servant to bring a bath."

Chapter Sixteen

Kate stepped inside the front room of the Bermondsey house. "Gentlemen," she said. "Mr Jay has a little job for you."

The three men looked up. Ned Hind held a pack of cards, one of the grenadiers was carving a piece of wood, and the other sharpened a knife. "What does he want?" Hind asked, shuffling the cards.

"Mr Jay wants you to discourage some youths." Kate remained by the door.

"Come in, Kate," Hind invited, dealing seven cards in front of him. "Sit down and tell us more."

The room contained a table, four chairs, a chest of drawers and a sideboard. The floor was swept and clean, and the window gleamed. Kate could not see a single speck of dust anywhere.

"Coffee?" the taller of the ex-soldiers invited and nodded to his companion. Within minutes, Kate was sipping at a mug of fresh coffee. "We don't drink until dusk."

"Coffee is good," Kate said. "Now, here's what I know so far." She told them about the youths, giving them a description and the address.

"Does Mr Jay want them killed?" Hind picked up his seven cards, added them to the pack and shuffled.

"Mr Jay wants an example made," Kate said. "He leaves it to you to decide what is best."

Hind nodded. "Usual rates?"

"Usual rates." Kate fished a small bag from her pocket and placed it on the table. Hind opened the drawstring and poured the contents onto the table. The heavy chink of gold was loud in the quiet room as Hind divided the guineas into three equal piles.

"Leave it to us."

"I will." Kate stood up. "Thank you for the coffee." As she stood, the smaller ex-soldier took away her mug and washed it in a pail of water.

"I HAD TO ORDER ONE OF YOUR HORSES SHOT," BESS SAID. "The poor beast had two broken legs."

Smith took a deep breath. "I remember hearing screaming," he said. "I wasn't sure if it was a horse or me. Which one?"

"The nearside lead," Bess said. "The whole weight of the equipage fell on him."

"Bloodhound," Smith said. "I named him after the second ship I sailed on in the navy. He was a willing animal, very amiable." He produced a pipe and thrust it, empty, between his teeth. "I don't like to see animals suffer."

"What are your plans now, John?"

"Build another carriage," Smith said. "And try again."

"No!" Bess stepped back. "You were lucky to survive, John! You're a bloody fool!"

"Maybe so," Smith said, "but I won't have Shapland and Copinger boasting that they got the better of me."

"You'll get no support from me," Bess told him severely.

Smith began to fill his pipe. "Yes, I will," he said. "I always do."

* * *

"SO THAT'S WHAT'S LEFT OF MY CARRIAGE." SMITH VIEWED THE wreckage with some dismay. "I was proud of that machine." The coach's body was a splintered mess, with the springs twisted and bent, while both nearside wheels were smashed beyond repair. Mud smeared the silver paintwork, and the name was reduced to the meaningless *uicksil*.

Harrison, the coachbuilder, nodded sadly. "It was the finest I ever made," he said.

"I heard something snap beneath the machine," Smith said, "and I lost control. Yet I don't believe the construction was faulty."

"The axle broke," Harrison explained. "It snapped in half." He knelt beside the wreckage and pointed, "And here's why."

"Why?" Smith crouched at Harrison's side and examined the heavy axle.

"Somebody sawed through the shaft." The coachbuilder ran a finger over the broken metal. "See the mark here? That's been deliberately cut."

Smith joined him, grunting at the pain in his ribs. Somebody had sawn the axle two-thirds of the way through, so the weakened metal would snap when any extra pressure was applied, as in turning a steep corner. "I see," Smith said. "Somebody must have been very keen to win a wager. Or they just don't like me."

Harrison stood up. "I can assure you, Mr Smith, that it was not shoddy workmanship." He sounded anxious.

"I didn't think it was," Smith said. "Can you make me another carriage, exactly the same?"

"I'd be honoured, sir," Harrison said, evidently relieved.

"As quick as you like," Smith said.

I can't prove Shapland had my carriage sabotaged, but I'd lay money that he was responsible. I'll find out, by God.

"IT MIGHT NOT HAVE BEEN SHAPLAND," BESS SAID AS THEY SAT in the study. "It could have been Copinger. He was the man who insulted you, remember."

"I remember," Smith said. "But I don't think he has the iron in him. Shapland is a hard man, while Copinger is a blusterer. He could be a bully at Eton or some other public school where authority backed him, but I can't see him putting himself at risk."

"He might have sent somebody else to saw the axle," Bess said.

"That's a possibility," Smith admitted. "I'll have a word with William at the coach house."

"William would not have sawn the axle," Bess said.

"He might have seen something," Smith said. He looked up when somebody tapped on the door.

"Come in, Mr Judd," Smith said.

"Excuse me, sir and madam." Judd bowed to both. "A Mister Redpath handed this document in. He particularly ordered that I passed it to you, Mr Smith, and none other."

"Thank you, Mr Judd." Smith accepted the folded piece of thick paper. He broke the seal, read the contents, and swore.

"What's the matter, John?" Bess asked as Smith crumpled the paper and threw it over his shoulder.

"Shapland again, I think," Smith said. "That's a note from Redpath telling me that the Runners have arrested Abe Reeves for fencing stolen goods."

Bess drew in her breath. "Can you get him off?"

"I don't know, but I'll try." Smith shook his head. "I'll see who I can bribe, but I fear Abe will end up in Newgate or worse."

"Transported?" Bess asked.

"Transported, although with the American colonies slipping away, I don't know where they'll send him."

"They'll find somewhere equally unpleasant," Bess said. "They can always find somewhere to send the unwanted or erect gallows to string us up."

Smith grunted. "That's true. Win a war or lose a war, the powers-that-be will still trample over the ordinary people."

"What will you do now, John?"

Smith pondered for a moment. "I'll speak to William first," he said, "and then work out how to free Abe Reeves."

Bess smiled. "That's more like you, John, except you're still reacting to Shapland. The only attack you've made is with young Peter."

Smith stood and stepped to the window. "My plans are slowly maturing, Bess. They'll take time."

"You wasted time in that foolish race," Bess scolded. "At present, Shapland is winning every hand."

Smith felt the ache in his ribs. "It's the last hand that counts," he said. "And I'm working to hold all the aces."

Bess reread the note. "I hope so, John," she said. "And so does Abraham Reeves."

***

"WILLIAM," SMITH STOOD AT THE DOOR OF THE COACH HOUSE. "Somebody damaged my carriage before the race."

William Harmon stepped back from the closed carriage he had been cleaning. "It wasn't me, Mr Smith," he denied quickly. "I wouldn't do such a thing."

"I didn't say it was you," Smith stepped inside, wincing at his still painful ribs. "Did you notice any strangers looking at the chariot?"

Harmon nodded. "Why, yes, sir. After you brought *Quicksilver* here, we had crowds of people coming to admire her lines. Mr

Jackson visited, and Mr Bancroft, Mr Judd, Lord George Gordon and even Sir Humphrey Waterson."

Smith swore quietly. He had hoped for a smaller list of suspects. "Did any of them seem unusually interested?"

Harmon thought for a moment before he replied. "Not really, Mr Smith." He hesitated. "It was busy the evening before you had your last inspection."

"Which last inspection?" Smith demanded.

"You came into the stables the night before the race, Mr Smith." Harmon looked puzzled.

"I did not," Smith denied hotly and moderated his tone.

It's no good berating the man for saying what he honestly believes.

"What makes you think I came into the stable, William?"

Harmon frowned and pointed to the door behind Smith. "The door was swinging open, Mr Smith and only you and I have the key, so I thought you had visited."

Smith clenched his fists. "You should have told me about the door, William."

Harmon's shoulders slumped. "I'm sorry, Mr Smith. I thought you had inspected your carriage and had forgotten to lock the door."

"I was not in here," Smith said, turned and stomped away.

William Harmon would never damage a chariot for which he was responsible, so somebody else entered the stable to saw through the axle. Somebody who had a key or was a skilled cracksman. I thought I had left the criminal world behind when I became a respectable businessman, but it seems murderers sit on the topmost branches of the trees as well as crawl under the stones at the bottom.

"Shapland was not in the house," Bess said as they sat in the study, "and I doubt he'd get access to the stable."

"That's what I think, too," Smith said. "That means we must suspect everybody."

Bess nodded. "That's right, John. We'll be very careful what we say and whom we trust." She looked at him over the rim of her coffee mug. "We've let our guard down recently, John, and now we're paying for it. We must remember the old rule, trust nobody, only say what you have to and always watch your back."

"It's just you and me, Bess, as it always has been," Smith agreed.

"You and me." Bess's mouth twisted into a smile. "That deserves a toast." She poured out two glasses of brandy. "Here's to us, John."

"To us." Smith lifted his glass. "And God help anybody who gets in our way."

Bess drained her glass. "Maybe we will be toasting three of us soon if we bring Peter into the family."

"Are you sure you want to?" Smith asked.

"I'd like a son," Bess said. "We didn't produce any, and it's too late now."

Smith finished his brandy. "If you're sure, Bess, bring Peter here tomorrow, and we'll see what he thinks."

Bess's smile broadened. "Maybe some good has come out of *Quicksilver's* wreckage then, John." She poured out more brandy. "Here's to a new addition to our family."

"A new addition," Smith said and smiled at the pleasure on Bess's face.

THEY FOUND PETER BROWN SHORTLY AFTER DAWN. SMITH had woken early, as he always did, and followed his usual routine of a three-mile walk through the streets of London, viewing his ships in the river and checking with the ship's watchmen. He refused the services of a link boy, one of the youths who carried lanterns to light pedestrians through the streets and returned home to Leicester Square. When Smith left his house, the square looked as it always did. When he returned, Peter's body was lying outside his front door.

"Oh, Peter." Smith looked down at the boy. Naked, bloody

and battered, there was hardly a square inch of Peter's body that was undamaged. "Who did that to you?"

Peter looked up through sightless eyes, a boy who had known little but misery, despair and hardship from the day of his birth.

Removing his coat, Smith covered the body, carried it inside the house and laid it gently on the settle in the hall. "You didn't have much of a life, Peter," Smith said. "I'll ensure you have a decent burial and a headstone to pronounce your existence to the world."

"Why?" Bess asked when Smith told her. She stared at Peter's lifeless body, holding her elbows and shaking. "Why murder my Peter?"

"A message to me," Smith said. "Shapland would have known I sent Peter and his friends to rob his ships."

"Poor little boy." Bess viewed the corpse. "He had a good heart. Poor little boy." She took a deep breath, visibly moved, with a single tear glistening in her left eye.

"Very few people have much of a life," Smith said. "That's why we turn to crime."

Bess shook her head. "We'd better get Peter seen to." She looked down, trying to control her emotions. "I want a Christian burial for him, not a pauper's grave."

"I'll take care of Peter." Smith put a hand on Bess's arm. "I've never seen you as upset."

"No," Bess said. "Peter was nearly family. I always wanted a son." She took a deep breath and stamped her feet on the ground, left-right, fighting to regain her composure. "Oh, God, John, it's not fair."

"No," Smith agreed. "It's not fair." He knew Bess would break down, and he held her when she did.

They stood together for twenty minutes with Bess sobbing into Smith's shoulder and Peter lying mute and cold. When Smith pushed the servants away, Bess removed his arms from her back.

"Get Shapland for me, John." Her voice was cold.

"I will," Smith promised. He had seen too many of his friends killed at sea to have much emotion for Peter's death. He had liked the boy but nothing more. However, he was angry because Bess was upset.

"I'll make Shapland pay, Bess," Smith said.

I'll free Abraham Reeves first and then grind Shapland into the dust.

"SHAPLAND IS MORE DANGEROUS THAN I REALISED," SMITH said as they sat in his office. "He seems to be able to counter my moves." He stood up and walked to the window, staring over Leicester Square. "We might find it hard to win this one, Bess."

"We'll win, John," Bess told him. "Remember where we started and how far we've come. We're not Kentish for nothing!"

"Maybe that's it," Smith said. "Maybe I'm too Kentish to win in the big city."

Bess's smile lacked any humour. "Can you recall what Redpath the Runner called Shapland?"

"Not exactly," Smith admitted.

"He called him a lewd profligate wretch," Bess said.

"And probably well deserved," Smith agreed.

"We can use that, John. A wretch he is, profligate perhaps, but lewd suggests he has a liking for a woman's skirt."

"Continue," Smith said.

Bess drummed her fingers on her desk, a sure sign she was agitated. "Why don't we use Shapland's weakness for women?"

"You have a plan, Bess," Smith said.

"I have a plan," Bess agreed. "Do you know any bunters?"

"Would I tell you if I did?" Smith searched for humour in Bess's face. There was none.

"You'd better tell me," Bess said.

"No, I don't know any prostitutes. I no longer come into contact with such people," Smith reassured her.

Bess nodded. "It won't be hard to find some bunters in London. I'll interview a few and select one or two."

"What do you have in mind?"

"I want to place a woman with Shapland," Bess said. "Exploit his weakness." She clenched her fists. "I liked Peter," she said. "I treated him like a son." She looked up with anger darkening her eyes. "Find out who did this, John, and kill them."

Chapter Seventeen

A thin wind sliced in from the sea, bending the rough grass around the graveyard and rustling through the leaves of the twin yews beside the square-towered church. A handful of mourners stood beside the newly dug grave as Smith helped lower the small coffin into the earth.

"The Kentish coast is a strange place to bury a waif from London," Bess said, holding her black comforter in place.

"He'll be among friends." Smith stepped back from the grave. "Look at his neighbour."

Bess read the words on the simple cross to Peter's right. "Abel Watson. That's your real name."

"It is. John Smith lies in that grave. I took his identity and gave him mine in return."

"Abel Watson lying beside Peter Brown," Bess said, "and neither name will be true."

"Only the Lord knows our true names," Smith said as he dropped a handful of dirt into the grave. The soil landed with a hollow patter on Peter's coffin. "As you know, I visit Watson's grave every few months. I'll say hello to Peter at the same time."

The Reverend Tyler opened his Bible and began the burial

service, putting meaning into the words as a lone kittiwake perched on Watson's memorial.

Bess stifled her tears. "I'll come with you," she said.

Smith put an arm around her shoulders, feeling her tremble as Tyler looked on, his eyes dark with sympathy. The bird began to preen itself as the gravedigger shovelled earth on top of Peter's grave, and the handful of mourners drifted away.

Sir George Danskin reined in his horse as they stood on the edge of Appleby Common. A thin mist rose from the ground, wrapping around the lone oak tree and disguising the steep incline where Smith and Quicksilver came to grief. "You're standing against me, my Lord?"

"I am," Smith said. "I am the landowner here and think I should represent my tenants in parliament."

Sir George shook his head. "Appleby has been Tory ever since God created England," he said. "The MP died last month, and there'll be a by-election to choose the next one. It's a pocket borough, for goodness sake, and there's never been a real contest here."

"There will be this time," Smith told him pleasantly. "I'm standing as a Whig, and I mean to win."

"I'll fight you, My Lord," Sir George promised. "I'll fight you tooth and nail." He looked over the Common, shaking his head.

"I wouldn't have it any other way," Smith told him cheerfully. "May the best Whig win." He flicked his reins and rode into the village, thinking that the little he knew about politics told him it was a dirty game of bribery, corruption and lies.

That's a bit like business deals in London, Smith told himself. *There are only a hundred and eleven voters in the seat, and fifty-nine are my tenants. I'll concentrate on them and work on the others later.*

Smith spent the remainder of that day touring the Appleby area, knocking on doors, and speaking to his tenants. He had kept a careful eye on his estate, ensuring the rents were afford-able and the houses wind and watertight, so the people regarded him as a caring landlord.

"Lord Fitzwarren!" With most of the men working the land, amazed wives and daughters answered the door to Smith's knock.

"Good day to you," Smith replied to the obsequious greet-ings. "I will contest this seat in the forthcoming by-election and wonder if I may depend on your man's vote."

Most of the women were unaware that an election was loom-ing, being too busy with their own affairs. Those that took an interest were so eager to promise their allegiance that Smith guessed they would be equally enthusiastic if Sir George asked them to vote Tory.

These people don't care which party sits in power. All they want is a decent home and bread on the table.

The villagers of Appleby were less pliable. While some immediately agreed they would vote for Smith, others were adamantly opposed.

"You Whigs support the rebels," one prosperous man told Smith bluntly. "You're nothing but a bunch of damned traitors."

Smith withdrew gracefully, knowing it was pointless to argue with a man who had made up his mind.

The next voter shook Smith by the hand a dozen times. "A Whig at last! Of course, I'll vote for you, sir; of course, I will. God bless you, sir, and more power to the cause of Liberty in the Americas."

"And Liberty in Great Britain as well," Smith reminded, smiling as he moved on to his next prospective supporter.

"It's customary to distribute largesse." Bancroft had appointed himself as unofficial supporter-in-chief and rode with Smith as he toured his prospective seat. "Grease a few palms, help your tenants out, make grandiose promises and so on."

"If any of my tenants need help, they only have to ask," Smith said.

Bancroft nodded. "Raising your profile might win votes, Smith."

"I may take your advice," Smith said. "Thank you, Bancroft."

———

SIR HUMPHREY FACED SMITH ACROSS THE WIDTH OF THE DESK. "I hope you are not here to influence my judgement in a forthcoming case, Mr Smith. You know I can't accept a bribe." He smiled and cradled the hot coffee cup in both hands.

"I would not dream of bribing you, Sir Humphrey," Smith said. "You are famed as an honest man."

"I am glad that's understood." Sir Humphrey sipped at his glass. "You are the last man I'd expect to attempt to pervert justice."

"I have every faith in your fairness, Sir Humphrey," Smith replied and poured out more brandy. "I understand you are judging Abraham Reeve's case next week?"

"I am," Sir Humphrey replied. "Do you know the fellow?"

"I know of him," Smith said. "I think somebody has falsely accused him."

"The evidence and the jury will decide, Smith." Sir Humphrey finished his glass. "This is excellent brandy."

"I have part ownership in a Burgundy vineyard, Sir Humphrey," Smith explained. "My brandy comes direct from the source, and I could let you have a barrel or two."

Sir Humphrey smiled. "I don't accept bribes, Mr Smith, not even of such quality."

"Surely you will accept a gift from a friend," Smith said. "If you have any doubt, I will ensure my carrier delivers the barrels after your verdict in the Reeves' case, whatever that happens to be."

"I would be much obliged to you, Mr Smith." Sir Humphrey nodded.

"Good," Smith said. "I do have one question about the case.

If the jury finds Reeves guilty, to which prison will you send him?"

"For fencing stolen goods?" Sir Humphrey frowned. "If the jury finds him guilty, and the evidence suggests that's likely, I'll commit him to Newgate and from there to the hulks for onward transportation." He paused for a moment. "Unless the evidence suggests he warrants execution, in that case he'll move from Newgate to Tyburn."

"Thank you, Sir Humphrey," Smith said offhand. "Now, permit me to tell you about my vineyard."

DRESSED AS A RESPECTABLE WOMAN, KATE WALKED TO THE Royal Navy Rendezvous at Wapping. It was a place that respectable seamen avoided, for the rendezvous was the Impress Service's headquarters, a centre of fear and intimidation. A group of men stood around a brazier outside the simple building. Some were sailors, others dockland toughs, and they passed a bottle around and intoned an old song celebrating pressing colliers.

"From the Black-Indies-men we gat,
Brave lusty seamen, plump and fat,
Out of the hold these men we hurried,
From down in the coals they deep were buried."

Ignoring the seamen's whistles, Kate stood in the rendezvous doorway, staring at the interior, dimly lit by three candles in brass candlesticks. Two navy officers sat around a table, drinking coffee and poring over a map of London. One looked up.

"Yes?" he said curtly.

Kate judged him between thirty-five and forty, with eyes like stones and a mouth made bitter by experience. He wore a lieutenant's insignia and the air of a man who knew he had already reached the summit of his career.

"I'm looking for the officer in command," Kate told him.

The stone-eyed lieutenant nodded, unsmiling. "That's me."

"My name is Kate Driver." Kate introduced herself with a little curtsey. "I believe your job is to find men for the navy."

"I am Lieutenant Keith Barrington, and you are correct." The lieutenant ran his gaze up and down Kate's body, assessing her. He considered she could either be a seaman's wife pleading for her husband's release or an informer hoping for her thirty pieces of silver for reporting a hiding seaman. Barrington would eject the former without a thought and pay the latter, despite his contempt for such creatures.

"I can help you find some prime seamen," Kate told him.

Barrington sighed and sipped at his coffee. "Why would you do that?" He could guess at many reasons, from being jilted by a seaman, left pregnant or hoping for some financial gain. He fished a shilling from his pocket and placed it on the scarred table. "Did a sailor leave you with a little extra?"

"I have my reasons." Ignoring the silver coin, Kate continued to stand, allowing the lieutenant to try and work her out.

Barrington's eyes narrowed slightly. He could see that Kate was not over-eager to grab the shilling and did not look pregnant. "Sit down," he said, suitably intrigued to delve deeper.

"Thank you." Kate sat down gracefully. The second officer wore a Midshipman's uniform and a face that had experienced nothing but disappointment. He allowed Kate a slight nod.

"Coffee?" Barrington lieutenant asked.

"I would be grateful," Kate said. "It's rather cold out there." She allowed the candlelight to reflect from her wedding ring.

"Coffee for the lady, Congreve!" Barrington snapped, and the midshipman rushed to obey. Kate hardly spared the midshipman a glance, working him out as poor and friendless, probably the younger son of a schoolteacher or clergyman.

"Thank you." The coffee was strong and sweet from an unwashed mug.

"How can you help me?" Barrington's voice could have penetrated the worst North Sea fog.

"I despise the rebels," Kate said. "They killed my husband, so I will do anything I can to hurt them."

"Ah, I understand." Barrington's gaze shifted to the wedding ring. "It can be hard for a woman alone in the world. Was your husband a seaman?"

"He was a merchant," Kate said. "A good man and a good husband." She dashed a tear from her eye and looked away. "I'm sorry, Lieutenant Barrington."

"No need to apologise," Barrington said. "I understand, and I'll do all I can to defeat the rebels and end this war."

"I hoped you would, Lieutenant," Kate said, allowing her hair to flop forward, so she looked up at him through an auburn curtain. "I am sure you are a very patriotic man as well as a brave officer."

Barrington grunted. "I do my duty, Mrs Driver. How can you help to defeat the rebels?"

Kate warmed her hands around the mug. "I know where some cowardly seamen hide from the press," she said. "They lack your patriotism, Lieutenant." She lifted her head, allowing her gaze to link with his.

"You intrigue me, Mrs Driver," Barrington said. "Please tell me more."

Chapter Eighteen

S mith sat in the small room overlooking the East India Company headquarters and looked up as a tap sounded at the door. "Come in," he said and mustered a smile as a young woman stepped in.

He had interviewed a succession of eager or hopeful women, neither of them certain what the job entailed but all desperate for employment to lift them out of poverty.

"Good morning, sir." The woman curtseyed as she entered and waited for Smith to speak. She wore good quality clothing, cleverly patched as if she had once known better times.

"Good morning," Smith said.

This one is different. The others were all feathers and curves, flaunting themselves with nothing behind the façade. This woman has intelligence in her eyes.

"What's your name?" Smith asked.

"Leah Lightfoot," the woman said and smiled. "It's a strange name, sir, but I was young when I was baptised and had no choice in the matter."

A woman with humour.

"Very few of us have a choice in our name," Smith agreed. *Yet I changed mine from Abel Watson.* "Sit down, Miss Lightfoot."

"Thank you." Leah sat elegantly, placed her hands in her lap and looked directly into Smith's eyes. "I am Leah Lightfoot, but also Mrs Blackstone," she said, and before that, I was Mrs Haliburton."

"You have been singularly unfortunate, it seems," Smith said, "to lose a husband so young."

"I have lost two husbands, sir," Leah said quietly.

"My name is John Smith," Smith said, "There is no need to call me sir." He frowned as the import of Leah's words hit him. "Two husbands? I know your face, Mrs Blackstone. Have we met before?"

"Yes, sir," Leah said. "I was married to Captain Robert Haliburton of *Kentish Princess* before you moved to London. You attended our wedding in Kingsgate, sir."

"I remember. You must have been very young," Smith said.

"I was seventeen," Leah said.

Smith nodded. "Now you are about thirty."

"Yes, Mr Smith. About thirty." Leah smiled.

"Your second husband, Mrs Blackstone?" Smith shook his head. "Would that be Isaac Blackstone, the mate of *London's Pride*?"

"That's right, sir," Leah said. "My first husband was fifteen years older than me, and my second nine years younger. Maybe my third will be the same age if I ever seek another."

"Maybe so," Smith agreed.

Leah held Smith's gaze. "Isaac drowned in the Atlantic when *London's Pride went down.*"

"I know," Smith said. "That was a terrible situation. Isaac was a promising officer and a good man." He saw Leah's face alter and quickly changed the subject. "What did you hear about the position I hope to fill?"

Leah straightened up in her chair and pushed back a stray strand of hair. "When Robert died, he left me with three children, ten guineas and a chest of clothes. I needed to feed the children, ten guineas do not last long, and the clothes were fast wearing out. I married Isaac for security, but he died the first voyage after our wedding." Leah lifted her chin further.

Smith nodded encouragingly. "Continue, Mrs Blackstone, or do you prefer Miss Lightfoot?"

"Either." Leah shrugged. "I need to earn money, Mr Smith, and I will neither beg nor cater to the needs of some sweating, panting drunk against an alley wall. I have three children to care for, and I will fill any respectable position I can find."

This woman understands the realities of life.

"You are a more than presentable woman," Smith said. "It should not be hard for you to find another husband."

"If I wanted one," Leah agreed. "What is the nature of the position, Mr Smith?"

"I want you to befriend somebody," Smith said. "And tell me what he is doing."

Leah nodded, immediately understanding. "Is this somebody a business rival?"

"Just so," Smith agreed with a smile. "Can you do that?" He paused for a moment. "For the sake of your family?"

Leah said nothing as the clock in the corner of the room ticked sonorously for thirty seconds. "Yes," she said slowly, "I can do that, as long as I don't have to share his bed. I am nobody's baggage, Mr Smith."

Smith smiled. "Prostitutes are ten a penny, Mrs Blackstone, and I'd value you a lot higher than that. Now, listen carefully while I tell you what I want and what I will pay for your help."

"Hot Press!" The alarm sounded along the Thames, through the Highway and into every dockside public house, lodging house and academy[1] within five hundred yards of the docks. "Hot Press!"

Kate watched the frenzy as men fled to escape the press gang. She saw burly seamen with faces seamed, weathered and scarred by hard service run like striplings to escape the horror of life in King George's navy. She saw young men scream in panic as they disappeared into any hiding place they could find. She saw women crying at the thought of their men being kidnapped to disappear for years, perhaps forever. She saw some more defiant men band together and draw knives or other weapons in the hope of defending themselves. Women joined them, wives, mothers and sweethearts, with various weapons, from mops and brooms to pokers and staffs, to fend off the might of the Royal Navy.

Behind the civilian clamour, Kate heard the tramp of feet as flint-faced officers and petty officers led the feared press gang through the streets. The men carried cudgels and cutlasses, while the midshipmen and lieutenants had swords and pistols at their belts. She noted that only some of the gang were seamen, with local London toughs helping to swell the ranks.

"Lieutenant Barrington," Kate lifted a hand and mouthed his name. "Keith."

"Kate!" Barrington said. "You're on time, I see."

Kate moved beside him and matched his stride, so her skirt snapped against her legs with every step. "I'll show you the way."

"How many men will be inside?" Barrington asked.

"I don't know," Kate said. "You gave plenty of warning, and two of Smith's vessels have arrived in the river recently, so I expect a fair number. Don't forget there are two entrances and a special knock. Three raps, a two-second pause, and then another four."

Barrington nodded without breaking stride. "I won't forget. Don't come with us, Mrs Rider, in case there is trouble."

"I won't." Kate slipped away, happy to watch.

Barrington's gang was efficient. While Lieutenant Barrington commanded half the force at the entrance to the church, Midshipman Congreve led the remainder to the dockside.

They're attacking the safe house by the back door.

Kate waited in a doorway in Atlantic Street, opposite the church but with shadows concealing her.

Go on, Lieutenant Barrington. Hurt John Smith's ships.

A fog drifted along Atlantic Street, part moisture from the river and part smog from London's thousands of chimneys. Kate coughed, covered her mouth and saw Barrington's men prepare to act. She heard the commotion inside the church; Barrington hissed final orders and slid his sword from its sheath.

The church door opened with a bang, and a flood of seamen rushed out, with the midshipman and his men following, waving cutlasses.

"Now!" Barrington led his section of the gang forward, cracking cudgels onto unprotected heads, wrestling furious men to the ground and holding the blades of cutlasses against bare throats.

Kate smiled as the press gang cut through their captives' waistbands, forcing them to hold their trousers up and reducing their mobility. One gaunt-faced man broke away, dodged a swinging cudgel and slipped left and right. Kate enjoyed the look of desperation on his face as he tried to escape while two predators hunted him. One of the gang grabbed his hair, gripping his pigtail in a calloused hand, while the other slipped a knife into his waistband and sliced upwards.

"Now we've got you, cully!"

The gaunt man swore and grabbed his trousers to stop them from sliding down. The knife man laughed as his companion released the gaunt man's hair and gave him a hefty shove in the back.

"Join your friends, and welcome to the Royal Navy!"

The gaunt man stumbled away, then pushed down his trousers, kicked them off his bare feet and ran away, dodging the surprised press.

"Stop that man!" the knifeman roared, but too late as the gaunt man sped down Atlantic Street.

Kate watched him escape with a smile.

You escaped, my bare-arsed friend, but the navy caught a score of Smith's men. He'll find it hard to replace them.

"Now that's unusual." Bess stared out of the bedroom window.

"What's unusual?" Smith asked from behind a newspaper.

"There's a man with no breeches running across the square," Bess told him.

"Probably a drunkard," Smith said.

"He's coming straight to our door," Bess said. "He looks like a seaman, with a canvas jacket and a tarred pigtail."

"The servants will take care of him." Smith put aside the newspaper, rose and casually glanced out of the window. "That's Davie Cupples, Bess!"

"Who?"

"The man who survived *London Profit's* sinking. Go and bring him in, Bess. Take him into the study."

Sweat had beaded on Cupples' face and soaked his shirt as he stood, panting in the study. "Thank you, Mr Smith. I thought you'd help me."

"What happened, Cupples?" Smith poured him a glass of rum. "Drink that and tell me."

"It was the press, Mr Smith," Cupples said, accepting the glass with a nod. "They rushed us at the Atlantic Street Church and knew exactly where to come. They gave the secret knock and barged in when we opened the door. They took us by surprise. Some of us made a break for the other door through the church, and they were waiting in Atlantic Street."

"Damn," Smith swore softly. "Somebody must have tipped them off. Somebody in their cups must have spoken."

"They might have spoken, Mr Smith," Cupples said, "but even a drunk man doesn't give away the secret knock. The press knew everything."

Smith nodded in agreement. "Has anybody else been in there? Anybody not from our ships?"

Cupples thought for a moment as Smith topped up his glass. "Thank you, Mr Smith. Nobody I can think of, Captain. We were always careful to follow your instructions." He frowned. "Wait, though. Yes, Mr Smith, there was somebody. A woman."

"A woman?" Smith repeated.

"Yes, Captain. One of the lads, Jem Diamond, I think, brought in a ladybird a while back when the press was hunting. She must have talked."

Smith glanced at Bess, who nodded.

"Describe her," Bess asked. "What was she like?"

Cupples looked blank. "She was a ladybird," he said at last. "A prostitute with ribbons and a short skirt."

"What colour was her hair?" Bess encouraged.

"Red, dark red," Cupples said at last. "I think. I didn't pay her much heed."

"Auburn hair?" Bess suggested.

"Yes, auburn," Cupples said.

"Was she tall or short?"

"Quite tall." Cupples struggled with his memory. "Taller than you, Mrs Smith."

"Average height, or a little above," Bess said. "How old was she?"

"I don't know," Cupples said helplessly.

"Was she a youngster, under twenty, mature, in her twenties and thirties, or older?"

Cupples screwed up his face. "I can't remember. I don't know much about women. Maybe she was about thirty or forty."

Bess realised she was getting nowhere. "Would you recognise her again?" she persisted.

Cupples frowned. "Yes," he said after a pause. "Yes, I would." He smiled as if he had achieved significant success.

"Can you draw?" Smith asked. He knew that many seamen were fair artists, although mainly of maritime scenes. Their sea chests were often highly decorated with ships, mermaids, and other nautical themes.

"Draw?" Cupples looked bemused.

Smith produced a sheet of paper and handed over a goose-wing quill. "I was at sea, Davie. I've seen the artwork seamen can produce. Draw me this woman as best you can."

Cupples held the pen in stubby, calloused fingers. He dipped it in the inkwell, made a few tentative marks on the paper and then produced a drawing that caused Smith to frown.

"I think I know that woman," he said. "I can't think where, but I'm sure I've seen her before."

"Thank you, Davie," Bess said as Cupples added some details to his drawing. "You've given us a lot to think about."

"I'll close off the Atlantic Street Church refuge," Smith said. "If the navy knows it's there, it'll only be a trap."

"Davie," Bess said quietly, with a slight smile. "I'd find myself a pair of trousers if I were you. I don't mind you showing off, but other people may object to you displaying all you have."

Cupples looked suddenly alarmed and covered up, which made Bess laugh.

"You're a bit late, Davie! I'm sure John can find you something to cover your decency." She leaned closer. "It's all right; you're shirt covered the essentials."

Smith nodded. "You'd best stay here for the rest of the day," Smith said. "You've already had one escape from the press, and that's enough for anybody."

Chapter Nineteen

A mounted magistrate led the coach, with two pistols prominent at his saddle and a sword at his side. Behind him marched four parish constables with long staffs and set, stern faces. The coach driver was middle-aged, with a broad hat partly hiding his face, while at his side sat a burly guard with a brace of pistols and a blunderbuss. Two more constables marched behind the coach, tapping their long staffs on the ground in time with their boots.

"That's an impressive display of authoritarian force," Bess murmured.

"It is," Smith agreed.

Three men and one woman sat on top of the coach, yelling and shouting as they rattled the manacles that secured them. Four more convicted criminals sat inside the coach, three hiding their misery behind false bravado, and the fourth sitting in despondent silence.

"Our man's inside the coach," Smith said. "Abraham Reeves. I want him freed and Will Wightman as well."

Bess frowned. "Who's Will Wightman?"

"Wightman's a highwayman," Smith said. "I want this attack to seem like an attempt to free Wightman, with Reeves' escape a coincidence. That way, we'll deflect all the attention from Reeves onto Wightman."

"Abraham Reeves," Bess repeated, studying the prison coach's escort. "This won't be easy. That magistrate looks like he'll fire at any excuse, and the guard holds his blunderbuss like a veteran."

"Josh Lennox is a veteran," Smith said. "He served eight years in the Fortieth Foot but lost his left leg below the knee on the Heights of Abraham in 1759. A French ball lodged in his shin, and gangrene did the rest."

Bess nodded. "This is like old times, John. You've got everything arranged, haven't you?"

"I believe so," Smith said.

"Who's the driver?"

Smith smiled. "Jeremiah Bragg. He's a Dover man who served as a quartermaster on *Maid of Kent.*"

Bess ran a finger down the scar on her cheek. "Did you know that before you arranged this escape?"

"Jeremiah got the job on my recommendation." Smith glanced at his watch. "It's nearly time, Bess. Get ready."

"I'm ready."

The magistrate led the coach into a broad street, where a crowd had gathered to watch, and a brewer's dray lumbered towards them. When the coach passed a public house named The Last Drop, a tall man in an old-fashioned wig blew on a hunting horn. As the sharp call echoed in the street, the dray's driver pulled his horses across the road, blocking it completely.

"What the devil!" the magistrate roared. "Get out of the way, you damned fool! Can't you see us coming?"

"Wightman!" the horn blower shouted, running toward the coach. "We want Wild Will Wightman!" He banged the flat of his hand on the door. "Are you in there, Will?"

"Wightman!" the crowd roared. "Free Wild Will Wightman!"

Led by a buxom woman, the crowd surged forward, surrounding the magistrate, and cramming the parish constables in a tight huddle, so they could not wield their staffs.

"What the devil is this?" the magistrate shouted as a section of the mob ran at him, shaking their fists and wielding makeshift weapons.

"Come on, Bess," Smith said, pulled a black silk kerchief over his mouth and nose and hauled his tricorn hat low over his forehead.

When Bess grinned, she looked fifteen years younger. "Come on then, John."

Emerging beside the dray, Smith pushed through the crowd with Bess a few steps behind. A dozen people surrounded the magistrate, two holding his horse's reins as eager hands removed his pistols from their holsters.

"You won't need these, cully," a man leered, passing the pistols to willing hands behind him. "You might hurt somebody."

"He's harmless," Smith said. The crowd treated the parish constables similarly, so they could not move. Only the guard showed fight as he cocked his blunderbuss, swivelled in his seat, and aimed at the prisoners on the coach's roof.

"You keep still," Lennox ordered, "or I'll blow your bloody heads off."

Without hesitation, Smith ducked under the horses, grabbed the guard by the collar and hauled him backwards from his perch. Taken by surprise, Lennox pressed the trigger of his blunderbuss, which fired its charge of buckshot harmlessly upwards. The blast momentarily stunned the crowd, and dozens of faces turned towards Smith.

"Don't stop!" Smith shouted. "Free Wild Will Wightman!" He wrestled Lennox to the ground, punched him once in the throat and dragged the pistols from his belt. "Lie still," Smith hissed, "or you'll be down for good." Stamping on the man's stomach, Smith unbuckled his false foot and threw it away, then pulled a length of cord from his pocket and tied his wrists and knees.

"Control these damned horses, Jeremiah!" Smith ordered, and the driver grinned.

"Aye, aye, sir!" He sawed the reins and murmured soothing words to the team.

Smith saw Bess wrench open the coach door and thrust her blunderbuss inside. "Where's Wild Will?" she asked. "Which one of you is Wild Will Wightman?"

"I am!" two men immediately claimed the honour. One was tall and lean, with deep-set dark eyes, the other very young, with a broad grin lighting his face.

"Two Wild Wills?" Bess asked. "Is one not enough for this world of woe?"

"Free them both," Smith ordered as he unhooked a bunch of keys from the guard's belt and joined Bess. He looked inside the coach.

"We'll free them all," he decided as the prisoners extended willing hands, with most now claiming to be Wightman. Only Reeves sat still, cowering in the corner as Bess pointed her blunderbuss inside the coach.

"Keep quiet, you!" Smith ordered roughly as he began trying the keys. He glanced over his shoulder, aware the crowd could only contain the escort for a short while. Either the mob would expand the riot, or the constables would regain control. Either way, the authorities would soon realise that something had happened and send a detachment of redcoats to restore order. That could mean musketry and a bloody bayonets, with dead and injured.

"Come on," Smith urged. "Get these men free!"

The prisoners on the coach roof were shouting, banging their feet, and crashing their manacles and chains together, demanding that Smith release them too.

"Don't forget us, cully! We're all Wild Will!"

"What do we do?" Bess asked as she freed a haggard woman from her shackles and shoved her roughly into the crowd.

"Free them, too," Smith decided. "The more we free, the harder it will be for the authorities to round them up."

"Not him!" The haggard woman pointed to a prisoner who

held out his manacled wrists. The man nursed a fresh black eye and bloody nose. "He raped a little girl and cut her throat."

"Not him," Bess agreed, working the keys as she glowered at the child rapist.

One by one, Smith and Bess freed the prisoners, who dropped their shackles and fled into the crowd without showing any gratitude. The grinning youth was second last.

"Much obliged to you, sir," he said. "Who are you?"

"A friend," Smith told him, "You must be Wild Will."

"That's me," Wightman said with a mocking bow. "If ever you want a favour, you only have to ask."

"I'll remember that," Smith said as Wightman slid away.

"Right, Abe." Smith unshackled Reeves last. "You're coming with us."

"John Smith?" Reeves stared at Smith.

"Keep quiet!" Smith warned as Bess unlocked his manacles and Reeves rubbed the raw marks on his wrists. "Come on!" He pulled Reeves from the coach.

Bigger, stronger, and better fed than most in the crowd, the parish constables had merged into a cohesive group and were beginning to push back the crowd, which retaliated with loud shouts and a volley of dead cats and rotten fruit.

Bess glanced at the prisoners on the roof and tossed up the keys. A man caught them expertly, unlocked himself, passed the keys on and jumped to the ground.

"Come on, lads!"

"Tommy Lobsters!" somebody in the crowd yelled, and Smith heard the disciplined crunch of army boots as a platoon of soldiers arrived to restore order.

"Hurry it up, Abe!" Bess grabbed hold of Reeves' sleeve. "Things could get unpleasant here."

The crowd greeted the soldier with a barrage of missiles and abuse.

"Go home, Lobster bastards! Get back to your whoring!"

Smith heard the lieutenant in charge shout sharp orders, and his men formed a double line, with their bayonets glittering silver on the end of the long Brown Bess muskets.

"Present!" the officer shouted, and the bayonets levelled, presenting the sharp points at the civilians. "Forward march!"

The soldiers stepped forward in a slow movement that pushed the crowd back. When a dead cat wrapped itself around one redcoat's face, the officer swore. "Load!" he ordered, and the soldiers stopped to load their muskets, jabbing the ramrods down the brown barrels, and their faces turned towards their tormentors.

"Come on!" Smith said. "We can't do anything here."

Guiding Reeves through the crowd, Smith ducked under the dray's horses and ran to the far end of the street. He stepped into a side street, removed his mask, and dropped it on the ground. Bess copied him, and both emerged quietly into the main road.

"Don't run now," Smith said. "We're innocent pedestrians out for a stroll."

The driver of the dray, job complete, pulled his horses around and moved away from the mob, which shredded before the soldiers' slow advance.

"Where are you taking me?" Reeves asked.

"You're staying with us for a few days and then boarding a ship," Smith said. "London isn't safe for you anymore. The judge sentenced you to hang, didn't he?"

Reeves nodded. "He did," he agreed. "Charles Shapland gave too much evidence against me."

"I'll sentence you to a lifetime of exile," Smith said. "With this war in the Americas, the authorities can hardly find you over there. I have friends on both sides in the Americas, so do you want to be a Patriot Whig or a Loyalist Tory? Boston or New York?"

Reeves did not hesitate. "A Patriot Whig," he said.

"Boston then," Smith said as they hurried to Leicester

Square. "I'll write letters of introduction to my friends and supply you with money."

"That's very generous," Reeves said.

"You're in this trouble because of me," Smith reminded as they walked casually towards his house. "Slow down." He nodded to a Charlie. "Good evening, Grieves, I think there's some trouble down that way." He nodded towards the riot.

"Yes, Mr Smith," the Charlie said. "That's why I'm over this way."

"Very sensible of you." Smith offered him a swig from a silver hip flask. "Here, have a little warmer against the cool of the night."

"Thank you, sir." Grieves drank heartily. "And good night to you."

"Good night, Grieves. Keep safe."

Judd was waiting for them with a silver tray when they arrived at Leicester Square.

"Welcome home, Mr Smith, Mrs Smith, and Mr Reeves. Will you take a glass of brandy?"

Chapter Twenty

Kate perused her new clothes. Ever since the affair at Atlantic Street, Shapland had been more than friendly, and when Kate hinted that her clothes were out of fashion, he asked what she wanted.

"French clothing," Kate replied immediately. "I want the latest styles from Paris."

Shapland smiled. "Then you shall have them, my dear. Write me a list, and I'll order them for you."

As soon as her clothes arrived, Kate spread them over her boudoir and admired them. She tutted impatiently when somebody rapped on the door.

"Come in!" Kate said and looked up when a woman entered and curtseyed before her. "Yes?"

"You advertised for a lady's maid and companion, Mrs Shapland," Leah said.

"I did." Kate looked Leah up and down. "Are you applying for the position?"

"I am, Mrs Shapland."

Kate frowned. "Do you have any experience?"

"I do not, Mrs Shapland," Leah said. "I am a shipmaster's widow with three children and will work hard at any position."

"And your name?"

"Leah Lightfoot, Mrs Shapland." Leah curtseyed again.

"You will work long hours with me," Kate said, "and you'll obey my commands immediately, without question."

"Of course, madam," Leah said.

Kate nodded slowly. "A shipmaster's widow, you say?"

"Yes, madam," Leah agreed.

"Which ship?"

"*Kentish Princess*," Leah told her. "One of John Smith's vessels."

Kate nodded. "Ah, John Smith. How did your husband die?"

"The ship was unsound," Leah said. "Smith sent it to sea, and it foundered." She lowered her voice. "I heard that Smith increased the insurance premiums before the voyage."

"Ah." Kate nodded again. "Do you blame Mr Smith for your husband's death?"

When Leah looked up, anger burned in her eyes. "I do, Mrs Shapland."

Kate smiled. "You can start immediately, Leah."

"Thank you, Mrs Shapland."

THE NEW YORK CONVOY LAY IN THE RIVER, MAKING FINAL preparations for the Atlantic crossing. Smith counted thirty-three merchant vessels, from two-masted brigs to a stately West Indiaman that looked disdainful to be in such lowly company. He saw three Royal Naval vessels beside the convoy, with a harassed-looking captain sitting in the stern of his barge as his men rowed him from ship to ship. Smith knew the captain was giving sailing directions and last-minute orders to the merchant masters, a breed who would be stubbornly reluctant to accept any authority except their own.

"Captain Campbell!" Smith stepped on board *Hermes*.

"Yes, Mr Smith." Campbell was amidships, supervising his crew.

"Are you nearly ready to sail?"

"Taking in water, Mr Smith," Campbell said. "The hands all have Protections, and we'll sail on the next tide."

"I'm coming with you," Smith said. "You have a spare cabin for passengers."

Campbell nodded. "Yes, Mr Smith. Are you taking charge of the ship?"

"I am not," Smith said. "*Hermes* is yours to command, Captain. I will not interfere, and all I want is a fast passage."

"You'll get one," Campbell promised.

"I also have a passenger for you." Smith motioned to the man who stood at his side with his hat pulled over his head and a comforter covering the lower half of his face. "This gentleman is Mr Jones."

"Good evening, Mr Jones," Campbell said, with hardly a trace of irony in his voice. "Are we bound for New York, Mr Smith?"

"Indeed, no," Smith said. "We are bound for Boston."

Campbell did not blink. "The Americans hold Boston, Mr Smith. We'll have to avoid the British blockade."

"We will," Smith agreed. "You command the fastest ship in the Atlantic, with a hand-picked crew. Can you slip through the Royal Navy's net?"

"Yes," Campbell said without hesitation.

"I wish to get to Boston as quickly as possible, and I want you to wait for me there, so that I can return equally quickly."

Campbell nodded again. "I have a cargo of munitions," he said. "Lightweight, so that it won't impair our speed."

"Whenever you are ready, Captain," Smith said. He nodded to the first mate. "Mr Burgess."

"Good to see you again, Mr Smith." Burgess greeted him with a smile, then ran forward to supervise a clutch of seamen checking the rigging.

Hermes slid down the Thames as dawn rose above London.

Smith stood at the taffrail on the quarterdeck, enjoying his last view of the city. Any voyage could be hazardous, but sailing in wartime was doubly so, with privateers and enemy government warships joining the usual hazards of bad weather and bad luck.

"I've never been to sea," the man Smith had introduced as Mr Jones said. "I've never been out of London."

Smith thumbed tobacco into the bowl of his pipe. "The world's a big place, Reeves," he said. "You might like it."

Reeves sighed. "It's sad saying goodbye to the old place."

"You'd be sadder with a noose around your neck." Smith fingered the red weal around his throat.

They made a fast passage across the Atlantic, with Campbell driving *Hermes* hard and a favourable wind filling the sails. They saw two vessels during the first eight days of the voyage, a labouring, pot-bellied British merchantman they overhauled and left in their wake and a rakish three-masted ship with no flag.

"She's either a slaver or a privateer," Smith said.

"Maybe so." Campbell chewed nonchalantly on a hunk of tobacco. "Either way, we have the legs of her."

"I notice you don't carry armament, Captain," Smith said.

"No, Mr Smith. *Hermes* is faster than anything afloat, and cannon would reduce our speed. I'm a sailor, not a fighter."

Ten days into the passage, the lookout shouted that he saw a flotilla to the north. Smith joined him at the masthead. "Four ships," he said. "French by their look, two frigates, a line-of-battle and a cutter."

The French ignored *Hermes*, who passed them without acknowledgement and continued her voyage west.

Twelve days into the passage, Captain Campbell eased up. "All hands!" He shouted, "All hands to paint the ship!" he faced Smith. "If we're to be a blockade runner, I don't want the navy to recognise us when we return home."

Smith nodded; he had used similar tactics as a Channel smuggler.

Campbell watched the hands scramble with paint pots and brushes. "What name shall we use?"

"*Grace of God*," Smith replied. "I already have false papers with that name."

"We won't need the papers," Campbell said. "They'll have to catch us to see them."

Smith laughed. "I hope you're right, Captain."

With Campbell's urging and Burgess's encouragement, the hands painted *Hermes* a dark red, with the name *Grace of God*, across her stern.

"It's bad luck to rename a ship," one of the crew grumbled.

"It's worse luck to be caught by the navy," Cupples replied. "Captain Campbell and Smithy know what they're doing."

Fourteen days into the passage, the lookout on the masthead shouted down. "Sails ho, Captain."

"Where away?" Campbell asked.

"Northwest by west, Captain. I see the topsails of three vessels. I reckon two frigates and a sloop."

"Keep your eye on them, Cupples! Let me know if they come closer."

"Aye, aye, sir!"

"Is that David Cupples?" Smith asked.

"Aye, Davie Cupples," Campbell agreed. "He signed articles the day before we sailed."

"Captain! The sloop is heading this way!" the lookout called. "One of the frigates is signalling, although I can't read the flags."

"I'm coming," Campbell said and scampered up the rigging like a fifteen-year-old apprentice. Smith joined him, with his old skills improving the longer he was afloat.

"That's a Royal Navy sloop." Smith borrowed Campbell's spyglass. "HMS *Snowdrop*, I think." He intercepted Campbell's quizzical look. "I served in the navy for years," he said, "and take notice of the ships that call into the Thames." Smith saw the flash of sunlight reflecting from glass on *Snowdrop*'s poop. "Her commander is observing us."

"That's as close as she's going to get," Campbell said and slid down to the quarterdeck. "All hands!" he bellowed. "All hands to make sail!"

Smith joined him on deck and watched *Hermes* leap ahead. Lightly built and with a vast spread of canvas, she seemed to dance across the sea's surface, with *Snowdrop* falling behind.

"Set stunsails and moonrakers!" Campbell ordered, and the hands ran aloft to add to the bulging canvas.

"We're losing her, sir!" Cupples shouted. "I can only see *Snowdrop*'s topsails!"

"Helmsman!" Campbell ordered, "Alter course to East north-east a half east."

"Aye, aye, sir!" the helmsman said, with his jaws working hard on a quid of tobacco. "East northeast a half east!"

Dusk eased over them, with *Hermes* sliding across the sea and *Snowdrop*'s topsails only a vague white speck on the horizon.

"Steer northeast," Campbell said as night fell. "They can chase shadows in the night."

"There will also be an inshore squadron," Smith warned, "and maybe some gunboats if the Royal Navy was vessels to spare."

"They're stretched too thin for a proper blockade," Campbell said. "We'll get through." He spared Smith a rare smile. "We'll have you in Boston in time for lunch, Mr Smith."

Smith realised that nobody had questioned his sailing into a supposedly enemy port. As he had suspected, few among his men disliked the Americans. To them, as to most people in England, perhaps in all of Great Britain, France was the real enemy, and this war was little more than a domestic dispute. The men did not care who won as long as they were paid and survived to return home.

ABRAHAM HARGREAVES NODDED TO SMITH ACROSS THE WIDTH of the table. "How many ships?"

"There are thirty-three ships in the British convoy from London to New York," Smith said, "with a single sloop, a privateer and a frigate as an escort."

Abraham Hargreaves noted down the details.

"I want you to capture five vessels," Smith said.

"Five?"

"*Amelia Kate, Amelia's Fancy, Our Amelia and Amelia Frances*," Smith named four of Shapland's ships in the convoy. "They are sailing together and may be mutually supportive." He gave details of each ship, with the master's names and the armament each carried.

"Each vessel has six four-pounder popguns on the maindeck, with a swivel on each ship's poop," Smith said.

"That's useful information," Abraham said and listened as Smith told him the strengths and weaknesses of each ship.

"*Our Amelia* is the slowest sailer," Smith said, "and *Amelia Kate* is the newest and fastest. She's Blackwall built so sturdy and only launched two months ago."

"She'll make a fine profit," Abraham said, smiling. "You only mentioned four vessels, yet you said I've got to capture five," he reminded.

"The fifth is the privateer," Smith said. "She's Shapland's prize pirate, an idea he stole from me, and I want him to lose by it."

"What's her name?"

"*Britannia's Reign*," Smith said.

"Privateers can be dangerous if cornered," Abraham said. "How many guns does she carry?"

"Twelve," Smith said. Eight four-pounders and four six-pounders."

"We have sixteen," Abraham said. "How many in her crew?"

"Seventy-two." Smith had studied his subject.

"I have two hundred and twelve," Abraham said. He looked up with a grin, "and a heavier armament of twelve and six pounders. I think we'll manage her."

"After you have captured the ships I mentioned, you are free to take any other," Smith said, "except those who wear a Union flag on their foremast. Those vessels belong to me."

Abraham nodded. "I'm aware of the private signal, Mr Smith. Your vessels wear the Union jack on the foremast by day and show a double lantern astern by night. All the American privateers and our Continental Navy know to allow them safe passage."

Smith nodded. "There is one more thing, Abraham."

"There usually is with you, Mr Smith."

"I'll come with you," Smith said.

"If they catch you, they'll hang you as a traitor," Abraham warned.

"Traitor to what?" Smith asked. "To the Crown? Was Cromwell a traitor? Or was he a patriot for fighting for the people against the divine right of kings? Is Washington not a colonial Cromwell, fighting for liberty against a tyrannical king? Or is he a traitor who's broken the oath of loyalty to the crown he took as a British officer?"

Abraham shook his head. "I don't know, Mr Smith. National loyalty seems to be based on shifting sands. When nations and boundaries change with every war, how can one know to which nation one belongs?"

"You have two loyalties." Smith pointed the stem of his pipe at Abraham. "The first is to your wife and family, and the second is to yourself. All else is smoke and lies as false rulers demand you fight and die for their profit and advantage."

Hargreaves smiled. "Profit? There is also the small matter of profit as you own *Liberty's Revenge*."

"That is also true," Smith said, "and that is my loyalty to my wife and myself. The New York convoy will be three days' sail away by my reckoning. Perhaps four."

"We'll leave tomorrow morning," Abraham said.

Chapter Twenty-One

"What's he like, ma'am?" Leah asked.

"Who?"

"Mister Shapland," Leah said. "You must be very proud to be married to one of London's most successful merchants."

Kate smiled. "He needs me as much as I need him."

"I am sure he does," Leah said. "I believe a man without a wife is only half a man."

They sat in Kate's boudoir on the upper floor of Shapland's Mayfair mansion as Leah helped Kate with her hair.

Kate laughed. "Charles was lost until I arrived," she said. "He wasted his time with all sorts of ladybirds."

"Ladybirds!" Leah repeated. "He was lucky to find you!"

"He was," Kate admitted. "But I found him, rather." She examined her hair in the mirror, turning her head to view it from different angles. "That's it, Leah. We have a ball tonight, and you can watch Mr Shapland dancing with me."

"Thank you, ma'am." Leah gave another curtsey.

Kate stood up and inspected herself in the mirror. "That will do," she said. "Now, Leah, when I am dancing, I want you to order the maids to clean my boudoir properly. No holidays, as our nautical friends say. I want it clean and orderly when I return and ensure they make up the fire here and in our bedroom."

"I will, ma'am," Leah said.

"Don't stand for any nonsense, Leah," Kate said.

"I won't, ma'am," Leah promised. She held the door open and watched as Kate glided away, with her silk and satin dress rustling as she descended the stairs to the great hall.

"There is the small matter of the British blockading squadron." Abraham studied a chart of the approaches to Boston. "They have two cutters inshore and three undermanned gunboats, with two frigates and a sloop further out, and two seventy-fours on patrol twenty miles east."

"The battleships and frigates will be distracted tomorrow," Smith said. "There's a small French squadron in the offing. We passed them on our voyage."

"That was fortunate," Abraham said. "Britain is not at war with France, though."

"They weren't at war when we left the Thames," Smith agreed, "but there are always rumblings of potential war, and one whiff of garlic will ruffle the navy's feathers. They'll be concerned that another French war has started and close ranks, which will leave gaps for us to exploit."

Abraham nodded and indicated his intended route on the chart. "Let's hope the Royal Navy is sufficiently distracted to miss us."

"And thank King Louis for his help," Smith said.

Liberty's Revenge sailed with bare poles on the ebbing tide, with sufficient wind to ghost them outward and a providential mist masking their passage. The most dangerous section was in the deep-water channel immediately outside Boston Harbour, and then Abraham ordered the men into boats to row them north of Bird Island. With their oars muffled, and every man an expert boatman, the crew towed *Liberty's Revenge*, listening for the British patrols. Avoiding the sandbanks on either side, the privateer passed one British guard boat whose crew huddled over their single nine-pounder in the deepest section of the passage.

"Fortunately, *Revenge* has a shallow draught," Abraham murmured, aware of how far sound travelled at night.

"Nothing fortunate about it," Smith said. "I wasn't a Channel smuggler for nothing."

Smith stood in the stern, watching Abraham Hargreaves take control of the privateer. The crew was far more numerous than a British privateer would carry, with every man an experienced seaman and about a quarter having British or Irish accents.

"Look ahead!" Smith heard the splash of a careless oar.

"Easy all!" Abraham ordered quietly, and the oarsmen stopped, rested on their oars, and allowed the privateer to drift on the tide.

Smith knew the water under their keel was sufficiently deep to float them, at between three and five fathoms, but if they drifted off course, they could grind onto treacherous shoals.

A sharp-eyed officer nudged Abraham. "There, sir." He pointed to larboard, where the prow of a gunboat protruded from a bank of mist.

"One shot will alert the inshore squadron," Smith murmured.

Abraham nodded. "All silent," he ordered, and *Liberty's Revenge* floated past with tendrils of mist trailing from her masts and the small boats pulling only when necessary. Smith saw *Revenge*'s hands waiting at the broadside guns, perhaps hoping to blast the British vessel to fragments, and then they passed, and a whisper of wind eased them towards Governor's Island.

"Topsails," Abraham ordered, and the topmen hurried quietly aloft. The sails bellied before the wind, and *Liberty's Revenge* raised her bows to kiss the first of the Atlantic rollers.

Abraham was a skilled mariner, and with a full crew, he handled the ship without difficulty. After leaving Boston

Harbour, *Liberty's Revenge* steered south and east without seeing the British blockading squadron.

The morning sun burned away the mist, and they cruised under easy sail, with sea birds keeping them company and waves breaking creamy white under their bow.

"How far is the convoy?" Abraham asked the next day as Smith stood at his side on the quarterdeck.

"We should sight their topsails in a couple of hours," Smith told him. "I'd change the lookout every hour to keep him fresh."

"I've given orders, Mr Smith," Abraham said quietly.

Smith nodded. "I'll leave the command of the ship to you," he said.

"Thank you, Mr Smith." Abraham shouted a string of orders that saw the ship alter course slightly and more canvas break up aloft.

"Deck, there!" a man hailed from the masthead. "Sail ho!"

"Where away?" Abraham shouted.

"Southeast by east," the lookout bellowed. "Two sails. No, make that three!"

"I'm coming." Abraham scrambled aloft. Smith followed more sedately, wishing he was young again or had been less keen on rich food the past decade.

I'm fitter than I was a few months ago; I've missed being at sea.

Smith balanced on the crosstrees of the mainmast and extended his brass spyglass. His view was more extensive eighty feet up, and he saw the three topsails, with others breaking the horizon as he watched.

"Over there," he pointed. "I see five ships and more coming. Six, seven and eight."

"That's the convoy," Abraham said with satisfaction. He scanned the horizon, snapped his spyglass shut and slid to the quarterdeck, shouting orders.

"Get the royals in, men! Helmsman, steer south by southwest!"

Realising he was in the way, Smith also returned to deck. He forced himself to keep quiet as Abraham steered his ship around the convoy, relying on superior speed to avoid a British sloop. The sloop pushed away from the convoy, her sails catching the wind and a bone in her teeth.

"We could fight her." Hermann, the Prussian mate, glanced at the ranked cannon on *Liberty's Revenge's* main deck. "She's only pierced for fourteen guns."

"That's what she wants," Abraham said. "If we stop to fight her, we might win, but the convoy will escape. The navy's task is to protect the convoy, so she'll have succeeded, whatever the result of the encounter."

Hermann looked disappointed. "If you say so," he said.

They watched the sloop pile on more sails to catch this strange ship.

"If she catches us," Abraham said casually, "half my men will be hanged as traitors. If she can defeat us."

"Let's hope she doesn't catch us then." Smith knew he would share the same fate.

Within five minutes, it was evident that *Liberty's Revenge* was the faster vessel, leaving the sloop trailing. Smith saw a puff of smoke from the sloop's bows and, a moment later, heard the crack as she fired her bow chaser.

"Too late," Smith said. "She's well out of range." He saw a fountain of water rise a good quarter of a mile behind *Liberty's Revenge*. The American seamen jeered and gestured in contempt until Hermann roared them back to their duties.

Abraham nodded ahead, where a dark cloud had descended to sea level. "We'll lose them in that squall, ease around the back of the convoy and cut out Shapland's ships." He focussed his attention on the sloop. "HMS *Nightingale*, I believe. The trouble with the Royal Navy is their ships are undermanned, under-gunned, and built for all conditions."

"That's the downside of defending trade routes that extend from the White Sea to Bengal," Smith agreed. He watched as Abraham eased *Liberty's Revenge* into the squall. Rain hammered onto the deck and ran in great rivulets from the sails as the wind howled through the rigging. "Great Britain would be better off with fewer commitments."

"I'll tell King George that next time I see him," Abraham promised, snarled orders to the helmsman and peered astern. "*Nightingale* won't catch us now."

When they emerged from the squall an hour later, only *Nightingale*'s topsails could be seen, and Abraham altered the set of the sails and steered northward to cut inside the convoy.

"We'll be amongst them in a quarter of an hour," Smith said.

Abraham nodded and lifted the speaking trumpet from its bracket on the mizzen mast. "Beat to quarters! Clear the ship for action!"

Chapter Twenty-Two

"Who's that woman?" Shapland asked in a break from the dancing. "She's been standing in the corner for half an hour, watching us."

Kate followed Shapland's glance and smiled, casually waving her fan to cool her glowing face. "That's Leah Lightfoot," she said. "My new companion and personal maid." She lowered her voice, although the noise of the ball would mask anything she said. "Her husband died on one of Smith's ships so that she might be useful. I am cultivating her."

"You clever woman," Shapland approved. "Bring her over here, Kate. I want to talk to her."

When Kate lifted an imperious hand and crooked her finger, Leah pointed to herself, curtseyed, lifted her skirt and scurried across the floor, avoiding the dancers.

"Yes, ma'am?" She curtsied again, avoiding looking at Shapland.

"Mr Shapland wishes to speak to you," Kate said.

"Oh." Leah glanced at Shapland and then down at the floor. "Yes, sir."

"I hear you are new in our employ," Shapland said, eyeing her up and down.

"Yes, sir," Leah replied meekly. "Mrs Shapland was good enough to offer me a position as her personal maid and companion."

"Look at me, girl," Shapland put a finger under Leah's chin and gently raised her head. "You've no cause to be afraid of me."

"No sir; thank you, sir," Leah said, meeting Shapland's gaze.

"No cause at all," Shapland said, admiring Leah's clear grey eyes and snub nose. "Leah, isn't it?"

"Yes, sir," Leah said.

"I am sure we will get on very well, Leah," Shapland said, smiling. "Very well indeed."

"Thank you, sir." Leah curtseyed and glanced appealingly at Kate.

"Thank you, Leah," Kate said. "You may go now."

"Yes, ma'am." Leah lifted her skirt and fled across the floor as the orchestra prepared for the next dance.

Shapland nodded as he watched Leah's skirt sway from side to side. "She seems very shy. Are you sure she could be useful?"

"I think so," Kate said. "If she's not, I'll get rid of her."

Shapland nodded and dismissed Leah from his mind. "Come, Kate, the floor is waiting for us."

THERE WAS AN IMMEDIATE FLURRY OF HURRYING MEN AS *Liberty's Revenge* reverberated to the sound of her drummer. The boatswain and his mate toured the ship, roaring to the hands to get to their quarters. The ship's boys sanded the decks to soak up any blood and provide better footing, and men poured water over the hammock rolls to prevent fire.

"You've trained them well," Smith said. "They act like a man-of-war's crew."

"If we're fighting the most professional navy in the world, we have to be better than the best," Abraham said.

Smith grunted approval as the boatswain supervised men

who dragged netting above the upper deck to catch any blocks, cables, men or other objects that might fall from above if *Liberty's Revenge* came under fire.

"Boarding parties!" Hermann shouted in his heavily accented German-American-English. "Make ready!"

The designated boarders grabbed their grapnels, axes, boarding pikes and cutlasses. Simultaneously, the gun crews ran to the cannon, with iron shot piled in iron monkeys, cartridges, sponges and buckets of water to hand.

"Convoy ahoy," the lookout shouted. "Eight ships to larboard!"

"Brace the yards!" Abraham ordered. "Steer to larboard, helmsman!"

Liberty's Revenge obeyed the helm, heeling into the wind as the sails flapped and boomed, dipping her bow into the blue-green Atlantic waves.

"This is sailoring!" Abraham said, glorying in the adventure. Showers of spray and spindrift spattered the forecastle, with an occasional wave breaking silver-grey on the hull, drenching the men.

"They're scattering!" the lookout shouted.

Smith clambered to the mizzen masthead and focussed his spyglass, searching for Shapland's ships.

There's Amelia's Fancy.

"Two points to larboard, Captain," Smith called down. "There's a prize worth the taking." He scanned the horizon, seeing the ships run from the American privateer like hens from a hunting fox. *Amelia's Fancy* crammed on as much sail as she could carry, but she was old and slow.

She has a foul bottom. I doubt Shapland's careened her from one voyage to the next.

Liberty's Revenge came within long cannon range of the merchantman within an hour and fired a single warning shot on the uproll. From his position on the mizzen masthead, Smith saw the passage of the shot as a black streak against the pale blue sky.

Amelia's Fancy tried to run, but *Liberty's Revenge* could travel three feet to her one and approached within ten cables' lengths within twenty minutes.

"Run out the guns!" Abraham ordered, and the crew opened the port lids, triced them fast and pushed forward the cannon. The sight of a battery of twelve and six-pounders glowering at him must have made *Amelia's Fancy* captain flinch.

"Heave to and lower your colours!" Abraham ordered. "Stand by to receive boarders!"

The instant the Union flag dipped, Abraham signalled for a boarding party to cross the two cables' lengths between the ships. He waited until the boarding party had taken control and *Amelia Fancy's* master and mate were safe on board the privateer before hoisting the sails again.

"The prize crew will take her into an American port," Abraham said. "The British are blockading Boston, but there are plenty of creeks." He grinned. "There aren't enough ships in the Royal Navy to watch even half the North American coast."

"Sail ho!" Smith was quite comfortable on the mizzen masthead, watching operations without taking part. "*Our Amelia* is half a mile to starboard!"

"Set the t'gallants and royals!" Abraham roared. "Come on, boys! Prize money for the asking!"

Elated by their early success, the crew cheered and worked with a will. Abraham used the same successful formula, firing a warning shot, sailing close and showing *Revenge's* teeth rather than subjecting his quarry to a damaging fire that might cost needless casualties.

When the master of *Our Amelia* tried to fight, firing her puny broadside at extreme range, Abraham shook his head.

"Brave but foolish, captain. Give her a shot through the rigging."

Liberty's Revenge fired a single twelve-pounder shot that parted a line aloft, and *Our Amelia* hove to and lowered her flag.

Smith checked the horizon. The day was wearing on, but he saw three sails, which meant three possible prizes for *Liberty's Revenge* and more losses for Charles Shapland.

"*Amelia Kate's* a mile in front," Smith shouted, "in company with *Amelia Frances*. But there might be trouble, for *Britannia's Reign* is half a mile to larboard."

"We'll capture them all, by God!" Abraham replied as the prize crew took control of *Our Amelia*. "T'gallants and royals! Stunsails and moonrakers! Damn it all, boys, hang your shirts out to dry if they can catch a breeze!"

Liberty's Revenge surged forward, with her bow throwing up spray and Abraham altering the angle of the sails to catch every whisper of wind. The crew responded eagerly to Abraham's commands, staring forward at the vessels they were pursuing.

"That British privateer is closing with the quarry," Hermann reported.

"They might operate as a team." Smith scrambled to the deck. He glanced upward, where the light was fading. "It will be dark in an hour."

"Mr Hermann," Abraham shouted. "Have the bow chaser fire at the first target to come within range."

Grinning, Hermann loped forward. Big, blond, and capable, he towered over the crew of the forward nine-pounder. *Liberty's Revenge* was faster than all three British vessels.

"We'll be in range of the merchantmen before *Britannia's Reign* closes," Smith said a moment before Hermann gave the order to fire.

The bow-chaser cracked out with a jet of flame and a gush of grey-white smoke. Smith did not see the fall of shot.

"Missed!" Abraham shouted. "Try again!"

Rather than continue to flee, *Amelia Kate* and *Amelia Frances* turned to face their attacker.

"They're going to fight, by God!" Abraham said.

"They're depending on *Britannia's Reign* to support them," Smith said.

"They're either very foolish or very brave," Abraham mused.

"Or they know something we don't," Smith pointed out. He lifted his head. "Lookout! Scan the horizon for a frigate!"

The bow chaser fired again, with the merchant ships replying with their broadsides. The closest shot raised a fountain three cables' lengths to starboard.

"They're game, at least," Abraham said calmly and raised his spyglass to *Britannia's Reign*. "The privateer is closing."

"We may have a fight on our hands." Smith glanced across the deck, where the hands stood by the guns or peered across the water at the rapidly approaching merchantmen.

"What do you suggest, Mr Smith?" Abraham asked. "You have more experience than I do."

"The privateer is the most dangerous of the three," Smith said immediately. "Defeat her, and the merchantmen will either run or surrender. *Liberty's Revenge* is far faster and can catch them if they flee."

Abraham nodded. "That's what we'll do." He raised his voice. "Hands to the braces! Prepare to go about!"

Britannia's Reign did not hesitate but opened fire at long range, with her first salvo surprisingly accurate. One shot crashed into *Liberty's Revenge's* hull, and another screamed aloft.

"Not bad shooting," Smith said as Abraham sent men to check for damage below.

"Hold your fire," Abraham roared. "We'll save the first broadside."

Smith nodded approval. The first broadside was often the most effective, as the gun captains selected the roundest shot and prepared their guns with care. Later, if the action continued, there would be no time to choose or aim properly and firing amidst the chaos of screaming casualties on a deck swimming with blood was harder.

The British privateer fired again, now half hidden by powder smoke, and again made good practice. Smith heard the crash as another shot thumped into *Liberty Revenge*'s hull.

"We're taking punishment," Abraham said.

"We have heavier metal than them and a larger crew," Smith reassured him. "Their crew will be nervous as we close, knowing we're reserving our broadside."

Liberty's Revenge caught a stray breeze that pushed her faster just as the sun set. Smith fixed his eyes on the British privateer's sails.

"That's your mark, Abraham," Smith said. "Cripple her aloft."

Abraham flinched when *Britannia's Reign* fired a third time, with one shot screaming a foot above the quarter deck and another spreading vicious splinters across the deck. A man fell, screaming, as a two-foot-long length of timber impaled him.

"Take him below," Smith ordered.

Darkness was falling fast, so when *Britannia's Reign* fired again, the muzzle flares from her cannon split the night, momentarily dazzling Smith.

"I think that's close enough now, Captain," he said quietly.

"So do I, Mr Smith," Abraham agreed. He raised his voice. "Brail the foresail and mainsail up to the yards." With the lower sails out of the way, *Liberty's Revenge* lost some speed, but there was less risk of fire. Abraham gave orders that took his ship to leeward of *Britannia's Reign*. "Open gun ports. Run out the guns!"

The men obeyed happily, cheering as the cannon rumbled over the scrubbed planking.

"On the uproll boys, fire at her rigging."

The gun crews cheered and bent to their task. A moment later, *Liberty's Revenge* fired her broadside, with some guns loaded with solid shot and others with chain shot, two half cannonballs connected by a length of chain. The object was to slice through the enemy's rigging and cripple her.

After waiting so long under fire, the American crew loaded quickly and added a second broadside before *Britannia's Reign* replied.

"We can't see what damage we've done," Hermann complained.

"We will soon," Smith said. "There's a full moon tonight."

Smith saw the American gunners working, cocking the firelocks, pulling the lanyards, firing, and reloading, with the flashes from the cannon revealing vignettes of men stripped to the waist, men shouting and the occasional casualty as the British vessel fought back.

"She's a tough one!" Abraham panted when a British shot crashed into the taffrail, spreading splinters.

"She's crippled aloft." Smith did not flinch. "Her mizzen's going."

As Smith spoke, the moon emerged, sending ghostly silver light across the sea. The scene looked eerie, an image from Dante, two ships containing men who were more similar than different, killing and dying for rulers who cared little for them and a vaguely understood philosophy.

A British shot ripped through the protective netting above *Revenge*'s quarterdeck, and another struck the foretopmast.

"Cross her stern," Smith ordered.

Abraham nodded and gave orders that saw *Liberty's Revenge* sail astern of *Britannia's Reign*. The British ship was a crippled wreck, with her mizzen and main mast trailing overboard and what remained of her rigging in rags.

"Wait!" Smith said. "She's struck."

"Hold your fire!" Abraham roared as the British privateer lowered her flag.

"That's the hard part done," Smith said as Abraham ordered a prize crew to take control of *Britannia's Reign*. "Now we can chase and find the two merchantmen."

"Then it's back to Boston for us," Hermann said with satisfaction.

"Oh, no." Smith shook his head. "We'll see if there are any volunteers from the British crews, increase our food and water supplies and head north."

"North?" Abraham repeated.

"We're going to hunt for blubber boats," Smith told him with a crooked smile.

Chapter Twenty-Three

"Have you settled in, Leah?" Shapland asked. He stopped at the angle of the stairs, with Leah a few steps above him and a longcase clock ticking softly at his side.

"Yes, sir," Leah replied with a curtsey. "I am quite comfortable, thank you."

"I thought you would soon settle," Shapland said. "I believe you had a personal tragedy before you came to us."

"I did, sir," Leah said. "I lost my husband."

Shapland sighed sympathetically. "That must be terrible," he said, patting her shoulder. "Come into my study and tell me what happened."

"Thank you, sir." Leah stood behind Shapland as he unlocked his study door and stepped inside. The room was large and airy, with a solid oaken desk against one wall. Shapland lit the four candles on an ornate candelabra, sat at his desk and invited Leah to sit opposite.

"If you could pour us both a glass of Madeira," Shapland indicated the bottle and glasses standing on a bureau in the far corner, you can tell me about yourself."

Leah placed the glasses on the desk. "There's not much to tell, sir. I have been a widow since my husband drowned at sea."

Shapland tasted his Madeira. "He was in one of John Smith's vessels, I believe."

"Yes, sir." Leah looked around the room as if afraid of being overheard. "They say Mr Smith neglects his older ships, sir."

"I've heard that." Shapland nodded understandingly.

"Yes, sir," Leah said. "They say Mr Smith insures his ships with two insurance companies, lets them sink and claims the insurance money."

Shapland finished his Madeira. "Who says that, Leah?"

"The other wives, sir," Leah said. "I'm sorry, sir, I am not used to strong drink, and I had no business telling you that."

"It's quite all right," Shapland said. "You must miss your husband terribly."

"I do, sir," Leah said.

"Well, you are among friends here." Shapland stepped across the room, retrieved the bottle of Madeira, and filled both their glasses. "Do you see the other wives often?"

"No, sir." Leah shook her head. "We only met after the ship went down. I haven't seen them since. I have no friends."

"You have me." Shapland leaned across the desk. "If ever you wish to talk or anything else," he smiled. "I am here for you."

"Thank you, sir," Leah said. "I can't, though. You're the master, and I'm only a servant."

"I don't think of you as only a servant." Shapland patted her arm. "I hope you don't only think of me as a master." He smiled and looked up when somebody tapped on the door. "I'd better get back to work, Leah. Shipping companies don't run themselves, you know."

Leah stood. "I'm sure they don't, sir." She stood, curtseyed, and stepped aside as the door opened and an anxious-eyed clerk looked in.

"Thank you, Leah," Shapland adopted a more business-like tone. "You may leave now."

"The whaling ships wait at the edge of the ice for the whale fish," Smith explained, "and drift down the pack ice, hunting. They kill the whales, flense them of their blubber and cut the bone from their jaws. The ships return home when they have killed sufficient whales, or the weather turns foul."

Abraham looked doubtful. "Is it worth the effort of capturing them, Mr Smith?"

"Very much so, Captain. A blubber boat with a full cargo can fetch five thousand pounds, and you don't have to pay the crew's wages from the profit."

"Five thousand?" Abraham raised his eyebrows. "I had no idea they were so valuable." He grinned. "Let's go hunting, Mr Smith!"

Sunlight glittered on an ice field that extended as far as Smith could see, with the sails of half a dozen ships puncturing the sky.

"Which ships?" Abraham asked.

"Shapland's," Smith insisted. "He has four that hunt in the Greenland Sea. They all stick together, and the Greenlandmen are a rough crowd, far more likely to fight than the fat merchantmen we met in the Atlantic."

Abraham nodded to his crew. "My men will handle them."

"Maybe," Smith said. "I think we should alter the ship's name, wear the Union flag and tell them we're here to protect them."

"Protect them against American privateers?" Abraham asked. "I like that idea. You're a devious man, Mr Smith."

Smith had no experience of high latitude sailing and looked all around as *Liberty's Revenge* scouted the edge of the ice. The Union flag at her mizzen gave her immunity from scrutiny as she passed half a dozen whaling ships that first day.

"*Dundee* of Dundee." Smith focussed his spyglass on the closest vessel. "Should we take her?"

Smith pondered for a moment, then took the speaking trumpet from its bracket on the mizzenmast. "*Dundee* ahoy! *George's Pride* here! Any success with the fishing?"

The mate in the stern of *Dundee* shook his head. "We're clean so far, *George's Pride*. Not a whisper of a whale fish!"

"Clean means no catch," Smith said, and they drifted on. He did not like whaling, with the utter desolation of the Arctic, nothing but snow and ice beneath a winter sky and cold so intense it hurt to breathe. After a week of dodging ice floes, Smith began to lose hope.

Maybe I've done the wrong thing coming north.

Desperate for success, Abraham captured the next vessel they found, a small, two-hundred-ton brig named *Delilah* of Shields, with only a single whale.

"We won't get rich on her," Abraham said gloomily.

"Bring her along with us," Smith said. "We may find a use for her."

With *Delilah*'s crew confined to the hold and a prize crew on board, she followed *Liberty's Revenge* along the edge of the pack ice.

The days merged into a week, with the sea surprisingly calm but no sign of whaling ships. On the eighth day, the weather turned boisterous, and *Liberty's Revenge* pushed through brash ice that had Abraham worrying about her hull.

"*Liberty*'s not built for the ice, Mr Smith," he said. "These whaling ships are double hulled with strengthened bows, and we are not. The ice could crush us like an eggshell."

"One more day, Captain," Smith said. "Then we can head for home."

"Yes, Mr Smith," Abraham agreed reluctantly.

At that latitude, there was no night, and Smith lost count of the hours. He was still determining the time when the hail came from the masthead.

"Another whaling ship ahead, Captain," the lookout shouted. "She's not carrying any boats!"

"That sounds hopeful," Smith said as Abraham steered *Liberty's Revenge* closer.

"Her name is *Amelia's Catch*," the lookout reported.

That's one of Shapland's ships. "Steer closer," Smith ordered and readied the speaking tube.

"*Amelia's Catch!*" he hailed.

"We're a bit busy!" the reply came over the sea.

"How is your success?" Smith asked.

"Seven fish," the reply came, "and maybe another. The boats are out."

Smith relayed the information to Abraham. "That's a good catch," he said.

"We'll take her," Abraham decided. "Lower the Union flag and raise our own!"

The crew of *Liberty's Revenge* cheered as they hauled up the new American flag and ran to the boats when Abraham ordered the boarding parties away.

Smith could imagine the consternation in the London whaling ship when they saw a predatory American so close to them and two boatloads of privateers bristling with weapons.

The captain of *Amelia's Catch* was no coward. Although half his crew were away hunting whales, he ordered the remainder to the guns.

"Heads down, lads!" Abraham ordered when *Amelia's Catch* rolled out her four-gun broadside. They fired, with the shots splashing around the approaching boats without causing damage, and then the American boarders scrambled onto the whaler's deck.

The whaler's crew fought back with flensing knives and harpoons but faced with a rush of determined men armed with cutlasses, pikes and pistols, their resistance was always doomed.

"Put your weapons down, boys," *Amelia's Catch's* captain called when two of his men fell to the deck. "We're just throwing our lives away."

The men dropped their makeshift weapons and glowered at the invaders.

"That was a dirty trick," the captain said as the boarders gathered the crew together.

"All's fair in love and war," Abraham told him.

"How about my men? I have six boatloads of men out hunting," the captain said as Abraham escorted him to *Liberty's Revenge*.

"We won't let them freeze," Smith promised.

"Will that do, Mr Smith?" Abraham asked as a chunk of ice scraped along his ship's hull?"

Smith nodded. "Not yet, Captain. I want another of Shapland's blubber boats. Send the crew to *Delilah* and bring the master and mates here as prisoners, and let's go hunting."

The crew cheered. As Smith had suspected, success had raised their morale, and they were hungry for more.

We have a long way to go, but we've dealt Shapland some shrewd blows. Now, all we have to do is capture another whaling ship and avoid the Royal Navy, and then I can return to London.

"BEGGING YOUR PARDON, MRS SMITH." JUDD STOOD AT THE corner of the office. "Do you want me to continue buying shares while Mr Smith is away?"

"Yes, please, Frederick." Bess favoured Judd with a smile.

"I'll need more money, Mrs Smith. I've been successful this week, but the price of shares has risen a great deal." Judd shuffled his feet apologetically.

"Do you want gold or a banker's draft?" Bess asked. She checked Judd's figures every week and appreciated his scrupulous honesty.

Judd hesitated. "Gold, please, Mrs Smith," Judd said. "I bought the final three shares in *London's Tower* yesterday, Mrs Smith. Mr Smith is now the sole owner."

"Well done, Frederick," Bess said. "You look agitated. Is there something else you wish to tell me?"

"Yes, Mrs Smith." Judd took a deep breath. "I saw Mr Anthony Jackson at the coffee house, Mrs Smith. He was also bidding for shares in Mr Smith's ships."

Bess raised her eyebrows. "Thank you, Frederick, but Mr Jackson is perfectly within his rights to buy shares in *London's Tower*."

"Yes, Mrs Smith," Judd said. "I've seen Mr Bancroft buying shares too, Mrs Smith, but Mr Jackson is a more frequent purchaser."

Bess nodded. "Thank you for the information, Frederick. I will relay it to Mr Smith when he returns."

Judd bowed. "Yes, Mrs Smith. I thought I'd better pass it on."

When Judd left the room, Bess scribbled a note and sighed.

I miss the old days in Kent. I don't like dealing with shares and finance; things were so much simpler when we were younger.

Chapter Twenty-Four

"Damned Yankee pirates!" Shapland stomped into the drawing room, swearing. "They've captured more of my ships!"

"How many ships?" Kate lowered her mirror and pushed Leah away. "Not now, Leah. Leave us."

"Yes, ma'am." Leah curtseyed and withdrew from the room, closing the door behind her.

"Four at the last count," Shapland said. "Only one damned privateer, and he captured *Britannia's Reign* as well. I paid a lot of money for that Letter-of-Marque. I may as well have tossed a hundred guineas into the Thames for all the good she did me!"

Kate stood up. "One privateer, you said. What was her name?"

"It was Abraham Hargreaves again, in *Liberty's Revenge*." Shapland crumpled a document and threw it on the floor. "That's seven of my ships he's captured. If he carries on like this, he'll possess more of my ships than I do!"

"Hargreaves? I know that name from somewhere," Kate shook her head. "I'm damned if I can remember where, though. Give me a minute, and it will come to me."

Shapland lifted a poker and attacked the fire Kate insisted on having whatever the weather.

"Sir." A clerk tapped on the door and pushed it open. "I have another message for you."

"What is it this time?" Shapland grabbed the scrap of paper, read it, and swore.

"What's the matter, Charles?" Kate asked.

"Two whaling ships now!" Shapland said. "That damned Abraham Hargreaves has captured two of my whaling ships and two full cargos of whales." He brandished the poker as if threatening the American privateer captain across thousands of miles of the Atlantic.

Kate lifted the mirror and patted her hair into place. "They were insured, weren't they?"

"Yes, and now the policies will rise again."

Kate watched Shapland curiously, wondering if he would either explode with anger or break into tears. "What was the name? Abraham Hargreaves?" she asked. "I've got it, Charles. Smith's senior captain in Kent was Hargreaves."

"Smith!" Shapland swore again, crumpled up the note and threw it at Kate. "I have enough bad news without you bringing me more! Get out!"

Kate shook her head, placed the mirror down and nodded. "I'm going, Charles. There's no talking to you when you're in this mood."

"And you!" Shapland pointed his poker at the clerk. "You've lost your position! Get out of my office. I'll set the dogs on you if I see you again!"

"Sir!" The clerk backed away, white-faced. "Sir!"

"Don't sir me, you fawning rogue!" Shapland stepped towards him, still brandishing the poker. "Get out of my house!"

The clerk ran from the room, with Kate hiding her smile and Leah standing on the carpeted staircase, watching.

SMITH SMILED ACROSS THE WIDTH OF THE DESK. "I HAVE insured my vessels with your company for some years, Mr Abergeldie."

Abergeldie adjusted his wig slightly before replying in his cautious Edinburgh accent. He opened the large, leather-bound account book that lay before him. "That's correct, Mr Smith. Twelve years, three months, and seventeen days since you paid your first premium to the London and Channel Ship Insurance Company."

"I believe I have been a good customer," Smith continued.

Abergeldie considered the question before he replied. "We value your custom, Mr Smith." He held Smith's gaze, waiting for Smith to reveal the purpose of his visit before committing himself.

Smith broadened his smile. "I intend to increase my fleet of whaling and trading ships, Mr Abergeldie, and hope to continue to work with you."

"We are always glad of your custom, Mr Smith." Abergeldie's eyes gleamed at the prospect of taking more of Smith's money.

"I wondered about the premiums," Smith said. "I believe Mr Shapland also insures with you and pays less than us."

"Less?" Abergeldie looked momentarily surprised that he might be losing money. "I will check on the figures, Mr Smith. Pray excuse me."

When Abergeldie left his desk to delve into the drawers in the adjacent room, Smith leaned back. The London and Channel Ship Insurance Company was well-established and among the most honest insurance companies in London, although the office was small and shabby. Abergeldie was a shrewd businessman, careful with money but sufficiently astute to pay promptly whenever a ship foundered. Smith allowed his eyes to wander across the panelled walls to the bookcases with their accumulation of journals and ledgers, wondering how much money was invested in this small office.

"No, Mr Smith." Abergeldie sounded relieved when he returned. "Mr Shapland does not have a lower premium on his vessels."

"Thank you, Mr Abergeldie," Smith said. "I rather wondered after his recent losses. He seems very careless of his vessels."

Abergeldie looked solemn. "War is always a bad time for shipping insurance, as I am sure you know."

"I know that Mr Abergeldie," Smith said. "And with these American privateers deliberately targeting Mr Shapland's vessels, I am surprised you gamble on him at all. You are a very generous man, sir."

Abergeldie looked up sharply. People had accused him of many things but never of generosity. "Gamble, Mr Smith? I am not a gambling man. Pray explain that term."

Smith lifted a hand in apology. "I meant no offence, Mr Abergeldie. I merely meant that you give Mr Shapland very generous terms considering the danger his ships are in."

Abergeldie stiffened in his chair. "Are Mr Shapland's vessels in greater danger than any other ship at sea, Mr Smith?"

"Why, yes, sir," Smith said. "I am surprised he has not informed you. Abraham Hargreaves, one of the most infamous of American privateers, seems to have a private war with Mr Shapland," Smith explained. "He captured half a dozen of his vessels only a few weeks back and has vowed to reduce his fleet further."

"Where do you get your information, Mr Smith?" Abergeldie asked, dipping his pen into the inkwell, and carefully noting Smith's words.

"I have people in North America," Smith said. "They pass intelligence to me." He produced a copy of the *New Hampshire Gazette* from inside his coat. "I have marked the article, Mr Abergeldie."

He passed over the newspaper with the article he had carefully drafted and sent to the newspaper before he left Boston.

Patriot privateer vows vengeance on London merchant.

Abraham Hargreaves, one of the most active of our privateers, has promised revenge on Charles Shapland, a London merchant known for his loyalist sentiments. Captain Hargreaves stated that he would retaliate for Shapland's deliberate provocation towards the American cause. He has recently captured four or five of Mr Shapland's vessels and vowed to continue his attacks until he drives Shapland's ships from the seas.

"I see." Abergeldie read the article, wrote another few lines and laid down his pen. "Thank you for the information, Mr Smith. I am afraid I may have to raise Mr Shapland's insurance policy in future and raise it quite considerably. If his ships are more at risk than others, I have little choice."

"I hope I have not caused you any trouble, Mr Abergeldie," Smith said smoothly.

"On the contrary, Mr Smith," Abergeldie said. "You may have saved me a great deal of trouble and expense. I am very much obliged to you, sir." He shook his head and unbent sufficiently to elaborate. "God knows, Mr Smith, if this American war continues much longer, we shall all die of hunger. Their freebooters have captured hundreds of our ships, prices are rising, and food shortages are on the horizon. Harbour dues are falling, charity rolls have multiplied, and some merchants send their cargoes in French bottoms."

"All wars come to an end," Smith assured him. "The rulers redraw national boundaries; the people bury their dead, widows and orphans lament and then trade resumes. Thank you, Mr Abergeldie," he rose and extended his hand.

They shook hands; Smith replaced his hat and left the office.

Only three more insurance offices to visit, and I'll have completed the rounds. Shapland will have to pay through the nose to insure his ships. I'll bankrupt that bastard yet.

"ARE YOU ALL RIGHT, MR SHAPLAND?" LEAH ASKED. "YOU look worried if I may make so bold."

Shapland stared at her for a moment. "You're a precocious piece, aren't you?"

"I don't mean to be forward, sir." Leah withdrew a pace. "I know my place."

They stood inside the drawing room, with sunlight streaming through the window and gleaming on the glass-fronted drinks cabinet. Shapland had a glass in his hand and anger in his eyes. "And where is that, Leah?" he asked.

"Why, sir, wherever you wish it to be," Leah said with a low curtsey.

Shapland smiled. "I recall you are no friend of John Smith."

Leah looked up sharply. "I lost my husband because of John Smith!"

"I remember," Shapland said. "That must be a terrible memory for you."

"It is, sir," Leah agreed.

"Smith is my enemy," Shapland said. "He and his friends are sworn to destroy me."

"I am not surprised, sir." Leah inched closer. "If there is anything I can do to help, anything at all, I am here for you."

"That's more than my damned wife is," Shapland said. "Mockery and abuse are all I get from her, and now the damned insurance companies either refuse to work with me or offer rates that would bankrupt Croesus."

"I am sorry to hear that, sir."

Shapland swilled more Madeira into his glass and swallowed it down. "I wonder if you are truly sorry, Leah, or if you're as false as the rest of them."

"Sir!" Leah stepped back. "I am sure Mrs Shapland is true, sir. I've never heard her say a bad thing about you."

Shapland eyed her for a long moment. "Where did we get you, Leah? You're a breath of spring air on a dull November day."

"Mrs Shapland hired me, sir," Leah reminded.

"Sit down and talk to me," Shapland invited. "Come, girl; you've no need to be shy with me." He took Leah by the hand and guided her to the Chippendale walnut sofa. "Come along now."

"If you are sure, sir." Leah perched at his side, keeping to the edge of the sofa.

"I am sure, Leah," Shapland said. "You are the most delightful of companions, demure yet intelligent, shy yet without fear. You are not scared of me, are you?"

"Scared of you?" Leah repeated. "No, sir. You have never given me any cause for fear."

"That's my girl." Shapland patted her thigh. "And I never shall." He smiled into her eyes. "You know that despite wars and disasters, people are the same. A woman needs a strong man to protect her, and a man needs a good woman to comfort him. I believe you are a good woman, Leah."

"Thank you, sir." Leah shifted her leg until it nearly touched that of Shapland.

"You are a very handsome woman, Leah." Shapland walked his fingers along Leah's thigh. "I am sure many men have told you that."

"No, sir," Leah said. "Only my late husband, the man John Smith sacrificed for profit."

"What? You have no followers? No trail of men eager for your hand in marriage?"

"I have not, sir," Leah said.

"You are alone in the world, then," Shapland mused. "Except for me." His hand patted softly as he inched closer.

"I am, sir," Leah said. "I am very grateful for the shelter and position Mrs Shapland has offered me in your house."

Shapland sighed. "I also feel alone, Leah, yet I sense that we can alleviate each other's loneliness."

"You have Mrs Shapland, sir."

"Only when she feels so inclined, Leah," Shapland said. "I'd rather have you."

Leah hid her smile. "Thank you, sir," she replied.

"Charles," Shapland patted her leg. "You may call me Charles."

Chapter Twenty-Five

Bess lay on her side, wondering what had awakened her. It had been something out of the ordinary, not the usual creaks of the house, the patter of a running servant or the night-time noises from the streets.

"John." she nudged Smith in the ribs. "John!" Bess hissed more urgently, shaking his arm.

Smith rolled over. "What is it?" He opened his eyes, automatically reaching for the gold watch on the table beside the bed.

"I heard something."

"What sort of something?" Smith sat up. Lifting his tinder box, he scratched a spark and lit the candle on the table. "It's three in the morning, damn it, Bess. Is this any time to wake a Christian gentleman?"

"Keep your voice down!" Bess hissed. "Somebody is moving around the house! It may be a burglar."

Smith slid out of bed and reached for the pistol he kept on top of the chest of drawers. "You stay here." He checked the flint was sharp.

"Put some clothes on," Bess hissed. "You don't want to scare the servants."

Smith nodded and pulled on loose sailor's trousers and a

linen shirt. He turned the door handle quietly, pulled it open a crack and slipped into the corridor outside. Knowing the house's layout better than any intruder, he left the candle with Bess, for he did not want the light to betray his presence.

The steady ticking of the long-case clock on the landing seemed loud in the otherwise silent house as Smith waited and listened. At first, he heard nothing except the creaking of furniture as it cooled, absorbed moisture, and expanded.

You're imagining things, Bess.

After a few moments, Smith heard the sound, soft but unmistakable. It was the pad of feet and a door opening and closing. Smith cocked his pistol, shielding the hammer with a cupped hand to keep the noise down.

The sound had come from downstairs, Smith decided. *Maybe one of the servants has a nocturnal visitor.* He shook his head. *They don't need to hide that sort of thing in my house.*

Holding the pistol before him, Smith crept downstairs. The ticking of the clock dominated the house, seeming to echo in the night, and the gilded mirror in the main hall appeared like a dark pool, an entrance to some subterranean world. The stone stairs down to the servant's quarters were cold under Smith's feet as he descended, listening for unfamiliar sounds, wary in case of a sudden attack.

Why the devil would a burglar choose the servants' rooms? There are better pickings upstairs.

Smith turned as he heard a noise behind him, levelling his pistol.

"John!" Bess whispered. She held the blunderbuss in both hands.

"I told you to stay in the bedroom!" Smith hissed.

"What? And let you have all the fun?" Bess wore a loose skirt and top, but the laughter in her eyes caught Smith's attention.

She's enjoying the excitement; God love her.

"Come on, then," Smith said and moved on with Bess a few steps behind.

"He's in the kitchen," Bess whispered and stepped into an inset doorway with her blunderbuss ready.

Smith nodded. He saw the flickering bar of light under the kitchen door and heard the soft sounds of somebody moving. He turned the handle slowly, took a deep breath, pushed the door open and barged inside, pistol in hand.

"What the devil's happening in here?"

Somebody gave a shrill scream and leapt for the window. Bess ran in behind Smith as he dived forward, reaching out with his left hand to grab the intruder.

"Get him, John!" Bess shouted, pulling the blunderbuss to her shoulder and resting her finger on the trigger. "I've got you covered!"

"It's a little girl!" Smith said as he clutched a pencil-thin arm in his hand.

"What?" Bess lifted the barrel of her blunderbuss, so it pointed harmlessly at the ceiling.

"Bring the candle," Smith ordered, relaxing his grip in case he hurt his prisoner. "I want to see what we have here."

Bess lifted the candle, pressed the wick against another and allowed the double light to spread around the room. Smith held a dirty-faced young girl by the arm, with tired servants roused from their bed and pushing into the kitchen to see what was happening.

"Who are you?" Smith asked brusquely, shaking the child. "What's your name, and what are you doing? Answer me!"

"John." Bess stepped over. "That won't work, and you're frightening the child." She released Smith's grip from the girl's arm and took a more gentle hold. "It's all right, my girl. Nobody's going to hurt you. Now, what's your name?"

The girl turned huge eyes on Bess. "Madge," she said, searching for weakness.

"Madge," Bess repeated. "And what are you doing here, Madge?"

"She's stealing food, ma'am; that's what she's doing!" The

cook bustled into her kitchen and pointed to the bulge at Madge's stomach. "Look!" Without hesitation, the cook lifted the girl's ragged dress to reveal a canvas bag with half a loaf and a block of cheese inside. "She's a thief! She needs a good thrashing; that's what she needs." The cook was a large woman in her forties with a broad red face and hands like a labourer's. "I'll fetch a birch rod."

"You'll do no such thing." Bess held Madge close. "I told this young girl nobody would hurt her, and nobody will."

Smith uncocked his pistol and placed it on the table. "Everybody get back to bed," he ordered. "Leave this to us."

"She needs a good whipping," the cook said, glowering at Madge.

"Good night," Smith injected iron into his voice as Bess nodded to the door.

Grumbling, the servants left the kitchen, leaving Bess and Smith with the child. Bess pulled three chairs to the table. "All right, Madge," she said. "Tell me what you're doing and how you got into the house."

"I've seen you before, Madge" Smith joined them at the table. "You were with Peter Brown."

Madge flinched at the name and hung her head. "Yes," she admitted.

Bess stiffened in her chair. "You're hungry, Madge." She glanced at the bread and cheese in Madge's canvas bag. "Did you come here to steal food?"

Madge lifted her dirty face. "Yes," she admitted. "Peter told me you always fed him here."

Bess nodded. "How did you get in? The doors and windows are all locked."

Madge shook her head. "Not all of them," she said. "The window above the front door is open."

"The fanlight?" Bess said, glancing at Smith.

"If that's what you call it." Madge smiled, pleased she could reveal her cleverness.

"I'll inspect that later," Smith said.

Once she started, Madge was eager to talk. "Peter told us that there's always food in the kitchen here, and he opened the window above the front door to let us in." She was smiling, proud to show off her skill. "He said we're not to touch anything except food, though."

"That was good of him," Smith kept the sarcasm from his voice. He slid a hand across the table and touched Bess's arm.

"I miss Peter." Bess tapped her fingers on the table and passed the bread and cheese to Madge. "You'll miss him, too."

Madge bit off a hunk of bread. "Yes," she said, chewing lustily. "Three men and a woman took him away."

"Did you see what happened?" Bess asked.

"Yes," Madge spoke through a mouthful of half-masticated bread. "We was in Peter's house when these men kicked the door down. We had come back from the docks and were seeing what we got from the ships. The men never knocked or nothing but booted in the door, and the woman pointed to Peter."

"A woman pointed to Peter," Bess repeated the words, glancing at Smith again.

"Yes," Madge said. "She never looked at the rest of us, just pointed to Peter, and the men grabbed him."

"Can you describe her?" Bess asked.

"Eh?" Madge looked confused. "What do you mean?"

"What was she like, this woman?"

Madge swallowed her bread and screwed up her face in concentration. "She must have been a bit of a dim mort once; that's a good looker to you."

"I know," Bess said. "Thank you for the translation."

She wasn't a baggage, though, not a prostitute from the streets anyway. Her ogles were stone-hard."

"A hard-eyed woman, then," Smith summarised, "and not a youngster."

"If you say so," Madge agreed.

"Was she tall? Short? Blonde? Dark-haired?" Bess asked.

"Tall," the diminutive Madge said, screwing up her face. "Taller than you and red-haired."

Bess hissed between her teeth and glanced at Smith. "That sounds like the same woman Davie Cupples saw at the refuge."

"I think so," Smith agreed.

"I want her, John." Bess clenched her teeth.

"I know," Smith said quietly. "We'll get her, Bess."

Madge looked from Bess to Smith and continued. "The woman stood at the door, and the twangs, the bullies, grabbed Peter. We tried to help, but they beat us off. Look." She lifted her dress to reveal an ugly purple bruise across her ribs. "And look." She pulled back her lower lip to show two missing teeth. "One of the twangs done that."

"Well done for trying," Smith said.

"The bullies smacked Peter across the jaw, lifted him and carried him away," Madge said, "with the woman watching and smiling."

Smith saw Bess struggle to control her anger. "Did you see where they took him?"

"Into a carriage," Madge said. "It had the curtains drawn at the windows, and I couldn't see inside."

"What sort of carriage?" Smith asked. "Dark, light, heavy, how many horses?"

"You ask too many questions!" Madge complained. "I can't remember. It was a carriage with two horses."

"That's enough questions for just now," Bess agreed. "Madge is tired. You stay here the rest of the night, Madge," she said. "We'll decide what to do with you in the morning."

"Yes, Mrs Smith," Madge said. "Can I sleep next to the fire?"

"Yes, Madge," Bess agreed. "I'll find some blankets for you."

"Don't leave the kitchen, Madge," Smith ordered. "Don't touch anything, or you'll wish the bullies had got you." He stepped away. "Come on, Bess. We have things to discuss."

"Not now, John," Bess said. "I'm a bit upset just now."

"I'll check the fanlight," Smith said. "Before we have half the cracksmen and thieves in London trailing in for breakfast."

The candlelight reflected from the glass as Smith climbed the wooden ladder to the fanlight. He placed the brass candlestick on the shelf above the door and checked the window. Peter had scraped away the putty from the central pane of glass and replaced the pane so anybody could remove it easily.

"Oh, you clever boy," Smith said, smiling. His respect for Peter increased rather than decreased. Peter's life experience had taught him to trust nobody, and yet he still tried to help Madge.

"I'll have that fixed today," he told Bess as he returned to the bedroom. "But what are we going to do with young Madge?"

"We're going to look after her," Bess said. "These bastards murdered Peter. Now we have one of his friends." She lifted her chin. "I'm not sending her out there, John."

"Dear God, woman." Smith shook his head as they slid back into bed. "We can't take in every waif and stray in London!"

"We're not taking in every waif and stray," Bess denied. "We tried to help Peter and left him to the wolves. We won't make the same mistake with young Madge."

Smith sighed and settled back in bed, although he knew he would not sleep. "Do what you like, Bess. You usually do, anyway." *I can organise smuggling trips, rob coaches and run multi-ship companies, but I can't control one woman.* He smiled. *Do I want to control her? No, of course now; if Bess were controllable, she'd be a different woman, and I don't want a different woman.*

MR JAY SAT WITH HIS BACK TO THE WINDOW, SILHOUETTED against the panes of glass. "I'll need you again," he said.

The two ex-soldiers and Edward Hind nodded. "Just say the word, Mr Jay, and pay the money." Hind slid a pack of cards from his pocket.

"I want somebody killed," Mr Jay said.

The ex-soldiers nodded without emotion. "That was our trade," the taller said casually.

Hind began to shuffle his cards. He placed three face-down on the circular table. "Pick a card," he invited.

Mr Jay leaned forward and touched the middle card, which the murderer turned over. "Ace of spades," he said. "Somebody will die."

"That's what I intend," Mr Jay said. "Who will do the deed?"

Hind reshuffled the pack, spread them in a fan and asked his companions to select a card.

"Don't look at it," Hind said. "Place it face down on the table in front of you."

The grenadiers did as Hind requested.

"Now you, Mr Jay. Pick a card."

When Mr Jay did so, Hind took the card and laid it before him, face down. He glanced at Mr Jay, who watched without comment.

"Whoever has drawn the highest card does the killing," Hind said and flicked his card face up. "Eight of Hearts."

The taller of the grenadiers smiled and turned his card. "Six of diamonds."

The remaining grenadier flicked over his card. "Queen of spades," he said without any emotion. The job is mine."

Mr Jay nodded. "I'll tell you what to do when I have more details."

The grenadier passed back his card. "You know where I am, Mr Jay, and how much you can pay me for the job."

Mr Jay nodded. "You may go, gentlemen." He waited until they left the public house before joining Kate at the darkest corner of the room. "We're making progress, Kate."

"Slow but steady," Kate said, "slow but steady."

Chapter Twenty-Six

"Well now, young Madge," Bess said, "I taught Peter to read and write, and I'll do the same with you."

Madge looked up. Scrubbed clean and dressed in the youngest maid's cast-offs, she looked nearly respectable except for her bleak eyes.

"What if I don't want to read and write?"

"Then you and I will have a falling-out," Bess said, "and neither of us wants that." She produced the books she had used with Peter and laid a rag doll on the table. "We'll start with the alphabet."

"What's that?" Madge asked.

"What's the alphabet?" Bess said.

"No." Madge pointed to the doll. "What's that for?"

"Oh, that," Bess said. "That's what good girls get when they learn their ABC."

"ABC," Madge said and reached for the doll.

"That's a start," Bess said. "You'll get her when you learn the whole alphabet." She began work with Madge's eyes fixed on the doll.

"WE NEED TO ACT!" LORD GEORGE GORDON STOOD IN FRONT of the crowd with both hands lifted. "We cannot allow the Catholics equality in our country when our entire constitution is founded on the Protestant succession!"

"No Papes!" a man in the crowd roared. "No Popery in England!"

The mob cheered, waving their fists in the air. "No Popery!" they chanted. "No Popery!"

"We must fight this assault on our Protestant liberty!" Gordon continued. "The government seeks to allow Catholics to buy land and even join the army!" He lowered his voice. "Could you trust a Catholic to fight against their co-religionists in France or Spain?"

"No!" the crowd yelled.

"Do you want the Spanish Inquisition in Great Britain?"

Standing at the back of the hall, Smith saw Jack Redpath, the Bow Street Runner, a few yards away, with his hat pulled low over his face.

"I didn't expect to see you here, Mr Smith," Redpath murmured.

"Nor did I expect to see you, Mr Redpath," Smith said. "Are you here officially or as an ardent Protestant?"

Redpath pushed back his hat. "I could be both," he replied, smiling.

"You could be the King of France, but you're not," Smith said. "Are you here as a Runner or for yourself?"

"For myself." Redpath failed to hold Smith's gaze.

Smith nodded. "I didn't know you were a dedicated Protestant."

They were silent for a few moments as Gordon continued his speech, extolling the advantages of the Protestant succession and the dangers of allowing Catholics any influence in Great Britain.

"I am, and I don't trust the French," Redpath said. "We have the most liberty and the fairest system of any country in the world. The Papist countries, Spain, France, and the like, all suffer under the dictatorial Pope and autocratic kings. Only Protestantism can offer true freedom."

Smith studied the Runner, decided he was genuine, and nodded. "We are of a similar mind," he said, probing to see how deep Redpath's beliefs descended. "My concern is also France," Smith said in another brief silence. "As Lord George said, if we allow Roman Catholics to have influence in Great Britain, they might support their French co-religionists in the next war."

"Will there be another war with France?" Redpath asked.

"Any time now," Smith told him. "They are already allowing American privateers access to their ports. All it needs is a glimmer of a victory for the rebels, and the French will be screaming about liberty and stabbing us in the back. Mark my words, Redpath, we'll be fighting France soon, and then Spain will declare war, and all the Powers will line up against us."

Redpath nodded. "I trust the Papes even less now, Smith. The ones who are open about their faith are bad enough, but some attempt to hide it and move freely among us."

Smith grunted. "We'll have to watch our backs, Redpath." He joined in a cheer for something Gordon had said. "There are already Roman Catholics hiding amongst us."

Redpath frowned. "Do you know of any in your line of work, Mr Smith?"

"I believe I do," Smith said.

"Who?" Redpath was instantly alert.

"I'll need proof before I accuse anybody," Smith said.

"Let me know if you find any," Redpath said.

"I will," Smith promised. Touching the rim of his hat with his forefinger, he slipped from the hall.

"SIR!" JUDD OPENED THE DOOR A CRACK AND PEERED IN.

"Come in, Mr Judd," Smith invited.

"Thank you, sir." Judd stepped inside the study.

"What is it, Mr Judd?" Smith put down his pen.

"I saw somebody else buying shares in your ships, sir."

"Who did you see?" Smith asked.

"Mr Bancroft, sir," Judd said. "He was in New Jonathan's Coffee House, asking to buy your shares.

"Did he see you?"

"I am only a clerk, sir," Judd said. "Nobody notices a clerk, even in a coffee house."

Smith grunted. Judd was correct. Judd was present in most of the partners' meetings, and nobody spared him a glance. He remained at the side of the room at his desk, with his quill scratching notes from beginning to end, quietly efficient and completely ignored. Smith recalled attending other meetings where clerks had been present, silent and invisible. He would not recognise any of them five minutes after the meeting.

"I see," Smith said. "You are correct; nobody notices a clerk. You are the most dependable of men, Mr Judd, underpaid and undervalued."

"Thank you, sir," Judd said. "Mr Jackson was also there. I have already informed Mrs Smith about Mr Jackson."

"Mrs Smith passed the message along," Smith said. Lifting his pen, he scribbled both names. "Thank you, Mr Judd. Is there anything else?"

"Yes, sir," Judd said. "I managed to buy three shares in *London's Capital*. You are now the sole owner."

"Thank you, Mr Judd. You are a very useful fellow." Smith favoured his secretary with a smile. "Please continue with the good work."

Judd bowed and withdrew, leaving Smith to reread the two names he had written down. Jackson and Bancroft.

I'll speak to James Bancroft next time we meet, Smith told himself. *Jackson? He always seems the unhappiest of men. Perhaps I should invite him for lunch and see what his plans are with my company. I am sure Bess will tease the truth out of him.*

KATE TAPPED ON THE DOOR BEFORE ENTERING AND SMILED AS she saw Mr Jay waiting for her.

"It's all going according to plan, Mr Jay," Kate said, striding into the hallway with the crystal chandelier swinging above her head.

Mr Jay nodded. "It's been a long haul, Kate, but we can see the light at the end of the tunnel."

Kate followed him under an arched doorway and into a room with plain oak panels and an oaken table with four chairs.

"We now own shares in two-thirds of Smith's ships." Mr Jay slid a leather-bound journal across the table. "But he's been busy buying as well. He has full ownership over the rest and has increased his shares in others."

"Does he suspect anything?" Kate asked.

"Maybe," Mr Jay admitted, "but we have the advantage. We've got Jenks standing by to kill him."

Kate smiled and handed over a small bundle of papers tied with a strip of white linen. "There are Shapland's latest ventures."

Mr Jay unfastened the linen and read the documents one by one. "His American ventures are not doing well," he said.

"That American privateer, Abraham Hargreaves, captured half a dozen of his ships a couple of months ago," Kate reminded. "I think Smith was involved."

"I wouldn't be surprised." Mr Jay took notes from Shapland's documents. "Smith has his grubby fingers in every pie."

"How long until we act, Mr Jay?" Kate asked.

"Not long now, Mrs Kay," Mr Jay said. He wrapped the tape around Shapland's documents and passed it back to Kate. "Then we'll control both Shapland's company and Smith's!"

"I want Smith dead," Kate reminded.

"You'll get your wish," Mr Jay promised.

"Have we heard from Leah Lightfoot yet, Bess?" Smith asked, returning from his morning walk, and striding into the study.

Bess looked up from her desk. "I have some news about that woman, John, but it's not what we want to hear. I fear that she deceived us both."

Smith sat at his desk, rang for a servant, and asked for a pot of coffee and two cups. "Tell me more, Bess."

"Leah told us she had three dependent children," Bess said. "That was not true. When Leah's first husband died, she had three children, but they died of a fever that same winter."

Smith tapped his fingers on the desk. "She has no children, then. That's discouraging," he said. "Why lie to us?"

"I don't know," Bess said. "It's a bit worrying. We're normally so careful, John, and we misjudged her."

Smith stood up restlessly, stepped to the window and watched the traffic in Leicester Square. "I wonder what our Leah is playing at. Try and find out, will you, Bess?"

"I'll do my best," Bess promised, "but I fear we've lost her. Perhaps Shapland has inveigled her to his side."

Smith broke off a fingernail-sized chunk of tobacco and thumbed half into the bowl of his pipe. "Perhaps he has," he mused, watching a tradesman's cart pass the house. "God, Bess, I'm sick of London and its traffic, stinks, and intrigue. Life was so much cleaner down at the coast."

Bess nodded. "I know you miss Kent. When we've finished our business here, John, we'll return to the Spike, at least for a few weeks."

"I might not want to come back to London," Smith told her. "I miss the sea air and the sound of the surf, the smell of the morning and," he stopped. "Sorry, Bess. On another matter," he said. "I was talking to Redpath the Runner the other day, and he is an ardent member of Gordon's Protestant Association."

"Does that interest us?" Bess asked.

"It could do," Smith said. "Redpath is concerned there may be Roman Catholics hiding in the business community."

Bess's slow smile caused her scar to writhe across her cheek. "What would he do if he found such a dangerous man?"

"I do not know," Smith said. "But wouldn't it be interesting to find out?"

Bess leaned back in her chair, immediately understanding. "You're an evil man, John Smith!"

"I've been called worse," Smith said. "I haven't given up on Leah yet, Bess, but I have another iron ready for the fire."

Bess looked up. "You mean you're going ahead with this crazy idea of standing for parliament?"

"Yes," Smith said, smiling, "in a few weeks, you could be married to a member of parliament."

Chapter Twenty-Seven

"Are you sure you want to be an MP?" Bess asked. "I remember you saying once that you wanted to be Lord Mayor of London."

Smith began to pace the room, his head busy with half-a-dozen ideas simultaneously. "It was something Gordon said," he explained. "If an eccentric like him can be a member of parliament, surely I can too. And then I heard that the old MP for Appleby had died and thought I should try for the seat."

Bess grunted. "What do you know about politics?"

"Not much," Smith admitted. "I asked Gordon his advice." He remembered the conversation, with Lord George Gordon shaking his head.

"I'm damned if I know, Smith," Gordon said, taking a pinch of snuff and sneezing. "As I told you, my constituency is in my pocket. I didn't have to fight for it. All I recommend is to wear a stiff hat and carry a stout cane on voting day."

Smith nodded. "I've heard that elections can get a little rowdy," Smith said.

"Rowdy is one word, Smith." Gordon put his snuffbox away. "A damned riot is another. I hope you have a bodyguard, for these Tories are a vicious bunch, up to all the tricks to stay in power."

"I'll be careful," Smith said.

Bess smiled at Smith's anecdote. "You've been a sailor, smuggler, highwayman, and merchant. Why not try your hand at a different type of skulduggery?"

"That's exactly what politics is," Smith said.

Bess shook her head. "One minute you want to retire to Kent, the next you wish to be an MP, where the corruption and backstabbing are worse than the business sector. Are you sure?"

Smith nodded. "As an MP, I will be able to influence matters."

"As you wish, John. Now, we don't have much time to make the arrangements. We'll need posters and advertisements, hustings and long tables, and a pile of food and drink."

Smith nodded. "Have you thought about this already?"

"Yes, I've been making lists ever since you mentioned the stupid idea." Bess opened a drawer of her desk and produced a large sheet of paper. "Here we are, John, listen carefully and only stop me if you think of something else."

SIR GEORGE DANSKIN ERECTED HIS HUSTINGS AT THE NORTH end of Appleby's Market Square, with Smith directly opposite at the south end. They draped party colours over the raw timber framework, buff for the Whigs and blue for the Tories, and stood to address the slowly gathering crowd.

"You all know me!" Danskin shouted, proud in his fine blue suit. "I have lived in this part of Kent all my life." He raised his hands and his voice. "My family has been part of the county for centuries. My blood and bone have created Kent's prosperity and fought for the true liberty of free-born Englishmen!"

The Tory-supporting section of the crowd cheered, waving

their hands, or pumping their fists while the Whig half booed, hissed, or stood in sullen silence.

"The authorities may call me Lord Fitzwarren," Smith countered, with his buff coat and breeches so new they crackled when he walked, "but I am plain John Smith, a man of the people, from the people and for the people!" He heard a ripple of applause and laughter. Many of the inhabitants of Appleby guessed at Smith's history of smuggling, and some suspected he had been a knight of the High Toby, a Highwayman. More importantly, they knew he kept the rents low and his tenants' houses in good repair and respected him for both.

"Vote for the local man!" Danskin roared, "A man born and bred within five miles of this village!" He ducked as somebody threw a half-chewed apple at him.

"Vote for me!" Smith shouted. "The man who saved your Common from being enclosed! The man with your interests at heart!"

"Bloody incomer!" a woman screamed. "Get back to Kingsgate!" She threw an egg, which splattered against the hustings.

"Nobody told me politics could be such fun," Smith said, grinning at the seething mob below him.

"The day is only beginning." Bess gripped the railing and forced a smile. "I feel we're here as targets for anybody with a grudge."

"It's the only real opportunity people have to strike back at the lawmakers that control their lives," Smith said. "I see their point."

Bancroft mounted the steps two at a time and shook Smith's hand. "Thought I'd join you, Smith. Good luck, old fellow!"

With the initial short speeches completed, the rival bands of each candidate marched around the square, blowing lustily on their instruments, and banging their drums to wake any potential voters still abed. Despite the early hour, many men and some women had already started the day's drinking.

"They're drinking well," Bess said.

"We have the advantage there," Smith agreed. "I've laid on sufficient rum, beer and ale to float a seventy-four!"

"That ought to convince the voters you are a suitable candidate for parliament," Bess agreed. She grinned. "I have another idea." Before Smith could prevent her, Bess ran to the foot of the wooden steps.

"Two kisses for one vote!" she shouted. "I will give a kiss to any householder who promises to vote for John Smith and another after he has voted!"

When two men came forward, Bess kissed both, linked arms and accompanied them to the voting booth to the cheers of the Whig section of the crowd. She returned a moment later, smiling.

"That's two votes secured," she said. "Let's see how many more I can pucker for you."

Beside the hustings, both candidates had erected long tables resplendent with food and drink. In theory, Smith's supporters would enjoy a feast at Smith's expense, but in practice, the crowds tended to eat at their rival's table.

"That's a strange system." Bess edged closer to Smith, watching the growing crowd.

Bancroft stood slightly further back, safer from any stray missiles. "It's quite clever," he explained. "The Tories eat at the Whig table and the Whigs at the Tory table, each tribe hoping to bankrupt their rival by eating them out of hall and home."

Bess nodded. "So the less we spend on food, the greater our chances of success."

"That's the idea," Bancroft agreed. He lifted a silver hip flask. "I've brought my own," he said. "I thought I'd save you a few coppers."

"That was thoughtful of you," Smith said.

As the daylight grew, the crowd in the square increased. Smith watched the numbers eating at his table and compared them to those gathered at Danskin's.

"We've got more customers," Smith said anxiously.

"It's early yet," Bess reassured him. "It's more important to watch the men voting than those eating." She touched the sheet of paper in front of her. "There's my estimated figures so far."

Smith glanced at the list. "How do you know who they're voting for?"

"Some wear their colours," Bess said, "and others, I only guessed; they looked like a Tory or a Whig."

"What does a Tory look like?" Smith asked.

Bess laughed. "Nothing like you, John."

A rising wind rustled the ribbons that adorned the voting booth situated midway between the rival hustings. Danskin and Smith had agreed on alternative ribbons of buff and blue to decorate the booth and the square, with both watching jealously as a team of workmen erected the colours.

"Look who's turned up." Bess nodded to the Tories' hustings. "That's Anthony Jackson talking to Danskin, isn't it?"

"It is," Smith agreed. "He seems to arrive at many of our events. He was at the carriage race as well, I remember."

"He was," Bess said. "And at Bancroft's birthday party." She stamped her feet on the plank floor, one-two. "That was the day somebody sawed through *Quicksilver's* axle."

"Yes," Smith said and repeated himself. "Yes, indeed, and Mr Jackson is always keen to reject my ideas."

"Which Shapland later accepts," Bess completed Smith's line of thought. "I'd keep my eye on Anthony Jackson," she said. "Judd warned me about him."

Smith nodded. "Judd told me Jackson's been buying up shares in our ships, too."

Bess nudged him as a group of men approached, all wearing buff waistcoats and sashes.

"Best of British luck, Lord Fitzwarren!" one portly farmer shouted.

Smith waved, leaned over the rail and shook the man's hand, with others hurrying to greet him.

"You're in demand, John," Bess murmured.

Bancroft stepped away. "I'll leave you with your supporters, Smith," he said and vanished in the crowd.

Smith spent the two hours talking to his supporters, laughing at their jokes, shaking a sympathetic head at their misfortunes and dodging the occasional missile from disaffected Tories. The Whigs and Tories, neighbours in the same village and with the same lifestyle and problems, glowered at each other like lifetime enemies, with fistfights breaking out from time to time.

By the middle of the afternoon, Smith and Bess were alone on the hustings as the crowd became more concerned about eating and especially drinking rather than greeting their prospective parliamentary candidates.

"When do we hear the result?" Smith asked.

Bess laughed. "Did you not learn anything before the election, John? We'll hear as soon as the votes are counted."

"When will that be?"

Bess nodded toward the voting booth where an elderly man hobbled forward, helped by two of Smith's servants. "I think that's the last of the voters now."

"Old Charlie Green," Smith said. "He's making no secret of his allegiance."

Charlie Green wore a knitted buff comforter with buff ribbons tied around both knees. He stopped at the top of the stairs that led to the voting booth, lifted a pewter mug of ale and croaked, "Three cheers and a bumper for Mr Smith! Lord Fitzwarren for parliament!"

The crowd cheered and booed in equal measure, with one man throwing an empty bottle that spiralled through the air before missing Green by two feet.

"That's a reduction in Old Charlie's rent," Smith said.

Bess grinned. "I'd agree with that!"

The buff section of the crowd surged forward to seek revenge for the thrown bottle, and the blue-wearing half retaliated by pushing at them, punching and kicking wildly.

"It's getting a little fractious," Bess said, smiling. "Here's Bancroft again, always in the thick of things!"

"Maybe it's time we left?" Bancroft suggested, ducking a thrown turnip, as Danskin urged his supporters to greater efforts.

"Not yet," Bess said. "It's just beginning to be interesting! Let's see how it turns out!"

The mayor of Appleby, a short-sighted, plump but astute merchant, had the unenviable task of announcing the winner. Half an hour after Old Charlie limped away, the mayor disappeared inside the booth, to emerge five minutes later.

"Here's the mayor with the results, John." Bess turned her attention away from the battling crowd.

"Gentlemen!" the mayor shouted, trying to make his voice heard above the growing clamour. "I have the results of the vote!"

"What's he saying?" Bess asked, cupping her hand around her right ear.

"He has the results," Bancroft told her. "We'll know in a minute if the fellow learns how to shout."

"I can't hear a blasted word in this racket," Smith said. "Come on, Bess. You too, Bancroft!" Mounting his horse, he pushed through the crowd with Bess at his back. On the opposite side of the square, Danskin was also heading to the voting booth.

As the crowd ignored the result and happily fought each other, Smith and Danskin mounted the steps to approach the mayor.

"Who won?" Smith and Danskin asked together.

"Were you not listening?" the mayor asked. "I announced the winner three minutes ago."

"We could not hear for the riot," Smith explained.

"Lord Fitzgibbons gained seventy-six votes and Sir George Danskin thirty-five, so Lord Fitzgibbon won by twenty-two votes," the mayor said. "Congratulations, My Lord. You are the new Member of Parliament for Appleby."

Smith held out his hand to Danskin, who immediately took it. "Congratulations, my Lord," Danskin said.

"Smith will do, Danskin," Smith said.

"Congratulations, Smith," Danskin amended. "Now that nonsense is behind us," he said. "I hope you and your lady wife can join us tomorrow evening. We were having a celebratory ball, but now it will be a congratulatory ball."

"We'd be delighted to attend." Smith had not arranged any such gathering. "Thank you, Danskin."

"Shall we say seven o'clock?" Danskin said. "We'll see you then."

Bess arrived at Smith's side and replied to Danskin's bow with a stiff curtsey. "Come on, John! The people want you!"

"Why?" Smith asked. "I was going down to the Spike."

"Your constituents want to see you!" Bess explained.

While the riot calmed down, a large section of the Whig supporters had brought up a large, ornately carved armchair decorated in buff ribbons.

"What am I meant to do with a chair?" Smith said, in an interlude between shaking hands and accepting kisses from an array of women of all ages from sixty to sixteen.

"You're meant to sit in it," Bess said.

"Why?" Smith asked. "I was going to get some work done tonight."

"Not tonight, you won't," Bess told him. "You have constituents to woo."

"But I've already won!" Smith's idea of politics was simple; gain the people's votes, then retire to parliament.

"Come on, John! Up you get!"

Smith obeyed, climbing into their and hanging on grimly as his supporters lifted him shoulder high and carried him through the town.

While the Whig supporters cheered, the Tories jeered and

catcalled, but none refused the beer Bess ordered distributed to every willing hand.

"Keep the people happy," Bess commanded. "It was bread and circuses in Rome; well, in Kent, it's beer, bread and cheese!"

"Take us right around Appleby, lads!" Smith ordered from his perch. "If I must endure this nonsense, I'll do it properly. Let's see the town I represent in parliament!"

The Whig supporters cheered and cheered again when Bess gave each man another tankard of ale.

"Where's Big Tom?"

"Here I am, Mrs Smith!" Big Tom was a diminutive man with a ready grin and blond hair he wore in a long queue halfway down his back.

"You'll find two barrels of ale and a keg of rum under the hustings, Tom," Bess said. "Load them onto your cart and follow us around the town."

"I'll do that right willingly, Mrs Smith!" Tom said, knuckling his forehead and grinning. He vanished into the mass and reappeared ten minutes later with his cart.

"Well done, Tom," Bess said and raised her voice to a shout. "Free ale, boys and girls! Free ale to celebrate John Smith, MP for Appleby! You're welcome too, Tories; drink away your sorrows!"

Smith looked over the multitude of heads. Some had wigs, some sported queues, many had hats, and a few were grey with age. The faces were smiling and animated as if Smith's success would affect them personally.

"Round the town, boys!" Smith ordered and waved to his constituents. He knew that most did not care who the Member of Parliament was and only came for the free drink and the chance of some excitement.

The crack was distinct above the hubbub, instantly recognisable as a rifle shot. Smith ducked instinctively as the bullet punched a neat hole in the back of the chair level with his head.

"John!" Bess shouted, whirling around.

The crowd continued, oblivious to the attempted murder.

One man was blowing a hunting horn while a group of women danced in a circle, skirts held above their knees as they kicked their legs high.

"Put me down," Smith roared. "Put the chair down!"

"Why?" Bancroft asked, lifting a tankard in celebration. "We're only halfway across the town."

"Dear God, I'm a sitting target here!" Smith tried to struggle free, but his carriers were too eager to prove their loyalty and increased their speed to a jog. He looked around, searching for the source of the shot. "Put me down, boys!"

"Smith!" Bancroft sounded alarmed. "What's the matter? You look agitated!"

The carriers realised that something was wrong and hurriedly lowered the chair.

"What's the to-do, Mr Smith? We're just getting started!"

Perhaps because he had expected it, Smith heard the rifle report again, and this time he saw the revealing puff of smoke from an upper window in a house across the market square. The shot whined high above his head.

"Over there!" Jack threw himself off the chair, to the consternation of his supporters. He felt for his pistol, swore when he realised he had come unarmed, and pushed through his constituents, trusting his luck to protect him. "Somebody's shooting at me!"

"John!" Bess abandoned the cart, lifted her skirt above her ankles and hurried to join him, leaving the crowd wondering what was happening.

"With you, Smith!" Bancroft said cheerfully. He pulled a large pistol from beside his saddle and handed it over. "Here you are. I have another."

Smith thanked him with a nod. "Make way!" he shouted, parting the crowd. "I'm coming through!"

The gun smoke had partially cleared when Smith arrived at the address, a substantial, brick-built two-story house with a thatched roof. Without hesitation, he threw open the door, brushed aside the decorative blue ribbons and plunged inside to find himself in a shoemaker's workshop.

"What's the to do?" An elderly man looked up from working at a shoemaker's last.

"Who's upstairs?" Smith asked, presenting his pistol.

"What's that?" The man put a hand to his ear. "Who are you? What's happening?"

Realising the cobbler was deaf, Jack strode to the wooden staircase, with Bancroft a few steps behind and Bess making up the rear. He took the steps two at a time and arrived at a small landing with three closed doors. Choosing the door that should open to a front room, Smith lifted his boot, poised, and kicked the door open. He flinched as the rifle fired again, with the bullet tearing a hole in the skirt of his coat.

"My new jacket!" Smith roared. He lunged inside the room as the shooter dropped the rifle and scrambled out of the window.

The man was tall, with broad shoulders and dark hair tied back in a neat queue.

"I'll get him!" Bancroft shouted and aimed his pistol.

"No!" Jack shouted. "I want to question him!" Thrusting the pistol through his waistband, he followed out the window, regretting his past sedentary years of good food and soft living. The shooter was surprisingly active for a large man and scrambled onto the roof, holding onto the thatch as he hauled himself to the apex. Smith was aware of the crowd watching, with people pointing and some shouting, although the words were lost. He realised a slight rain had begun, making the thatch slippery.

"Stop that man!" Smith roared, knowing he was wasting his breath. He turned with difficulty, grasped the thatch, and dragged himself up, feeling the straw brittle under his hands. His quarry was faster, scrambling along the roof as if he was used to such endeavours.

"Stop!" Smith shouted again. The shooter did not look back but leapt onto the adjacent roof and sped away.

"I'll get him, Smith!" Bancroft overtook Smith and strode ahead.

"I want him alive," Smith shouted, but Bancroft was already five yards in front and moving quickly. Smith swore, slipped, recovered, and continued, ignoring the gasps and shouts from the watching crowd below.

"That's His Lordship!" somebody yelled. "What's he doing?"

"He's chasing these two men!"

A man threw a bottle, which spiralled upward and narrowly missed Bancroft.

"Not him!" Smith roared. "The man in front!"

More missiles followed, with most falling short as Smith increased his speed to catch up with Bancroft and the shooter.

Bancroft was ten yards ahead and gaining on the fugitive, who stopped to glance over his shoulder. For the first time, Smith saw the shooter's face. He was no youngster but a mature man with features that had experienced great hardship. He hesitated when he saw Bancroft, raised a hand, and shouted something.

Bancroft yelled an obscene insult, raised his pistol, and fired. The shot was loud, with a puff of grey-white smoke. The shooter staggered backwards as the bullet caught him high in the chest.

Smith saw the shooter's mouth move, and Bancroft fired his second barrel, knocking the man from the roof. He landed on the ground and lay still.

Chapter Twenty-Eight

"**D**amn it!" Smith shouted. "I wanted him alive, Bancroft! I wanted to find out who he was and why he tried to kill me!"

Bancroft looked around with rain streaming from his face. "He was getting away, Smith!" He swarmed down the side of the house and bent over the body. "He's dead now."

A dozen people swarmed around the body before Smith climbed to the street.

"Here's your reason, Mr Smith." Bancroft held up a blue sash loosely wound around the man's chest. "He's a Tory. He must have been disappointed that a Whig won the seat."

Smith lifted the sash. "Maybe so," he said. "Maybe so. All the same, I'd like to have spoken to the man." He stepped away, noticing Judd standing beside Anthony Jackson at the fringe of the crowd. Judd frowned and shook his head as though trying to convey a message.

"Bring the body into the garret from where he fired," Smith ordered.

"You're a Member of Parliament now," Bancroft reminded. "Should you get involved in such sordid matters?"

"You're damned right I should!" Smith snapped. "I want to find out who tried to kill me."

"Come on," Bess ordered as four of Smith's constituents lifted the would-be assassin's body and carried it down the street. The crowd watched, with some pushing forward for a better view and some turning away. One woman closed her eyes while the parish vicar, Reverend Tyler, stepped forward with his Bible.

"May I accompany you?" Tyler asked.

"You are always welcome, Reverend," Smith told him.

The four bearers dragged the shooter's body carelessly up the stairs to the garret and dumped it on the floor.

"I'll examine him in a minute," Smith said as Tyler prayed over the corpse. "I want to see his weapon first." He lifted the rifle. "A Pennsylvania rifle," he said, pulling back the hammer to inspect the lock. "They're not common."

Bess nodded. "Very uncommon in England," she said. "And very expensive. It shouldn't be too hard to trace its provenance."

Smith examined the rifle. "It takes a good shot to fire one of these rifles," he said. "An American frontiersman, perhaps, or a soldier who had fought in the Americas." He handed the rifle to Bess. "Let's see the body."

Tyler stepped back, holding his Bible as Smith stooped over the dead man. Ignoring the congealed blood where Bancroft's bullets had hit, he stared at the shooter's face. "Well, my fine fellow, why did you try to kill me?"

"John." Bess pointed to the man's wrist. "He has a tattoo."

"He has," Smith said. "Help me take his coat off." He pulled the shooter upright as Bess dragged off his coat and ripped his sleeve. The number twenty-eight was tattooed in faded blue, with crossed muskets above.

"28th Foot," Smith said. "I'm sure they fought in the Americas, and by the size of this fellow, he'd be a grenadier."

"That explains how he learned to fire a rifle," Bess said, "but not where he obtained it. I doubt he carried it across the Atlantic." She lifted the weapon. "I'll see what I can find."

Smith searched the body. "No identification," he said. "I doubt we'll ever know who he was."

"A stray Tory." Bancroft had been a quiet spectator. "Military men are often Tory, especially in wartime."

"You may have saved John's life, James," Bess said.

Bancroft looked down at the dead man. "Maybe," he agreed. "It would be a shame for somebody to shoot your husband so soon after his success." He faced Smith with a grin. "May I offer you my congratulations, my Lord? My Lord and Member of Parliament, now!" He held out his hand.

"Thank you, Bancroft." Smith shook the proffered hand.

Tyler approached Smith. "I think you should thank the Lord for delivering you, Mr Smith."

"I am not sure the Lord would want me," Smith said.

Tyler lifted his Bible. "We are all sinners, Mr Smith, and God's arms are open when you repent."

"Thank you, Reverend," Smith said. He saw Judd waiting patiently, stepping back whenever somebody entered or left the room.

"Oh, well, Smith, if you have no more attempted assassins for me to dispose of, I'll be on my way." Bancroft glanced at Tyler, lowered his voice, and winked. "I have a woman to meet, Smith."

"I won't hold you back," Smith promised. "Thank you for your support, Bancroft."

Only when Bancroft sauntered away did Judd approach Smith.

"Congratulations on your victory, sir," Judd said. "And congratulations on escaping the murderer."

"Thank you, Mr Judd," Smith replied solemnly.

"Sir," Judd said and cleared his throat. "When that man fell, I swear he wasn't wearing any colour of sash. I saw the whole thing."

Bess gave Judd a sidelong look. "Are you sure, Frederick?"

"Yes, Mrs Smith. "I was moving towards the houses, wondering if I could help, and I saw the man running across the rooftops, with Mr Bancroft and Mr Smith following. The man turned to say something, and Mr Bancroft shot him, and then shot again."

"He turned to say something?" Bess repeated.

"Yes, ma'am. Mr Smith was trying not to fall at the time. The man shouted something just before Mr Bancroft shot him."

"Did you hear what he shouted?" Bess asked.

"I am not sure, ma'am, but it sounded like Mr Jay."

"Mr Jay?" Smith repeated the words.

"He was not wearing a sash when he fell," Judd said. "I have an eye for details, sir. I have to in my position, and I can say with absolute certainty he wore only his dark trousers, linen shirt, and dark jacket." Judd looked away for a moment. "I can still see him falling, with his arms flapping and mouth open."

"Is that the first violent death you have seen?" Smith asked.

"Yes, sir. I'm a clerk, not a soldier."

"What happened next, Frederick?" Bess asked, touching his arm. "How did he get the sash?"

"A whole crowd of people got to his body before me," Judd said. "I don't know most of them, but I saw Mr Jackson."

"Anthony Jackson?" Bess asked, with a glance at Smith.

"Yes, Mrs Smith, Mr Anthony Jackson; he owns shares in some of Mr Smith's ships. He was one of the first to arrive, and then Mr Bancroft nearly jumped from the roof. When I saw Mr Smith was unhurt, I wanted to see who tried to kill him, and the sash had appeared."

"Why the devil would somebody put a blue sash on a dead body?" Bess asked.

"As a distraction," Smith replied immediately. "Somebody wanted us to think this fellow," he pointed to the dead body," had a political motive."

Bess nodded. "That could be so."

"Now there will be an enquiry, and the local magistrate will make a ruling," Smith continued.

"Who is the local magistrate? Is it you?" Bess raised her eyebrows.

"No, it's Danskin," Smith said. "My erstwhile opponent. He's a good man, whatever his politics, and he'll make a fair ruling."

Bess looked out of the window. "Your supporters are waiting for you, John. An attempted murder and a chase over the rooftops have not diminished their enthusiasm."

"It's all in the day's work for a politician," Smith said. "Come on, Bess. Let's greet my constituents." He nodded to Judd. "Thank you for your information, Mr Judd. I'll see you back at the office tomorrow."

"Yes, sir," Judd said.

Tyler blessed Smith as he left the room. Downstairs, the cobbler continued with his work, ignoring the commotion in his house.

Chapter Twenty-Nine

"You always appear very composed, Leah," Shapland said, smiling. "Are you content in your position?"

They stood in the inner hall, with the marble staircase rising behind them and an array of swords and firearms decorating the wall above a carved oak settle.

"Yes, sir," Leah said with a brief curtsey. "I am very happy in your employ."

"I do wish you would call me Charles." Shapland held out his hand. "We are old friends now, Leah, and there is no need for formality between us."

"It's not fitting that I use your Christian name, sir," Leah said. "I am your wife's companion and maidservant, and you are a great man."

"Come and sit beside me, Leah." Shapland led her into the drawing room and deposited her on an armed chair beside the fire. "I have a confession to make, Leah, and something to tell you."

"Have you, sir?" Leah asked, holding his gaze.

"I have." Shapland pulled his chair closer. "Kate and I were never formally married. She only calls herself Mrs Shapland as a precaution in case other people become inquisitive about our relationship."

"Oh!" Leah covered her mouth at this admittance of scandal. "I had no idea, sir."

"Charles, my dear," Shapland reminded. "Please call me Charles." He put a hand on her thigh.

"Yes, Charles." Leah patted his hand. "Thank you for confiding in me."

"So you see, your idol has feet of clay," Shapland said, smiling. "And you need not concern yourself about becoming friendly. You will not upset my wife, as I have no wife to upset." He broadened his smile. "You see how much I trust you?"

Leah allowed herself a small smile, although her hands twisted together.

"A few moments ago, you called me a great man," Shapland said. "I may be great in business, with a fleet of ships, a grand house and money in the bank, but I am only a man."

"But such a man, Charles," Leah said quietly.

"An unmarried man," Shapland reminded. "And a man needs a companion in this world, somebody in whom he can confide. Somebody he can trust with his innermost thoughts and desires."

"You have Mrs Shapland, my mistress, sir," Leah said, with her hands still wrapped around each other. "I know she is not your wife, but surely still your friend and companion."

"Kate is not what she seems." Shapland looked away. "She is not right for me, Leah. She belongs to a different world, whereas you." He hesitated, sighed, and looked at the fire. "I think you understand me better. You are a good woman, Leah, quiet, undemonstrative, demure; the sort of woman a man like me can marry."

"Marry, Charles?" Leah looked up with her hands suddenly still. "I could never marry a man of your standing! I was only a seaman's wife, and you are a gentleman."

Shapland smiled, shaking his head. "I am only a man, Leah; beneath these fine clothes, I am only a man."

"Yes, sir," Leah said, looking down again and shifting her hips slightly.

Shapland removed his hand from Leah's thigh. "I hope I have not frightened you, Leah, in this public demonstration of my feelings."

"Frightened me? No, sir." Leah shook her head vigorously. "I admit that I am surprised. I have admired you from afar for years, sir, but finding employment in your establishment was the height of my desire." She shook her head. "Oh, sir, Charles, I don't know what to say."

"If you are with me, Leah, you'll never have to worry about money or anything else again," Shapland said. "You will have the run of this house, my other houses, my carriages and everything a woman could desire. What do you say to that, Leah?"

Leah shook her head. "I am not sure what to say, Charles. I am overwhelmed."

Shapland smiled. "Don't be overwhelmed, Leah, be pleased. Would you consider becoming my wife?"

Leah closed her eyes. "Charles, if I were your wife, I would do things to you that no woman has ever done before. I would be the last woman you would ever look at."

Shapland touched her arm. "Leah, I can quite believe that. In return, I will treat you like a queen."

"Queen Leah Shapland." Leah smiled and shook her head. "You'd be my king, Charles." She smiled at him, allowing warmth into her eyes. "I have quite fallen under your spell."

"We might not have to wait until marriage to prove our feelings," Shapland hinted, and Leah's smile broadened further.

"My cup runneth over," she quoted from Psalm Twenty-three and allowed Shapland to kiss her.

"THAT BUSINESS OF THE SASH WAS INTERESTING," BESS SAID AS they prepared for bed.

"It was a little disturbing," Smith said. "I doubt any villagers would carry a spare blue sash, leaving only two possibilities."

"Jackson or Bancroft," Bess agreed. "Then there is the name that the man shouted. Mr Jay."

"Mr Jay," Smith repeated. "That name follows us from the Americas to Appleby."

"That might not be somebody's name." Bess poured water from the ewer into the basin and washed her face and hands. "It might be a false name, a nickname or even his initials."

"We've known for some time that somebody is informing Shapland of our plans," Bess reminded. "We've seen Anthony Jackson on every occasion there has been trouble. He was at the race when somebody cut through your axle, at the meetings where you discussed buying licences for privateers and now at the hustings when somebody attempted to shoot you."

"He was," Smith agreed. "I don't like Jackson, but I never thought he would try to murder me."

Bess dried her face and slid the ewer across to Smith. "Nor did I, and don't forget that Jackson's initial is J," she said. "Mr Jay."

Smith stripped off his shirt to wash. "Judd was also there, and his initial is also Jay."

"Judd?" Bess shook her head. "Frederick Judd told us about the sash and the man shouting Mr Jay." She shook her head. "He'd hardly incriminate himself."

"No, perhaps not." Smith washed hurriedly in lukewarm water. "He's too cautious a man for that."

"Judd has warned us about Jackson more than once," Bess reminded, slipping her nightdress over her head. "And don't forget that Bancroft was also there."

"Bancroft shot the assassin," Smith reminded coldly, "and his initial is B."

Bess sighed. "He did, John, but I was pointing out that Jackson was not alone."

"I know," Smith said. He began to pace the room. "I wonder why Bancroft killed the man when I wanted him alive."

"Perhaps he was excited," Bess slid into bed. "He's not as used to such adventures as you and I."

Smith nodded. "That was probably it. I'm looking for motives where none exist."

"It's your suspicious mind, John." She pulled back the covers. "Come in, and let's celebrate your new status. I've never made love to a Member of Parliament before."

"No?" Smith raised his eyebrows as he peeled off his tight breeches. "Well, I've never made love to an MP's wife, so we'll both have a new experience!"

THE COFFEE SHOP WAS QUIET, WITH ONLY A HANDFUL OF customers in separate booths. Mr Jay sipped at his cup and glowered across the table at Kate.

"That attempt was not successful," Mr Jay was tense. "I wanted Smith killed, and he's still alive."

Kate nodded. "I heard what happened," she said. "I am not pleased."

"Neither am I," Mr Jay said. "We lost a good man there and failed to meet our objective. We'll have to find another method of ridding ourselves of Smith."

Kate leaned back. "We have two killing men left," she said. "We pay them well, and I am not giving up yet." She waited until a man in an old-fashioned wig walked past. "Why do you want Smith dead, Mr Jay?"

"I don't care if he's dead or alive," Mr Jay said. "As long as he's out of the way. I want control of his company, but he's a damned sharp operator."

Kate nodded thoughtfully. "I can get him out of the way," she said. "Maybe I'll settle for sending him to a living hell rather than the real one."

"Tell me more," Mr Jay said and listened as Kate explained. He smiled. "Try that," he said. "If it doesn't work, I'll use Hind and the remaining grenadier."

"I rather like my idea," she said. "I'd like to think of Smith suffering while we take over his business and ships. It may be even better than killing him, and if he does come back, he will find only poverty."

"There's the woman as well," Mr Jay said. "His ugly, scarred wife."

"Bess Webb," Kate said softly. "I'm looking forward to dealing with her." She signalled for more coffee. "When we've disposed of Smith, I have plans for scar-faced Bess. I know an academy off the Highway specialising in freaks and no questions asked."

Mr Jay laughed and lifted his coffee cup. "Here's to a bright future," he said, and Kate smiled into his eyes.

THEY LAY SIDE BY SIDE, WITH THE HUGE MIRROR ON THE FAR wall reflecting the light from a dozen candles and gleaming from the varnished mahogany of the four-poster bed.

"You are even better than I imagined," Shapland said, lying on his back. "I thought Kate was good, but your imagination surpasses anything she could do."

"I have imagined this evening a thousand times." Leah ran her nails down Shapland's smooth back, around his shoulder blades and down the length of his spine.

Shapland shivered. "You are unlike any woman I've been with before," he said.

"Thank you." Leah dashed the tears from her eyes.

"Have I aroused you to tears?" Shapland asked, pleased to see her emotion.

Leah nodded, looking away. "I'm going to be the last woman you ever sleep with," she said. "After me, you'll never have another."

Shapland shifted to lie on his back, smiling at the ornate plasterwork of the ceiling. He thought of the women he had known, a long procession that stretched back to the twelve-year-old chambermaid who had squealed loudly until he slapped her to silence. He thought of the five women he had promised to marry and Kate, the one-time prostitute who had been helpful to his business objectives.

"When you die," Leah said, "the last thing you will think of is my face."

Shapland laughed. "That won't be for some time yet," he said.

"You're wrong," Leah said, pulling a knife from under her pillow. "So very wrong." She plunged the knife into Shapland's stomach. "I told you I'd do things to you that no woman has ever done before," she said as Shapland gave a long, gurgling scream. "Well, Charles, no woman has ever killed you before."

"Leah! Why?" Shapland gagged in agony as Leah began to rip her knife sideways. "Oh, god, why?"

"Why?" Leah twisted the handle to enlarge the wound. "Do you remember a ship called *London's Pride*? She sank in the Atlantic, and you left the survivors to drown."

Shapland began to scream as Leah pulled the blade further down, tearing his intestines.

"One of the men you abandoned was Isaac Blackstone, my husband," Leah explained, twisting the knife and ignoring the blood.

"I didn't know!" Shapland screamed, writhing on the bed.

Leah gave her knife a final twist and pulled it out. "You're going to die, Charles, but not before you suffer." She slid from the bed, watching Shapland's agony and listened to him plead for help.

In her head, Leah was walking hand in hand with Isaac, watching the ships on the Thames and planning their future together. Although she listened to Shapland's desperate screams, she only heard seagulls and the soft ripple of the River Thames.

Kate heard the screaming as she returned early from her shopping trip.

"It's upstairs, ma'am," a terrified servant said. "It started a minute ago."

"Take these into the drawing room!" Kate thrust her purchases at the servant. "Don't come upstairs if you value your situation!" She ran upstairs, pushed two agitated servants out of the way and slammed open the bedroom door.

"What the devil is happening in here?"

Leah was standing beside the bed with a bloody knife in her hand. Beside her, Shapland wriggled, retched, and whined on the sheets with both hands on his stomach. Blood covered his naked body.

"Help me, Kate," Shapland pleaded as blood seeped through his fingers. "She stabbed me!"

"Why did you stab my husband?" Kate asked mildly, eyeing the knife in Leah's hand. "Why are you two naked in my bedroom?"

"We were making love," Leah said. "And I stabbed him."

"Why?" Kate asked, watching Shapland writhe. His eyes were desperate.

"Please," Shapland said. "Please help me!"

"He was responsible for my husband's death," Leah explained.

"Was he indeed." Kate shut the door and sat on her seat. "And now you are responsible for his."

Leah nodded as Shapland's moans grew weaker. He reached out a hand to Kate.

"Don't let me die, Kate."

"Why not?" Kate asked. "You cheated on me with this woman and maybe with others."

"*London's Pride*," Leah hissed, bending over Shapland. "Isaac

Blackstone was the second mate, and you left him to drown." She leaned closer. "You murdered my husband."

Kate waited until Shapland died before attracting Leah's attention. "Leah," she said.

When Leah turned around, Kate dropped the pistol from her sleeve and shot her in the head. Leah fell backwards, smiling.

Isaac? Are you there? Isaac Blackstone was waiting for her in the corner of the room. They left hand-in-hand, drifting through the walls to walk along the banks of the Thames, planning their future.

"Help!" Kate screamed as the acrid gun smoke drifted around the room. "In here!"

The door crashed open, and a press of servants rushed in, staring at the carnage on the bed.

"I tried to save him," Kate sobbed. "I tried to save him, and that woman ran at me with her knife. I had to shoot her!"

"Oh, ma'am," the housekeeper said. "The poor master!"

"Fetch a magistrate," Kate ordered. "For God's sake, fetch a magistrate!"

Chapter Thirty

"Yes," Twigg said from the opposite side of the counter. "I buy and sell firearms as well as make them." In his mid-forties, John Fox Twigg was among London's most celebrated gunsmiths, respected by his peers and sought out by hunters the length and breadth of England. Bess had called into his Piccadilly workshop after a tour of all the gunsmiths in the city.

"Robert Wogdon recommended that I try you, Mr Twigg." Wogdon was one of London's finest pistol makers, and Bess was never averse to name-dropping.

"Robert is rightly famed for his duelling pistols," Twigg informed her. "But perhaps not as well informed in colonial long arms. May I?" He took the rifle from Bess and stroked it almost sensually.

"This is a lovely example of a Pennsylvanian rifle," Twigg said. "You'll note the exceptionally long barrel and the small calibre, which European weapons seldom possess."

"I prefer a blunderbuss," Bess said.

Twigg shook his head disapprovingly. "The blunderbuss is a bludgeon of a weapon, Mrs Smith, while the Pennsylvanian rifle is a rapier." He peered down the barrel. "The rifling, the spiral grooves within the barrel, spins the ball, increasing the stability of its trajectory and improving the accuracy."

"Yes, Mr Twigg," Bess said patiently. "I know the Pennsylvania rifle is a fine weapon, but could you tell me anything about this particular example?"

Twigg sighed and put the rifle on his counter with a last fond stroke of the barrel. "Oh, yes, Mrs Smith, I know it well."

Bess waited for further information. "Could you educate me, Mr Twigg? Could you tell me who owns this piece?" She smiled. "I'd like to return it to its correct owner."

"Goodness me!" Twigg looked alarmed. "Has he mislaid it? Such a careless fellow does not deserve such a fine piece." He held the rifle close as if hugging an infant.

"Do you know the owner, Mr Twigg?" Bess persisted as her patience thinned.

"A gentleman handed it to me to be repaired." Twigg refused to be hurried as he cast a longing look at the rifle. "I'll consult my records." Still holding the weapon, he slipped away and returned within five minutes. "A Mister Jay owns this rifle," he said. "I have his address as "Montjay House, Surrey.""

"Thank you, Mr Twigg," Bess said and held out her hands.

Twigg sighed and relinquished hold of the weapon. "Take good care of her," he said. "Mr Jay does not deserve such a pearl."

"CHARLIE SHAPLAND'S DEATH ALTERS THINGS." KATE GLANCED around Mr Jay's small office overlooking the Ratcliffe Highway. "We can't get rid of Smith so easily now. It would look too suspicious having two of London's leading merchants dying so close together."

Mr Jay nodded. "That woman Leah spoiled our plans, yet she also helped. Scores of Shapland's shares have come onto the open market. I bought a dozen yesterday alone, but Smith and another buyer are equally interested."

"I suspect the rats will be scrabbling to see who is king of the dung heap." Kate swirled the dregs of her coffee around the cup.

"That will be John Smith," Mr Jay said. "Unless he vanishes for a while. If he's out of the way, we can snap up all Shapland's remaining shares and control his empire." He swore softly. "Leah Lightfoot has speeded things up, Kate. What the devil was Shapland doing with her?"

"He was a womaniser who constantly had to prove his manhood," Kate said. "He wasn't even very good in bed." She laughed, with Mr Jay joining in slightly uneasily.

"I won't ask for details." Mr Jay stirred uncomfortably.

"This is a very small office," Kate changed the subject. "But at least you furnished it with quality." She smoothed a hand over the desk. "Pure oak, I see, and with the best writing paper you can buy." She lifted a sheet of paper.

"Alexander Wilkinson's," Mr Jay said. "It's what Shapland used."

"I thought it might be," Kate said. "Once I learn to write, you can stop scribing for me." She smiled. "We'll move to a better location once we dispose of Smith permanently." She crumpled the paper into a ball and threw it across the room. "I know a way of getting Smith out of the reckoning without killing him. I can put him where he can do no harm, and his company will stagnate."

"Where?" Mr Jay asked.

"Leave it to me, Mr Jay," Kate said. When she looked at him, Mr Jay shivered at the cold hatred in his eyes.

SMITH PASSED THE NOTE OVER TO BESS. "SHAPLAND IS DEAD," he said. "Our Leah Lightfoot stabbed him."

"That was not what we intended," Bess replied as they stood in the drawing room. "Who will take over his company?"

"It's open to speculators," Smith said. "Judd brought me the news about Shapland." He poured them both a glass of brandy. "The coffee houses are rife with speculation."

Bess sipped at her brandy. "I expect that's why Leah took the position."

"I expect so," Smith said. "Shapland's stock has slumped already. I've instructed Judd to buy as many shares in his ships as he can when the price falls to its lowest and sent other men to do the same."

"How will Judd know when the price has bottomed out?"

"Judd will know; he's a clever man," Smith said. "Did you find anything with the rifle?"

Bess nodded. "Mister Jay handed it in with an address of Montjay House." She put the glass down. "There is no such place."

"He's given a false address," Smith said. "Probably a false name, too, as we already guessed. We're no further forward."

"We know Mr Jay exists, and he's nearby," Bess said. "That's a start. We also know he's dangerous but not infallible, or you'd be dead."

"That's a comfort," Smith said. "What next, Bess?"

"Next, I'll ask if anybody knows about Pennsylvanian rifles," Bess asked. "Then I'll look for soldiers from the 28th Foot and question them."

"The odds are against you on both these lines of questioning," Smith said.

"I know," Bess told him. "I'll keep pushing and asking questions. We'll offer a reward of fifty guineas for information about this soldier. Somebody, somewhere, will know something, and money attracts the greedy like a magnet."

"You'll have half the beggars and liars in London banging on the door claiming the money and telling you all sorts of nonsense," Smith warned.

"Poor Frederick will have to cope," Bess said, smiling.

"Judd copes with all the administrative jobs," Smith said. "He's becoming more valuable by the day."

"You like him, John," Bess said.

"I do," Smith agreed. "Unfortunately, like most clerks, he lacks imagination. He is the master of ledgers, accounts, and letters, but ask him to do anything outside his routine, and he'll flounder."

Bess sighed. "Poor Frederick Judd. He's such a conscientious man, never late, always polite and accurate, yet destined to spend his life in the employ of others."

"A man has to take a chance to advance in this world," Smith said. "Judd is naturally cautious."

Bess stood up. "I'll get busy with my enquiries," she said.

"Good luck, Bess," Smith said. "I'll expect a host of clutching hands and storytellers."

KATE BRUSHED THE HAIR BACK FROM HER FACE. "WELL, Keith, have I helped you in the past?"

Lieutenant Keith Barrington smiled across the rim of his glass of rum. "You have indeed, Kate. The Admiralty is promoting me into a seagoing command. I'll be a seaman again, not a shore-bound ruffian tearing unfortunate sailors from their wives and families."

Kate knew that career naval officers viewed the Impress Service as a blight on their service record, a place where the old and inefficient officers ended, those with no hope of future advancement.

"Congratulations, Keith." Kate leaned across the table and kissed him on the forehead. "I have one more man for you, a prime seaman with a wealth of experience, a man any captain would welcome to his crew."

Keith nursed his rum. "If that's the case, Kate, why has

nobody already grabbed him? At this stage of the war, prime British seamen are as rare as hen's teeth."

"He pretends to be a gentleman," Kate said. "He dresses, acts and looks like a gentleman, but beneath the fancy clothes, he's a rough-hewed tarpaulin with salt water and Stockholm tar in his veins."

Barrington smiled and intoned the famous lines, "Begotten in the galley and born under a gun, with every hair a rope yarn, every tooth a marline spike, every finger a fishhook, and his blood right good Stockholm tar. Where is this paragon of seamanship?"

"He takes a morning constitutional at six, rain, hail or shine," Kate said. "Always around Leicester Square, down to Westminster Bridge and back through St James's Park."

Barrington smiled. "Then we shall take him in the morning. Don't you like the fellow, Kate?"

"I like him as little as I like the King of France," Kate replied. "And Keith, I have a favour to ask of you."

Barrington chuckled. "You find me a prime seaman, and I'm all yours, Kate."

"Don't make it easy for him," Kate said.

Barrington nodded. "I understand," he said. "What has he done to offend you, my pretty?"

Kate's eyes darkened with memory. "I once was promised in marriage," she said. This fellow Smith ensured the marriage did not take place."

"That was unpleasant of him," Barrington said. "How did he manage that?"

"He caused the death of my intended," Kate said.

"Ah." Barrington tossed back his rum. "I shall ensure he has an uncomfortable voyage, Kate."

"John!" Bess nearly ran into Smith's office in Leadenhall Street.

"You look agitated." Smith looked up from the invoices he was preparing. "What's the matter?"

"This is the matter!" Bess nearly slammed a sheet of paper on the desk.

Smith scanned the document with his quill poised, dripping ink. "What's wrong with it? It looks like a perfectly normal Bill of Lading to me."

"It is a normal Bill of Lading," Bess said, "but look at the writing!"

Smith frowned. "It's Bancroft's," he said and stiffened when Bess thrust another crumpled piece of paper beside the Bill of Lading.

"This is the note we found when we searched Redpath," she grated. "Compare the writing, John!"

"They're the same," Smith said quietly. "What does this mean, Bess? James Bancroft is my most particular friend."

"James Bancroft," Bess emphasised the first name. "James. Mister Jay! We concentrated on the surname and forgot the Christian name."

"Damn the man," Smith said softly as he crushed his pen to fragments. "Damn him to an eternity of hell, the backstabbing, double-dealing, murderous, betraying traitor!"

"Yes." Bess took a deep breath to calm herself down. "It's no wonder Shapland was able to counter all our moves. Bancroft must have told him everything in advance."

Smith felt his hands curling into fists. "Bancroft ordered that man to shoot me. I'll tear his heart from his living body," he promised.

"You could do that," Bess agreed.

"He's cost us thousands of pounds," Smith said. "And he's probably responsible for Peter's death." He saw Bess stiffen at his words.

"Yes, John, have you got the notes from Baltimore?"

Smith grunted and dived into the drawers, swearing before he found a folder. "Here we are," he said.

"Give it to me." Bess unfolded the paper and placed it on the desk. "I thought so," she said. "It's the same writing. Bancroft's." She sat down heavily. "We'll treat the turncoat bastard as he deserves." When she looked up, Smith saw the cold hatred burning in her eyes. "Bancroft posed as a friend and acted against us all the time."

"So it seems," Smith agreed, staring at the writing. "He fooled me completely."

"And me," Bess said. "Madge told us three men grabbed young Peter, with a woman in charge. You think that Bancroft was behind that as well."

"Maybe," Smith struggled for words.

Bess stared at the writing. "I thought of Peter as a son."

Smith nodded. "So did I," he said quietly. "So did I."

Bess shook her head as she pieced the fragments together. "I want to strike back at them, John. We have two enemies, Bancroft and this red-haired woman."

"We have," Smith agreed.

"Bancroft must have sawn through your axle," Bess said. "When we had a birthday party in his honour. William Harmon said he came to admire your chariot." She shook her head. "We trusted that man. I can't believe how stupid we've been. Are you going to confront him?"

"No," Smith said. "If I face him, I'll kill him and swing for murder. I'll hoist him on his own petard. Where's that young friend of yours."

"Madge?" Bess looked alarmed.

"Yes, Madge. I have a job for her." Smith grinned. "It's time she earned her keep."

"Don't put her in danger," Bess warned, "or you'll have me to deal with."

"Madge will be in no danger," Smith assured her. "I'll be with her all the time."

"That's no guarantee," Bess said. "Remember the carriage race? I can't let you out of my sight without you breaking something." She forced a smile. "Be careful, John. I've taken quite a liking to that little girl, and I don't want another Peter."

"Neither do I," Smith assured her earnestly. He did not want Bess to suffer as she did when Peter died.

For that reason, if for no other, he told himself, *I'll ensure that Madge is safe.*

Chapter Thirty-One

S mith swung his cane as he walked, enjoying the warm summer air. London was at its best in the morning, with the criminal element returned to their squalid haunts and the bustle of the day barely begun. Birds sang and flittered among the trees, the sun was pleasant, and the streets showed the glory of the greatest city in the world.

Humming *Amazing Grace* and *British Grenadiers,* Smith extended his walk to the Ratcliffe Highway and viewed Bancroft's newly purchased office above a tobacconist's shop. *We'll soon have you out of there, my boy.* Hurrying south, he stopped at Westminster Bridge to view the traffic on the river. *Less than usual,* he told himself. *This war is taking its toll on shipping.* Smith noted two of his vessels preparing for sea and nodded in satisfaction.

He heard the patter of feet without any alarm and turned to see who was running at this early hour.

The press gang surrounded him, with a tall, serious-faced lieutenant at their head and a score of men at his back. Most were grinning as they tapped heavy cudgels in the palms of their hands.

"What's the to-do, lads?" Smith asked, knowing that the Impress Service would never take a gentleman.

"That's the man!" a female shouted.

"He's a gentleman," a petty officer protested.

Smith saw a red-haired woman with the gang. She pointed to him, her mouth twisting in anger. "He's no gentleman!"

"He looks like one," the petty officer said doubtfully.

"A beggar can wear royal robes, but he's a mendicant at heart!" the woman replied. "That man's a prize seaman, I tell you, with the marks of pussy's claws on his back!"

"I am John Smith," Smith told them calmly. "Lord Fitzwarren and the Member of Parliament for Appleby."

"And I'm the Queen of China," the woman said. "He's a deserter, boys! Cut him, and he'll bleed salt water and rum."

"Take him, men," Barrington ordered. "The lady's never been wrong, yet!"

Smith stared at the red-haired woman, knowing he had seen her before but unsure where. He had only a second, and the press gang fell on him with flailing fists and cudgels.

Smith held his cane like a sword, poked the first attacker in the throat, sending him gasping back, slashed the second across the face and thrust the ferrule into the groin of the third.

"Get him, boys," the woman shouted.

The gang attacked Smith again, with some circling behind him. Smith stood on guard, wishing he had brought his pistol. "Murder!" he shouted, the universal cry for help in London. He glimpsed a brown-coated Charlie at the edge of the square, and then the gang were on him.

Two came from the front, wary of his darting cane, and others from the side and rear. Smith slashed sideways, ducked and weaved, hoping to force a passage, but the gang were experienced in trapping seamen. Somebody grabbed his arms, and another smashed a cudgel on his head while a third punched him in the stomach. The blow on the head staggered Smith; he felt his senses reel, with his attackers wavering as his sight failed and he crumpled to the ground.

"Don't damage him too badly," the lieutenant ordered. "We want a valuable seaman, not a crippled wreck."

Outnumbered and outmuscled, Smith began to shout until a sturdy petty officer stuffed a wad of oakum into his mouth and somebody cracked a cudgel over his head for a second time. Smith tried to fight the blackness that overcame him, but the world dissolved into a whirl of flashing lights and colours.

Smith heard the lieutenant order, "Take him!" and grinning seamen grabbed his arms and legs and carried him at a trot through the streets. Unable to resist, Smith took a last glance at the red-haired woman.

I know that woman. I've seen her before, but I am damned if I can remember where.

"COPINGER NEXT," MR JAY SAID WITH SATISFACTION. "NOW Smith's out of the picture for a while; we can concentrate on our other rival."

"Henry Copinger's only a minor concern," Kate said. "The American war has cost him dearly, and he had to resort to asking for loans from the moneylenders to keep his business afloat."

"The banks turned him down as a bad risk." Mr Jay smiled. "He had to ask all his friends, and one man loaned him five thousand at a high rate of interest."

"Who was that?" Kate asked.

"Me," Mr Jay said, leaning back in his chair. "The insurers have all tripled or quadrupled their rates, and shipping costs have escalated. Crews demand higher wages, especially for voyages to the Americas, and poor Copland couldn't cope."

Kate laughed. "Poor Henry Copland. That's Shapland gone, Smith in the navy and Copland in deep debt. The way is clear for us, Mr Jay."

Mr Jay lifted a bottle of gin. "Let's celebrate our good fortune, my dear Mrs Kay. We have a golden future in front of us, and we'll reign over the shipping interests in London." He filled two glasses and passed one to Kate.

Kate lifted her glass. "Here's to a long and fruitful reign, Mr Jay and Mrs Kay. King and queen of London shipping!"

They emptied the glasses and laughed.

SMITH FELT AS IF HE WAS REPEATING A NIGHTMARE. MANY years before, a magistrate had ordered him hanged for horse stealing and only reprieved him when he had swung on the end of a rope for a long thirty seconds. The reprieve had been partial, for instead of death, the magistrate condemned Smith to a lifetime in the navy. Now he was back in a Royal Navy ship, no longer a frightened young boy but a middle-aged man with his head pounding and his mind unable to focus.

As a scarred petty officer pushed him into the hold of the receiving ship, moored off the Tower, Smith relived those far-off days. He remembered the confusion and fear, the bullying and comradeship.

"That one." Lieutenant Barrington pointed to Smith. "He claims to be some sort of lord."

The petty officer's smile was entirely without humour. "He dresses like a lord, doesn't he, sir? In seaman's trousers and a linen shirt, and with a simple Malacca cane."

"That's what I thought," Barrington said. "A lord wandering on foot through London without a single servant in sight."

The petty officer laughed. "That's just how lords act, sir. Lords of Newgate Prison!"

"My informant told me he was a deserter from the navy," Barrington said.

"He might be branded then, sir," the petty officer said. "Hey, my lord! Come here, handsomely now, or it'll be the worse for you."

Smith remembered the petty tyranny of petty officers and stepped forward, with his mind clouded, so the past and present merged into a single confused mass.

The petty officer called up a trio of seamen. "Off with his shirt, lads! We think we've got a dirty deserter here!"

"A dirty deserter!" the men echoed. "We think we've got a dirty deserter here!"

Knowing it was useless to resist, Smith stripped off his shirt and stood in front of them, swaying as he sought to focus.

"No brand," the petty officer sounded disappointed. "But he's been flogged, that's for sure." He pointed to the scars the cat of nine tails had left on Smith's back. "What was that for, cully?"

"I was in the wrong place at the wrong time," Smith answered, trying to remember.

"Oh, my lord!" the petty officer mocked. "Well, you'll be on a man of war in a trice. We'll soon be at war with France now, and we'll need every able-bodied man, including lords of the manor."

"He says his name is John Smith," Barrington said and withdrew a step.

"Lord John Smith?" the petty officer asked.

"Lord John Smith," Barrington confirmed. "I'll leave him in your care, Dowell."

"He's safe with us, sir," Dowell replied. "Come on, Lord John Smith, I'll keep you in irons for now."

As Smith tried to struggle, the seamen cracked him across his aching head once more and shoved him into the hold. Practised hands thrust him to the deck and slammed him in irons.

Smith had seen men in irons before but had never experienced the cramped frustration of the punishment. The iron, or bilboe, was a long iron bar set into the deck, with manacles attached so Smith could neither sit nor lie comfortably. When they fastened Smith onto the bilboes and padlocked him, the seamen stepped back, smiling. One cuffed him again, and another kicked him in the ribs.

"You stay there, my lord Smith," the petty officer said. "It's not the silk cushions and satin sheets you're used to, but better than Davy Jones' locker." He swaggered away, laughing.

The night passed slowly, with Smith cramped and frustrated in his confinement. The memories crowded into his head, the old crew mates he had known, the tedious hours on blockade duty and the vicious ship-to-ship battles when the French tried to escape. Smith's head ached, and he knew something was wrong. He could not think straight and wavered from his present predicament to the past, so he was unsure whether he were John Smith or Abel Watson. He knew that Smith was a ship owner and respectable London merchant while Watson was a youthful smuggler accused of horse theft. Blood from the cudgel blows congealed on Smith's scalp and down his face, adding to his discomfort.

Who am I? Smith asked himself. *Why am I here?*

He rattled his manacles helplessly and looked over the collection of human misery that shared his accommodation in the ship's bowels. He breathed in, smelling the stink of bilge water, human waste, fear and rotting wood.

"Where am I?" Smith asked, feeling the throbbing bump on the back of his head.

"You're on a hulk, mate," a rough-voiced man informed him from the dark. "A receiving tender moored off the Tower."

Smith pondered the words. He knew a receiving ship was an old vessel moored offshore, where the navy confined press-ganged men before sending them to seagoing ships. "But why am I here?"

"The press caught you, mate," the unseen man spoke from the dreary gloom. "Keep your chin up. Nothing lasts forever."

"Who am I?" Smith asked as the images circled inside his head.

"I don't know, mate," the reply came. "Just pick a name and

use it if you're on the run. The navy doesn't care much, as long as they have hands to haul on braces and man the guns."

Smith lay against the damp planking and closed his eyes. The repeated blows on his head had concussed him, so he could not order his thoughts.

Am I John Smith or Abel Watson? Maybe I am both.

"YOU! SMITH! YOU'RE BOUND FOR HMS *HAZARD*!"

Smith opened his eyes. The bullying petty officer from the previous night – or was it the night before that? - stood over him, kicking at his legs. A seaman unfastened the manacles, grabbed Smith's hair and hauled him upright. "Get up, you lubber! There's work to do!"

Smith looked around, wincing at the pain in his cramped limbs. His head still ached, but not with the same intensity. He pushed the seaman away as something of his old spirit returned. "I can stand without your help, cully!"

"Cully, is it? I'll teach you cully, you jawing bastard!" The seaman lifted a knotted rope's end.

"Touch me with that, and the fish will feed on your guts," Smith warned. The seaman snarled, looked into Smith's eyes, and decided to back away.

For a moment, Smith contemplated bursting free and breaking for freedom, but he knew it was pointless. The navy was vastly experienced in holding reluctant seamen; they would have armed guards on the hatches and ventilating scuttle and have closed and barred the ports. Even when they allowed men on deck for exercise, the navy had armed men constantly watching.

"I wish to speak to your captain," Smith said.

"You can wish to speak to Jesus Christ for all the good it will do you," the petty officer snarled, pushing Smith in the back. "Get on deck, you idle bastard!"

"I wish to speak to your captain," Smith repeated, aware that the other pressed men were listening. "I am John Smith, Lord Fitzwarren!"

He said no more as a seaman stuffed a gag in his mouth and tied it tight while another gave him a hefty push towards the hatch.

"Get over there, your bloody Lordship," the petty officer said. "Any more trouble from you, and it'll be a dozen at the gratings, and you already know what that's like."

When Smith tried to struggle, a man punched him on the head, nearly knocking him down. Rough hands manhandled him on deck, where he blinked in the summer sunlight.

It's daylight. How long have I been on the receiving ship?

"Into that boat, you lubber!"

A longboat lay alongside, with an oarsman fore and aft and a young midshipman at the tiller. Five pressed seamen sat in the middle, one in tears and the others sulking at the unfortunate turn their life had taken. A flaxen-haired man with a lengthy pigtail sat beside the midshipman, holding a blunderbuss. He watched the recruits in case of resistance.

"In there, you!" A seaman shoved Smith onto the wooden bench. "That's the last one, sir!"

The midshipman nodded. "Very good! Push away and head for *Hazard!*"

The oarsmen pushed away from the tender and dipped their oars, pulling for a sloop on the opposite bank of the river.

Smith closed his eyes, with part of him nearly resigned to his fate. He was back where he belonged at the bottom level, a pressed ordinary seaman with no hope and no prospects. Smith knew he could accept his position and fit in with his companions, drink his daily rum, obey orders and dream of runs ashore, cheap prostitutes and alcohol-induced escapism. He was a before-the-mast seaman; he was a fool to believe he could maintain his elevated position as Lord Fitzwarren and a London merchant.

265

The Thames swept past HMS *Hazard*, lapping onto her hull. A dozen men worked on her planking, removing barnacles and long strands of seaweed, while others scrubbed the deck with holystones.

Hazard's master keeps a tight ship, Smith approved. *He might have the humanity to listen to me.*

"Get them on board!" the midshipman ordered, and the petty officer reinforced the words with casual cuffs that sent the pressed men up the hull and onto *Hazard's* deck. Smith automatically looked about him, noting the snowy cleanliness of the planking and the demeanour of the men. They were alert, not cowed, and the marines on deck were helping with menial tasks rather than guarding the seamen.

That all points to a happy ship.

A stocky lieutenant approached them. "How many new hands, Mr MacBride?"

"Only six, sir," the midshipman answered. "All pressed men, no volunteers, and the regulating captain recommends we watch for the one calling himself Smith."

The lieutenant nodded and glanced over the new additions to his crew. "Only six, and we are twenty-five men short." He stepped closer. "Right, you men. You may think yourselves hard done by to be pressed, but you are entering an honourable and noble service where you can serve your king and country. On board *Hazard,* all an officer orders you to do is your duty, and you must obey willingly and cheerfully. Any refusal is mutiny. Remember that, and you will find yourself contented with your position."

The lieutenant studied each man intently. "You look a handy bunch. Once we wash the stink of the receiving ship off you, we'll introduce you to our ways. Which one of you is called Smith?"

"I am, sir," Smith stepped forward.

"Well, Smith, I hear you've been troublesome in the past.

That's behind you now, and you start on *Hazard* with a clean sheet, so let's have no more of it."

"Aye, aye, sir," Smith answered automatically. "May I have permission to speak to the captain, sir?"

The lieutenant looked Smith up and down. "Captain Lambert will join us at sea, Smith. Until then, I expect you to knuckle down and obey orders. Dismissed."

"Sir," Smith protested. "I am not liable to impressment! I am Lord Fitzwarren, a ship owner and merchant!"

"Sir, if I may," the midshipman intervened. "Men! Show the lieutenant Smith's back!"

Two seamen grabbed Smith, ripped his shirt open and turned him around, revealing the furrows of the cat-of-nine-tails visible across his shoulders and back.

"You were a seaman," the lieutenant said. "Don't try your tricks on my deck, by God! Take them away, hose them down and teach them their duty." He marched away, with his feet clicking on the deck.

"Sir!" Smith shouted until the petty officer punched him on the jaw, and a bosun's mate arrived with a length of knotted rope.

"Start some manners into him," the petty officer ordered, and the bosun's mate laid on with the rope, knocking Smith to the deck and hammering him until an older man intervened.

"That's enough! There's no need to kill the fellow!"

"Cast off fore and aft!" the lieutenant ordered. "Hoist the anchor, and we'll catch the last of the tide! Hands to the braces!"

With the older man watching, the bosun's mate kicked Smith in the ribs. "Get up, you bastard. We've got work for you!"

Back in the king's navy, Smith thought, dragging himself to his feet. *Survive, Abel, survive whatever happens.*

Chapter Thirty-Two

The past had returned. Smith felt the blisters forming on his hands as he hauled on the rope, dragging the mainsail up to catch the offshore breeze. London lay astern, with its smoke and bustle, hope and despair. The marshes of Essex lay to larboard and the coast of Kent to starboard, with *Hazard* already lifting her bows to the first of the North Sea rollers.

Smith had nearly forgotten how life at sea would make his soft shore-side muscles ache and how bells, whistles and blows from the bosun's mates regulated a seaman's life.

"Move, you lubber!"

"Handsomely, you dirty buggers!"

"You're moving so slowly I can see the dead lice falling off you! By the living Christ, I'll make seamen out of you even if I kill you in the attempt!"

Life was one long torment, made harder by the knowledge he belonged here. Smith knew this was his proper station in life, serving before the mast rather than standing on the world's quarterdeck, reigning over his subjects. Already Leicester Square and the Spike seemed a dream, Bess a surreal memory and soft beds and good food were things that happened to a stranger. Smith glanced at the ranks of six-pounder cannons beside the bulwark and wondered if he could evade the patrolling marine sentries, leap over the rail and swim the two miles to Sheerness on the Isle of Sheppey.

Even as he contemplated freedom, Smith knew it was impossible. If the marines did not shoot him, *Hazard* would launch a boat and drag him back to face the cat or the noose as an example to the rest of the crew. He felt as trapped as securely as any prisoner within the stone walls of Newgate. For the foreseeable future, the navy owned him, body and soul.

"Sir!"

Smith instinctively looked up at the word to see a midshipman addressing the first lieutenant.

"A cutter is approaching, sir! It may be the captain!"

Smith knew that *Hazard* was a fourteen-gun sloop, small, handy but too small for a post captain to command. Her master would hold the rank of commander yet have the courtesy title of captain without his seniority or wages.

The Bosun cracked his cane across Smith's shoulders. "Did I say you could stop working? Haul, you useless bastard!"

Smith bit back his bitter retort and hauled, yet watched the cutter slide closer.

"Cutter ahoy!" a man shouted.

"*Hazard!*" the reply came, signifying that the captain of *Hazard* was coming aboard.

"Make ready!" the lieutenant shouted, and a dozen men ran to the entry port, with the bosun ready to pipe the commander on board. *Hazard* hauled her wind and eased her passage, with the landsmen and idlers cleared off the deck in case their presence offended the august gaze of the commander.

"Get forrard, you bastards!" The bosun's mates drove away the unwanted with their canes and ropes' ends. "Make way for the captain!"

"I want to speak to the captain," Smith reminded, to have two of the bosun's mates hustle him forward.

"Get below, you bugger! We'll deal with you later. You'll see the captain all right when he sends you to the gratings!"

Two men stepped aboard *Hazard*, Captain Lambert and a nondescript figure in civilian clothes carrying a leather case. Then somebody shoved Smith down a hatch into the stuffy atmosphere below.

"Get your filthy body out of the captain's sight!" a thin-faced bosun's mate snarled.

"What's happening?" another of the pressed men asked.

"The captain's coming aboard to take command," Smith explained. "The first lieutenant wants us off the deck so the ship looks its best."

Smith felt *Hazard*'s motion alter and knew she had slowed further. "Something's happening," he said.

"What?" a man asked from the gloomy depths.

"I don't know," Smith said. He heard a rush of feet on the deck planking above, and somebody dragged the hatch open. Even after such a short time, the daylight and fresh air were welcome.

"Smith!" the thin-faced bosun's mate roared. "John Smith! The captain wants you!" He reached down and grabbed Smith by the hair. "Get up here, you idle vermin!"

The cutter still lay beside *Hazard*, rocking on the chopped waves, but Smith was more concerned with the small group of men who stood on the quarterdeck. Captain Lambert was splendid in his blue and gold, with the first lieutenant slightly behind him and the civilian a few paces to the side. A section of scarlet-coated marines stood at attention, overlooking the main deck with Brown Bess muskets in hand and blank faces.

"We're going to see your backbone, Smith!" the thin-faced bosun's mate gloated. "Six dozen at the gratings and you capering and bawling for mercy!" He laughed and pushed Smith ahead of him. "Get up there!" The bosun's mate propelled Smith up the ladder that led to the minuscule quarterdeck.

Smith drew himself to attention, prepared to state his identity and defend himself from whatever accusation the first lieutenant levelled at him.

Captain Lambert stepped forward. "Are you John Smith, Lord Fitzwarren and the Member of Parliament for Appleby in Kent?"

"I am," Smith answered as if in a dream.

"Then please accept my profuse apologies, sir." The captain bowed and held out his hand. "I have no idea how this most unfortunate incident occurred, your Lordship. If it was not for this gentleman here," Lambert indicated the civilian, "God knows what would have happened."

For the first time, Smith looked at the civilian, who bowed. "My Lord," he said.

"Mr Judd?" Smith said in some surprise. "What the devil are you doing here?"

Judd permitted himself a rare smile. "One of the Charlies told me the Impress Service took you, my Lord," Judd explained, as the seamen on the quarterdeck looked embarrassed. "By the time I came outside to help, the press had hustled you away."

Captain Lambert cleared his throat. "I think we should continue this conversation in my cabin, gentlemen."

"No, Captain Lambert," Smith took command. "There is no more to be said. You should make sail while the offshore wind holds. Mr Judd and I will return on that cutter."

"I have given her commander orders to wait for you, sir," Lambert said. "And once again, I offer you my apologies. The Impress Service overstepped their authority in taking a gentleman, and Lieutenant Lawkins should have listened to you, sir." He glanced at his first lieutenant.

Smith stepped back. "I will take action against the Impress Service in due course, sir. Thank you for your courtesy." He stopped at the head of the ladder, aware that everybody on deck was watching him. "I wish you fair weather and a successful voyage, Captain, and I harbour no ill will towards Lieutenant Lawkins. He was acting in the best interests of the ship."

"Thank you, my Lord," Lambert said.

"Come on, Mr Judd, let's get home." Smith descended from the quarterdeck. As he passed the thin-faced bosun's mate, he turned and landed a single punch that knocked the man off his feet. "I suggest you disrated this man, Captain Lambert. His job is to encourage the men, not bully rag them."

Smith heard the muted cheer from those hands who witnessed his punch. "Take us back to London," he ordered the young midshipman in charge of the cutter. "And be quick about it."

"Aye, aye, sir!" the midshipman piped. "Come on, lads, cheerily now!"

The lads in question were twice the midshipman's age but responded happily, bringing the cutter about, and heading upriver.

Smith leaned against the single mast as the midshipman gave the orders that saw the cutter tack against the wind. "You're a good man, Mr Judd. How did you manage to convince Captain Lambert who I was?"

"Thank you, sir." Judd stood at Smith's side. "When I heard the Impress Service had taken you away, sir, I was tempted to run out and attack them."

"I am glad you did not, Mr Judd," Smith said.

"Yes, sir. I am not a physical man, sir, and I knew they would overpower me," Judd said.

"The press would have taken us both," Smith said grimly. He watched the midshipman control the cutter as it eased westward upriver.

"That's what I thought, sir," Judd said. "I know the navy works on administration and rules, so I approached the officer in charge of the local rendezvous. Lieutenant Barrington was most unhelpful when I informed him of your rank and position."

Smith nodded. "You were brave approaching him, Mr Judd. He could have grabbed you as well."

"I know, sir," Judd agreed. "However, I am only a clerk, and nobody notices a clerk."

Smith realised he had barely glanced at Judd when he first boarded *Hazard*. "Perhaps not, Mr Judd."

"After I left Lieutenant Barrington, I was unsure what to do, sir. I know I should have informed Mrs Smith, but I thought it best to strike the iron while hot, sir. I ran to the Tower and caught the Impress men taking you to the receiving ship, but they sent me away. The officer in charge there said I was no good to them as a seaman."

"You were lucky, Mr Judd."

"I believe so, sir," Judd said. "There was a woman at the Rendezvous, sir, and she laughed when I mentioned your name."

Smith nodded and frowned. "Red-haired?"

"That's correct, sir," Judd said. "Do you know her?"

"I might do," Smith did not give details.

The cutter was approaching London, with the first smoke of the city acrid in the air. Smith saw the Tower in the distance and St Paul's emerging above the roofline.

"When the gang took you to the receiving ship, I ran to the Admiralty," Judd said. "I took the liberty of calling in at the Leadenhall Office, sir, and taking some documents from your desk. I hope you don't mind."

"Not in the slightest, Mr Judd," Smith said.

"I showed them to the gentlemen at the Admiralty, sir, a Viscount Keppel, the Senior Naval Lord."

Smith raised his eyebrows, wondering how much Judd was leaving unsaid. "Did you indeed, Mr Judd."

"I thought it best to go to the top." Judd allowed himself a smile. "As soon as I explained what had happened, Admiral Keppel wrote me a letter ordering your immediate release." He delved into his leather bag and handed Smith the letter.

It was short and to the point, stating that the bearer, Mr Frederick Judd, carried documents that proved John Smith to be

Lord Fitzwarren MP and exempt from naval service. It was signed "Keppel, Senior Naval Lord."

Smith handed back the letter. "Why, Mr Judd? Why have you such loyalty to me? You must know I am a rogue and a lawbreaker."

"Yes, sir," Judd said. "I know all about your activities, the smuggling, the highway robbery and the privateering." He faced Smith without any expression on his face. "I don't care a button, sir. You always treat me with respect, which is what matters to me."

"Good God, man," Smith said. "I rely on you."

"Thank you, sir," Judd said. "I hope you're back in time for the funeral, sir."

"The funeral?" Smith had been too intent on his troubles that he had forgotten the outside world.

"Yes, sir," Judd said. "Mr Shapland is being interred this afternoon."

Chapter Thirty-Three

The convoy of black carriages drove slowly through London, with a long column of mourners following close behind. Black horses pulled each carriage, with black-draped men walking at the side and a varnished oak coffin in the hearse. It was a funeral that befitted one of London's most prominent merchants, with all the great and good of the business community present and a few gentlemen with titles and lands.

Bess was standing alone, dressed in mourning black. She lifted her face as the hearse passed, with her veil obscuring her scarred cheek and the worry in her eyes.

"Bess!" Smith stepped beside her.

"John!" Bess started and stared at him with mixed relief at his safety, concern at his appearance and anger. "What happened to you? Where have you been?"

"Press ganged," Smith said shortly. "I'll explain later."

"I thought you were dead! I didn't hear anything." Bess hugged him briefly and touched the raw bruise on his head. "Who did that?"

Smith held her tight. "I will tell you all later. Just now, I'm going to Bancroft's house in Grosvenor Square."

"John! Be careful; you look terrible."

"Thank you. You don't." Smith said. He stepped back, holding her at arm's length. "You look perfect."

"John?" Bess shook herself free. "You're hardly dressed for a funeral."

"I'm not staying for the funeral," Smith said. "I only wanted to see you."

Bess frowned. "What are you planning, John?"

"Striking back." Smith rasped a hand over his unshaven face. "We're striking back, Bess and this time, we're going for the jugular. I'm going to borrow your little friend."

The colour drained from Bess's face. "Madge? Are you taking Madge?"

"Yes," Smith said. He saw some of the mourners staring at his battered clothes. "I'll have to go, Bess. I'll see you later."

"John!" Bess held out her hand, but Smith turned and strode away, walking with the peculiar rolling stride of the seaman. "Take care," she whispered. "Please take care."

Behind her, the funeral cortege entered the cemetery, with the column of solemn respectable people calculating how they could gain by Shapland's demise.

"You're with me, Madge," Smith said as he walked into the small room they had given to the young girl.

"Where have you been?" Madge asked, playing with her doll. "Dolly has been worried about you."

"I'll tell you later," Smith promised. "Get your boots on and put the doll down."

"Where are we going?" Madge held her doll tight. "Are you taking me back to the Rookery?"

Smith winced. The St Giles Rookery was one of the worst areas of London, a sprawl of filthy streets and courtyards where people lived by crime and prostitution. Every kind of depredation flourished in St Giles, and nobody responded to a scream for help. "No, Madge," he said. "I'm not taking you back to the Rookery. I need your help."

Madge smiled. "What do you want me to steal?"

Smith stared at her. "What makes you think I want something stolen?"

"Stealing is the only thing I can do," Madge said simply and lifted her doll. "Ask Dolly if you don't believe me!"

"I don't want anything stolen," Smith said. "We're going to leave a present for somebody."

"A present like Dolly?" Madge held her doll up for Smith to inspect.

"Not quite," Smith said. "We're leaving some documents, papers, for somebody to find."

"Come on, then." Madge slid on her boots and stood up, ready to leave. "Does he know we're coming?"

"No," Smith said. "It's a surprise, so we'll have to sneak in unobserved."

Madge gave a small, understanding smile. "You want to break in," she said.

"That's right," Smith agreed.

"I'll need a knife," Madge said. "Do you have a lockpick?"

"Yes," Smith said, dismayed at the knowledge of such a young girl. One moment she acted like a three-year-old, and then she displayed the cynicism of a jailbird of fifty.

"Give it to me," Madge said. "I might need it."

Smith smiled. "Give me a minute." He ran to the study, retrieved his lockpick and added a couple of knives. On an impulse, he brought a small pistol, determined that the press would never capture him again.

I'll shoot them next time.

Dressed in dark breeches and a grey shirt, with a tricorne hat and a black kerchief, Smith slipped on soft-soled shoes and left the house. With Madge beside him, he hired a closed carriage under an assumed name.

"Who's Mr Black?" Madge asked when he lifted her to the driving seat.

"I am," Smith said and drove in the opposite direction from the hiring stables before turning the coach around.

"Where are we going?" Madge asked.

"Grosvenor Square," Smith said. "It's where my friend lives."

"Why are we in a carriage?" Madge asked.

"So people can see us and don't know who we are," Smith told her.

Madge smiled. "If you wanted to be known, you'd use your own chariot," she said.

You're far too clever for a seven-year-old. "That's right," Smith said.

Smith drove the carriage to a stable near Grosvenor Square, lifted Madge from her perch and walked to Bancroft's house. The square was surprisingly empty, with a single carriage rolling past and a courting couple and their chaperone strolling through the central garden.

Bancroft's house was quiet, with no sign of life inside, as Smith took Madge to the front door.

"Can you sneak into the house and open the door to let me in?"

"Easy!" Madge said. "Just find me a window, and I'll get in."

"Plenty to choose from," Smith said.

"That one." Madge pointed to the fanlight above the front door. "It's always loose." She smiled. "Peter taught me that."

"Up you get." Smith hoisted Madge to the top of the door. "Don't make a noise."

Madge threw him a disgusted look. "I know what I'm doing," she said.

Smith had only to wait a minute as Madge scraped the putty from a single pane of glass and slid her scrawny frame inside the house. He shrank into the doorway as the courting couple strolled past, but they were too involved with each other to notice him. The chaperone, possibly the girl's sister, watched them closely without looking around.

"Come in then!" Madge hissed.

Smith had not heard the door open. He slipped inside the house and closed the door. "Well done, Madge!"

Madge smiled at him; a practised and expert housebreaker with a doll inside her jacket.

"Now, where?" Madge asked, inspecting her surroundings. She pointed to a portrait of Bancroft that hung inside a heavy gilt frame. "I could pawn that for a few shillings!"

"Thomas Gainsborough painted that." Smith recognised the style. "It would cost him around two hundred guineas."

Madge screwed up her face. "I don't like the picture; the Runners could trace that too easily. I meant the frame."

"Upstairs." Smith had never been in Bancroft's house but guessed that his study would be on the upper level. Any servants would either be in the basement or the garret. "Don't make a noise."

"You're noisier than me," Madge told him sharply.

Smith grunted and led the way upstairs. An Axminster carpet softened their footfall while the ubiquitous long-case clock ticked softly from the landing.

Are all houses in London furnished in the same pattern? I'll have to talk to Bess about changing ours; I like to be different.

Bancroft's house was on four levels, with the basement below, the ground floor and an upper floor beneath the garret. Smith led the way to the short landing on the upper floor, with a magnificent glass chandelier hanging from an ornate plaster ceiling and sombre paintings on the wall.

Madge stood behind him, staring at the splendour on display. "This house is richer than yours," she said.

Smith nodded. "I noticed," he agreed. Five panelled doors led from the landing, with large keys in each lock. The first opened into a guest bedroom that smelled musty and unused. The second was a reception room with a large oval table and eight chairs, and the third was the master bedroom.

"Bancroft's trained his servants badly," Smith said when he saw the unmade bed and a pile of ashes in the fireplace. He smiled at the full-length mirror and frowned at the mound of female clothing on one of the three chairs.

I didn't know Bancroft had a lady friend.

"This isn't the study." Madge lifted an auburn wig from a wig stand and tried it on, posing in front of the gilt-edged mirror.

"The wig is as big as you are," Smith said. "I've never seen Bancroft wearing it."

"It's a lady's wig," Madge told him severely, replacing it carefully on its stand.

"I believe you," Smith said. "This room will do."

"It's a bedroom, not a study." Madge was inspecting the contents of Bancroft's drawers, laughing at his underwear and stockings. "Your friend is a macaroni," she said.

"Maybe so," Smith agreed. "I'll hide the documents in here," he said. "Somewhere Bancroft won't find them by mistake."

Madge rifled another drawer, taking out a selection of cravats and tying them around her doll. "Not in the drawers then, Mr Smith. They're such a mess he must go through them every day."

"Not in the drawers," Smith agreed. He glanced around the room, contemplated sliding the documents under the mattress and decided the maid may turn it at some time.

"Put them under the carpet," Madge said helpfully. "Nobody will look there."

"Good idea," Smith said. "Help me here." He rolled the carpet back, exposing unswept wooden floorboards, and slipped the packet of letters from inside his coat.

"What are these letters for?" Madge asked.

"To get Mr Bancroft in trouble," Smith said.

"Was he the man who tried to get you killed?"

"Yes," Smith said.

"Why not kill him?" Madge asked, chillingly cold-blooded.

"That would get me hanged," Smith told her. He removed the letters from the packet and spread them out so there was no unevenness on the carpet.

"Oh." Madge understood Smith's technique. "I hear voices!"

Smith swore softly. "The funeral must have ended sooner than I thought. Replace the carpet where it was!"

They rolled back the carpet in a desperate rush, and Smith looked for somewhere to hide as the voices came closer.

"Under the bed!" Smith nearly threw Madge under the bed and shrank into the corner between the wardrobe and the corner of the room, holding his breath. He heard footsteps in the corridor outside and tried to make himself invisible as the door opened.

Bancroft entered the room, dressed in mourning black. He admired his reflection in the mirror for a moment and began to undress, throwing his clothes on the floor.

Dear God, he's going to come to the wardrobe, Smith thought and squeezed closer to the wall. He saw Bancroft hesitate and lift something from his dressing table. It was Madge's doll, with a royal blue cravat around its neck.

He'll know! That will give us away for sure.

Bancroft lifted the doll, shook his head, and, dressed only in his shirt, carried it out of the room. "Mrs Kay!" he shouted. "Is this yours?"

"Not mine," a woman's voice replied.

"It must belong to one of the servants." Bancroft returned to the bedroom without the doll and dressed hurriedly in tan breeches and a blue jacket. Pulling on a pair of short boots, he left the room.

Smith emerged from behind the wardrobe. "Madge!" he whispered.

"Where's Dolly?" Madge asked, crawling from under the bed.

"I don't know," Smith replied. "We must get out of here."

"Not without my dolly," Madge said firmly.

"We haven't time!" Smith said. He opened the door quietly

and looked up and down the corridor. "Come on; there's nobody out here."

"That man stole Dolly," Madge complained.

"I'll get you another one." Smith was not experienced with children.

"I want that one!" Madge's voice was getting more strident. She's mine!"

"Come on!" Smith pulled her out of the bedroom and along the corridor, hoping to get downstairs without meeting anybody.

"My dolly!" Madge cried, pulling at Smith's hand to escape. "I want Dolly!" Her voice rose with every word.

"Come on, Madge!" Smith hissed. He heard murmuring voices behind him and ducked into a doorway, dragging Madge behind him.

The voices rose and a young maidservant pattered along the corridor. She passed the doorway without a glance and hurried downstairs. Madge tugged at Smith's sleeve.

"She had my dolly," Madge told him in a conversational tone.

"I know," Smith said and sighed, beginning to realise how much the doll meant to Madge. "We'll get no peace until we have your doll back, will we?"

"No," Madge said happily.

Holding Madge by the hand, Smith scanned the corridor and led her downstairs. He knew he would be better off leaving Bancroft's house immediately but felt responsible for Madge. He had brought her here and had to bear the consequences.

"Stay here!" Smith pushed Madge inside an empty room. "Don't move until I come back for you."

Madge looked at him, huge-eyed. She nodded and moved further into the dark room. Closing the door, Smith negotiated the stairs, listening for voices or footsteps, ready to fight or flee, whichever was better.

He heard people talking on the ground floor, with Bancroft's hearty laugh and a woman's thin, London-harsh tones.

The servant will have taken the doll downstairs.

The stairs to the basement were bare stone, painted a dull ochre and without any ornamentation. Smith descended slowly, knowing he was foolish wasting time looking for a doll. He heard a man's deep voice and a lighter reply from a female.

Where the devil would a servant put a child's doll? In her quarters?

The kitchen was busy, with servants running in and out and the cook shouting orders. Smith avoided that room and found himself in a stone-flagged corridor with half-a-dozen plain doors leading off.

Smith eased the first open, glanced into a storeroom and withdrew. The next was a male servants' bedroom, judging by the clothes, and Smith hurriedly closed the door.

That's more like it, Smith told himself when the third door opened into the maids' bedroom, with two double beds side by side and articles of female clothing protruding from a wooden chest. Smith stepped inside and saw the doll's head on the pillow as if it were a child. He picked the doll up, thrust it inside his jacket and left.

When a maid ran from the kitchen carrying a pot of something hot, Smith slipped inside the storeroom, waited for a moment, and emerged. He ran up the stairs two at a time and swore when he saw Bancroft standing outside an open door.

Move, you bastard, or I'll end this affair here and now.

Bancroft laughed, and a female replied. Smith lay on the servants' stairs, keeping in the shadows. When the door opened wider, the woman stepped out, tall, red-haired, and smiling.

Smith started. *I know you,* he told himself. *You're the woman who betrayed me to the press, but I've seen you before.*

"Come on, Mrs Kay. Come on, Kate," Bancroft said. "We've done our duty by Shapland. Now we have his business to take over."

Kate laughed. "There's time for that, Mr Jay."

Kate! Kate Rider! Damn it all, that's Kate Rider. That explains it all.

Chapter Thirty-Four

"Kate Rider?" Bess stared at him across the table. "Are you sure?"

"I saw her as plainly as I see you," Smith said. "You'll remember that I was responsible for the death of man, Lightning Bowlt, years ago."

"I remember," Bess shook her head. "Dear God in heaven. She's the red-headed woman who's been causing all the trouble. Our past has returned to haunt us."

"It seems so," Smith said.

"She had Peter killed." Bess gripped the table's edge so tightly her knuckles gleamed white. She controlled her anger when she saw Madge standing at the door, holding her doll. "You'd better get to bed, Madgie. It's late."

"Yes." Madge looked from Bess to Smith and back. "Who's Kate Rider?"

"Never you mind, Madge." Bess rose and took Madge's hand. "Come on; I'll tuck you up."

Smith poured himself a glass of brandy and drank it without tasting a drop. He remembered those hectic, crazy days when he had acted the highwayman on the roads and lanes of Kent. His exploits gained him a house, lands and his title of Lord Fitzwarren, but now they had returned to torment him. Lightning Bowlt had been a typical highwayman, and Kate Rider had been his girl.

Smith poured more brandy. The combination of Kate Rider, who hated him for being the cause of Bowlt's death, and James Bancroft, who knew his business secrets, was formidable.

Damn them both, Smith said. *Damn them both. I'll see both in hell for killing Peter and having me press-ganged.*

Smith was on his fourth glass of brandy when Bess returned, took the bottle from him, and replaced it in the cabinet.

"That's not the answer," Bess said sternly. "We've worked too hard to drink everything away."

"Damnit all, Bess." Smith did not object to Bess's interference. "I trusted Bancroft. Why has he stabbed me in the back?"

"Money and power," Bess said. "The Bible says the love of money is the root of all evil, and we know its lure."

"We do," Smith agreed.

"Are you going to confront him, John?"

Smith pondered for a moment. "No," he said. "I'd kill him, Bess, with witnesses present." He fingered the scar around his throat. "I've been hanged once, Bess and have no desire to repeat the experience."

Bess sat opposite him, placed her elbows on her knees, and stared into his eyes. "What's your plan, John? I know you'll have one."

"Listen, and I'll tell you," Smith said with a slow smile.

───────

THE BOW STREET MAGISTRATE'S OFFICE WAS AS CLEAN AND efficient as always when Smith walked in. Fielding smiled from behind his desk and lifted his head.

"Mr John Smith, isn't it?"

"It is," Smith agreed, "although I don't know how you know. You can't see me, and I had not spoken yet."

Fielding chuckled. "You use a distinctive type of Virginia tobacco, Mr Smith, and you were drinking brandy before you left the house. Both have a unique scent, and the combination screams John Smith of Leicester Square and the Spike as clearly as if I saw your face."

"You're a clever man, Mr Fielding," Smith said. "Is Jack Redpath available?"

"He is through the door on your left, Mr Smith," Fielding said. "And I must congratulate you on your election victory. You are now a Member of Parliament and that is quite a climb for a foremast hand and a Kent smuggler."

"Alleged smuggler," Smith corrected.

Fielding chuckled again. "Walk through that door, honourable gentleman, and you'll find Jack Redpath."

Four officers lounged in the small room beyond the door. Smith knew them all by sight, name and reputation and nodded acknowledgement. Three sat on hard chairs, quietly smoking pipes, and the fourth was busy with paper and pen.

"Mr Smith." Redpath looked up and placed the pen in its stance. "What do you have for me?"

"I have a rumour," Smith said and glanced at the other officers.

"Ah," Redpath said. "I understand."

"Walk with me, Mr Redpath." Smith held the door open.

Fielding smiled as they left the office. "Good hunting, gentlemen," he said.

"Thank you, sir," Redpath replied.

"This may not be Bow Street business," Smith said as they strolled through London's streets, both clicking their walking canes from the ground. "It concerns the Protestant Association and possible treason."

Redpath pointed his cane at a begging blind woman. "On your way, Lily! You're no blinder than I am!"

Smith said nothing but flicked a silver shilling to the beggar, who thanked him with a gap-toothed grin.

"Treason, Mr Smith?" Redpath asked when Lily had slouched away. "Tell me more."

They walked side by side with traffic rumbling along the road and low clouds pressing smoke onto the streets. A chimney sweep hurried past with his diminutive climbing boy at his heels, carrying a collection of brushes. Both avoided Redpath's eye.

"No thieving today, Davie, my lad," Redpath said. "I know your little games." He glowered at the sweep and repeated, "Tell me more, Mr Smith."

"I heard a rumour that a friend of mine is a secret Roman Catholic," Smith said. "I can't tell you how shocked I was." He shook his head. "I've known this man for years, Mr Redpath. He owns shares in many of my ships, and I've invited him to my home." They turned a corner and headed toward Covent Garden, with a flight of pigeons exploding from the ground in front and a group of children poking in an ashpit for anything they could sell.

"Does this traitor have a name?" Redpath asked.

"James Bancroft," Smith said. "He was my most particular friend."

"Bancroft?" Redpath sounded surprised. "The ship owner?"

"That's the fellow," Smith said sadly. "We were close, he and I."

"You mentioned treason," Redpath reminded. "Please explain."

They altered direction to head for the river, where the ships crammed the roadway, and sea birds circled overhead. A Thames barge ploughed downriver with her master at the tiller and two young boys trimming the spritsail.

"My informant told me that Bancroft was in direct communication with France," Smith said. "I trade with France, Redpath. I import brandy, wine and silk and export wool and leather goods, but my informant thinks Bancroft has political and theological motives."

"Who is this informant?" Redpath asked.

"I am not at liberty to say," Smith replied.

"I see. What's Bancroft's address?"

When Smith told him Grosvenor Square, Redpath smiled. "He must be a successful traitor to afford property in that neighbourhood. I'll watch the house for a few days, and if I see anything untoward, I'll act."

Smith nodded. They stopped at the side of the river as a Royal Navy cutter eased downstream with a slender midshipman proud in the stern. "I don't like to betray a friend," he said, "but I've no time for traitors."

"Neither have I, Mr Smith," Redpath replied solemnly. "Neither have I." He was silent for a moment as he filled his pipe. "I can't act officially in this case," he said quietly. "I shall inspect the house for another reason and see if there is any incriminating evidence."

"Yes, Mr Redpath, that would be best," Smith said. "My informant mentioned some sort of papers, documents, but he did not have any details."

"Documents are easily concealed." Redpath puffed smoke over the Thames. "You would be surprised, Mr Smith, where I have located such things in houses and secreted on the person."

"I don't want to imagine," Smith said. "When we were at sea, we hid valuables under the decking, but the petty officers always found them."

"Valuables?"

"Rum, Mr Redpath, rum." Smith considered he had given sufficient hints. "I'd better be getting along. I am attending parliament for a debate on the progress of the American War this evening. Good luck with Mr Bancroft." Lifting his cane in farewell, Smith sauntered away.

Chapter Thirty-Five

"Mr Judd," Smith said, "do you know anybody who can speak French?"

"I speak French, sir," Judd said without a change of expression.

"You are a man of constant surprises, Mr Judd. How on earth did you learn French?"

"In my last position, sir," Judd said, "I was an agent for a company that imported wine from France and Spain. I learned both French and Spanish."

"What a treasure you are, Mr Judd. Are you willing to do something else for me? It's quite simple, but I don't want anybody to recognise you."

"Nobody will, sir," Judd said. "Nobody ever notices a clerk. We are invisible." His smile was part self-deprecating and part rueful. "What do you wish me to do, sir?"

"I want you to find a companion and deliver a package to Mr Bancroft's house," Smith said. "You will see a man standing in the gardens outside."

"Yes, sir," Judd replied.

"The man is tall, with a three-cornered hat and a long dark-green cloak, and habitually carries a cane with a silver mounted handle."

"Mr Redpath, sir," Judd said. "The Bow Street officer. I believe the cane is a sword stick."

"How the devil do you know that?" Smith asked.

"I notice details, sir," Judd replied. "It's part of my job."

Smith smiled. "You astonish me, Mr Judd. Yes, the man is Redpath the Runner. I want you to pass Mr Redpath and speak French to your companion."

"Yes, sir," Judd said without a change of expression. "What do you wish me to say?"

"I don't mind, Mr Judd. Just ensure that Mr Redpath hears you speaking French."

"Yes, sir." Judd hesitated for a significant moment. "Does it matter who my companion is, sir?"

Smith shook his head. "Not in the slightest, Mr Judd. All you have to do is walk past Redpath speaking French, knock at Mr Bancroft's door and hand in a packet."

"Yes, sir," Judd nodded. "When shall I go?"

"Tomorrow morning," Smith told him. He waited a moment. "Do you have a companion in mind, Mr Judd?"

"Yes, sir." Judd looked uncomfortable. "A young lady of my acquaintance, sir. She is a French tutor for gentlemen's daughters."

Smith hid his surprise. He had never thought that Judd would have a woman friend. "She sounds perfect, Mr Judd. Come to my study in an hour, Mr Judd, and I'll have the package ready for you."

"Yes, sir," Judd nodded, bowed, and withdrew.

Smith trawled through his drawers and retrieved a bundle of documents concerning his vineyard in France. Reading them to ensure nothing connected the business to him, he tied them together and wrapped them in a cover sheet from the same address.

"Mr Judd!" Smith shouted.

Judd arrived within a minute.

"Please write Mr Bancroft's address on this package. It's..."

"I know the address, sir," Judd replied. "May I?" He lifted Smith's pen and wrote the address in his neat handwriting. "There we are, sir. I'll deliver that tomorrow, and don't worry, sir, Mr Redpath won't be able to follow us here."

Smith smiled. "I knew I could rely on you, Mr Judd."

With the trap set, Smith waited until Judd left for Bancroft's house and sauntered out, wearing dark clothes and with his hat pulled low over his face. Striding through the streets, he arrived at Grosvenor Square before Judd and waited at the corner. He could not see Redpath for a few moments and then noticed him leaning against the bole of a tree, calmly stuffing tobacco into the bowl of his pipe.

Judd arrived ten minutes later, arm-in-arm with a woman wearing a long blue skirt and a fashionable hat. Smith studied her, seeing her proud carriage and firm chin. *You've chosen well, Judd,* he thought, and saw Judd casually steer his companion through the gardens near Redpath.

Well done, Judd, you're a natural.

Smith saw Redpath move slightly closer as Judd said something to the woman, who replied with a laugh. They stopped beneath a tree, Judd kissed her lightly, and they walked on. Redpath clenched his pipe between his teeth and followed, stopping to examine one of the trees.

Judd and the woman stepped to the front door and knocked loudly as if they hadn't a care in the world. Redpath sauntered past, trying to shield his pipe from the breeze as a servant answered the door and accepted the package.

That went smoothly, Smith thought. *Let's see if Redpath takes the bait.*

"The carriage as well," Bancroft ordered. Other customers in the coffee shop ignored the quiet group in the corner.

"You want my carriage?" Copinger looked startled.

"Yes," Bancroft said. "I loaned you sufficient funds to keep your company afloat, and now you must repay your debts. As you don't have the readies, you must pay in kind." He smiled across the table. "Gentlemen keep their word." He emphasised the word *gentlemen*.

"I have every intention of keeping my word," Copinger said. "This American war has ruined me. I've lost nearly all my ships to American privateers, with that fellow Abraham Hargreaves capturing most." He shook his head in despair. "I am sure he knew where my ships were."

"He captured many of poor Shapland's as well," Bancroft said. "However, that is neither here nor there. I loaned you money to keep you afloat, and now I am calling in the loan."

"My carriage is not part of the company," Copinger said.

"The debt was personal," Bancroft told him. "I'll take your watch too; it must be worth a few guineas," he smiled. "Come now, Copinger, don't welch on me."

"I thought we were friends, Bancroft." Copinger unfastened his watch from its chain and nearly threw it across the table.

"There are no friends in business, Copinger," Bancroft told him. "Only colleagues and rivals. The chain too, and that fine ring. If you don't pay up, I'll have you in the debtor's prison until you find the rhino."

"You're a bastard, Bancroft," Copinger said.

Bancroft laughed. "Take me to your house," he ordered. "I am sure we'll find more items to help pay your debts."

"Mr Judd." Smith called on Judd's small office, where two candles pooled yellow light onto the ledger on his desk. Five more ledgers sat in a neat pile on a small table, with an array of goose-wing pens upright beside a deep inkwell.

Judd looked up from his work. "Mr Smith! Sir!" He struggled to his feet. "You could have called for me, sir. There was no need to trouble yourself coming here."

"It's no trouble, Mr Judd," Smith assured him. "How are Shapland's shares coming along?"

"I'm checking the figures now, sir." Judd sprinkled sand over the still-wet ink of his ledger, brushed it into a wooden pail and turned the page for Smith's perusal. "As you see, sir, shares in his ships dipped after his unfortunate demise."

Smith studied the figures. "They did," he agreed. "This second column shows the number of shares you purchased, I see."

"Yes, sir," Judd said. "The first column is the date, the second column the shares we purchased, the third the buying price and the fourth the amount of shares others own. I have one page for each of Mr Shapland's vessels, and this ledger," he lifted the top book from the pile beside him, "shows the estimated shares of our rivals."

"Show me." Smith held out his hand, and Judd opened the journal at the correct page.

"Here we are, sir," Judd said. "Here's a list of the vessels and the owners. I have been as accurate as possible, using Lloyd's List when I could and keeping my eye on the market." He cleared his throat. "Since Mr Shapland's departure, Rogers, his clerk, has entered Mr Bancroft's employ. I have continued our previous relationship, sir. I trust that meets with your approval?"

"It does, Mr Judd," Smith said. "I see that Mr Bancroft now owns shares in most of the late Mr Shapland's vessels."

"He does, sir," Judd confirmed. "And he's the majority share-holder in the few vessels Mr Copinger used to own. Mr Bancroft has called in his debt, and Mr Copinger is at present in the Fleet, sir, the debtor's prison."

"So I understand. You're a meticulous man, Mr Judd," Smith said. "I see the buying price has increased recently."

"Yes, sir. It recovered from its initial fall and is slowly rising. In some cases, the price has more than doubled in the last few days, as demand increases." Judd coughed into his hand. "I am afraid our interest in the shares has helped push the prices up."

"I can understand that," Smith said. "Well, Mr Judd, I believe that the shares of the vessels Mr Shapland and Mr Copinger used to own are about to fall dramatically."

"Are they, sir?" Judd looked concerned.

"I want you to sell, Mr Judd," Smith said. "Hold what you have today, and be ready to sell. I'll give you only a few hours' warning and rely on you to get the best price possible."

Judd looked pained. "I always do, sir."

"Of that, Mr Judd, I have no doubt," Smith said and left the office. He turned at the doorway to see Judd already busy with his head down and his pen scratching at the ledger.

"A soldier who used a Pennsylvania rifle?" The veteran shivered at the corner of the street. His begging bowl was at his feet, while his scarlet coat was faded and patched. "Corporal Jenks was best with the rifle."

"Do you know him?" Kate asked.

"Used to." The veteran lifted the stump of his left arm. "He was a champion at the arm wrestling was Jenks. I was good, but I never beat Jenks."

"Do you know where he lives now?"

The veteran screwed up his gaunt, weather-tortured face. "I heard he's taken up with Private Harkness of the 34th, and some wealthy merchant pays his rent."

Bess's interest increased. "Which wealthy merchant?"

"Somebody called Jay," the veteran said with a wry smile. "If I knew more, I'd knock at his door and ask for charity."

"Mr Jay?" Bess controlled her excitement.

"That's right." The veteran lifted his cup with his remaining hand. "Could you help a crippled soldier, ma'am? I lost my arm in Cuba."

"I could." Bess dropped a guinea into the cup. "If you could tell me where Jenks and Harkness live, I'd be more helpful."

"Out at Bermondsey." The veteran eyed the gold coin with a mixture of avarice and disbelief. "That's all I know, ma'am."

"Thank you," Bess said and added two more guineas. "Take care, my friend."

"God bless you, ma'am. You're a princess, and you'll reign in heaven."

"WELL, SMITH." REDPATH HAD CALLED ON SMITH'S OFFICE IN Leadenhall Street. He took off his hat, shook off the water droplets and sat uninvited. "It's raining outside."

"I'm sure you didn't come in to tell me that," Smith said.

"I did not," Redpath agreed. "I've been outside your friend Bancroft's house every day this week, duty permitting."

"Did you discover anything?"

"I did," Redpath said. "He has had a constant stream of callers, including two undoubted prostitutes, a woman with red hair and a French couple."

"A red-haired woman?" Smith asked. "There are a few of them in London."

"She's been in Bancroft's house twice this week," Redpath said, "but it's the Frenchies I'm concerned with."

"Are you sure they were French?" Smith asked.

"They spoke French," Redpath said curtly, "and the man had a French face."

"Ah," Smith nodded. "That settles it, then."

Redpath nodded. "I thought I'd let you know your information was helpful, Mr Smith. I'll pursue my enquiries further."

Smith poured them both a glass of brandy. "What do you plan next, Mr Redpath?"

Redpath sipped the brandy. "I will call on the house in the dark hours, Mr Smith, and see what I can find." He finished the brandy. "We must root out the traitors and Catholics, Mr Smith. We must dig them out root and branch!"

"When will you strike, Mr Redpath?"

"Thursday night, Mr Smith." Redpath put down his glass with a bang. "I'll search this traitor's house on Thursday night." He jammed his hat on his head, lifted his cane in a gesture of farewell and swept from the office.

I'll be watching, Mr Redpath.

Smith was in Grosvenor Square when Redpath arrived. The Runner arrived shortly after midnight with a small group of muscular men, two carrying an eight-foot-long log and others with lanterns. Redpath hammered on Bancroft's door with no pretence of subtlety.

"Open up!"

When nobody replied, Redpath signalled the two burly men, who lifted their heavy log and smashed it against the door.

That will awaken the neighbours, Smith thought.

The sound echoed around the square, and then a servant opened the door and blinked nervously into the dark. "What's happening?"

"Protestant Association!" Redpath states as if the group possessed an official sanction. "Stand aside!" He pushed past the startled manservant and strode into the house with his men following. Their lanterns bobbed inside the house, and then they closed the door.

Smith saw lights appear at other windows in the square as the inhabitants opened the shutters and peered outside, wondering what had disturbed their sleep. With Bancroft's shutters closed, Smith could only guess at the progress inside the house. He waited for fifteen minutes as a thick mist rolled in from the Thames, carrying the sour smell of the river, and then the front door opened again.

Redpath was first to emerge, grim-faced and carrying a packet under his arm. His bullies followed, laughing, and Bancroft made up the rear, shouting and waving a fist.

"I've never seen them in my life!" Bancroft complained and slammed the door shut.

That will do, Smith said and slipped away. He strode back to Leicester Square, swinging his cane.

"You look pleased with yourself," Bess said as Smith entered their bedroom. "Was it successful?"

"I believe so," Smith said and related the night's events. "Redpath looked satisfied."

"What now?" Bess sat up, scratched a spark from her tinder box, and lit the candle beside her bed.

"Now we sell all our shares in Shapland and Copinger's ships," Smith said. "I don't know what Redpath will do next, but I expect the share prices to fall."

"What will he do about Bancroft and Kate Rider?" Bess asked.

"I think we can leave Bancroft to Redpath and Gordon's Protestant Association," Smith said. "I am not sure about Kate Rider."

"Jenks and Harkness," Bess threw out the names. "I haven't seen you since I learned about them."

"Who?" Smith asked.

"Corporal Jenks of the 28th and Private Harkness of the 34th Foot," Bess explained. "Jenks was good with the Pennsylvania rifle," she repeated what the veteran had told her.

"Mr Jay hired them," Smith said. "So Bancroft ordered Jenks to shoot me, as we thought."

"If that's correct, why did Bancroft kill Jenks?" Bess asked.

"Bancroft killed him to prevent Jenks from telling me anything," Smith said. "Judd heard Jenks shout "Mr Jay" before Bancroft shot him. He must have been pleading for his life."

"Bancroft killed his friend," Bess said, "I don't like that man."

Smith nodded. "Nor do I," he agreed. "Who was this other fellow you mentioned?"

"Private Harkness," Bess said. "Corporal Jenks' friend."

Smith nodded. "I'd better watch my back for him."

Bess nodded. "I'd wager a thousand guineas that Bancroft will set him on you next."

"I won't take that bet," Smith said, stepped to the bedside table and pulled out a brace of pistols.

Chapter Thirty-Six

S mith!" Kate shouted and glared at Bancroft. "I'll wager
everything I own that John Smith is behind this."

Bancroft slumped on a chair with his head in his
hands. "I've heard of the Protestant Association," he said, "but
I've never paid them much heed. Why would they search my
house? I'm Church of England, for the love of God!"

"They've paid heed to us now." Kate controlled her temper.
"What documents did they find, Mister Jay?"

"I have no idea. We had something delivered a few days ago,
rubbish that I threw away and these people found in the ash pit,
and some sheets of paper under the bedroom carpet."

"Which sheets of paper?" Kate asked. "What did you hide
under the carpet, Mister Jay?"

"Nothing," Bancroft said. "I've never hidden anything there.
All I know was the writing was in French."

"Who put it there?" Kate asked. "Not you or me, so either a
servant or an intruder. This has the mark of John Smith." She
frowned. "We found a doll in the bedroom, too, didn't we?"

"We did," Bancroft confirmed. "I don't see the connection."

"There will be a connection," Kate said. She raised her head.

"We'll end this now, Mr Jay. I'll lead Harkness and Hind to Smith's house."

Bancroft looked up with a new resolution on his face. "Kill him, Mrs Kay," he said. "No mistakes this time."

"No mistakes," Kate agreed softly.

I haven't forgotten you, Lightning. You were a better man than James Bancroft will ever be.

"SEND THE PAPES HOME! NO POPERY IN ENGLAND!" THE chant increased in volume as the crowd in St George's Fields swelled. Lord George Gordon marched at their head with a small group carrying banners behind him.

"No Popery! No Popery!"

Jack Redpath remained at the fringe of the crowd, automatically watching for pickpockets.

"No Popery in England!" The mob cascaded from their meeting, shouting their slogans. The members of the Protestant Association wore blue cockades to announce their loyalty to the Protestant cause and protest any leniency to Roman Catholicism. Others joined the march, some out of curiosity but most in the hope of causing trouble. Redpath jerked a thumb to warn the criminal element to leave.

"Shall we join them?" Bess asked as she heard the commotion and saw hundreds of people swarm past.

"We'll keep to the back," Smith said. "Pull your hat low and your collar up. I don't want anybody to recognise us."

Bess nodded to the rapidly swelling crowd. "Do you believe all these people are good church-going Protestants?"

"No more than I believe in the man in the moon," Smith said. "Some might be sincere, but most are troublemakers, thieves, and rogues from the rookeries hell-bent on mischief. They're out for what they can steal and who they can hurt."

"Did we start this, John?"

"No," Smith shook his head. "London's always simmering. The London mob takes any excuse to vent their frustration; it could be a hanging, the king's birthday, an election or anything else."

Followed by the constantly swelling crowd, Gordon marched to Westminster, where the mob gathered outside the Houses of Parliament, shouting insults and throwing missiles at the building. Gordon led a few of the boldest inside while the majority demonstrated in the surroundings.

"I hoped you'd be here, Smith." Redpath stepped to Smith's side.

"What's the to do?" Smith asked mildly.

"We're showing everybody that King George's Protestant subjects rule London rather than the Pope," Redpath told him. "The nation and constitution won't stand for any of this Catholic nonsense."

"I'm glad to hear it," Bess said and raised her voice. "No Popery in London! Drive the Papes into the Thames!"

The people closest cheered, while those wearing a blue cockade joined in.

"I know where a Roman Catholic lives," Bess shouted. "And the scoundrel's in league with the French!"

"That's correct!" Redpath roared, forgetting that as a Bow Street officer, he was responsible for keeping the peace. "Follow me to Grosvenor Square!"

Smith pulled Bess aside as the mob followed Redpath, some bearing banners with anti-Catholic slogans while others carried crude weapons.

"Stay back," Smith grabbed Bess's arm. "This could get violent."

When Bess looked at him, her eyes were wild. "I want it to get violent! I want to see Bancroft and Kate Driver swinging from a gibbet!" She shook her arm free. "Come on, John!"

"I don't want you hurt!" Smith shouted above the crowd's increasing roar.

Bess glared at him. "I know who's getting hurt," she snarled, lifted her skirt, and ran to join the crowd.

"Bess!" Smith roared and staggered as a score of men shoved him aside.

"Burn the Papes! Send the Pope back to Rome!" the crowd chanted.

"There's a Frenchie in London! Swing him from the gallows!"

"Bess!" Smith yelled, realised she would ignore him and thrust forward into the mass. Redpath marched in front with men holding banners at his side and the mob following, shouting slogans and threatening anybody they fancied might be a Catholic.

They surged through the frightened streets to Grosvenor Square, where Redpath pointed to Bancroft's house.

"That's the place," Redpath shouted. "That's where the traitor lives! He's got letters from France wanting to make Britain a Catholic country, and I saw the French agents at his door!"

The crowd howled in anger and threw a volley of stones, bottles and other missiles. Most bounced harmlessly from the walls, but some smashed the windows with a satisfying crash of breaking glass.

"Burn it down!" a woman wearing a blue cockade screamed. "Burn the Frenchie to the ground!"

Looking over the heads of the crowd, Smith saw Bess at the head, waving her fist as she encouraged them to boot in the door.

"Come on!" Bess shouted. "Haul the murderer out!"

The screaming woman elaborated on Bess's words. "They're murderers!" she said. "They murder good Protestants!"

"Murderers!" the mob took up the cry. "Get the Papist murderers!"

The door held for the initial assault, but the weight of numbers and sheer desperation burst it open, and the screaming mob crashed inside. Smith saw Bess at the forefront and pushed forward.

"Burn the French!" the mob chanted. "Send them back to Rome!"

The frantic-eyed woman with a blue cockade threw a stone at the nearest window, smashing a pane of glass and rebounding from the stout inner shutter. "No Popery!" she screamed.

The mob surged inside the hall, intent only on destruction or looting. Already Smith saw people sliding away with anything they could carry. Others tore the pictures from the wall or hammered at priceless furniture with cudgels and boots.

"No Popery!"

"Bess!" Smith pushed people aside, ignoring their protests as he searched for Bess. He saw two men and a woman lift a beautifully carved Jacobean chair and carry it away, chortling that it would make fine firewood, and another woman taking a knife to the Gainsborough portrait of Bancroft.

"Bess!"

Smith knew his voice would be lost in the commotion and pushed up the stairs for a better view. More people crammed into the house, screaming and yelling. Some wore rosettes; others seemed to be the dregs of humanity as they looted or destroyed, with motives that encompassed neither religion nor politics.

"She's up there." Redpath gasped from the landing, adjusting his hat, and slashing with his cane at the howling rabble. "I didn't expect this to happen!"

"What did you expect?" Smith snarled and thrust further up the steps.

Bess was in Bancroft's study, glaring about her with her blunderbuss in her hand. "He's not here," she said. "I wanted to blow his head off, John, but the bastard's escaped."

Smith dragged her out of the room. "Put that bloody thing away, Bess!"

"He murdered Peter." Bess's eyes were wild, and the scar on her face glowed white with her anger. "Where is he?"

"Not here." Smith staggered as a press of people crammed into the room, screaming obscenities.

"He could be hiding in his bedroom," Bess said.

"Maybe. This way." Smith guided her through the press and into the bedroom where he had left the incriminating documents. A dozen people were busily engaged in looting everything of value and destroying what remained.

"Look!" Bess lifted a silk-and-satin gown from the floor. "We were right about one thing, John; Bancroft or Kate Rider has a French connection."

"What?" Smith had lost interest when Bancroft was not in the room.

"This dress is this year's style, so it's fresh from Paris," Bess said and laughed in near hysterics. "Kate Rider has expensive tastes!"

"Bancroft's not here." Smith was not interested in Kate's clothes. "He might be in his shipping office."

"Where's that?" Bess grabbed Smith's sleeve. "Where's the bugger hiding, John?"

Smith pulled her from the room as a man threw a lighted candle onto the desk and laughed as flames licked across the papers. "Come on, Bess; these madmen are setting the place alight."

"Where's the murdering bastard hiding, John?" Bess repeated.

"He's got an office on the Highway," Smith remembered. "Near the docks."

"Come on, then!" Bess shoved the blunderbuss under her coat. He's mine, John. I want him and that bloody woman!"

"Come away, Bess!" John dragged her onto the stairs as blue smoke coiled from the desk. The mob cheered, throwing papers onto the flames. One blonde-haired virago lifted a portrait from the wall and added it to the fire, laughing.

Redpath was in the hall, vainly trying to restore order.

"You're wasting your time, Redpath," Smith told him. "They've gone crazy and started a fire upstairs!"

Redpath swore. "Where are you two going?"

"The Highway," Smith replied. "Bancroft has an office there to watch over his ships."

"Ships!" A swarthy faced gypsy caught Smith's words. "The Papes have got ships in the Thames!"

"They're invading us!" a black woman shouted. "The French are in the river!"

"Send them back!" somebody screamed. "The French are going to hang the king and turn us all into Papes!"

"Come on, Bess, before this rabble scares Bancroft away!" Smith took hold of Bess's arm and dragged her out of the house. The crowd outside had grown, with anti-Catholic banners held high while people shook fists and cudgels as they screamed abuse of Catholics and the French.

"This way!" Smith rammed through the crowd with Bess behind him.

"Now, this is what I call a riot," Bess said. Her eyes were calmer now as she looked around her.

Smith stopped in a side street to control his breathing. "Do you still want Bancroft and Driver?" he asked. "Or do you want to get away from this nonsense? The army will be out soon, and there'll be blood on the streets."

"They murdered Peter," Bess reminded, lifting her chin. "I'll not let them off with that."

"Very well, then," Smith said. "Keep your temper under control, Bess. An unsteady head is the fastest route to failure."

Bess nodded, taking deep breaths. Behind them, tall flames licked from Bancroft's house, brightening the night-dark sky. I will," she promised.

"Come on, then," Smith said. "Steady pace and ignore the idiots."

They moved toward the Ratcliffe Highway, striding through

the night that drunken screeching and the crash of breaking glass made hideous.

As the mob moved in an aimless parade, stopping to attack any building they thought might have a Catholic connection, Smith and Bess trotted in front. They ignored the people who peered out of their windows to see the cause of the commotion.

Despite the nearby riot, the Highway was busy with seamen, prostitutes, and thrill-seeking gentlemen. Smith dodged groups of drunken men, checked the side streets and arrived at a heavily-shuttered corner shop. Candles glowed behind the windows above the shop.

"This is Bancroft's little office," Smith said. "The viper's nest."

"He seems to be at home," Bess's voice was savage with satisfaction. "Let's hope that woman is also here."

"Smith! John Smith!" the voice was hard-edged. "Now there's a coincidence!"

Smith halted as three people emerged from a narrow alley beside Bancroft's office. Two carried pistols, and the third was Kate Rider.

Chapter Thirty-Seven

"I thought you'd come here," Kate said. "I could always anticipate your movements, John Smith or Yellowhammer, whichever name you prefer."

Smith calculated the odds. One of the men moved like a soldier, holding his pistol with professional ease; that would be Harkness. The other had the evilest face Smith had ever seen, with basilisk eyes and a mouth like a man-trap.

"We've been searching for you, Kate," Smith said, feeling the comforting weight of his pistol inside his coat. "And the soldier is Private Harkness, late of the 34th Foot." He stepped back slightly to shield Bess, giving her time to draw her blunderbuss. "The other fellow, I don't know."

"Ned Hind," Hind introduced himself. "You may know my name."

Edward Hind, a triple murderer with a reputation for brutality.

"Ned Hind?" Smith shook his head. He heard the roar of the approaching mob and played for time. "No, I don't know the name. And you, Private Harkness, you'll miss the late Corporal Jenks."

"You killed him." Harkness had a northern accent, *Yorkshire, perhaps*, Smith thought, *or perhaps even further north.*

"Bancroft killed him," Smith contradicted, "Bancroft shot him like a dog." He lunged to the side, knocking Hind against Kate. Harkness fired at once, with the crack of the pistol loud in Smith's ear. Smith felt a tug on his sleeve, and then Bess returned fire with her blunderbuss.

Bess's shot spread, hitting Harkness in the chest, and blasting him backwards. He died with an astonished look on his face, and then Hind also fired, swore as his ball whined wide, and pulled a second pistol from his pocket.

Smith fell to the ground, dragging his pistol from its holster. He saw Kate snarling at him and Hind aiming at Bess.

"Bess! Duck!" Smith shouted and squeezed the trigger. His ball took Hind in the shoulder, spinning him around. Blood splashed over the wall behind Hind as he gasped, then yelled shrilly.

"You can't shoot me! I'm Ned Hind!"

Ignoring the screaming Hind, Bess ran at Kate, holding the blunderbuss like a club. Kate dropped a pistol down her sleeve, aimed and fired. The powder in the pan flared without igniting the charge in the barrel.

A flash in the pan, Smith thought as Kate swore, turned, and ran half a dozen steps before stopping to cock her second barrel.

"Get Bancroft," Bess shouted. "I'll take care of Kate Rider!"

Smith nodded. Leaving Hind screaming on the ground, he lifted his boot and crashed it against the door leading to Bancroft's office. When the solid wood held, he kicked again, using all his weight. On his third effort, the door crashed open, and Smith burst in, shouting.

"Bancroft!" Where are you, you bastard?"

The stairs were narrow, ancient, and smelled of new paint covering old decay. Smith ascended carefully, fearful of standing on rotted wood. There was a landing at the top, with three doors, each of which boasted a name. The central door read *James Bancroft Shipping* and lay ajar.

Pausing to reload his pistol, Smith stood at the side of the door and slammed it open, expecting Bancroft to be waiting with a loaded gun.

"Bancroft!" Smith shouted as the door banged wide. He crouched and entered, holding his pistol at arm's length.

The office consisted of two rooms. The first held a desk, chair, and piles of documents, with a candle burning in a simple brass candlestick. The second had a rumpled bed, a sea chest, and a gaping window.

"Where are you, Bancroft?" Smith uncocked his pistol and returned it to his holster. "Where the devil are you hiding?"

BESS GRABBED AT KATE'S COAT AND MISSED. "COME BACK, YOU murderous bitch!" Bess shouted as Kate passed her. "I want you!"

Kate snarled and fired the second barrel of her pistol. Expecting the move, Bess ducked to the side. She heard the ball whistle past her, to land with a meaty thump in Hind's belly. Hind screamed and looked down at himself, seeing the small puncture wound but feeling nothing for a second. Then the pain hit, and he yelled again, high-pitched and frantic. A pack of cards slipped from his pocket, with the ace of spades detached from the rest. It lay face up as Hind slid beside it, dying.

As soon as she fired, Kate threw her pistol at Bess, turned again and fled. The gun barrel caught Bess a glancing blow on the side of the head. She winced, grunted, and put up her hand. The metal had cut the skin, with slow blood dribbling down her face.

That's more I owe you, Kate Rider, you murdering bitch!

Bess followed Kate, taking long strides and ignoring the howling mob that had taken control of much of London. Kate ran, gasping as the smoke from burning buildings rasped in her throat and glancing over her shoulder as Bess kept pace.

"That woman!" Bess shouted as she neared a crowd of men stoning a chapel. "She's one of them!"

"One of who?" a woman wearing a blue cockade asked.

"She's a Roman Catholic!" Kate yelled.

"I'm not!" Kate protested as faces in the crowd turned towards her. "I'm English!"

"That makes it worse," Bess countered. "She's an English traitor taking pay from the French!"

"I don't!" Kate denied shrilly, but with their temper up, the crowd would not listen to reason. They chased after Kate, throwing missiles and howling threats and imprecations. Bess followed in the fringe of the crowd, encouraging them to greater effort.

"She's in French pay! A child-murdering spy!"

When a second group exploded from a corner, they trapped Kate between them.

"I'm not a Catholic!" Kate yelled. "I'm as English as you are!"

As the crowd hesitated at the sound of Kate's accent, Bess remembered the clothes in Bancroft's bedroom. "She might be English," Bess shouted, "but she has French friends! Even her clothes are French!"

A score of women dived on Kate, ripped the clothes from her back and left her defiant and cursing in her underwear. The woman with the blue cockade held the expensive gown and passed it around.

"It looks French," a stout apple seller said, fingering the silk with grubby, calloused fingers.

"It is French," a one-eyed vixen announced. "I've never seen English clothes like this before!"

Convinced by this proof, the crowd roared furiously.

"What will we do with her?" a man asked, waving a long staff in the air.

"Hang her!" somebody shouted.

"Burn her alive!" the one-eyed vixen suggested, leaning closer to Kate.

"Tar and feather her!"

"No" Bess stepped forward, determined to make Kate suffer as long as possible. "Make her ride the stang!"

"You bitch!" Kate hissed as half a dozen people held her tight.

The idea caught on as people repeated it to one another. "Ride the stang!" they chanted. "Make her ride the stang!"

"Fetch a stang!" the one-eyed woman shouted, and men climbed a nearby wall and hacked down the red-and-white striped pole outside a barber's shop.

"Too easy," the one-eyed woman said, fingering the smooth wood. "Find some brambles!"

Brambles were hard to find in the heart of London, but some enterprising men cut bundles of stinging nettles from run-down courtyards.

"That will do," the one-eyed woman said. "Wrap them round the pole!" She added details that raised a cruel laugh from the crowd while Kate cringed and tried to pull free.

"You're not getting away, you French bitch!" the one-eyed woman gloated. "Bring her over!"

A group of women dragged Kate to the stang, as four men held it at waist height.

"Get on it!" they ordered. "Sit astride!"

Kate's reply was short and obscene.

Bess watched with bitter satisfaction, allowing the one-eyed woman to take control. Grabbing Kate's hair, the woman forced her astride the pole with her now sadly torn petticoats around her waist.

"Up with the Frenchie!" The crowd cheered, and the pole bearers lifted the pole on their shoulders and bounced it to increase Kate's discomfort.

"Round the parish!" the one-eyed woman ordered, and the bearers jogged through the streets. Kate hung on, trying to alleviate the sting from the nettles and the pain from the bouncing. The crowd added to Kate's torment with a constant barrage of rotten fruit, eggs, dead cats, mud and filth.

Bess followed the stang, with her memories of Peter killing any sympathy she might have had for Kate.

"Bounce her!" Bess yelled. "Bounce her hard!"

The bearers complied, bouncing Kate astride the stang until they reached a large heap of human and animal waste beside a tannery near the Thames.

"Throw her in!" the one-eyed woman screamed.

The bearers crouched then sprung up, tossing Kate head-first into the filth, with her petticoats ballooning and her bare legs kicking.

"That's what we do to French Catholics!" the virago said. "Get back to Rome where you belong!"

As the crowd dissipated, Kate gradually extricated herself from the pile. Battered, bruised and stinking, she crawled onto the street and looked around. A small group of children and youths waited. Mudlarks, scuffle-hunters, and night-plunderers, they were the refuse of the city, the unwanted, uncared-for children born with neither hope nor love. A thin youth adjusted the silver-braided three-cornered hat he had inherited from Peter and gave orders to his followers.

Cursing, Kate tried to remove the worst of the filth and realised the crowd of children had increased. Some carried broken bottles, others with sharpened animal bones, and all had tangled hair and feral expressions.

"That's the woman who had Peter murdered." Bess emerged from the middle of the group with Madge at her side. "Her name is Kate Rider, and I'll leave her to you."

The boy with the three-cornered hat nodded. "We'll look after her."

"You murdered my son," Bess said and walked away. She heard Kate scream in terror as the children advanced on her but did not turn around. "Come, Madge. We have things to do."

Chapter Thirty-Eight

Firelight from burning ships reflected from low clouds along the River Thames, turning the water into molten gold and causing consternation among the seamen. Smith stopped one of the crowd, who gathered to gape at the scene.

"What's the to-do?"

"They're burning Catholic ships," the man informed him. "Lord George Gordon discovered that Bancroft and Shapland were agents of the Pope and King Louis of France."

How quickly false news spreads and expands.

"I wasn't aware of that," Smith said and hurried to find a viewpoint. He watched anxiously to see if any of the two vessels he had in the Thames were in danger.

London's Capital was safely moored in mid-river, while *London's Tower* was only three cables' lengths from the fire and swinging with the current. Smith swore; his search for Bancroft would have to wait. The safety of his ships must take priority.

Despite the excitement and the lateness of the hour, Smith found a boat woman willing to row him to *London's Tower*.

"It would normally cost sixpence, dearie." The woman was

about fifty, with grey hair and forearms that any prizefighter would envy. "A shilling tonight, with the fire."

"I'll give you two shillings if you get me there quickly," Smith promised.

"For two shillings, Captain, I'd row the devil to hell with a cargo of brimstone." The woman ejected a stream of tobacco juice into the river. "In you get!"

Smith climbed into the open boat, and the woman plied her oars like the expert she was. "What's your interest in *London's Tower?*" the woman asked.

"I'm one of the owners," Smith said, watching as the sails on the nearby *Amelia's Hope* caught fire, sending orange flames crackling skyward. Fire on a ship was every seaman's nightmare, with highly combustible wood, canvas, and tar ready to welcome the flames.

"Ah." The woman bent to her oars. "Worried about the fires, are you, Captain?"

"I am," Smith admitted.

The woman chuckled. "Aye, the boys started them when somebody said James Bancroft was a French Catholic in league with the Pope." She shook her head. "Nonsense, of course. He's no more French than I am."

"You might be correct," Smith agreed, watching as *Amelia's Hope's* mizzen collapsed in a horror of flaming spars and canvas.

"Here we are, Captain.," The woman lay her boat alongside *London's Tower* and held out a calloused hand. "Two shillings, you said."

Smith fumbled in his pocket and produced a handful of coins. "Here." He dropped them in the woman's palm.

She looked at them suspiciously. "That's too much, Captain."

Ignoring her, Smith threw himself on board *London's Tower*. "Where's the watchman? Who's in charge here?"

The deck was deserted, with the ship swinging to its cables and the mercy of the river.

"What the devil's happening?" Smith bellowed. He flinched

as *Amelia's Hope's* mainmast collapsed in a welter of flames and sparks. The current pushed a burning spar towards *London's Tower,* and Smith grabbed a boathook from beside the mainmast and pushed it clear. He raised his voice to a shout, "Where's the bloody watchman?"

Has the pressgang stripped my ship clean?

"Smith! John Smith!"

Smith looked towards the quarterdeck. A tall man stood there, silhouetted against the burning *Amelia's Hope.*

"Bancroft?" Smith shouted. "Mister Jay?"

"You've ruined me, Smith!" Bancroft said. "You've burned my house and my ships."

"You're a back-stabbing bastard, Bancroft!" Smith narrowed his eyes against the glare. "I trusted you! I thought you were my friend!"

"There are no friends in business, Smith!" Bancroft replied.

"What are you doing on my ship, Bancroft?"

"I knew you'd come to try and save her!" Bancroft shouted. "You wouldn't let your precious vessel burn."

"I'm coming for you, Bancroft," Smith strode over the deck, with his boots thudding on the scrubbed pine planks.

As Smith came closer, Bancroft stepped sideways, and Smith saw he had commandeered a swivel, a vicious weapon similar to a large blunderbuss. Loaded with grapeshot, the charge would hardly damage the fabric of a ship but was highly effective against boarders.

Hoist with my own petard! I insisted that my ships were all armed against privateers with cannon and swivel guns.

"Goodbye, Smith!" Bancroft shouted and fired.

The gun barked, with a jet of flame and smoke gushing from the muzzle. Smith threw himself sideways and downward and felt a searing pain across his left shoulder. He saw the grapeshot chew up the pine planking, wondered what the captain would say, rolled away and rose quickly to his feet. His shoulder was aching abominably, but he could move his arm, so the wound was not significant.

"I'm coming for you, Bancroft!" Smith moved quickly before Bancroft reloaded. He hauled his pistol from its holster and swarmed up the ladder to the quarterdeck.

Bancroft crouched over the swivel, ramming a cartridge into the muzzle. When he looked up, Smith saw the hatred in his eyes.

I want to kill him, but first, I must find out why he turned against me.

"Why, Bancroft?" Smith levelled his pistol. "Why stab me in the back?"

"You've got everything, Smith," Bancroft replied at once and gave a high-pitched laugh. "You've got all the money, power and position, and I was only hanging onto your coattails." He rammed home a bag of grapeshot. "I want your money, Smith! I want to be on top of the tree! I want your success!"

Bess is correct; the love of money is the root of all evil. Seeking wealth has driven all morality and perhaps most sanity from Bancroft's mind.

"Where is the ship's watchman, Bancroft?" Smith levelled his pistol. "Did you kill him, too?"

"No," Bancroft sounded surprised at the question. "Why would I do that? I want you, not him."

"Step aside from the gun, Bancroft," Jack ordered.

"I'm going to kill you," Bancroft said. "I tried with your phaeton, but you survived, damn your eyes, and I tried to ruin you by sinking your ships."

"You were a shareholder in these ships," Smith reminded. "You lost money, too."

"I was a minority shareholder," Bancroft explained reasonably. "You lost much more than I did."

"Men drowned," Smith said.

"I know." Bancroft remained at the swivel. "I didn't mean that to happen, but they had to drown, don't you see? If I am to reign in London, I must eliminate lesser men."

"Lesser men?" Smith repeated the phrase. "What is a lesser man, Bancroft?"

Bancroft faced him, frowning. "One who fails," he said thoughtfully. "The poor are lesser men because they lack wealth. The rich are great because they are successful, Smith. You understand that. The poor are here for men like us to use. That's their function in life."

"Only in your warped mind, Bancroft," Smith said.

Bancroft had nearly finished loading the swivel. If he fired at such short range, he could not miss, with the charge of grapeshot blasting Smith off the deck and into the burning river.

SMITH GLANCED UPSTREAM. *AMELIA'S HOPE* WAS SINKING INTO the Thames, with pieces of timber breaking off to float downstream. A ship's launch, blazing from aft, slid from her deck and hissed into the water.

Smith swore. "Stand clear, Bancroft!" He realised that Bancroft was insane. The pursuit of wealth had driven all humanity from his mind, and only personal success mattered.

Bancroft's voice rose to a scream. "I'll kill you, Smith, and rise to rule in London!"

Smith levelled his pistol, pulled back the hammer and swore as the current rammed a section of *Amelia's Hope* against the hull of *London Tower*. Flames licked onto the deck, already spreading glowing sparks.

"Leave the gun, Bancroft," Smith yelled, "or we'll both die!"

Bancroft giggled like a child. "Then we'll die, Smith; you, me and all the crew."

"The crew?" Smith winced as the sparks took hold, with tiny flames licking along the oakum between the deck planking.

"They're locked in the foc'sle," Bancroft shouted. "Lesser men, Smith, only here as sacrifices to our ambition! Don't you see? The poor don't matter!"

"Dear God!" Smith looked forward. The flames were growing

in intensity, running along the deck seams, and gaining strength by the second. He had a choice, leave Bancroft and save the men, or kill Bancroft and avenge the death of Peter and all the men who had drowned at sea.

Let the dead look after the dead.

Uncocking his pistol, Smith rammed it in its holster, turned and ran forward, avoiding the tall flames and leaping over the smaller. He coughed as he breathed in acrid smoke, swore as something hot licked at his wounded arm, and plunged on.

London's Tower was a hundred and eighty feet long, with a crew of twenty-seven men. Smith intoned the statistics as he ran. She was due to sail in two days, so only a fraction of the hands would be on board; the others would be ashore, either with their families or enjoying the delights of London's taverns and academies. How many would have crammed in the foc'sle?

Maybe ten or a dozen.

Twelve lives depend on me.

Smith swore as he heard a loud bang behind him as Bancroft fired the swivel. Instinctively, he threw himself down, yelled as his left arm landed on a smouldering plank and swore again when something ripped into his right thigh.

Bancroft got me. Is it serious?

Smith looked down, saw a long tear in his breeches and felt the slow flow of blood.

Can I walk?

He stood carefully, tested his leg, winced at the pain, and limped on. The deck seemed to stretch forever, with the foc'sle far in the distance and thick smoke partially concealing the entrance. Bancroft had wedged two spars against the door to prevent the hands from escaping.

"Is anybody in there?" Smith shouted.

He heard hoarse voices from the foc'sle and shoved at the spars, gasping at the pain of his injuries.

"Let us out!" The hands were panicking as they kicked at the door. "Let us out, you bastard!"

Putting his shoulder under the spars, Smith threw them free, and the door crashed open. A press of men tumbled out, some holding knives, as they sought vengeance.

"John Smith! Mr Smith's freed us, lads!" David Cupples put away his knife.

"David Cupples," Smith said. "We seem to meet whenever there is trouble."

"Yes, Captain." Cupples glanced at the fire, frowning.

"What happened?" The watchman was an elderly one-legged veteran with a face seamed by decades of harsh weather and hard living.

"The ship's on fire," Smith explained, "and there's a madman aft with the swivel." He pointed to Cupples. "Davie, take the lads and man the pumps, break out the hoses and douse the fire." He pushed them to the aft hatch. "Handsomely, now!"

"How about the madman, Captain?" Cupples asked.

"Leave him to me," Smith said.

I've done enough talking. The hands will douse the fire before it takes hold.

Smith pulled his pistol from its holster and strode aft, coughing at the smoke and jumping over the burning planks. Bancroft remained at the swivel, ignoring the smoke as he reloaded again.

"I knew you'd come back, Smith!" Bancroft aimed the gun. He looked up, laughing as he saw the flames licking across the deck. "We'll die together and rule in hell, John Smith!"

"Not today, Mr Jay." Smith did not hesitate. He lifted his pistol and fired, with the ball catching Bancroft between the eyes. Bancroft died instantly, falling backwards to lie on the quarterdeck.

Smith did not look at the body. He had a ship to help save.

Chapter Thirty-Nine

A warming fire crackled in the grate as Smith sat at the head of the table. He looked over the partners of John Smith and Company.

"Gentlemen," he said, nodded to Bess and added, "and lady." He waited for the inevitable laugh. "As you know, there have been some changes since our last meeting. Mr James Bancroft has left us, and we have a new partner in my wife, Bess Webb or Mrs Smith."

The partners murmured their congratulations and nodded to Bess. One or two extended their hands in welcome.

"It won't work," Anthony Jackson gave his expected objection. "Women don't have the brains to help run a company like ours."

Smith smiled. "Time will tell, Mr Jackson, time will tell."

"Godsakes," Jackson said. "We'll be educating them next, or giving them the vote, like as not." He shook his head. "Blasted bluestockings."

"I sincerely hope so, Mr Jackson," Bess said, smiling. "I am glad you remain a constant in an ever-changing world."

"Eh?" Jackson glowered at her. "I'm not going to change, Mrs Smith."

Bess curtseyed from her chair. "I hope not, Mr Jackson."

"When you have all settled down," Smith said and waited until the murmur died away. "I have other news. You all know Mr Judd, our efficient secretary." He indicated Judd at his desk in the corner of the room.

"Judd? Is that your name? I didn't know your name," Jackson said.

"Yes, sir, I am Judd." Judd stood, bowed, and sat down again. "Nobody notices a clerk, sir."

"When this present war is over, I will appoint Mr Judd to be our agent in France. He will be our eyes and ears for business affairs on the Continent."

"Sir?" Judd stood in surprise.

"Sit down, Mr Judd. Your promotion is well deserved," Smith said.

"We'll lose this war," Jackson grumbled.

"That is probable," Smith agreed. "But don't worry, trade will continue after the war and anyway, we'll probably win the next one." He smiled, stuffing tobacco into the bowl of his pipe. "We must give the Frenchies a chance for some success, hey?"

The board members laughed. Although they preferred victory to defeat, profit mattered more than either. Smith allowed them a moment of levity.

"In this war, the odds are stacked against us. Most of Europe is fighting on the opposite side, as well as Mysore and the Americans." Smith sugared the pill. "That is one reason why this company is investing heavily across the Atlantic." He winked at Judd, who produced a sheaf of papers and placed one in front of each partner.

"What's this?" Jackson asked suspiciously.

"This document shows details of our investments in the United States," Smith explained. "You will see we have bought over some New England whale-fishing companies. After the war, they will lose the British market, and many of the best whaling masters will immigrate to this country." He waited for the wise nodding of heads and murmurs of agreement. "We will use the Americans' experience in our adventures to the Arctic and Southern whaling. Bess, Mrs Smith, has created a list of our current and projected ventures and profits over the next ten years."

The partners scrutinised the paper, with Jackson making disparaging comments.

"What's this?" Jackson pointed to the lower half of the page. "A. H. and Company? What's that?"

Smith had thought it best not to print Abraham Hargreaves' name or privateering voyages in full. "It is a speculative venture," he said smoothly. "As you see, it is making solid profits."

Jackson nodded. "Who's managing these American operations?"

"Abraham Reeves," Smith said. "Bess has added his name at the bottom of the page."

Jackson nodded. "The country might lose, but we're making a profit from this bloody war." He glanced at Bess. "I apologise for the language, Mrs Smith, but I am not used to having women on the board."

"That's all right, Mr Jackson," Bess replied evenly. "I am sure we will both adapt."

"Now." Smith beamed at the partners. "I think that is all the current business unless anybody has anything else to add?"

"I have, sir," Judd said. "A messenger brought this package for you five minutes before the meeting started." He held up a sealed letter.

"Well, open it, Mr Judd," Smith said. "It may be important."

Judd lifted a whalebone paperknife and meticulously slid it under the seal, and prised open the letter.

"It's from the Lord Mayor, sir," Judd reported quietly. "It says that at a meeting of liverymen of all London's livery companies at Common Hall, you have been elected Lord Mayor of London for next year."

Smith took a deep breath, knowing the elation would strike

later. "Thank you, Mr Judd. It seems that celebrations are in order."

He remembered his dream of Bess riding in the Lord Mayor's carriage. That would soon be a reality. His plans were coming true.

"You are reigning now, John," Bess said, "Lord Fitzwarren, Member of Parliament for Appleby and Lord Mayor of London. Do you have anything else in mind?"

"I might try for Prime Minister," Smith said. "That's the next logical step for a rogue and a Lord Mayor." He grinned. "There's a bottle of brandy and half a dozen glasses in that cupboard, Mr Jackson. Would you be so kind as to pour for us?"

Jackson sighed. "French brandy?" He shook his head. "We may as well toast the victor."

Bess met Smith's eye. "Well done, Abel Watson," she said. "We'll drink a toast to the future prime minister."

Historical Note

Lord George Gordon

One of the many eccentrics of the eighteenth century, Lord George Gordon was a London-born, Eton-educated anti-Catholic agitator. Having failed in a career in the Royal Navy, perhaps because of his desire to help the ordinary seamen, he turned to politics. Rather than nail his colours to any party, he attacked both Whigs and Tories.

In 1778 an Act relieved some of the disadvantages that Roman Catholics suffered from, and Gordon founded a Protestant Association to attempt an appeal. In 1780, he addressed a rally in London and headed a mob of some fifty thousand people who rioted and attacked various Catholic institutions, as well as Newgate Prison.

The authorities called out the army, and over two hundred and eighty rioters were killed, one hundred and seventy-three wounded, and nearly a hundred and forty arrested. The authorities arrested Gordon and tried him for high treason, but he escaped conviction. Gordon later converted to Judaism and was jailed for libelling Marie Antoinette. He died of gaol fever in Newgate.

About the Author

 Born in Edinburgh, Scotland and educated at the University of Dundee, Malcolm Archibald has written in a variety of genres, from academic history to folklore, historical novels to fantasy. He won the Dundee International Book Prize with *Whales for the Wizard* in 2005 and the Society of Army Historical Research prize for Historical Military Fiction with *Blood Oath* in 2021.

Happily married for over 42 years, Malcolm has three grown children and lives outside Dundee in Scotland.

To learn more about Malcolm Archibald and discover more Next Chapter authors, visit our website at www.nextchapter.pub.

Notes

Chapter 18

1. Academy = Brothel

Reigning
ISBN: 978-4-82416-646-3

Published by
Next Chapter
2-5-6 SANNO
SANNO BRIDGE
143-0023 Ota-Ku, Tokyo
+818035793528

20th January 2023

Lightning Source UK Ltd.
Milton Keynes UK
UKHW011917270223
417761UK00003B/159